Passing Place

LOCATION RELATIVE

Mark Hayes

Salthomle Publishing

Copyright © 2015 by Mark Hayes

All rights reserved. No part of this publication may be reproduced, distributed or transmitted in any form or by any means, without prior written permission.

Saltholme publishing
11 Saltholme Close
High Clarence
TS21TL

Publisher's Note: This is a work of fiction. Names, characters, places and incidents are a product of the author's imagination. Locales and public names are sometimes used for atmospheric purposes. Any resemblance to actual people, living or dead, or to businesses, companies, events, institutions, or locales is completely coincidental.

Book Layout © 2016 Saltholme Publishing

/ Mark Hayes. -- 1st ed.
ISBN-13:
978-1533106100

ISBN-10:
153310610X

This one is for my father, John Hayes
Who taught me everything I ever needed to know
about been a man, simply by being himself.

Additional thanks to my wonderful proofreaders
Katie Salvo and Andrew Hawley.

To dozens of others over the years who have read
scraps of this work and offered advice
and encouragement.

And to all those tellers of tales,
Without which there would be no stories.

Authors note.

This is a novel about many things, but more than anything else it is a novel about stories. The ones we tell, the ones we here and the ones we all know. How they influence our lives and our perceptions of the world around us. How they teach us about ourselves.

I have begged, borrowed and stolen ideas from other tellers of tales, because that's what writers do, we are all thieves of the rich history of tales which permeates human culture. The good ones, of which I can only hope I am, add to that which they steal and make it their own. The truly great ones, which I can only aspire to be, do this so well that they become the source of the tales they tell for a new generation.

In this tradition, the tradition of literary thievery, I have plundered here and there a few tales, true and imaginary. I won't be telling which is which, but if you want to know more about anything within these pages the internet is at your disposal.

I am at heart, an honourable thief of stories, however, if I steal from the real world I try to stay true to the source. If I steal from other tale-tellers, I try not to twist their visions round too many corners. The eagle-eyed reader will spot some of the references to my plunder. Many are hidden in plain sight after all.

Moorcock, Gaiman, King, Pratchett, Verne, Wells, Orwell, Gemmell, Adams, Bradbury, Eddings, Gibson, Holt, Rankin and many more have been subjects of my thievery. My thanks then to them, tale tellers all. Without which none of this would be possible.

Beyond artists of a literary kind, there are others who tell tales. The ones who set them to music and sing the words, weaving their tales with sound walls of passion and grace. Without them this novel more than most would be a poorer tale.

It was written over the course of five years, somewhere in the middle of writing it, I wrote Cider Lane, my first novel, a tale which had much to do with silence and silences.

Passing Place, on the other hand, is a tale which has much to do with music. As such it comes with a playlist of songs, one for each chapter, from those other tale-tellers who influenced this tale…..

Mark Hayes 2016

Playlist by chapter

Minutes to Memories	John Mellencamp
My Hometown	Bruce Springsteen
As Time Goes By	Herman Hupfield
The band played waltzing Mathilda	The Pogues
Hey Jude	The Beatles
When the Man Comes Around	Johnny Cash
Emmylou	First Aid Kit
Absolute Reality	The Alarm
Christine	Siouxsie and the Banshees
Paranoid Android	Radiohead
Parisian Walkways	Gary Moore
I Bleed	Pixies
Between Dog and Wolf	New Model Army
There's a Plan	Waiting for Wednesday
Dead is the New Alive	Nervous 'Orse
One Too Many Mornings	Bob Dylan
Tears dry on their own	Amy Winehouse
Little Face	The Cult
Demonic Phenomenon	Rob Zombie
A Forest	Bat for Lashes
Powerless	Nelly Furtado
All hope in Eclipse	Cradle of Filth
Stuck in the Middle With You	Stealers Wheel

CONTENTS

Authors note
Playlist

The Bus Stop of Lost Hopes
Relativity of Location
As a Passing Place Passes By
The Ballad of Pvt Burbank
Do You Know 'Hey Jude.'
A Stranger Rides In...
Jolene Followed the Morn
Causality Sandwich
The Girl in the Nightmare
Rhapsody in Grey
Parisian Walkways
World Tree in the Garden
The Wolf King of Winter
Existential Meanderings of Gaia
Pretensions Afterhours
Dylan on the Keyboard
Weaver of Tears
Faces in the Dark
Demonic Home and Garden
The Forrest in the Cellar
Power according to LaGuin
Striking the Wrong Cord
Back in the Middle Again

Also by Mark Hayes

CHAPTER ONE

The Bus Stop of Lost Hopes

The Greyhound pulled away into the thunderous summer storm, leaving in its wake a dishevelled, world-weary figure in the dark, deserted bus station. The night was lit only by a faltering street lamp, which occasionally blinked fractiously at odd moments and the blue luminescent glow of a bug killer. The electric device crackled under the eaves of the ticket office roof, a stray moth enticed to its death, burning on the filaments.

As is the way of the western desert states in

high summer, the air was hot and humid, despite the rain. The traveller chose, though, to ignore the urge to seek shelter. Opting instead to enjoy the cooling rain, he was aware that it would prove to be a mistake, knowing it was not wise to let himself get soaked through to the skin. But a day spent on the back seat of a bus, sweltering in the heat with no air conditioning, meant he felt more than half roasted, and the refreshing rain was a welcome relief.

The heat of the day was persistent even this deep into the night. While the temperature would drop through the night, and being soaked would run the risk of catching a chill, at that moment he did not care. Cooling off in the rain won out over common sense.

The traveller had three dollars and change in his pocket and little hope of more coming his way anytime soon. All he had was the contents of his pack and the clothes on his back. He was not even sure where he was. All he knew was that it was as far as the bus ticket he purchased that morning would take him. Which was nothing like as far as he wished.

He knew all the same that getting soaked to the skin in a rain storm was foolish. It was not as if he had the money to buy shelter, or even a place to dry off and change. It was the essence of a stupid thing to do. He should be running for what shelter there was, trying to keep as dry as he could. Self-preservation was, however, not high on his list of priorities. Indeed, there was little on that very short list.

This was finally the end of the line, figuratively at the very least, if not actually. He had no more places to go, had no more money to go there with, and less motivation to do so than money. So he stood in the rain and enjoyed the simple pleasure of it falling on his skin, taking the heat of the day from him. Simple pleasures, the only pleasures he had left to him.

Moments passed, the rain running down his face, a welcome cold sinking into his bones. Until his revelry was broken as he became aware he was being observed. He could see no one, but he could feel it on his skin all the same. A prickling feeling like an itch he could not scratch. A feeling colder than the rain. Yet a cursory glance about revealed no one else around. All the same, he shivered, half from cold and half to rid himself of the feeling of being observed he scanned around, finally taking in his surroundings.

Wherever the bus had landed him, it seemed no more than another average dust bowl of a mid-west town. A lost soul of a place that a century ago would still be in the badlands, all flat featureless horizons, and a huge sky. Somewhere in between rolling farmland of the Corn Belt and encroaching desolation of the desert, it was a place as barren as he felt.

The buildings near the bus station had a temporary look about them. The kind of temporary you only get when buildings have been around for a long time.

The bus station lay on the outskirts of the town itself, separated from the huddling buildings of the main drag by a junkyard. Rusting Studebakers were piled four high. Written off Cadillac's were stripped of anything valuable. Chevys and Pontiac were shells devoid of engines, windows, and wheels, corroding away, not even worth the effort of crushing. At the back of the lot there were small hills of worn out tires, stacked high till they loomed above the rusting stacks. It was an elephant's graveyard for the automobile, the last resting place for the chipped paint and battered bones of America's love affair with big v8 block engines and gas-guzzling excess.

Opposite the junkyard, there sat a desperate, dispirited drudge of a motel, in little better repair than it neighbours across the road. A neon hotel eight sign was mostly flashing in the night, 'mostly' because the M had long since burnt out and the dim looking E destined to join its departed brother any day. It looked to be a flea pit of a place. The kind of place where the sheets had indescribable stains that no washing powder would ever remove. As well as strange moulds on the shower curtains on the verge of becoming a new form of life. Ancient black and white TVs that buzzed with static, and also more than likely an odd blood stain no one ever bothered to scrub away, probably out of fear that a clean spot on the carpet would stand out all the more.

The ticket office for the motel was a small ovular trailer of ancient aspect, with a ripped awning hanging limply in the dead air. A coke machine stood next to it, offering some light amongst its shadows. On the trailer's wall was what the traveller guessed was a condom machine rusting in the desert air, its casing smashed and hanging limply open. He wondered if someone had tried to rob it for cash many moons ago. Or perhaps a young buck braving the motel's stained sheets with a date had been desperately in need of what they used to call a Johnny where the traveller came from and had at the machine to get one. Preferable no doubt to running down to the local store and giving his girl a chance to sober up. After all, if she did she might think better of a night of passion with someone cheap enough to bring her to such a shit-tip.

The traveller half smiled as these thoughts crossed his mind. He wondered idly how many cherries had popped in that desperate place over the years.

Then he sighed to himself as he reflected that there were probably worse places to lose your virginity. The motel at least would have a bed. A rather better place to lose it than in the garden shed at his mate's sixteenth birthday party on a pile of potato sacks, after four tins of passion inducing special brew. The girl he was briefly with summed up his performance with the words, "Is that it?" as she pulled up her knickers and went in search of her Alcopop, clearly less than impressed by his prowess. Leaving him wilting into a shrivelling condom he had barely had time to put on.

This was not a memory to which he had grown fond over the years. On reflection, he considered, the motel was probably a palace of romance in comparison to his teenage fumblings on a council estate in Tadcaster.

The bus stations ticket office was also a trailer. A larger one of the static kind, which was at least in reasonable repair compared to the one at the motel. One side had been cut out and replaced with long windows, around a set of double doors, Half the trailer formed the waiting room, the other half the office itself.

Both were closed.

Just as the rest of the town seemed closed. A few lights were on in trailer homes further down the strip. A few more where trailers got replaced by actual subprime track housing. Further still where the strip became Main Street there was a small commercial district, with better street lighting. All told it was about a quarter mile from the station to heart of town. It was not a beating heart. However, Main Street looked as closed as everywhere else.

Wherever he was, it was dead time, 2 am. The only things in the streets at this time were stray cats, or perhaps a foraging coyote, come in from the desert to raid the trash of civilisation. Hicksville mid-west was closed for the night and sheltering from the unusual summer storm. The traveller, whose name was Richard Barrick, found himself wondering if there would be much more life there in the middle of the day, deciding in all likely hood it would be equally dead at 2 pm. Such was the run down, broken nature of the place: the back end of nowhere in the mid-west. A place half forgotten by the world, and probably by those who still dwelled there.

Richard could not shake the feeling of being

watched by someone or something all the same. For a second, he thought he saw a face in the shadows, but that was nothing new to him. He saw faces everywhere. A flash of red reflected in the glass of the windows, which may have been a car's brake light, though he heard no car. He closed his eyes and let the rain fall on his face, letting his paranoia fade. Till a cold breeze came out of the dead air and he felt a shiver of cold against his spine.

The shiver broke the spell of the rain, suddenly it was no longer refreshing, and so he moved into the shelter of the ticket office awning. Through the glass, he looked longingly at the hard plastic seating of the waiting room. Feeling cold from the raid and bone tired, even the crappy looking coffee machine looked appealing. Though he hated the taste of cheap machine coffee in tiny plastic cups, at this moment he would be thankful for one. Not that he could afford to waste the fifty cents.

Occupying his mind to shrug off the feeling of being watched if nothing else, he tried to take in every detail of the waiting room. Mostly, though, it was to avoid making a decision about his next move. He knew he should be moving on, but had nowhere to go or money to go there with. Standing around and sheltering from the rain was as good an option as he had.

Dirty vinyl tiles covered the floor, scuffed and longing for a polish they badly needed. If they had a pattern upon them, it was indistinguishable beneath the grim. The over-filled ash trays, forgotten on the chrome topped pedestal bins, were equally untended to. The usual detritus of any waiting room was all the worse for the level of neglect about the place. Half-filled forgotten plastic cups no doubt sprouting mould, mingled on the dusty corner tables with out-of-date magazines no one would wish to read. While beneath hard utilitarian plastic seats, designed with an equal lack of comfort for all in mind, lay fast food cartons and cigarette ends. Kicked, or occasionally brushed to one side, they gathered in mounds in defiance of fire regulations. A single match could set the place ablaze in minutes.

In one corner a ragged plastic plant, probably placed in the vain hope of adding some semblance of nature to the room, instead served as an extra ash tray.

The door to the unisex toilet had a heavy padlock and a sign saying '*Request the key at the counter.*' If the worry-worn battered door was any guide, then he was not sure he wanted to imagine the state of the facilities beyond.

Waiting rooms the world over inspire little in the way of human warmth, at least in Richard's opinion. This one was no exception. Indeed, in utter fairness, it was a damn sight worse than most he had had the displeasure to spend any time in.

Looking for a further distraction from the cold and the numbing relentless beat of raindrops on the tarmac, Richard found the Grey Dogs Bible in the corner of the window, posted with small ads. In his last few months on the road, he had found himself seated next to more than one old hand in the vagrant lifestyle. He had come to realise there was a whole subculture out there he had never previously imagined. Travelling the length and breadth of America on Greyhound buses, there were those who referred to themselves as the Grey Dogs, or collectively as Grey Dogger's.

The name amused Richard more than it should have done due to his British upbringing. It conjured up the image of a bunch of ageing men standing in bushes, watching parked cars with steamy windows.

Grey Dogs travelled the back ways of America on busses and picked up work where they could for a few days or weeks, never staying still for long before they hopped the next Greyhound out of town. The Dogs held themselves aloof in their chosen path of vagrancy, different from the 'rail riders' or common hoboes. They had a place in the world, even if that place was the back seat of a Greyhound and ill kept bus station waiting rooms. In their minds, at least, it raised them above the average hobo. They paid their way, or at the very least their fares.

Richard had found their pride odd and the station it assumed laughable at first, though he had the good grace to keep his opinion to himself. As his time on the buses went on however he came to understand the Doggers more and more. He realised that even on the fringes people needed something to cling to. Something that allowed them to feel better about themselves, giving them a place in the world and someone to look down upon, no matter how close they sat to the bottom of the pile.

He hated the idea that even down there at the

bottom people were as conceited and bigoted as anywhere else in society.

He hated the idea even more once he realised he had been thinking in similar terms, rationalising that he wasn't himself a transient, if for no other reason than because his decision to live as he did had been entirely his own. In his own mind, this placed him a step up from the bigoted self-worthy Grey Dogs.

Until his realisation that he was doing the same as them, finding people to think of as lesser than himself, to boost his own self-esteem.

For the Grey Dog's the Bible was the bus station pin board. Every small town bus station had one. They were full of little ads selling old worn out things which, had little or no real value. Short term let ads for run down rooms and the cheapest end of the hotel market; lost pets posters with pictures of the loved animals their owners desperately wanted back, enough so to put signs in bus stations. And, of course, there were the want ads, offering short-term employment: picking fruit, packing meat, fence painting, labouring or other jobs. Jobs so short-term and poorly paid, only the Grey Dogs and others in the transient community would be likely to take them up. Everything a Grey Dog needed could be found on those pin boards.

The boards offered a short-term reprieve from the life of a bus-bound vagabond. Work, shelter and a way to make a quick buck or two. Enough, at least, to keep body and soul until next time you had to move on and to earn the price of the bus ticket to the next town.

Stood there now with only three dollars and change in his pocket, no bed to go to, no dry change of clothes, and no food in his stomach, Richard guessed that made him as much a Grey Dog as anyone else.

So he scanned the little cards and posters on the pin board, more in hope than expectation.

The itch of being watched returned, but he suppressed the urge to look over his shoulder, into the dark of the night and the faces he might see there. The haven of the lamp light, intermittent though it was, gave him a vague sense of security, despite him being all too aware that bus stations at night were not the safest of places. He closed his eyes for a moment and let himself find some calm, before looking at the reflections in the window to assure himself he was alone. Putting the feeling down to nothing more than paranoia, he focused once more on reading the pin board.

He skipped over the twelve dollars a night boarding houses beyond his means, which was unlikely to be found open at 2 am in any case. Then paused for a moment to take in the picture of a cocker spaniel called Alfie, posted by a loving owner willing to pay ten dollars for his return. It's sad eyes gazed back at him from the badly photocopied photograph.

Richard thought absently to himself that *'Anyone who really loved their dog would have had a better picture to use, and would offer more than ten bucks to get him back.'*

He was still half pretending to himself that he was only looking at the pin board to pass the time.

Trying, as he did so, to ignore the deep-seated ache in his joints and the hunger pains of a stomach, left empty for more than a couple of days, when he found in the corner of the pin board something he would never have expected.

Which ripped him in two.

> ## Piano Player Wanted
> ## Must know Forever Autumn
> ## Room, Board, Plus Tips
> ## Esqwith's Passing Place
> ## Piano Bar and Grill
> ## Location Relative

Forever Autumn…

It had been her favourite song.

From the moment he had first played the album for her. She had loved it with an abiding passion. The name of the song had brought him up short. Cutting him to the quick, deep within his soul.

Forever autumn…

He had not listened to the song since she died. He sold his copy, along with everything else, six months after her death.

He had quit his job a month after her funeral. It seemed a worthless, hollow, and pointless thing. The support group told him it was one of the stages of grief. His boss told him they would hold his position open. Everyone told him to, "*Take some time.*" Just as well-meaningly they all told him, "*It will get easier.*"

"Horse shit!" he had told them in reply.

Nothing got easier, it never got easier. Nothing filled the gaping hole in his life. Six months after she died he could not take the reminders anymore.

In a crappy little bar off Main Street, while he drown his sorrows, a fellow drunk offered him some sage advice…

"Sell up and move on."

It seemed like the best advice in the world. So that was what he did.

He let the rent on the apartment run out and held a garage sale to turn all the detritus of his life into cold, worthless cash.

The garage sale to end all garage sales:

"Come. Buy my shit. Everything for sale. Take my life in exchange for your cash."

"These china cups, ten dollars and they're yours, five then since you want to haggle and I'll throw in the saucers for free."

"The brass-framed bed we slept in, argued in, ignored each other in, made up in and fucked in, two hundred bucks, take it, take the mattress and, while you're at it, take the linen we stained with our love making as well."

"The wide screen, which we watched Casablanca, Star Wars and Jaws together on. That we snuggled up in fount of on the couch, with popcorn and coffee. Hell, buy the couch while you're at it, the DVD's, the player, the lot, give me the dead presidents and carry them out with you."

"The silver frames with our wedding

photographs in, twenty dollars the pair, fifteen then, okay twelve greens and it's a deal, no don't give me the pictures back, take them, chuck them, burn them, whatever, just don't leave them with me."

"The clothes she wore, the smell of her perfume and sweat still on them. Haunting my senses each time I go near the washing basket. My clothes, the ones I wore when I was with her, the ones that remind me of our life together each time I pull them on. Shit, just take everything in the wardrobe and the damn wardrobe itself, make me an offer for the lot, taking any bids any price, take my junk, take my life,, take it all."

He had flirted with the idea of piling up the cash afterwards and dropping a match in the middle, just to watch it burn. His life was gone, ended with her, with just some half-life left that had no worth or substance. So all that was left was to sell it all, and burn the proceeds.

Richard fell short of that at the last; the match burning down to his fingertips while he held it. Instead, he took the cash, found a cheap rental car and set off to see America. Trying to find a point in it all, a reason to go on, or an answer, any answer, to the question that burned within him.

Why?

Three letters and a question mark, one word.

An endless black hole of a question.

"Why?"

Their last few months together she seemed happier and more at one with herself than at any time he had known her. Throughout the five years of their relationship, Carrie had fought off bouts of depression more than once. But they had become more fleeting over the years. He had always known she had issues with events in her past. Dark memories that could be brought to the surface by the smallest of things, a newspaper article perhaps, or an unexpected scent in the air, or just the colour of falling leaves, triggers all of those memories long suppressed, that languished unresolved in the darker corners of her mind.

Her psychiatrist, a charmless individual who viewed things with cold detachment, had broken her confidence after she died and spoken to Richard over the phone.

"You have my deepest sympathies, Mr Barrick. I am sorry for your loss. It is tragic when depression leads to this but, much as we would wish it otherwise, some things can never be resolved. The best we can achieve is to lessen their impact over time. Dampen, it down as it were. Sadly, it can resurface when least expected."

It had been only a few days after her funeral, a call not so much made out of sympathy, Richard suspected, but in order to present his bill to the grieving widower.

The court injunction had arrived two days later. The good doctors' deepest sympathies did not extend to a waiting period for payment. Richard had written a long angry letter, filled with bitterness and grief, taking pains to point out that his wife had been receiving treatment for her depression, which obviously had not been successful. He stated he would see the doctor in court and told him to stick his bill where the sun did not shine. He stamped it, posted it and punched the post box in frustration, before walking back to the apartment feeling terribly alone.

He woke that night in a cold sweat, and remembered how much she had hated unpaid bills. The next day he posted off a cheque and an apology.

Richard had always struggled to deal with her bouts of depression. He had tried to help in any way he could. He would give her space, making himself scarce around the apartment, or stay close and hold her through the night. Treat her to her favourite food, or take her to a happy movie. He tried talking her through it. He tried keeping silent and just being there to listen. At times the frustration got beyond him. It had turned to anger and he had despised himself afterwards.

No matter what he tried, she just seemed to sink deeper into herself. Adrift somehow in what the Japanese call a cold of the soul.

"This is not yours to deal with, Richard, honey, I know you want to help but you can't," she told him once. He refused to accept that, and kept on trying.

Even now, a year after her death he could not accept that it was not in some way his fault. That he could have said the right thing at the right time, done some little thing that would have made a difference. Not been out working perhaps, stayed home and held her close with coffee and cookie dough ice-cream. If he had smiled as he walked out the door and said he loved her. Or just given her just one more hug. A little thing that could have made her decide not to take her own life that night. Put it off for another day, another week, forever.

That was another question that woke him in cold sweats at night…

"What if?"

"What could I have done differently?"

"What could I have said to make her think twice?"

'What if?'

He had asked himself, asked his friends, asked his colleagues, asked the mailman, asked the girl behind the counter at Starbucks, asked the guy on the subway, asked a stranger in the park, asked anyone who cared to listen. Asked whether they cared or not.

Just another question with no answer, but it kept on occurring to him all the same.

He remembered the day they met for the first time, one of those mad little coincidences, nothing more.

They had both missed the same subway train by a few moments, arriving on the platform just as the train pulled away. He would not have missed the train at all if he had not dropped his keys while struggling for change at the ticket booth. While he scrambled for the keys his place in the queue was taken by a less than polite fellow ticket buyer, who took their own sweet time choosing their ticket.

He recollected, muttering something under his breath about *'fucking tourists'*, and being rewarded by a sharp look of disdain from the queue jumper, who then snorted at Richard and returned to deciding between an off-peak roamer and an all zones travel pass. A choice which it seemed was far more difficult than the twenty cents price difference suggested.

In all, he was only delayed a few minutes, but it was enough that even half jogging, half running towards the platform his reward had been the sight of the back end of the train pulling away with a thirty-minute wait for the next one.

She entered the platform from the other entrance as the last vestiges of the train vanished into the darkness of the tunnel. That was his first sight of her, frustrated and red-faced, angrily stomping across the platform to the solitary line of blue plastic seats.

They sat two seats apart in silence for the better part of ten minutes, though he had found himself glancing in her direction more than once between staring at his feet and looking up at the arrival/departure screen to see how much longer the wait would be.

Each time he looked her way he found his eyes dwelling upon her a moment longer than was strictly polite, before catching himself doing so and snapping his gaze to the track in front of him. The third or fourth time, however, he found her smiling back at him, returning that odd embarrassed, but interested gaze.

Somehow that shared gaze had led to an edgy broken conversation. One in which he had felt more nervous than he had any right to be. As nervous as himself as an awkward teenager talking to girls for the first time back home in England.

He could never recall now what she was

wearing, or how the conversation between them began. All he remembered was at some point he had invited her to Lincoln's Lizard Lounge, the crappy little venue he was playing at the following night. He'd had a spare flyer on him, half crumpled in his pocket, which he had nervously handed to her. Mostly, in truth, an attempt to prove it was not just a line he was swinging by her.

When the train finally arrived they sat opposite each other on long bench seats in an empty car, continuing the strangely awkward conversation as the subway train rattled through the tunnels. Lights flickering each time the train jumped the rails.

They parted when his stop came up, Richard feeling an odd twinge of regret as he rose from his seat. All too sure he would never see her again, while desperately hoping he would. But it was, after all, just a coincidental meeting. Nothing but blind luck, one of those moments when you touch another's life as they touch yours for a few minutes, perhaps, or an hour. Then never think of them again.

He thought about her all night, the sound of her voice, that soft accent which he could not quite place. Wisconsin perhaps or Maine or any of a half-dozen other states.

Her sad green penetrating eyes, the way they gazed back at him, and into him as they talked.

Her laugh, a throaty chortle, which uttered from her lips at the oddest moments in their conversation.

And mostly her face, her strangely awkward, quirky, beautiful face. The face looking back at him, into him, and smiling.

The following morning he awoke from a dream of that smile. The morning was spent half in a day dream of that smile. By noon, reality kicking in, he had resigned himself to never seeing her again, with an evocative curse uttered against the gods of coincidence.

That night looking beyond the keyboards to the dimly lit club, awash with dry ice to hide the tiny audience and the state of the floor, he saw her sitting by the bar. Her eyes watching him with an intense, sad kind of joy, he dropped several notes. His eyes locked on her, and she broke into a smile, which melted his soul.

He struggled his way through the rest of the set. For his pains, he received disgruntled looks from both the lead guitarist and the bass player for messing up his notes. Though the singer, a prima donna named 'Slick' Steve Snake (real name Tony Mills) didn't seem to notice. Instead, he sang as badly and as out of tune as ever.

When Richard joined her at the bar, they fell back into the same awkward, delightful conversations which were to become the norm between them.

A year to the day after their first meeting in the subway, they married in a small ceremony before a judge upstate. The guests extended only to a couple of his friends who served as witnesses, toasting the happy couple with cheap, not quite champagne, and waving them off to a honeymoon weekend in St Paul.

Life settled down. She was working on her

doctorate part time at NYU, while teaching gym at the Y. He'd worked in the parts department of a Queens car dealership through the day, and played keyboard in a string of unsuccessful bands on the suburban New York circuit. They found a small apartment on the better edge of Queens. Times were good. Money, though never plentiful, was not a problem. What problems they had, their love carried them through.

Carrie never spoke of her past, of her family, friends, or lovers from before him. She never spoke of anything from before that day on the subway. When he asked, she would grow dark and troubled. When he pushed too hard, his questions would lead to arguments, and throw her into odd depressions and silences. By the time they married, he had stopped asking and tried to think of it as just one of the quirks of her character. Eventually, he just accepted his wife's missing past. Whatever she hid from him, it was her business, not his.

It was a few months after their wedding that she fell into her first deep depression, and a cycle began that he came to know only too well.

She would slip into dark mindsets, which would lead to suicidal thoughts, and anger; a deep raging anger which often seemed directed at him, though in truth, he was just the one she could vent her anger with. He struggled to cope, yet loved her more deeply than he had imagined possible all the same.

She would accuse him of taking hold of her life, tying her to it, so she could not move on. Because she loved him, she was locked into this life, chained to living in this world, trapped, when she should have returned long ago.

The things she said in her rages made little sense to him. for all he tried to follow her reasoning. When she was calm, he would ask her to explain what she meant, convinced that it was tied up with her mysterious past. He thought perhaps she was running from someone. Even feared she may have been married before, or was a runaway from some strange cult, or something like that. But asking her would only lead to her withdrawing from him, refusing to answer, or just dismissing the questions. So, in the end, he stopped asking her to explain those rages as well.

She started therapy, partly at his suggestion, after their third year together. It was costly, but they managed the bills for both the sessions and the medication which followed, though Richard was left speaking lyrically of the wonders of the NHS back home. They both took extra shifts at work to find the money. The sessions helped a little for a while, but the effect was fleeting, while the drugs mostly made her nauseous or withdrawn and passive. For the first couple of years, it seemed to do little beyond manage the worst of her depression, but the blackest days were still as black as ever. She often talked of ending it all, for him as much as for herself. He hated those conversations, which always led to the same arguments.

Then it all changed over the course of a summer. Suddenly she began to smile more. She laughed freely at his jokes. She smirked with joy at the shared references of a long relationship. Her days seemed full of joy, and there was an exuberance about her he had never seen before.

She was off the medication and did not have an episode for months. She was happy and as in love as was he. Richard harboured the hope that the depressions were finally behind her.

Then she ended that hope it in the most final and absolute of ways.

> Richard My love
> I could not stay, it has grown harder each day.
> Do not mourn me. I am going home at last.
> I will see you again in another life
> I will love you always.
> Carrie

A brief note, he found by the sink, simple and lacking in anything he could grasp towards as an explanation. There was no distraught phone call, as there had always been in the past. No finding her weeping on the floor and not going through with that final act of choice. No waking in the night to find himself being held as if the world was collapsing around them. All the things he had been through with her before, in her darkest moments, had not prepared him for the finality of that letter.

He came home late on that fateful night from a gig with a small jazz band two towns over and thirty miles upstate. Came home to find her lying dead in the bath. The water a deep red sickening colour.

Cold and clammy. The deep cuts in her wrists brutally final. Her eyes open and staring endlessly at the polystyrene tiles on the ceiling.

She had ended it all and left him behind, stuck with one unanswerable, painful, question. "Why?"

Three letters, a question mark, and a black hole in which to drop his every emotion.

"Why?"

Six painful months had followed, waking each morning alone in the shell of their life, empty, cold and soulless without her. The funeral had been a blur; every day after was a blur.

Then came the garage sale to end them all.

Richard took the money he decided not to burn and hit the road. It lasted him six more months. The rental had lasted the first three before he decided it was cutting through his funds too quickly, and he had dropped it in favour of the good old Greyhound. The first week of bus rides left him regretting the loss of the car. Stale smells and stale conversations on late night journeys between states had put pay to his romantic idea of the old grey working dog. But he had stuck with it and in those six months he had seen America from one coast to the other, mid-west to Texas, the Everglades of the sunshine state, to the endless rain of Seattle. The Grand Canyon and Disneyland, the Joshua tree to the giant redwoods, Old Faithful, and the great lakes, he had seen it all, and none of it touched him, cheered him or filled the hole she had left.

Six months on the road, and he was down to

loose change and a bag of dishevelled clothes, looking for a job in a hick town he could not even remember the name of; just another mid-west outpost with a Baptist church, tavern and an empty bus station where the Greyhounds were kenneled each night. He found himself staring at a sign in the grimy bus station window offering work to a piano player who knew Forever Autumn.

Carries favourite song.

He read it for the third time, with the same disbelieving eyes. "What's wrong with this picture," he muttered to himself under his breath, falling into an old habit of thinking out loud when alone.

"Hicksville bar seeks piano player, fair enough. Hell, they probably even have MTV out here so it's not all Tammy and Dolly. Maybe Hicksville has a yearning for a piano bar and the best of Gilbert and Sullivan. But shit! Come on, give me a break. *Forever Autumn*? Who the hell in this back end of nowhere knows a song from a 1978 concept album?"

He read it for a fourth time, trying to ignore the rest of his thoughts: that voice inside him which wanted to add painfully, '*It was her favourite song. Of all the songs in the world, her favourite song.*' Even if he could suspend his disbelief about everything else, even if he could accept the unlikeliness of the card naming such an improbable song. It was her song. She played that album to death, Jeff Wayne's *War of the Worlds*, a double album, retelling the H G Wells classic. All powerful vocals, odd keyboards and majestic rock guitars, a weird synthesis of rock music and storytelling you would never get past a record producer in these more cynical days of pre-made formulated mass music. Richard Burton was the narrator. Hollywood Royalty—the Tom Cruise of his day—he gets involved in this weird little concept album, written by a virtually unknown composer at the time. It was unique. Carrie had loved it, cherished it even despite it being a decade older than she was. *Forever Autumn* was her favourite track on her favourite album.

She would play it over and over.

.A gentle rain falls softly on my weary eyes,

She was so pleased when he had shown her how to get the CD player to repeat one song on a constant loop.

As if to hide a lonely tear,

She had smiled for what seemed like hours as she sat writing the last draught of her thesis while it played over and over.

My life will be forever Autumn,.

Driving him to distraction but he loved to see her smile so never moved to change the song.

Cause you're not here …

It was the CD in the player the night she took her life, playing on that selfsame loop. She had slit her wrists laying in a hot bath while she was listening to her favourite song.

Like the sun through the trees, you came to love me.

It was still playing when he found her. It echoed through his head for an hour while he waited for the ambulance he had called four hours too late to mean a damn thing.

Like a leaf on a breeze, you blew away.

The police came next with forced sympathy, edged with questions he could not answer. Questions which amounted to "Did he have any idea why she did it?" Why? Same old unanswered question.

Cause you're not here.

It was one of the police who finally turned off the CD player, filling the apartment with a silence that was terrifying in its own right. Richard had never played the song again. But it echoed through his nightmares.

Cause you're not here.

Waking with cold sweats in the night, the song strolled through his mind as he found himself reliving the moment of finding her. Or just having those endless "Why's?" staring back unanswered in the darkness.

Cause you're not here.

"Cause you're not here."

It became his plaintive cry to the world ever since. Life was without worth; it had no taste nor meaning.

Cause you're not here,
Going on made no sense anymore
Cause you're not here ……….

He stood staring at the card in the window through the grime, refusing to believe his eyes. Breathing deeply of the warm dead air, he wondered to himself if he had become light-headed from lack of food. It had been a couple of days since his last proper meal. A couple of candy bars were no substitute for actual food. Perhaps then this was just some kind of hunger delusion.

A short gust of wind whistled through the dead air, pushing his long, lank hair across his face. The unexpected breeze made him shiver slightly as the temperature dropped a degree or two.

A half bored yowl filled the silence of the bus station, shaking him out of his self-indulgence, bad memories, and uncomfortable questions. Surprised and suddenly paranoid once more, he looked around for the source of the noise. It turned out to be a tortoiseshell cat. Laying a few feet away on the asphalt pavement.

The cat seemed to be languidly examining Richard amidst a bored yawn, while its tail, a fluff of fur, stretched out into the night air, arching above it. Its green eyes were staring straight back at him, its head at a slight tilt. It showed nothing of fear or even concern, just lay there watching him with an air of supreme indifference and giving out the impression of owning the pavement in that way only cats can.

He remembered Carrie telling him once that cats considered anywhere they were belonged to them, and to them alone, as a matter of course. Which he had come to think was probably not far from the truth. It was one of those odd little insights which he had loved her for. She had always managed to find strange ways of looking at the world.

Carrie would have liked this particular cat, he considered, tortoise shells were always among her favourites. His thoughts straying to her he felt that same deep well of grief threaten to flood over him, and he snatched the thought away before he could dwell on it, not wanting to think of her again so soon.

To distract himself, without really thinking about it, he found himself staring at the cat as it slowly, with artful laziness, stood and stretched its limbs, before strolling towards him.

It captivated his attention in much the same way as the card in the window had, but without the feeling of grief, the cards words had inspired. For a moment at least it was forgotten.

The tortoiseshell had that sleek elegance only a cat can muster. Yet its green eyes never left his as it walked, before it leapt up to the window sill and stalked along it with self-assured grace. Finally coming to a halt right next to the card in the window, where it started purring gently as if it was purposely dragging his attention back to the card.

Dragging him back to the memories again in the process, he felt a lump in his throat as it tightened, but the cat continued to purr softly and almost seemed to be speaking to him.

Telling him, *'Take the job'*, telling him *'It's Okay,'* telling him there were answers to be found. "*Take the job. Time to start rebuilding your life Richard. Only then will you find an answer to your why,*" it purred.

After what seemed like an age, but was probably less than a minute, the cat leapt down from the windowsill and stalked off into the night.

Richard watched it go, its tail high in the air. Bemused, somehow sure, despite knowing it was impossible, that the cat had spoken to him. That the cat had even known his name. Known him in fact.

Once it was gone, he looked back at the card in the window. "*Esqwiths Passing Place*. Weird name for a bar... But what the hell it's probably that or starve, I guess," he muttered to himself.

Resolved to take the job, he picked up his backpack and set off in search of the bar, thankful that the rain was at least easing off. He headed, somewhat without direction, towards the centre of the nameless town, in the hope it would lead him to wherever the bar was. With an odd sense of purpose, without aim, he started walking. Stepping through the puddles on the tarmac, not noticing the odd pulse of red light reflected there which had no source.

He did not notice either that his choice of direction meant he was following the tortoiseshell cat as it led him through the heat of the night ...

CHAPTER TWO

Relativity of Location

Finding Esqwith's Passing Place was both easier and harder than Richard expected. It only occurred to him as he made the quarter mile walk towards the centre of town that the address given on the card had seemed a little on the odd side.

Location Relative.

It did not tell him anything. Unless Relative was a street name in whatever Hicksville town actually was called. Which seemed a little unlikely. Medwest towns tended to go with the usual bunch of unimaginative street names, Main Street and Madison and the like.

Not wishing to ask directions until he had to, while figuring a small town like Hicksville would have most of its bars and businesses in and around Main Street, he headed there. He knew it was a possibility that Esqwith's was a roadhouse out near the interstate. He ruled out that option for no other reason than the centre of town was closer.

Location Relative, it prompted the question relative to what? Possibly it was a joke of some kind, or perhaps an oblique reference he was just not getting. It occurred to him the whole thing could just be a joke, though he would be damned if he could figure out the punch line. He found himself pondering this and other questions as he stalked through the drizzling rain.

The name of the bar, if it was a bar, was an oddity in of itself, he realised.

'Esqwiths Passing Place.'

It should have been '*The Watering Hole*', or '*The Dew Drop Inn*' or some other staple bar name in places like the Hicksville town he'd found himself stranded in.

If anything it sounded more like some half-assed sophisticated New York or LA name. The kind of bar that would be all the vogue, for six months or a year at most, among the yuppie crowd. Before its inevitable fall from grace and then being closed down to make way for the next trendy wine bar to spring up.

For that matter, a Piano bar and grill sounded an improbable combination. "After all," he mused verbally "*How many steak houses have a pianist playing requests for the carnivores for Christ sake?*"

Smiling at his own dismissive incredulity, as he made his way down the main drag of a town he thought would have to grow some to become a backwater. It was not that he did not want to believe the card, he just found it hard to credit. More the whole idea inspired a grim humour within him.

"Could I get a rack of ribs, loaded potatoes skins, corn on the cob, a rib eye, a draught of Bud? Oh, and ask the piano player to bash out *Unchained Melody* will you?" He joked to the night air.

The more he thought about it, the funnier it seemed to him, and the more unlikely.

As he reached the start of Main Street, however, it started to rain heavily again. Dampening the levity of his mood. Instead, he began thinking the whole thing a fools errand.

Unable to find suitable shelter between store fronts, he was soaked to the skin once more in a few minutes. He resolved to ask directions from the first local he came across. Which struck him as another fools errand in a town as dead as the desert air on a weeknight at 2 am.

The seven eleven had been shut for hours, its neon sign switched off for the night, as had everywhere else. Though the sign seemed to flicker with a dark red for a moment as he passed, which caught his eye and for no reason he could fathom made him shiver. The reflection of a stop sign on the window he caught himself thinking, without knowing why he felt the needed to rationalise.

Even the local sheriff's department was closed

for the night. Emergency calls probably just went direct to the duty officer's home and got him out of bed. If you did so, you better have a damn good reason for waking him up unless you wanted to get an ear full about why your problems were not his problems.

2 am in Hicksville's streets was dead time.

Not a time to be asking for directions in the rain, Richard realised grimly.

Giving up on the hope of finding the bar in the storm, let alone that it would still be open so late into the night, Richard looked for shelter. Somewhere he could at least sit out the worst of the downpour. Eventually, he ended up under the eaves of the local farmers union and tucked himself tightly into the doorway. It offered little enough shelter but at least kept him dry enough to roll a cigarette and have a drag, while he considered his options.

He stood in that debatable shelter and looked out across a slowly dying main street, all too reminiscent of so many other small towns. Having seen the same pattern so many times before he had no doubt that the local mall took much of the business away from the centre of town. One in four lots were vacant. The ones in use showed all the hallmarks of struggling businesses, store fronts in need of a lick of paint, and a modicum of investment which their meagre turn-overs would not cover. Sale signs hung in most windows, Sale signs that looked like permanent fixtures.

He looked out into the darkness, trying not to see the faces in the shadows, knowing they were phantoms of his own creation. He felt a shiver run down his spine for a moment, which may have been because of the rain, but may have been for other reasons. He took a deep breath trying to calm himself. The cold and the wet were dragging at him, he knew. A numb ache behind his eyebrows was a sign of a headache to come. He tried to relax his tired mind, closing his eyes for a few moments. Lack of sleep was not helping. Though there was little chance of bedding down in the doorway in this weather.

He opened his eyes once more. The ache at his temples fading. The faces gone, for a while at least. He surveyed the street once more.

Across the road from the Farmers Union, there was another seven eleven. Long closed for the day, metal shutters had been pulled down over the store front. Beside the store was a vacant lot, fenced off with chain link and full of weeds and trash. Beyond the vacant lot was a gentleman's barbers which looked like it hadn't done good business for a decade or more. The obligatory red and white pole sticking out of the wall was flaked and rusting.

A car dealership further up the road looked like the kind of place which had done good business in the fifties and had limped on ever since, was now a second-hand dealership, Crazy Dave's. "D*eals so good I must be crazy.*" A banner proclaimed.

Richard had no doubt the local FM station would feature the owner singing his own praises. A sticker on a station waggon windshield proclaimed that Dave had the, "*Best deals in Nebraska*" while a sign over the car lot said *Providence Automobiles*.

All of which probably gave Hicksville a name, though Richard cared little which part of the mid-west he was currently standing in, drenched to the skin.

He stood in the Farmers Union doorway smoking and watching the rain flush dust and trash down the gutters of the main street. Staring out towards the vacant lot opposite him for almost half an hour, tiredness seeped over him until he was half drifting off leaning against the doorway.

He was shocked back to wakefulness when something brushed against the leg of his jeans. He looked down in the kind of mild panic you only get when unexpectedly roused from a dozing dream.

It was, to his surprise, the cat from the bus station. The tortoise shell was determinedly pressing up against him, sharing his sanctuary from the downpour.

"Hey there fella," he murmured, finding himself unexpectedly pleased to have the company. The cat, however, hissed back at him. Looking up from his feet with an expression, which Richard somehow instinctively knew was irritation. For a moment, he wondered what he had done. Then realised his mistake and smiled apologetically. "Sorry lady," he amended.

Richard fished about in his coat pockets for something to make reparation with, finding, much to his own surprise, the last of a square of a Hensley chocolate bar in the recesses of his coat pocket. He bent down to offer his token of appeasement to the cat. His reward was a deep rumbling purr. The tortoise shell rubbed its neck and back hard against his leg, nibbling the chocolate out of his hand.

It did not occur to him to question how he had guessed her sex. Somehow he had just known his error. Nor did he question the way she seemed to know what he had said. Instead, what occurred to him as the cat nibbled away at the chocolate was how it reminded him of Carrie, odd though it seemed. She'd also had a love of nibbling away at chocolate bars. She could make a bar last a couple of days, taking tiny bites every now and again and savouring the treat rather than eating it all at once. It was a strange thought to strike him, he knew. But then so many things would bring back memories of Carrie. She always lay at the back of his mind.

That small reminder of his grief dampened his mood. A wave of it slipping over him, as it always did. So he tried to push it out of his mind and stared off across the main street again towards the vacant lot.

Vacant no longer.

It was the brightness of the neon sign that first surprised him. Not that it was overly brash or ostentatious, just a sudden bright point in the darkness of the downpour. The windows of the bar were tinted glass affairs, which looked a little out of place in Hicksville's broken streets, yet seemed to suit the bar all the same.

'*Esqwiths Passing Place, Piano Bar and Grill* ' it read.

Pale blue in the black, without a strobeing flash or any other low-brow tricks to draw attention to it, a simple small neon sign in a window and a pair of heavy doors.

After he got past the shock of seeing the bar appear in what he had sworn was a vacant lot. Richard rationalised its appearance to himself, speaking out loud, half to the cat at his side.

"Of course, it's nearly 4 am, I just didn't see it because the lights were off. Someone just turned them back on. That's all. It just looked like a vacant lot in the darkness." He found himself chuckling at his own foolishness. Then glanced down at the cat and added, "Bars don't just appear in vacant lots."

Returning his gaze the cat seemed to be giving him a dismissive, almost unbelieving look. Almost saying '*Sure Richard, if that makes you feel better.* '

He knew he was tired, but he could have sworn he actually heard the cat purr out those words. He wondered for a moment if he was starting to lose his fragile grip on reality. Then found himself shaking his head and muttering. "I must be more tired than I thought."

The cat just stare back at him, almost seeming to shake her head at him in disbelief.

Disconcerted, Richard looked up and across at the bar again. As he did so, he saw the bar's main doors swing open. A huge man dressed in a black tuxedo stepped out into the rainy night. Propping the door open somehow, he stood in the shelter of the overhang, like some mythical portal guardian. He was built well for the role, the archetypal club doorman. Richard found himself musing about the doorman verbally, "I guess if that guy bounces you, you stay bounced."

The cat purred at his feet in what Richard half believed was actually a chuckle.

The doorman's skin was as black as his tux, his face covered in a neatly trimmed but beard of thick, coarse black hair. His hair was platted into tight cornrows and equally dark, only the whiteness of his shirt and eyes broke up the patch of darkness he made. He had an aura that was at once both welcoming and held menace, the kind only a true bouncer could achieve. He stood there looking across the main street. Straight at Richard, who felt the hairs on the back his neck stand up.

They locked eyes for a moment. Then the doorman seemed to lose interest. He reached into his jacket and took out a half crumpled packet of Marlboro, deciding there was no immediate call on his doormanship. He pulled a cigarette free from the packet and lit it with a Zippo.

'*Well, you going to stand in the rain all night Richard, cause it will be a damn sight warmer in there*' said the voice of the cat.

It definitely was not actually the cat. He was sure of that, because cats don't talk, and there was enough strangeness in the air tonight as it was. His imagination, he was in no doubt, was getting the better of him. The desire for the shelter that warm glowing doorway across the street offered, playing tricks on his mind, he assured himself.

'*Which doesn't mean the cats wrong*,' he thought to himself.

He looked down, and found himself unsurprised to see the cat stalking off across the road, heading towards the bar. Richard felt equally unsurprised when it turned to look at him at the half way point and motioned with its head for him to follow.

'Come on then slack Alice,' the cat said as clear as day, Richard was sure, before resuming its crossing of the road.

'Slack Alice'... that phrase stung him.

He had not been called that since Carrie died. It brought him up short, more than a little shocked for a second. Then he rationalised once more that it was his subconscious, doing its best to fool him. Sure that it was his own mind striving to convince himself he was talking to the cat. He felt the familiar emptiness of grief inside and pushed it down.

"Slack Alice…" he whispered to himself. Shaking his head for a moment and doubting his own sanity.

Then, a decision made, he grabbed his soaked backpack from the doorway, and headed across the road.

As he walked, Richard watched as the cat got a polite nod from the doorman, who stepped to one side to let it disappear through the door. He racked it up to just another little bit of the strangeness of the night, musing to himself, *'The doorman likes cats, So what? Can't blame him for that.'*

Sadly for Richard, it appeared that the doorman did not feel as welcoming in regards to half drowned transients, particularly ones who probably did not look like they had the price of a drink on them. He moved to block Richard's entry before he was even halfway across the road. A feat he easily accomplished by his sheer bulk, which in consequence, also effectively blocked out most of the light coming from within.

"Good evening Sir." the doorman said politely but with a voice which had a definite hint of malice behind the pleasantry, a voice which clearly said it's a good evening for now, whether it continues to be a good evening for you remains to be seen.

"I'm afraid we are not open in this relative at this time." The doorman added after waiting for Richard to complete his crossing of the road. His voice was even and friendly, but a passing note of warning remained.

Richard stood at the curbside, his feet still in the gutter. A gutter which ran high with sluice water which soaked through the fabric of his trainers.

He felt a sudden longing for the warmth that lay beyond the beckoning portal of the doorway, as the rain ran down the back of his collar.

His eyes went from the light seeping passed the doorman to the doorman's eyes, and for a long moment he struggled to find his voice. The whole night had been so strange. The cat seeming to talk, the sign in the window, those words, '*Must know Forever Autumn.*' The sudden storm from dry air. A Bar which he could not find that was suddenly right there in fount of him.

Everything was too strange by far.

He had reached a point where he was passed questioning the strangeness.

He tried to explain to the doorman that he had come about the piano player's job that had been advertised in the bus station window. But all that came of his first attempt was, "Piano job."

He coughed and tried once more, breathing in deeply before he started again, and managed the only slightly less garbled, "I've come about the job as a piano player. I know Forever Autumn, and it said there was a job here. There was a card in the window. And the cat sort of lead me here... I think... well I'm not sure."

The doorman greeted all this with a stoic silence, his face impassive. Richard waited till he could not stand the silent giant's cold stare anymore before beginning to explain once more, "There was this card in the window of the ..."

The doorman held up an imposing hand to stop him.

"I heard you the first time my friend," he intoned, before resuming his silence again for a few seconds. He seemed in the depths of consideration or something and waiting for inspiration to strike. If it was anything, Richard was sure, it was for some profound or witty reply to come to him. At which point, he did not doubt, entry would be refused and the Doorman would tell Richard that he should move on.

Richard felt himself deflating, resigned to a miserable end to this fool's errand, and was all for turning back to the limited sanctuary of the doorway across the street. Then the Doorman seemed to reach a decision and spoke again with words which Richard would never have expected.

"Tell me, my friend, did the cat talk to you as well?"

Richard's first assumption was that he was being mocked.

The doorman having a joke with the half-crazed and all soaked man in the gutter. The one who knew himself to be spouting mad ideas about a job. *"Did the cat talk to you as well?"* seemed mockery at the very least.

Richard felt a swell of anger, sick of being wet and tired. He was about to respond angrily when it suddenly struck him there was no mockery in the doorman's tone.

The question was actually a genuine one, at least, it seemed to have been asked in nothing but seriousness.

"Erm... Yes, I mean she seemed to, I followed her I think, at least I seemed to hear the voice in my head,, erm... This is nuts, right?" he replied, shaking now. Deep down he wondered if this was all down to lack of food and sudden exposure; If it was, in fact, the early signs of hypothermia or something else brought on by poor diet and a transient lifestyle. *'Perhaps I am finally losing my grip on it all completely,'* he thought, somewhat bitterly.

The doorman smiled, white teeth cutting through the darkness of his face in the dim street lights.

"I think you better step inside my friend, we're leaving this relative in a few minutes anyway. I guess she's been collecting strays again," he uttered, there was a sigh in his voice at this last bit. His whole tone had softened suddenly. He stepped to one side and ushered Richard past him into the doorway. A second set of doors with misted glass stood between the outer portal and the bar itself, but even getting this far and out of the rain cheered Richard considerably, the warmth coming from inside a welcome relief.

"Wait here a moment," the Doorman said before rummaging through a small cupboard beside the door. After a few moments search, he produced a soft pink towel and tossed it to the bedraggled Richard. "Dry yourself a little before you catch something nasty."

Richard thanked him and began to towel down his hair and face, feeling a little warmer and less like a human river bed. He risked a smile in return. "The cat ...." he began inquiring only to face the hand of silence once more.

"All in good time, I suspect we will have plenty of it, my friend," the doorman said, then relaxed a little. "I'll tell you what though, I'll stand you a brandy at the bar to warm you up. Sound good?"

Richard nodded to this.

"Yes, brandy's good for a drowned man. Piano Players job, you say? Well, I guess I shouldn't be surprised. Still never thought we would be getting a new piano player," he said grinning.

Richard felt a moment's apprehension, then risked a question.

"Whys that?"

The doorman chuckled for the first time, more a booming hearty laugh than a chuckle, which seemed to come from somewhere deep within his chest. "Because my friend, I didn't know we had a Piano."

CHAPTER THREE

As a Passing Place Passes By

The glass the brandy came in was exactly the right shape and size. The type you could hold cradled in your palm, the stem held between your thumb and ring finger. Then you could rotate your hand slightly to make the brandy swirl around in the belly of the glass.

Richard was aware this was the correct way to hold a brandy glass, allowing the brandy to warm to room temperature with the heat of your hand. He had always suspected that this was to allow you to take a moment to consider a question being asked of you, if you were of a mind to play the intellectual.

Swirling the brandy was not seen as stalling. Instead, it was just observing the correct way to appreciate fine French brandy. If, by chance, this also allowed you time to formulate the most witty intelligent, and exacting of replies, without looking like you were trying to do so... Well, that was just a bonus at the end of the day after all.

Richard however, suddenly aware of how wet and cold he felt, simply picked up the glass and threw half its contents down his throat.

Afterwards, he put the glass down sheepishly and surveyed the Bar room in silence. There was, he concluded, something definitely not right about it. If asked, Richard could have described it in many ways and in great detail. But 'Not right' seemed to sum it up.

It was too large for one thing, Larger than the building he had entered had looked on the outside, certainly, though this for some reason surprised him less than it should have done. The strangeness of the last few hours had worn down his ability to feel surprised at the anomalous.

From the entrance, the room seemed to wander off in random directions. Broad archways ran over a vaulted ceiling. Small and, for that matter, large alcoves sat in deep shadows that may have led to further rooms or other areas of the bar. They might, for that matter, have just lead to walls with benches on them. The way the shadows hung in the corners made it hard to be sure.

In all, it gave the impression of being a large

cellar, with brick pillars supporting the arched ceilings which were higher than they should be. There just seemed so much of it, and yet at the same time, it had a homely closeness to it. It gave Richard the feeling he was in some small welcoming place. A local bar he was familiar with and would know most everyone who walked through the doors. Yet at the selfsame time it just happened to be huge, it was more than a little disconcerting.

The lighting of the place was strange, too. It seemed at once both well lit, and yet hung with shadows around its edges. Shadows which seemed to ignore the sources of light and just hung where ever they wished.

The effect made it hard to be sure of the dimensions of the place. Richard could almost understand how the doorman would be unsure they had a piano if it sat in one of those strange dark alcoves. You could lose a four piece band in some of them. That one could hold an old upright honky-tonk key hammer covered in dust, that was long forgotten, was not beyond his imagination.

However, the upright piano that sat so obviously on the small raised area in what may have been the middle of the room suggested that the doorman was either blind or joking. Yet strangely all the same Richard felt sure that neither was the case.Though he could not explain why he felt so, but something about the doorman made he feel an honest sense of trust in his words.

The piano itself reminded Richard of another bar room piano. The one Sam had famously, but not actually, been told by Bogart to *'play it again'* on. Richard remembered being told once by Carrie that the actual line had been "*Play it Sam, you played it for her, so play it for me*," They had argued about it playfully in the way only couples in love could argue for two weeks afterwards. Before it occurred to either of them to go and buy a copy of Casablanca from the local DVD store.

The store had to order it in. Classic or not, there was little call for old black and whites movies in Lower Queens NY. So there was a further week of loving argument and discussion before they actually managed to watch the movie together for the first time.

Carrie had cried at, *"Maybe not today, maybe not tomorrow, but one day and for the rest of your life…"* He hugged her tightly, smiling happily at her emotion.

Neither of them had pointed out she was right when the line came up, they had been too busy enjoying the movie. They had watched together again a few days later, snuggled up together in bed, and making love as the credits rolled after Bogart finished the film with the infamous, "*This could be the start of a beautiful friendship.*"

That had been a month to the day before she died.

Richard winced as the memory was provoked, but continued to stare at the piano. Lacquered white, and polished to a high shine, with baroque embellishments on the panelling, it was a beautiful instrument in its own right. The key cover was up, and the bright rows of ebony and ivory looked pristine.

He felt it was calling to him, demanding to be played. "I wonder if it's in tune?" he mused without realising he spoke aloud.

The doorman chuckled at this, drawing Richards's attention back to him.

"Oh it will be, no way has she gone to all the trouble of putting it here, just to have it out of tune," he replied with a smile, picking up his own brandy, after loosening his collar.

Unlike Richard, he took a moment to swirl the brandy respectfully before taking a short drink.

"She being?" Richard enquired, mostly because he felt the question was required of him.

"She, who decided we need a piano player that swills his brandy like cheap wine," came the reply and slight chastisement, with a chuckle to accompany it. The doorman seemed to find his cryptic utterings amusing.

Richard, for his part, was finding them both confusing and frustrating.

He waited silently all the same as the doorman took another sip of brandy, watching him intently as he swirled around the glass, before taking a slow savouring drink. He was hoping for a more forthcoming answer. The doorman, perhaps sensing this was the case, sighed and shaking his head slightly while cradling his glass, added, "Esqwith, she of the Passing Place." and raised his glass slightly in a mock toast to the name.

"Esqwith… That would be the owner I take it?" Richard asked simply, while hoping the doorman would be more forthcoming with an answer to direct questions. The doorman however just laughed loudly at this, the smiled broadly.

"Guess you could say that, though I sometimes think the queen over there owns the place." He said motioning over at the cat which was now prowling along the lid of the piano. He smiled again then for a second he looked more serious, taking on the aspect of a teacher trying to explain something complex to a slow student. "Esqwith, well, she is the bar my friend. If you can follow me. Not sure she would allow anyone to actually own her. In fact, I suspect she would take such a notion as an affront to her dignity. If anyone owns her, it's herself."

Richard just felt more confused and returned to gazing around the bar, which was empty save for him, the doorman, and the cat.

The bottle of brandy had been sitting on the Bar with two clean glasses next to it when they entered as if was waiting for them. He had assumed the doorman had put it there before he took the air. But that did not explain two glasses.

Come to that, he realized that they had sat at the only two barstools not stacked up for the night on tables, almost as if they had been placed there just for them, however unlikely that seemed.

He felt like Alice falling down the rabbit hole.

The whole place had an unreal quality about it and yet it felt safe somehow. It reminded him of every bar he had ever been in, while being completely different at the same time.

An abstract thought struck him that this was perhaps not a bar at all, but 'The Bar.' The bar from every old movie he had ever seen. The archetype for all other bars.

Once the notion had occurred to him, as ridiculous as it was, it seemed to be the only correct explanation. Not a bar, but every bar. It had the feel of every bar. Or perhaps closer to the truth, the ghost of every bar at 4 am, after the customers had gone home for the night and the bar was empty but for a couple of staff, enjoying a quiet moment before shoving off home for the night themselves.

"What is this place?" he found himself asking without meaning to say his question aloud.

The doorman's face took on a serious aspect once more, the easy humour gone from his eyes. It struck Richard that the doorman must feel this was a question which required reverence when answering. Far too important a question to be dismissed with a half-smile. Taking a deep breath while he gathered himself, the doorman replied…

"Esqwith's Passing Place."

As if that explained it all, then his smile returned.

"Or to be more exact it is Esqwith, and Esqwith is a passing place. Perhaps the passing place, can't say that I know whether it's the one and only. Try to think of it as a place between here and there, a place of passing through. Like…" he seemed to be considering his words for a moment, the seriousness in his eyes returning, even in the face of Richard's obvious confusion. Then he continued, "You know how on a single track back road out in the sticks, you get these bits which are a little wider than the rest, so if two cars are coming along in different directions one can pull over to let the other pass?"

Richard nodded, taking a sip of his brandy, while making no effort to hide his confusion. Even with all the weirdness of the evening this seemed a weird line of conversation. He felt it was getting away from him, but was past the point where he was expecting anything to make much in the way of sense.

"Well, they call that a passing place, they even have it written on signs sometimes, and Esqwith's is like that. It's a place you can pull over into to let what's in the way pass. A passing place, a place to let the things in your way go past. You see, at least that's how I like to think of it."

The doorman smiled what seemed to Richard, for a moment, was a condescending smile, but then realised there was genuine warmth behind it. He realised too that the doorman did not expect to be understood but was trying to explain as best he could all the same.

Richards lack of comprehension must have been written on his face, however, so the doorman continued.

"Let me try that another way, it's like…" he said then seemed to grope around for another analogy, covering his indecision by taking another drink of his own brandy, after a long swirl of the glass.

"Okay, it's like a bridge between different places. You can use it to pass between one place and another, hence passing place. Esqwith though, now she just prefers to move around a little, so I guess she's a passing place that passes through," he smiled at his pun.

Richard remained silent, hoping perhaps, that if he listened long enough to the cryptic doorman, he would come to understand where he had found himself. He had lots questions, but none of them made much sense to him, so he kept them to himself, hoping the doorman might start to make more sense if he listened long enough. The doorman, however, decided to change tack and asked a question, rather than trying to explain further.

"You're a piano player right, I mean that's probably not what you are exactly, but it's something you can do, right?"

"Yes."

"Well it seems to me Esqwith has decided you're to play the piano here for a while, don't know why, can't say I care much for why either. If Esqwith wants you to play that there piano, then that's her business. She'll have reasons and no one around here is gonna question the why of them."

"Hang on. You said Esqwith was the bar, are you telling me the Bar decided it wanted a piano player?"

The doorman chuckled loudly and then replied, "No, I am telling you the Bar decided you were to play the piano here, not that she needed just any old piano player; She chose you."

Richard breathed deeply for a second, and then admitted, "I'm confused,"

The smiling doorman replied, "Hell I know that feeling, I was too. Sweet lord but was I confused,"

"Hang on, you're saying the bar chose me. Not the owner, the bar. Not any old piano player, me?"

"That's about the size of it."

"You realise how insane that sounds?"

The doorman laughed, a hard hearty laugh and then smiled a smile the Cheshire Cat would have been proud of. Richard was about to say more when the doorman raised his hand to silence him once more.

"A moment," he said, picking up the bottle of brandy and slowly pouring them both another drink, before smiling again and holding the bottle up to the light.

"You see this bottle, it contains the finest French Armagnac. And I mean really the finest. I know this piano man because I happen to have a taste for all things French. Lord, you may not think it to look at me, or hear this southern drawl of mine, but I am something of a Francophile." He paused for a moment, making a show of examining the label. Then continued.

"But I did not get this bottle off the rack back there and set it down here between us, which is not to say I wouldn't have done so if it was my choice. Cause I tell'ya, if I were planning to have a quiet hour, in good company and talk the talk, then this is the bottle I would have chosen." He looked at the label once more before placing the bottle back down on the bar.

"But I didn't choose it, and yet here it was. Sat down here on the bar waiting for us. Finest French Armagnac, of 1913. Rare… mark me well… Rare… Is not the word. Why, you could not find this vintage outside of the finest of cellars. And I am as sure as I can be, it was not on that rack behind the bar tonight and never has been. Yet, all the same, it was sat here on the bar when we walked through those doors, if you remember, sat here with two glasses. Real brandy glasses, mind me, which was a nice touch," he said and mimed tipping his hat towards some invisible barman.

"Now you see piano man, brandy as good as this needs to be drunk right… slow and steady… from the right glass if you want to savour it. And me, I like to drink my brandy real slow, as a rule, piano man. I don't drink anything when I'm working, and it's damn rare I ain't working, so I like to savour it a little when I do, you hear me? But as I say I didn't get the brandy out. It and these here glasses weren't on the bar when I stepped out to take the air and let the queen back in from her prowling."

He let go of the bottle, with due reverence, and picked up his glass, gently swirling the brandy clockwise while seeming to take a moment to consider it. Then smiled warmly once more.

"Seems to me Esqwith, bless her, is dropping us a hint. She's subtle that way sometimes. Reckon she wants me to take my time and tell you a story, least that's what I suspect anyway. She is fond of stories you see, and the telling of them. Who knows, maybe my story will help you to understand, maybe it won't. But if Esqwith arranged this bottle of brandy, I damn sure ain't gonna to snub my nose at it and haul my ass to bed without drinking it all. So I'll tell you a story. It will pass an hour while we drink. But mind me well, a good listener listens to the whole story and doesn't ask questions till it's over, and I'll mind you to that."

Richard nodded and took a moment to refill both glasses, before the doorman began his tale.

CHAPTER FOUR

The Ballad of Pvt Burbank

"Let me tell you something, Piano Man, and take it from one who knows. There ain't no place in all of God's creation as miserable and soul-sucking as death row.

"Now there was a guy by the name of Sonny Burbank, who could have told you that way back in 1925. No place worse. But Sonny had been in plenty that came close, damn close, I tell you. Right then though, in that stinking little cell, those places, well, they seemed like paradise in comparison."

"In a death cell, your life's behind you. Nothing ahead of you but the chair and a few thousand volts. Hope, well shit, hope packed it bags and took a hike. And you? You're just counting down the hours till they throw that switch."

"You may have heard tell of the five stages of grief, some psychologist came up with this is the 1960's. Kubler-Ross or something, though that was a long time after. But Sonny Burbank, when he was sat in that cell, well I reckon he would have recognised them right enough. Course he weren't going to live long enough to hear about them."

"In a Death cell, you go through your own five stages of grief. Only the one you're grieving for, well that's your good self."

"First, you just deny it's happening. Simpler not to think about it I guess. It has an unreal quality to it. Takes some getting your head around. You're sat in this tiny room on your own just waiting to take one last walk. But denying don't last and before long you get to the next stage, anger."

"Now Sonny, he could tell you all about anger. See Sonny was an innocent man. And, sure, you're thinking everyone on death row says their innocent, least ways, innocent or a victim of circumstance I guess. But in Sonny's case, well, he really was innocent. For that matter, a genuine victim of circumstance."

"Course, his circumstance being that he was a Black man in South Carolina, accused of the rape and murder of a white woman. The jury, every one of them white as snowdrifts, would have convicted him even if the Lord God himself had come down and spoken in Sonny's defence."

"See in South Carolina in the twenty's a black man was guilty and for hanging if he raised his head and looked a white man in the eye. Hell, the way Sonny saw it, it was a miracle he'd lived long enough for a trial. That he did not end up just '*strange fruit on the popular tree*' as the song has it. Let's just say he was lucky to be in that cell all things considered. Thought I dare say he didn't see it that way at the time, if yer mind me."

"County sheriff must have put his re-election on the line simply by not leaving the jail unguarded for an hour and turning Sonny over to the mob. Believe me, when I tell ya that must have taken some stones on his part. The guys in the white hoods probably did not take too kindly to it going before a jury."

"As it was, though, that just meant swapping a lynch mob for the chair. No white Carolinian jury was ever going to be convinced with Sonny's skin was innocent."

"He was, though, and he was damn angry about it for a while. Punching the walls angry, pacing up and down the floor of that cell. Kind of angry that's all the worse when there is no one to throw it at. Though truth be told, Sonny had been angry most his life, with one thing or another."

"Now if I remember this right, according to our friends, the shrinks, after anger there comes bargaining. Well, Sonny came to that in a few days, even his kind of anger could only burn bright so long, I guess."

"Trouble was that the only bargaining you can

do on death row is to try for an appeal. And there weren't a judge in South Carolina back then who'd listen to an appeal from a nigger on death row. Hell, even before you got to the judge you'd need your lawyer to set up an appeal, and there was fat chance of that."

"Sonny's lawyer was not gonna waste his time coming to see a dead guy. Probably didn't give Sonny a second thought once the case was lost, him being court appointed and all. Honest enough about it though, straight off the bat he told Sonny he'd only taken the case for the advocate's fee. '*The state pays its bills on time, and it's been a quiet year.*' Which is as straight up as you can get, I guess. No abiding sense of justice or the right to a fair trial. His right to a payday he was in it for."

"Now, to be fair to him, the CA tried to earn his money. Not that Sonny felt a whole lot like being fair, you understand, but the lawyer really tried. Cause, mostly he just tried to convince Sonny to plead guilty. He told Sonny that if he did, then he would push for a life sentence instead of the likely alternative."

"Sonny though, why he was prideful, hell that and he considered himself righteous. There weren't no way he was gonna hold his hands up to what he ain't done. Told the lawyer straight. '*I ain't saying I did when I didn't...*' "

"The lawyer, no surprise, told him he was a fool. That what he did or didn't do, did not come to much, it was what he represented that matter in court. Black skin before a white jury was guilty of something that was for sure, so best find him so.

'Don't you see son, they're gonna find you guilty no matter so we need to make the best of it...' "

"Sure Sonny knew, but it stuck in his craw that his public defender came straight out and said it to him. He used some choice words at the time that don't need repeating."

"Still for all his realistic approach to the situation the Lawyer tried to put together a defence and earn his crust. Sonny had to give him that. Built a case based on the evidence, or, more to the point, the lack of any actual evidence. It was solid lawyer work. Sure it was doomed to failure and the lawyer knew it, but solid all the same."

"Sonny could see in the lawyer's eyes he had no fire in him all the same. He knew his client was going to the chair and that was all that she was gonna write. No matter what his lawyer did, and he weren't no Atticus Finch."

"So, fair to him, the lawyer tried his best at the time, but after the case? Well, the state didn't pay court appointee's to take up appeals. 'They do not waste tax dollars keeping people alive on death row for a few extra months,' as the lawyer put it to Sonny in a letter. Frankly, it was a surprise he even bothered to write him back."

"Only other hope was a governor's reprieve, and the state of *'smiling faces and beautiful places'* had a governor who wasn't a man to smile. Least of all on a Negro waiting for the chair on a rape and murder conviction. Hell, I doubt the governor gave it a moment's thought. Particularly as it was an election year. A reprieve for some Negro rapist killer would definitely be a vote loser back in the twenties in South Carolina."

"Doubt that's changed much since then now I think on it."

"So anyways, bargaining didn't exactly last long as a stage. Even a fool would have known the cause was lost when it came to bargaining. Whatever else he was, Sonny wasn't no fool."

"Shrinks say that when bargaining ends, the next stage is depression. Well, Sonny slid deep and hard into that. Truth be told, he had teetered on the edge of depression more than once in the past. Life hadn't been pretty to Sonny Burbank, no sir."

"He'd grown up in a place called Ledford, South Carolina least ways two miles out of town in the Gabon's or *'Nigga town,'* as the whites had called it back then."

"Calling it a town, now that was a stretch. Truth is it was not much more than a couple of dozen shacks nailed together with a little hope and a whole lot of belligerence."

"The Gabon's was a back road leading to an old plantation house, far enough out of town to be forgotten about. When slavery ended after the Civil War, the old masters kicked the freed chattel off their land. Sent them to build homes elsewhere. So the black folks moved closer to town and walked five miles to the plantation each day, working their old jobs for money that wasn't enough to feed them."

"Top of that, he only store was white owned, prices high and measures short, but it's all there was. You lived on the Gabon's, you didn't go into Ledford lest you were there to work."

"Sonny's mother once told him her grandfather used to say he'd never gone to bed hungry till he was a free man."

"He'd been dead a long time when young Sonny was around, playing in the mud stream behind the Gabon's. Far as Sonny could see, not a great deal had changed since his grandpa's time. Sonny, well, he had plenty of hungry nights himself as a child."

"Now the Gabon's wasn't a fixed place you understand. It moved more than once over the years of Sonny's childhood. Always further out from town and always more cramped up. When he was twelve, there was a fire that burned most of the township to the ground. It had started while most of the families were in church a mile up the road. The fire spread fast, faster than could be stopped anyways. Before long, the town was all but burned out."

"It was, *'A blessing they were all in church,'* according to Sonny's mother. She told him, *'It's the good Lord keeping us safe.'*"

"At the time, Sonny thought that if it was a blessing, it was a *'Damn shitty one'*. And told her so, only time he ever swore in front of her, she looked so disappointed in him for that, that he half wished she had taken a broom to him instead of just turning her back and walking off."

"The sheriff, a whIte guy, of course, came down and told them they should rebuild, *'A little further out of town where there was less chance of another fire…'* "

"Course they knew it was set deliberately, even before the sheriff pretty much confirmed it. Moving further out of town had been suggested before, in those subtle little ways the whites of Ledford had of making such suggestions to their black neighbours. Black eyes and busted ribs to some poor random picked up late at night."

"If they were feeling subtle that was…"

"Sonny's neighbours had plenty of anger, three people had died in that fire. Old man Smithson had been too writhen with arthritis to walk to church. His shack burned around him while he lay in bed. That wasn't the worst of it. Mara Phelps was at home with her baby Florence, poor child had been ill for days. Mara stayed home to nurse her. She should have got out when the fires started, but a beam from the porch fell blocking the door. Trapped them both inside."

"No one knew how the beam fell, though there was more than one willing to guess it had some help."

"Mara's husband hit the bottle hard, Reggie Phelps never needed much excuse, God knows, but he had a good one now."

"Night after, all drunk and angry, he picked himself a fight with a couple of whites in town and found himself invited to a lynching party as the guest of honour."

"So I guess the fire took four lives in the end, one way or another."

"There was plenty of angry talk, plenty who wanted to stand up and fight. Lots of talk about rights and the law."

"But the only law worth its salt in South Carolina back then was white man's law. Rosa Parks and the civil rights movement were half a century away. They argued and raged for a few days. Then they did what the oppressed normally do. Try to forget about it and start again."

"Twelve-year-old Sonny saw all this and made his mind up to get out of the Gabon's. Out of there and as far away from South Carolina, dirt road towns and white man's justice as he could get. Took him four years, but when he did get out, he went further than he could ever have expected—by way of New York City, the army and a ship to Europe's war."

"Yet eight years later, he was back in South Carolina, in a death row cell, and depression hit him damn hard."

"Hell it hit him harder than his mother's death, and that was nigh on crippling. He had seen his buddies die in those godforsaken French trenches and never gotten so low. He sunk down into a pit of despair that seemed so dark, so deep, he just curled up on the cold concrete floor of his cell shivering and wished for it to end, for a while at least."

"They say acceptance follows depression, Sonny had a hard time coming to acceptance, truth told I ain't so sure he ever did. Instead, he just left depression and moved to some uncaring state. Death row was his final destination after a long journey. It's not something you accept, it's more something you just know. Only place left was a quarter mile walk to the chair and the wait for the switch to be thrown."

"When you have nothing to look forward to, you

stop look forward. You just let the days slip past."

"Perhaps that's acceptance of a kind. After a while he just wanted it over with. *'Slap that sponge on my head, strap me down, and throw the damn switch.'* Least ways that's how Sonny started to think. If nothing else it would get him out of that damn death cell."

"Like I said, life hadn't been good to Sonny Burbank. Never showed him much in the way of kindness. He grew up fatherless and beggar poor, which did little for a sense of self-worth."

"I guess everyone needs someone to look down on. Those in the Gabon's looked down on Sonny and his mother for the unforgivable crime of being a little poorer than everyone else."

"His mother used to scratch out a living, taking in laundry or sewing and working the cotton fields come harvest time. Sonny's father, he'd gone from their lives before Sonny was old enough to remember him. Not that Sonny's mother would hear a bad word said about Jeremiah Burbank.

"*'Why am I a bastard?'* Sonny asked his mother once."

"*'Burbank's bastard don't you play with him,'* he'd hear from those that should have known better."

"He was too young to know the meaning of it. When he asked her, Sonny's mother, why she flew into a rage and beat him with the broom. He ended up fleeing the shack rather than face her anger. His mother, she was a woman of peace; don't think he ever saw her as angry as he did that day."

"He came back an hour later to find her sitting

on the bed they shared, weeping. She hugged him tight and told him in a whispered voice never to say the word again. To his credit, he never did in front of her."

"He came to hate that word for the stigma it attached to him, and for the taunts of other children whose parents didn't want them playing with Burbank's bastard, which hurt, as only children's taunts can."

"Some will tell you that you have to wear such things as a badge of honour and make armour out of them. Grow harden to them till they mean nothing. Easy to say, damn hard to do when you're nine."

"Weeping while hugging him tight, angry at herself for the beating she'd dished out, she tried to explain to her nine-year-old son about his father, the man she'd loved. Still loved, come to that, just as his father had loved her; tried to explain to him that his father hadn't known she was with child when he left. Else ways, he would have never gone, or better still taken them with him."

"*'He went north to the cities to look for work,*' she told him. '*There's good money for black folk up there, working in factories and having real houses. He promised me he'd send for me when he had sorted out a good job. He really loved me child, he's a good man, the best of men. No matter what those fools say. He will love you, too, child. We'll be a real family and happy. You're his son and have his name child. He would never deny you that and nor shall they. If he had known about you, he'd have come back for us already. One day he will.*'"

"Sonny's mother believed her words, Sonny knew that much. She wanted more than anything for her son to believe them too."

"So he did, for a while at least, with all the trust a son has in his mother's words."

"'*The pride of the poor is a thing to behold,*' someone famous said that, though it escapes me for the moment just who. But that was the way of things with Sonny's mother. She'd look her neighbour's in the eye at church on Sunday and dare them with that look to repeat to her face what they'd say behind her back. Hell, when you have next to nothing you take pride in every little thing you do have. His mother, she pushed that pride into Sonny no matter how bad things got. But pride buys no food. Doesn't pay the rent either. There was more than one night the two of them starved for want of an unpaid bill."

"The years took their toll on Sonny's mother. By the time of the fire she had aged four maybe five years for each one passing since he was able to walk upright. An old woman by thirty-five. Hair gone grey and eyes failing. She couldn't see to sew. She'd pass on meals to make sure Sonny was fed more times than anyone has a right to expect. Fourteen months after the Gambon's fire her kidneys failed."

"Hell, I guess life had weakened them enough before that, but the water supply of the new shacks was gritty, at best, and poisoned what was left."

"Sonny came home one evening, dog tired from working in the cotton fields and found her curled up in agony on the floor of their single room. His mother was a tough woman; Life had been cruel, but she had fought it all the way. Now she fought death."

"It took her three days to die."

"The Ledford town doctor was not in the habit of making house calls to '*Nigga town*'. Guess he didn't believe that charity to black folks was a virtue worth pursuing. So when Sonny went seeking aid for his trouble, he got a door slammed shut in his face."

"Three days to die. Her insides bled out with her urine. If God granted any mercy to her for her years of faith, it was the delirium she fell into after the first day. The pain was too much so I guess her mind went elsewhere. But even that was just a temporary respite. She slipped out of it, into a world of agony and pain every few hours, before it took hold again. If it was God's mercy, it was a damn thin mercy at best."

"Sonny could do nothing to ease her pain, but he stayed with her and tried all he could. In the end, that just meant he watched her die and ran out of tears before she was gone. Her last words, uttered as the delirium slipped away for her last moments '*He never came back, he never came back…*'"

"Two months after they laid her to rest in a pauper's grave Sonny headed north. Just like his father before him. Riding in one freight car after another. He was fourteen by then. Owned nothing but what he stood up in. He stole food and cursed himself for doing so, knowing his mother would have been horrified that her son turned thieving. Even if it was to avoid starvation."

"Sonny had a whole world of anger inside him.

Anger at his mother's death. Anger at how his neighbours had treated his mother, at how they treated him. They were full of kind words at her funeral but damn few offers of help. He'd sold what little they'd had, for less than it was worth because the buyers all knew he was desperate. He'd felt so powerless watching her die and he was angry that he was left so powerless after her death. He took what he could steal and made his way north, in short jumps. Trying to get odd bits of work as he went and mostly failing to do so. There were cold nights, hungry nights and a painful night too when he took a beating for being caught in the stockyard."

"Going north took a month or more. Slow progress up through Virginia, Maryland, and up into New Jersey. But he ended up in Harlem, New York in nineteen sixteen."

"It was a boom time in a boom town."

"Yet a black face from the south still had a hard time finding a steady place to sleep. Let alone a steady job. He slept rough most nights and did so hungry as often as not. When the army came recruiting in the June of the next year, he saw it as a way out."

"In some way, I think, he also saw it as a way to be a man, I guess. Sonny wanted to feel like a man. He was sick to the stomach of scrounging a life out of nothing. The idea of regular meals, a real bed and clothes that didn't walk about on their own, seemed to be a damn fine thing. Trouble was he was too young to join up, and had less meat on him than a dog's bone. But hell, you know, '*What's a few months between you and the government.'* Least that's what he thought at the time.

"He perjured his age by a year, though I suspect the recruitment officer didn't care a great deal. At basic training, he found he wasn't the only one who had added a year or two to his age. One of his fellow privates, a guy called Jacobs, was only thirteen. That poor swine never got much older, took a bullet in the throat in a muddy trench a few months later."

"Anyway, at fifteen years of age, Sonny Burbank left New York harbour on a cold December day, sailing across the Atlantic to a hell worse than any man ever has a need to see."

"That crossing was awful for Sonny and the other men of the 15th New York Infantry. The Brass didn't want them above decks mixing with the other regiments. The 15th was all black you see. Those days regiments weren't mixed any more than busses were. The brass was afraid of trouble between the 15th's negroes and the white regiments. So the instruction came down from the top. The 15th was to stay down in steerage for the duration of the seven-day voyage to France."

"The seas pounded that ship, rough and nasty, for most of those seven days. The constant noise of the engines and the constant swaying made for little sleep in that hold. And that's what it was, a hold. They were packed in like cargo, and the doors kept shut. Not much different than when their forefathers made the journey from Africa in chains if truth be told, and weak stomachs with bad food made for less than desirable air. Free men off to fight for their country they might have been, but 3rd class freemen at best. Cattle would have been treated better."

"Things didn't improve all that much once they arrived in France. Brass gave them a new name, the 369th, and then set about forgetting about them."

"They christened themselves *'The Harlem Hellcats'*. Pride, you see, no matter how low you are, you have to have it, even if you make it yourselves. And they were proud, God help them, proud of being Harlem's finest, the fighting 369th. Damn, if they would be proud of that, even if no one else was."

"The Brass didn't know what to do with them. Sure as hell didn't want them fighting alongside white GI's in the trenches. Far as the Brass were concerned the all Negro regiments would cause trouble mixed in with the real soldiers. Those being the white ones you see."

"Bad for morale, that was their opinion. Old divisions ran deep, particularly with southern regiments. As if being shot at and shelled into oblivion, living in a muddy trench six inches deep in water and piss for weeks on end ain't bad for morale to start with. Somehow sharing that hell with a few Negros would make it all but unbearable. Insane, I know, but that's how it was back then in the minds of the Brass. The only thing worse to them would be mixed regiments."

"Black regiments then were only good for menial labour behind the line far as the Brass were concerned. Loading waggons of shells, cleaning the latrines and any crappy job no one wanted to do. Travel half way around the world to fight and end up doing the same shit you always did. Now I dare say had Sonny and the rest of the 369th known what the trenches were like, then they would have been glad of it. Behind the lines doing menial work was better than that manmade hell. But they didn't know that at the time. So they bitched and moaned about *'Polishing the white man's turds'* as one of his comrades eloquently put to Sonny.

"Now, you'll need to mind that Sonny wasn't much enamoured of the white man back then. You keep kicking a man down for long enough he'll start to hate, and Sonny hated real well by then. He'd never known a white man give him an even break in his life. He wasn't the only one either. The 369th was full of men who had taken white man's crap for most of their lives. What trouble started between them and white enlisted men was not all started by the other side. Though you can guess which bunch got the blame when it came to handing out punishment details. Least ways I guess the Brass thought they had a problem unit and got inventive about solving their problem."

"The French wanted the Americans to reinforce their 16th division in the trenches. The 16th had taken a pounding and more in the last year. The French command was desperate to re-enforce. But out brass couldn't warrant putting American soldiers under foreign command. '*It's against the US constitution'* was the line the brass trotted out each time they were asked."

"Which as it happens is true enough. *'No*

American shall be made to bear arms under the command of another nation' or something like that. Dates way back to the early days of the independence war. But the French kept asking anyway, and our brass kept saying no. Till there was someone in the brass came up with the idea that it need not apply to that troublesome all black regiment they wanted to get rid of. After all, they weren't real Americans, you know, the white ones. So the constitution need not apply..."

"So anyway, Sonny and his buddies got issued with French helmets and learned to take orders from people who didn't even speak the same language. Truth told, seemed little different to Sonny. It was still white men giving the orders, and black men under the screw, even if they had accents and silly hats. It was still the same crap he had been taking all his life."

"May the 8th in the spring of nineteen eighteen a few days after turning sixteen, Sonny Burbank got his first taste of the trenches, and discovered there were worse things than polishing the white man's shit behind the lines."

"In his death row cell a few years later, though Sonny would have given much to be back in those trenches. The trenches were hell picked up and put on earth. But at least there you had a chance of getting out alive. In death row, you're just waiting for death and the only way out was the walk to the chair."

"The war changed a lot of things; killed a lot of men for very little, but changed a lot of things. For Sonny, it changed his view of everything. The

French treated him and the rest of the 369th like equals. As far as they were concerned, you fought alongside a man. You didn't care about the colour of his skin. Plenty of French troops were coloured's from the colonies. The French got rid of slavery a long time before the US. Their attitude was, a little more civilised, shall we say. In the trenches the only colours that mattered were the uniforms."

"French soldiers christened the 369th 'Black Death'. A name they damn well earned, and so did Sonny Burbank. It may seem a strange thing to say, but he found himself in those trenches. For the few short months he fought in them, he felt he'd a purpose, something he'd never felt before. Those trenches killed a lot of men, ruined many more, but Sonny came out a stronger man."

"Ironically, that was partly the reason he ended up on death row."

"The French officers didn't look down on the 369th's enlisted men. Not the way the American brass had done. Sonny and his unit got awarded the Croix de Guerre, the cross of war, bronze with decorative crossed swords, with a green and red ribbon. Even in that damnable cell years later, Sonny remembered with pride the day it was pinned on him by General Le Bouc."

"He went to war for his country, but it took a Frenchman to give him a medal for it."

"He carried that slab of bronze with him everywhere he went from that day on. Even hollowed out the heel of his shoe and slotted it in there to keep it safe when he got back to New York after the war. To keep it safe and to remind himself he was a man. In South Carolina, hell, in the states in general, Sonny Burbank was a second class citizen. In the heel of his shoe was proof to him that he was more than that. He was gonna be damned before he would let anyone take that from him."

"Late at night, in his cell, Sonny would slip back the shoe heel and hold the medal in his hand. Tightly, so tightly, in fact, the points of the cross swords would dig deep into the palm of his hand. He'd hold it there so long that he could still feel the ghost of it when he put it back in his heel. That medal, proof to himself, if no one else, that he was a man. Proof of his honour. Proof of his bravery. Proof of all those machismo things that take on such important sometimes. When no one else treats you like a man, I guess you need to feel it for yourself."

"It was holding the medal, a few nights before his execution that Sonny decided that if he were to die it wouldn't be by another's hand."

"They take everything from you when they put you on death row, everything that you could use leastways if you wanted to save the state electricity. No belt, no shoe laces, light cotton clothes that rip before they take your weight. They fed you on a tin tray and gave you a spoon to eat with."

"Oh, they take no chances that you could deny the state its pound of flesh. But they weren't about to put their hands in their pockets to give you a new set of boots when they could just take out the laces. So Sonny had his Croix de Guerre, and it didn't take much over a couple of nights of scraping it on the wall to turn an edge on it. Till it was something close to a razor."

"Nietzsche said '*It is always consoling to think of suicide. In that way, one gets through many a bad night.*'

"Not that Sonny Burbank's had ever heard of Nietzsche. German philosophy wasn't exactly a vogue in South Carolina back then. It's a sentiment he'd have agreed with, though. As he lay there, sharpening his medal on the wall, the slow scraping of bronze on stone strangely a comforting noise as he set about rationalising the taking of his own life."

"Sonny's mother raised him with the church, and for all that Sonny was a wayward son, he was a son of the church all the same. He believed suicide was a mortal sin. But is it suicide to take your life when you're going to die anyway? Does God care if you slit your wrists when you're on death row? You're just goin' to fry after all if you don't take matters into your own hands?"

"Well, Sonny got to thinking in those dark nights that any God who would call that a mortal sin and condemn you to hell for eternity it, was no god he wanted a part of. A God no better than the all-white jury that convicted him of a crime he didn't commit. Hell, you could have driven trains through the holes in the evidence against him. But he was black, and that was that."

"Black in South Carolina, guilty till proven innocent with the devil's chance to prove it."

"No, if God was like them then Sonny wanted no part of him. Could an eternity in hell be worse than being born black in the old south? But he hoped the good Lord was more charitable than Carolina justice. So he kept on scraping his medal on the wall each night, praying for the strength of his convictions."

"The strength to use it, and praying for a god who'd forgive him the doing."

"From New York, after the war, Sonny had drifted south over the course of a few years, older and wiser than the kid who'd once gone north. He found work as he went and knew when to move on. Most times he slept in small hotels or hostels on the dark-skinned side of town."

"He was a big man, grown strong in the war, and found work on the doors of the black clubs that were springing up just about everywhere at the time. He even worked the Cotton Clubs door after old Mr Bojangles himself got him a job there."

"Bill 'Bojangles' Robinson had served in the 369th you see, and recognised the young kid who'd been there with him in the trenches. James Reese Europe, also ex-369th got him work when he toured his ragtime band down through Virginia. There were others too. The 369th fraternity looked after their own, and Sonny earned a reputation as a cool hand on the door. Good at spotting trouble and moving it on before it started."

"Sonny liked the work. He liked the authority of the doorman as well if truth be told. Hell, he could say no to a white man who looked like trouble and get away with it. Sad to say, but such things pleased Sonny a whole lot. Maybe pleased him too much in the end. He got a taste for it and didn't always make the wisest choices. Once in a while, he would refuse entry to someone whom he shouldn't have done, and the club owners would give him a good reference but ask him to move on."

"Cause of that, he was often on the road from one town to the next. Things being what they were back then, this led to sleeping rough between towns or if he couldn't find a place without an ominous '*No Negros*' sign on the door."

"Further south he drifted, the more of those signs he saw."

"But work was easy to find. Jazz and ragtime, man, that was where it was at. Even in the most segregated of towns you'd get young whites who would want to go to the black clubs. And the white clubs wanted black artists, too, cause you could pay them cheap and they brought in the crowd. Either way, a Black guy on the door added a kind of authenticity to the whole thing. Christ only knows why but it was true all the same. Work was never hard to find."

"So he would move from one town to the next and occasionally sleep in stations or on a cemetery bench for the night before he moved on to the next door job. It wasn't like he hadn't slept in worse places than cemeteries, they're only full of the dead after all, unlike the trenches back in Europe, which had been full of the dying. So truth told he did not mind it so much. Hell, at least the dead were quiet, and weren't throwing shells at you."

"Then one late spring in North Carolina he found his father. Sonny had spent the night sleeping a few yards from him on a bench in fact. His black doorman suit in the battered suitcase he used as a pillow. That morning as he was setting off in search of breakfast, a crow flapping up from a gravestone and the name on it caught his eye."

Jeremiah Burbank
1903
May he find rest.

"1903 a year after Sonny was born. He knelt next to the grave feeling numb for a moment or so. Then found tears for a man he'd never known. And tears for the woman who'd waited for so long while never knowing his fate."

"'*He never came back ma, at least now we know why,*' he whispered loud enough for only the dead to hear."

"He never found out how his father died. It occurred to him to check with the local newspaper or the town hall records. But he somehow never got to it. It was enough for him to know where his father was buried, I guess. That and to know why he never came home. Sonny spent some time by that graveside, telling his father all about his own life, about how his mother had waited, having those conversations he always wanted to have with a man he had never known."

"He moved on again in a few days, south again. Perhaps he had buried some ghosts at that graveside. He felt he had, I know that much."

"Whether that was the case or not, he kept going south with each new job, crossing the Mason Dixie line along the way. I'm not sure if he knew or not at the time, but his feet were dragging him home."

"A few months later in South Carolina, in a town

no more than twenty miles from where he was born, Sonny was working the door at the Richmond Club when the deputies came for him."

"A white woman was dead and had been raped beforehand. A white woman, which as the deputies said, was '*Known to have frequented the Richmond several times in the last few weeks.*' Adding that, '*The sheriff has a few questions to ask.*'"

"They were friendly enough for white deputies; he should have probably realised he was in serious trouble right there. Deputies in South Carolina weren't friendly and nice to a Negro unless they had good reason to be."

"Sonny Burbank was a big man you understand. He didn't get door work for his personality. The deputies, well, I recon' they didn't want a struggle taking him in. It would be bad for their dignity for one thing. So they told him the sheriff just wanted to ask some questions, '*What with her being known to come to the club an' all. Seems you'd be the right man to ask.*' they told him. Nice and polite about it too."

"Nice and polite till he was in the sheriff's office, at least. Once he was there, they took to him with the billy clubs. Six of them, while two more stood with shotguns in case he got out of hand. Then threw him to the floor of the cell and dished out some more."

"They took to him hard with those clubs, busting three ribs, blackened an eye, split his head open and broke three of his fingers in the process."

"He was laying on the cold concrete of the cell floor, spitting blood from a busted lip, and twitching a little when they brought their witnesses through, a couple of local farmhands and their foreman."

"Rough men, Sonny had refused entry to at the Richmond two nights previously, for good reason in his mind. They had a look about them, like they were trouble just waiting to happen to someone. That someone, well, she was the foreman's girlfriend. She'd been *'Hanging around in this fucking Nigga dive,'* as the foreman eloquently put it to Sonny at the time."

"He had argued politely with them on the door for five minutes before they moved on. Nothing physical had happened. But, as we are being truthful here, it has to be said that Sonny had been tempted to lay out all three of them. In the end, though, they moved on, spitting curses back at him, humiliated by being refused entry to the club. That humiliation pleased Sonny more than it should have done. But as I have said, Sonny wasn't overly enamoured of white Carolina's. I think a part of him revelled in refusing entry when he could to men like that. Exercising power over some white folks, in a world where you normally have none, well, that can be mighty enticing."

"Anyway, as they were to do in court a month later, all three of these *'fine upstanding citizens of Carolina'* identified him, claiming they'd seen Sonny forcibly escorting Miss Parker away from the Richmond club the night she disappeared. They also claimed they'd seen him force her into the old barn up behind the club, decrying the fact that they thought it was a simple argument and had thought no more of it till the next day when they heard Miss

Parker had been found dead."

"The foreman, whom you would be insulting brutes to call one, admitted he'd been walking out with Miss Parker till they had argued a month or so before. He had even managed to look suitably outraged about the *'Dirty nigga bastard!'* He went on record saying, must have raped and murdered her."

"The judge had warned him against using such working language in the court room. So the foreman apologised to the court, before being told by the judge he, *'Understood why feelings ran high, what with a Negro been involved and all.'* But there's South Carolina justice in the twenties for you."

"The prosecutions three *'eye witnesses'* were the only evidence against him. Sonny had several witnesses who saw him leave the club and return to his boarding house. Another one that had seen him there playing cards for several hours with a couple of the musicians from the club. That wasn't including the two musicians themselves. But his witnesses were all just as black as Sonny, and they were all too well versed in good old southern justice to not to smell the wind in the courtroom."

"None of Sonny's witnesses turn up at court. Their stories were changed at the suggestion of a group of local men. Men in white hoods who put burning crosses outside the Richmond club and the boarding house. The warning was all too clear. The locals were feeling fractious enough what with a white woman being dead. The prevailing feeling among Sonny's friends was, *'They ain't going to believe you, so no point antagonising them by testifying.'* None of them wanted to pay the kind of price Sonny was going to pay. Better one dead black man than another burning black township."

"Guess Sonny understood that as well as they did. But I can't say in all honesty that he felt that at the time."

"Those key witnesses for the prosecution men who moved on after the trial, seeking work further west. Nothing surprising there; farm workers moved around a lot in those days. They were gone from town, and the town was glad to be rid of them, no doubt. Probably the townsfolk were happy just let the whole thing be forgotten."

"Half an eye could have seen there was more to this than a black doorman who hung around long enough to get arrested. But the judge, the lawyers, the town, and the newspapers all kept that eye firmly closed. Everyone had known the Parker girl hung around '*that Nigga club.*' Local scandal merchants had long whispered she would sometimes go home with those Negro musicians. Some of the locals no doubt thought she just got what was coming to her for that. Fraternising with Negroes was not what a good white girl should be doing. Complaints about the hedonism of the youth and the corrupting influence of jazz led to a petition at the local Methodist church to close down the Richmond."

"Johnny *'the horn'*, was one of the musicians Sonny had been playing cards with that night. He admitted to Sonny when he visited him in jail, that he had drank at the bar with the Parker girl a couple of times. But he also told him that she was far from the hedonist they were making her out to be in the papers. She just liked the music. Came to the club mostly to escape the attentions of her previous boyfriend, a farm foreman. You know, the one also known as chief witness for the prosecution. Apparently, she hated her ex with a passion, and knew hanging in the *'nigga club'* would piss him off. She loved the jazz, but according to Johnny, she never went home with anyone. She just sat at the bar, tapping her foot, too shy to even get up and dance."

"The Richmond closed down. The moral outrage of God-loving white folk saw to that. The musicians moved upstate with rest of the clubs workers, and Sonny sat on death row sharpening his Croix de Guerre, waiting for the inevitable, and determined to beat the inevitable to it."

"The day before his execution they brought him breakfast as usual. Unusually, there was a newspaper with it. The short guard, the one who sniffed a lot and was always looking for a reason to be hateful to a prisoner, took great delight it pointing out the newspaper, *'Read page seven.'* he told Sonny. It didn't take a genius to figure out why."

Burbank to fry tomorrow, convicted rapist and murderer Sonny 'the beast' Burbank goes to the electric chair tomorrow at 11 am. Burbank, who brutally murdered Miss Emilie Parker in September last year, will not receive any clemency according to the office of South Carolina state Governor McHale ... '

"Sonny, well, he ate his breakfast in silence and contemplated the night ahead."

"'*May the good Lord forgive me this trespass from his commandments. That I be spared hell and this unrighteous punishment they would do unto me.*' He whispered that prayer each morning and night for two weeks, a mantra said in preparation for what he was about to do. I guess in the hope it would carry him through. When he was saying it, he would think of the medal he took such pride in. And of the one side of that bronze cross, now as sharp as a razor, still hidden in his boot heel."

"Breakfast over, he flipped through the paper, just for the novelty of being able to, I guess. This being the first newspaper he had seen since entering that damn cell three months before. Yer I guess it felt good to do something normal for once. So Sonny read it methodically, taking his time. He knew he had an hour before they returned for the breakfast things, and he guessed they would take the newspaper away with them. He wanted to savour it. To soak in news of the world beyond his cell. To know it was real, I guess."

"But before long he returned to the page where he was the headline and reading it once more, he'd a strange sense of detachment. This was about him, you see, and yet he did not recognise himself in those words. The repetition of the crime he was to fry for, told in exaggerated detail. A short biography of Sonny 'the beast' Burbank, which never mentioned his war record or anything else that had more than the slimmest grain of truth to it."

"The anger returned then, not only were they killing him, they were killing the memory of him as well. Painting him the savage, the criminal, the dirty villain. He started to rip the newspaper apart, wanting to rid himself of those lies."

"It was only then, as he tore shreds away from the newsprint, he saw the small want ad on the bottom right-hand side of the page."

"Which seemed odd in of itself, as want ads were normally all in the classified section. It read:

Wanted, Doorman
Experience with lively bars,
Used to travel and loud noises,
Esqwiths Passing Place,
Location Relative

"That was the first time since his arrest that Sonny Burbank laughed and oh how he laughed, and as he laughed all the rage and anger draining from him."

"*'Used to travel and loud noises, wonder if half way around the world and German shelling counts for that.'* He said to the world in general and laughed some more at his own joke."

"Then this voice from nowhere said, '*Probably*.'"

"So anyway, a little surprised, Sonny looks up and sees, of all things, a tortoiseshell cat sat outside the bars looking at him, purring softly to itself while it gazed straight back at him."

"When I say Sonny was surprised, that was the

least of it. Not because it had talked, you understand. Hell, he just assumed he'd imagined that. But a cat in the cell block, he couldn't imagine how it got in there. He was even more surprised when it wandered through the bars and started to rub the side of its head against his leg. Affectionate, in a place utterly devoid of affection."

"Sonny had a liking for cats that came from his childhood, I guess. See you can train a dog to attack—hell, you can train a dog to attack on command—and some South Carolinians had a thing for training them to attack those of a certain skin colour."

"You're hard pressed to train a cat to do anything. Like as not, they will wander off if you try. They don't give a damn about the colour of your skin, or human prejudices. A cat will like you or hate you for no reason other than its own. I think he admired that about them."

"Anyway, so Sonny leant down and stroked the cat a little, feeling its fur run through his fingers. Doing so he felt all his anger slipping away, I guess."

"*'Pretty little thing ain't you.'* he told it or something like that."

"*'Thank you.'* Purrs the cat, plain as day. Least ways Sonny would have sworn it had. Then it just lays down at his feet and snuggles up next to him."

"Now this shook Sonny up, as I am sure, given recent events, you can imagine. He took a moment or two then decided he was probably going a little stir crazy. Hell, there was probably no cat in his cell at all. And it sure as hell wasn't talking to him. But then he thinks to himself, crazy, well that don't seem so bad all things considered, and he asks the cat. '*So how did you get in here anyway?*'

"The cat, well, she just purred some more, then said to him in this impertinent little voice. *'Through the door behind you of course.'* stood back up and wondered, casually, in the way only a cat can be casual, around him."

"'*What door?*' Sonny says, watching the cat. So he turns around, following her with his eyes intently like as she struts away. So that he barely noticed the large wooden door hung in the air behind him, just hanging there on nothing but thin air, in the middle of his cell."

"Then that damn cat seemed to smile at him and says, '*This one… Now are you coming or do you have an appointment you want to keep tomorrow?*' and wondered through the half-open door."

"So Sonny gets up and followed her. And he says to himself. '*No, I guess I don't,*' and then left the cell by the only door available to him."

....

Richard drained the last of the Brandy in his glass and glanced at the now empty bottle. They had worked their way through it over the last hour.

With the ending of the tale, Richard felt himself relax from the tension of listening. The doorman had a way with a story. He had felt drawn into the world of Sonny Burbank. He had almost smelt the stale odour of the death cell; tasted the ash in the air of the trenches; felt the intrinsic warmth of the jazz clubs. The whole tale had seemed palatable to him, real almost, surrounding him. He put it down to the brandy. It all seemed too strange to be anything but the effect of the drink.

The doorman smiled at him and emptied his own glass then stood slowly up from the bar stool. "A good tale told is told till the bottle is dry. Time to get some sleep I think," he told Richard. "There's a spare bedroom up the stairs behind the bar. Think you'll find it's yours now. I'll be about in the morning no doubt, but for now, I'll bid you good night, Piano Player," he said, making to leave.

Richard shook himself out of his mild stupor and, slightly worse for the drink, said louder than he meant to "You expect me to believe that ending? I told you I followed the cat here, and you tell me some convoluted tale that ends the same way? You're claiming you're this Sonny Burbank, right? And the cat saved you from the electric chair? Are you trying to put the wind up me?"

The doorman laughed and tossed something small and metallic to Richard. He gave a yelp of pain as he instinctively caught it. It dug into his fingers on the sharpened side. He opened his hand and saw a medal in it, one edge sharpened up. The central circle still clearly read '*Croix de Guerre.*' He said nothing, turning it over in his hand and reading the inscription.

' *Pvt Sonny Burbank,*
Pour la Bravoure.'

"Night Piano Player," the doorman said, "And

don't cut yourself on that thing. I didn't in the end, sure would hate someone else to," smiling as he headed to his bed.

Richard watched him go, his palm sweating slightly as it held the sharpened brass, which had a slightly oily feel to it.

He wondered, not for the first time if any of this was real, and where he had found himself.

Standing, he looked back towards the doorway, tempted to just leave, though it was the smallest of temptations. The sighed to himself and decided to go in search of the promised bed, suddenly feeling tired to the bone.

As he raised himself and turned towards the stairs, he caught a flash of red light in his peripheral vision that made him feel itchy somehow. It was from beyond the windows out in the darkness of the night, a passing cars tail light he assumed. Though it explained nothing about the odd feeling it gave him.

He put it down to the brandy and the lateness of the hour and headed for the stairs.

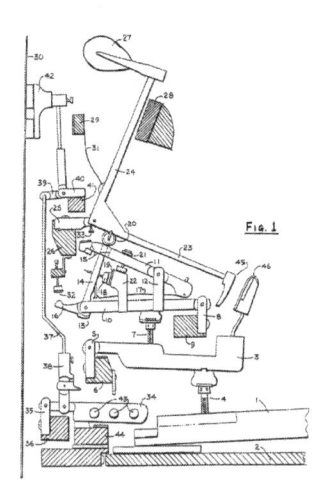

CHAPTER FIVE

Do You Know 'Hey Jude'

The grey man pushed the mop around the floor in an elaborate waltz to a tune only he could hear and apparently had nothing to do with the one he was whistling. His grey features lit with a broad smile that gave life to his face. Richard watched him from the doorway, fascinated by the man's evident joy in so mundane a task and just as equally fascinated by the alien quality of the man himself.

The impression which first sprang to Richard's mind was that he should be wearing a grey suit rather than overalls, even though he was obviously the cleaner. It was not the overalls, in a practical dark grey, which lead to the description that came to Richard's mind when he first saw him. Nor was it his hair, which was a silvery wispy grey in a mad tangle of curls, which did not suit their owner's face. Some men, in Richard's opinion, should never wear their hair long, and the grey man was defiantly a man who should have had short, perfectly groomed hair, short back and sides in a utilitarian style. Somehow that was the impression he gave all the same.

It was however not his hair that gave him the name 'Grey Man' in Richard's mind, it was his complexion. His skin was a monotone grey as if the colour had been drained out of it. He would not have looked out of place on a black and white screen, sat in Rick's café in Casablanca, except he would never have been somewhere so interesting.

He belonged in some monotone cubicle; in the monotone world of the civil service. Even with the odd hair style he looked like a man who sat behind a desk making humourless bureaucratic decisions. The only colour on the grey man was the yellow smiley comedian badge on the pocket of his overalls, noticeably missing the extra splash of colour from human bean juice.

Richard was watching the Grey Man's dance from within the doorway at the bottom of the steps behind the bar. He was feeling more himself than he had in months, thanks to a solid night's sleep in a real bed, rather than hugging down on a Greyhound seat. That and the almost forgotten luxury of a long hot shower that morning, which had burned away the cobwebs from the night before and months on the road.

Waking in a clean, soft bed had, he decided, much to recommend it, though he had gone through his normal morning moments of insecurity while he tried to remember where he was. The feeling of being out of place was made oddly worse by the warm, soft body purring beside him while cradled in his arm. The cat clearly had decided to join him at some point in the night, awakening memories of another soft, warm body cradled in his arms.

As always when his wife was brought to mind there had been a fresh moment of loss in the pit of his stomach. A strange sense of guilt curdled uneasily within him as well, ridiculous as it was to feel guilty waking up next to a feline.

The cat's presence was not the only surprise that morning. His backpack and clothes from the night before had gone. His belongings, such as they were, had been neatly arranged on the dresser opposite the bed, along with a note in intricately scrawled handwriting which informed him, simply, his clothes were being washed, and he would find suitable attire in the wardrobe.

Richard was, in truth, more than a little put out to discover someone had been in the room while he slept, not least because he had always been a light sleeper. Either he had been drunker than he thought the night before or whoever had arranged his belongings and taken his clothes away must have moved as silently as a ghost. The whole idea had a disconcerting edge to it.

His general feeling of unease worsened when he realised what it was about the neat arrangement of his belongings on the dresser which bugged him so much. It was exactly how Carrie used to arrange things, hair brush to the right, with a tin of deodorant and loose change in a bowl to the left, next to his wallet. The battered paperback he had been carrying around with little interest in reading for months sat on the corner of the dresser. The same place she would habitually pile books to read. A square of paper had been inserted within it for a place marker—another of Carrie's quirks. Richard tended to splay open books he was reading, just putting them down on whichever page he had reached. Carrie had always hated him leaving books like that.

"It ruins the spines!" she would tell him. A favoured complaint whenever she caught him doing so. She always said it with a smile, but there would always be a world of seriousness and exasperation in her voice. Invariably she would then find a piece of paper and mark his page for him, putting the book down with enough force to underline her irritation. It was the book that really bugged him about the top of the dresser. It was exactly how she would have placed it.

The Unease he felt only increased after he had showered. It had come to him that the book had been stuffed at the bottom of his pack both closed and unmarked. He stood there wrapped in a towel staring at the book for an age. Slowly dripping dry while feeling, quite reasonably, in his opinion at least, too nervous to look and see if the page marker was in the right place, he convinced himself even before looking it would be on the exact page he had last read.

Another twinge of grief hit him then, for his wife had an unerring ability to find whichever page he was reading at the time.

He had sat upon the end of the bed staring at the dresser for ten minutes in a stupor while he fought back the tears from the sudden wave of grief. Then the cat stirred from its sleep and broke him from his torpor by pushing up against him purring loudly. Richard found himself stroking her fur absently, and the grief fading into the background as he calmed down. He even managed a playful half laugh to himself a few moments later, when his hair dripped on her, the cat spring away and out of the door, with a mildly indignant yowl.

Watching the cat stalk through the partially open bedroom door had made Richard suddenly aware that, but for the towel around his waist, he was naked. Pushing the door shut behind her, he went in search of clothes, which, thankfully, he found in the wardrobe. He was slightly disturbed however to find the clothes were uniformly in the guise of a row of black tuxedo suits. Hung next to which were a row of pristine white shirts, with straight black ties on hangers. While below them on the wardrobe floor sat three pairs of highly polished black leather shoes. All of which were in his size.

Everything, in fact, was in his size.

Bewilderment gave way to simple acquiescence. Everything here was just too uncanny to be mere coincidence. Faced with the constant onslaught of oddity it was easier just to accept it all and go with it.

"Black tux it is then..." he half muttered to himself and got dressed. The bar obviously had a dress code for its piano player. He guessed he had no real option but to follow it.

A few minutes later found himself, black tuxedo and all, wondering down the steps into the bar, which was where he had halted in the doorway to watch the man, as grey as monochrome, mop the floor, doing a half waltz with the mop and bucket.

"There's some would say it rude to stare at a man when he's working..." a brisk nervous sounding voice, with an unplaceable and slightly lisped accent said from behind the bar. Followed by what might have been a thoughtful pause before the voice continued at a slightly higher pitch. "Of cause, that said, you being a performer yourself, you probably think the opposite..."

Richard stepped down into the bar and turned to look at the speaker. He found himself half expecting someone with green scaled skin or a huge mop of hair and fangs. Someone who would not have looked out of place as an old Doctor Who monster of the week.

It was the lisp, that and the way Richards's morning had been going.

He was relieved to see a fairly average and in fact decidedly normal looking young man in a white shirt and a dark waistcoat, who stood polishing shot glasses on a tray behind the bar. Richard guessed that was almost mundane in the circumstances and, therefore, the best he could hope for, because he had reached the conclusion that no one connected to the bar was likely to be entirely normal.

The other conclusion he was quickly reaching was it was simpler to just accept all this oddity, treat things as normal even. With this in mind, he decided to introduce himself properly to the guy behind the bar. "Hi... I'm Richard, I'm the new piano player I guess..." he said holding out his hand and smiling at the barman.

The barman smiled back, putting down the cloth and shot glass he was working on, before wiping his hands on his jeans with absent-minded vigour. He was, Richard judged, about normal average height, with average length brown hair oiled back and, to Richard's mind, a fairly average face. Average, that was definitely the thought which the barman brought to Richard's mind.

It did not occur to him straight away to think that was in itself peculiar.

The barman looked quizzical for a moment, his head doing an odd little twitch to one side, before taking Richard's hand for the obligatory shake, and replying, "You guess you're the piano player?" He paused and looked quizzical once more, with the same odd twitch of his head. "Is it not a bit silly to take the job unless you're sure you can play the piano?"

Richard tried to let go of the handshake, but the barman seemed insistent on shaking as long as possible. He also felt somewhat off balanced by the barman's reply.

"Sorry, I meant I am the new piano player," he restated. "My names Richard,,, Richard Barrick," he added in the hopes that giving his full name would at least be taken by the barman as a cue for ending the handshake.

"Richard… Richard? Parents lack imagination?" the odd bartender asked, still shaking his hand and his head doing the same odd little twitches at the end of each question. Richard found himself wondering if they were caused by the barman trying to shake the ideas into place in his mind. It was only afterwards he realised what an odd thought that had been.

"Erm… no, just the one Richard." He replied.

The barman tilted his head at an odd angle, twitching slightly. Richard considered he must be trying to figure it out, though why this would have confused him, Richard could not guess, while he was conscious of the barman's hand still firmly grasping his.

Then a smile, with slightly too many teeth, crossed the barman's face. A look passed over him like a light bulb being lit in an old Lonnie Tunes cartoon.

"Oh, I see, I'm Lyal, Lyal Sometimes, and I have heard all the questions before you ask..," the bartender replied, finally letting go of the handshake. Then added while looking oddly thoughtful, "Everyone just calls me Lyal, or Literal, don't know why they call me that. So you play the piano?"

Richard smiled while he absently rubbed the palm of his hand, left aching from the barman's unusually firm grip. Ignoring the question about the barman's last name that came to him.

"Yes, there was an advert for a piano player. I answered it." he replied, deciding it was probably best to ignore the '*Sometimes*', though he was already beginning to suspect the reason why Lyal was occasionally referred to as '*Literal.*'

Lyal nodded knowingly as if that explained everything, which Richard mused it probably did to anyone working here.

There was an awkward silence for a few moments as Richard waited for the barman to continue the conversation, but after a minute or so had passed Lyal twitched his head once more then returned to polishing his shot glasses, seemingly happy to leave Richard to his own amusements. Richard sighed to himself, having reached the point he was going to cease to question things once more. He looked across the bar room to the piano, shrugged his shoulders, and set off to try out the ivories.

He began with a few simple tunes, little more than a few cords with simple melodies to them. Not even songs really just notes which followed each other. It had been over half a year since he had last played a keyboard. More like three since he played an actual piano.

Synthesisers were not the same. The key action was different for one thing.

The notes were always different as well. He had forgotten just how natural and earthy a piano could sound. It took a while to come back to him, but he found himself gradually ignoring everything around him and just playing—simple tunes, simple songs, half-forgotten light classical pieces and the melodies behind modern pop songs mixed in with other tunes from the fragmented memories of a lifetime listening to music.

Richard found a kind of catharsis in the music. There always had been for him.

Playing, he slipped out of his troubles for a while and just felt the notes gently roll out of him. Something from Rogers and Hammerstein rolled out across the keys, before being mixed into a section of Holst planet suite. Then there was some old Beatles favourite followed by a rendition of a Nirvana song, before he went slipping back to something from a musical. At some point someone, who may have been Lyal, brought him a coffee and sandwich from behind the bar. They were drunk and eaten by him respectively in little breaks between tunes, before continuing on.

The theme from the Lion King was wandered through, followed by one of Bach's simpler affairs. Then *Wonderwall* was followed by *Your So Vain*, before, with no irony intended, he slipped into *As Time Goes By*.

At some point, the cat made an appearance on top of the piano. Leaping up from a nearby table and then after a few moments prowling, settling down with something akin to intent, to lay on top listening to the music.

Some Gilbert and Sullivan trickled out of the keyboard, followed by a passing interpretation, though admittedly heavily slowed down, of Motorhead's *Ace Of Spades*, which he found himself singing along to with the words no one really hears Lemmy sing.

Patrons had been wondering into the bar for the past couple of hours or more by this time. Richard, however, took no great notice of them and lost himself in teasing music from the keyboard, letting the melodies take him along without paying any great regard to where they were taking him.

He was half-way through the opening bars of *Forever Autumn* when he realised what he was playing. His fingers jumped back from the ivories as if they were charged with electricity. Horrified.

Memories that had been held in check by the act of playing, flooded over him once more. Her favourite song and he had played it without a thought. The song he had played her the night he proposed. The song they had danced to. The song that had so often been playing in the background while they made love. The song that made her smile. The song that filled her eyes with joy. The song which she had been playing as she ended it all.

He snapped his fingers away from the keys and sat there staring at them, feeling betrayed by his own digits, remembering them bright red with her blood as he held her. Cradled her in his arms. Weeping as he lay there. Carrie still in the bath where she emptied her veins. That song playing over and over as he wept. Betrayed by his own fingers, as they played that same song now.

'*Don't stop now, I like that song*' said the voice of

the cat, staring down at him from her perch on the lid of the piano.

Richard's eyes snapped up to the cat, wide and full of disbelief. She stared right back at him, with a cold even unforgiving gaze and pointedly said nothing. It was the same voice he remembered from the night before, the voice he was firmly convinced he had imagined. Did he imagine it now? If so, it was a cruel trick his imagination was playing upon him. Not only a talking cat but one that was telling him to play '*that song.*'

The murmur of voices in the bar filled the air where previously Richard had only heard the notes of the piano as he played. A wave of self-consciousness swept over him, making him aware he had left a void where music had been, and done so mid-tune. He could pick out words from the numerous conversations, and a realisation struck him. '*That's it,*' he thought, quite reasonably to himself, '*I just heard voices and filled in the words in my head.*' He continued to stare at the cat, however, whose stare back was unrelenting. A long moment passed, in which he started to doubt his own reasoning.

The cat stretched its paws, its back arching up in a long drawn out yawn and its tail swinging up to form what could have been a question mark of fur. Then its eyes once more bore directly into Richard's, blinking once.

'*I said don't stop now, I like that song. Besides it was on the card for a reason you know, play it, you'll feel better once you do,*' the cat said in a voice which purred with sincerity. Richard could hear the voice as clearly as he heard his own thoughts. Attempts at rationality fled in the face of the irrational but unquestionably real voice. He found himself swallowing hard, still staring at the cat. He had heard the voice, he knew he had heard the voice.

He broke the stare and glanced about him, taking in the oddity of the bar room, and the strangeness of the customers he had barely noticed before. It was all far too surreal, but there seemed little point in trying to ignore the voice. He decided, in that moment, that it was simpler and better to accept the difficult truth than worry about it. If things which were an impossibility were happening, then let them happen. He looked back at the cat once more.

Quietly he asked, "You really are talking to me?" It wasn't entirely a question.

The cat stretched again, like a wave of fur moving down its body and then up its tail, before padding down to lay on the top of the piano once more. Something about the way she did so conveyed her distaste for the question. Richard got the impression she disliked stating the obvious. If he could not grasp the obvious, that was his fault, not hers. She seemed to express this without words, leaving him in no doubt that replying to the foolishness of his question was something she considered beneath her.

Richard heaved a sigh, forcing himself to look down at the keyboard and away from the cat. Then slowly, with a horribly deliberate forethought, began playing the first notes of *Forever Autumn* once more.

He had reached the chorus after the first verse when he heard the cat plainly say *'Thank you Richard."* He managed to only drop one note before he carried on.

The Cat had been correct. He admitted as much to himself once he had moved on a couple of songs. Playing it had made him feel better. While it reminded him of his wife's death, it also reminded him of the good times with her. At least once he had got past the first few bars. The nights laying on their battered sofa, naked under a quilt drinking wine and sharing a chocolate box while it played in the background. The day he gave her the CD, and she played it for hours while they both read books in bed, pausing only for hot bagels with cream cheese and ham. Of kissing in the shower while it played at full volume on the stereo so they could hear it over the water. And all the other times. The good memories pushing away the bad. By the time he finished he felt as if one of the demons he had been carrying with him for so long had finally lifted from his back.

He reconciled all this with the thought that If he could play it, he could get past it and move on, if only in that one little way. It was a start, if nothing else, though it was a start that he was not fully convinced he wanted. He had lived with his grief so long. To feel a small part of it peel away felt wrong. Like losing part of his skin.

It was three songs later when he said in as simple a way as he could, "Thank you," to the cat.

Another song later the cat purred out a *'Your*

welcome, Richard.' This time, he did not drop a note and played on in silence.

A couple of hours slipped by, passed with songs played and a smattering of conversation between them punctuating the songs. At one point the doorman, whose name he remembered was Sonny, arrived with a coffee in each hand. Richard smiled up at him, seeing him for the first time since the night before. The big doorman just winked at Richard putting one coffee down on top of the piano, next to the cat, before wondering off, his own coffee in hand to a stool by the door.

'*Big dolt could have brought me some cream,*' the cat purred sleepily at him while staring after Sonny.

"Isn't cream bad for cats, you're all lactose intolerant aren't you?" Richard replied, taking the opportunity to engage in a conversation beyond '*I like that one play it again,*' and '*oh that one's a dirge don't play it again*'. The cat seemed to have strong opinions on musical taste. He had adjusted his world view, somewhat, to one which accepted hearing the cat talk in his head. While it had taken some adjustment, he now wished to see what the cat's conversation was like beyond musical criticisms. It seemed the right thing to do, though his actual knowledge of cats was limited at best. The lactose intolerance was something he remembered hearing at some time.

The cat gave him a withering look and stared down its nose at him. '*Smoking and drinking are bad for humans, doesn't stop you liking them does it!*' the cat replied with disdain, '*If I want cream I shall have it,'* she added with a note of indignation.

Richard smiled, then found himself chuckling quietly, mildly amused and mildly appalled to recognise that kind of righteous indignation. It reminded him of Carrie. Somehow it failed to cause the usual pangs of remorse that such reminders normally brought, though. He carried on playing for a while, only to find he was back on *Forever Autumn* and, despite whatever cathartic properties it had achieved earlier, this time, it brought back a flood of grief. Despite the wave of loss, he did his best to ignore those feelings and play through anyway, something which the cat seemed to appreciate.

He played on, moving from song to song as the day wore on. Losing time and feelings in the music. For a while, he ceased talking to the cat, who seemed to know instinctively that he needed to be left to himself for a while.

"Do you know '*Hey Jude'*?'" Asked a voice that sounded as dry as a desert wind.

Richard was just coming to the end of a long, curvaceous melody he could not remember the name of. The voice pulled him from his own thoughts which had been drifting as he had played for the last hour or so. He looked up from the keyboard, trusting his fingers to remember the last few bars on their own, and found himself staring at a gunslinger.

That was the first word that first sprang to Richard's mind as he looked at the bars patron who stood before him at the piano.

Gunslinger…A man who had stepped right out of the old west.

Or perhaps it would be truer to say a particular idea of the old west, a Clint Eastwood spaghetti western maybe, *High Plains Drifter* or *A Fist Full of Dollars*.

Tall and imposing, with long, lank sandy hair, framing a face of impassive granite, narrow lipped, with sharp-edged features. It was as weather-beaten and as harsh as the old west itself. The stranger's eyes were shaded by a wide-brimmed hat, which looked equally battered by the elements, as did the rest of his apparel. A heavy, full length, dirt brown duster dropped from his shoulders, bulging unnaturally at his hips, where his gun belt undoubtedly hung. *'A desperado,'* thought Richard, *'a cowboy,'* and most of all *'a gunslinger.'* He seemed out of place in the well-lit piano bar.

'He seems out of place in this century,' Richard added as a mental note to himself.

"Presuming you do requests pilgrim?" the grim gunslinger said, filling the silence as Richard ceased to play.

"Guess I do," Richard replied.

In truth, it had not occurred to him that playing patron's requests would be part of the job. But he had played in hotel bars, and cocktail lounges enough over the years, earning a few bucks a night, so it seemed natural enough that he would. Besides, it was a way to earn tips back then, though he was unsure what kind of tip he might receive in Esqwith's bar. The strange thought occurred to him and then glossed over swiftly. The patrons seemed an odd bunch, as odd as the bar. What tips they might give, well best not thought about too deeply, he decided.

His fingers found the opening bars of the Beatles classic, and the gunslinger nodded approvingly. Almost without thinking about it, Richard found himself gently singing along with the words, while finding himself wondering absently why someone who looked like they were from the 1880's would want to hear a 1970's Beatles song.

The gunslinger listened impassively at the foot of the piano, his face not cracking much, despite a thin smile on his lips. All the same, he seemed to be appreciative of the song, which Richard took to be a good thing. It did not bear thinking too deeply what the gunslinger's response to disappointment might be, after all. He gave the impression of being a man of violence. Not that Richard was scared exactly, but he was more than a little intimidated by the desperado's general appearance. Not that he would have admitted that for the life of him.

"Not bad, different version to the one I know but appreciated all the same, Piano Man," the gunslinger said at the end of the song, dropping a couple of coins as ancient looking as himself on top of the piano. "Brought back a few memory's, most of them good," he added in the same dust-dry voice before stalking off to the bar.

Richard stared after him, feeling slightly bemused by all this, '*different version,*' there's some other version? He wondered to himself absently.

The cat, which had given the impression of

being asleep for a while on top of the piano, seemed to smile in her sleep, before a lazy eye opened betraying the sleep as a ploy and a soft purr issued forth. Richard let his fingers find a song and played on, finding himself smiling back at the cat.

It was a while later when Richard found his gaze wandering to the gunslinger once more. He stood with his back to a recess wall by the side of the bar. It occurred to Richard that, in this way, the gunslinger could view the bar room with ease, assured that no one could come at him from behind. A wise move if you had half an eye for some danger. Richard tried to shrug off the odd observation, but could not help but perceive a tense readiness about the gunslinger. He seemed to be inherently dangerous in nature—like a wolf in amongst the sheep—his eyes always wary and scanning the bar every few moments, looking for something or someone perhaps. Richard had an itchy feeling that trouble would follow should the gunslinger find what he was looking for. At some point those cold slate blue eyes locked with his.

Richard was not aware he had stopped playing; nor more so than he was aware his eyes were locked with those of the gunslingers. Until the cat's voice interceded the strangely mesmerising stare he had encountered there. '*He has a story to tell you might find interesting,*" said the cat, her tone mysterious.

The moment passed, and Richard snapped his gaze away, his fingers finding the ivories once more.

He was halfway through the next piece when he half whispered a conspirator's reply, "A story to tell me? Is that why I am here? Am I here to listen to stories?"

He was not sure where the question came from, or why it occurred to him. It just sort of felt right, correct somehow. He could not explain it to himself, but he knew the question was all but rhetorical. It was a feeling that had come upon him.

The cat, it seemed, decided it was a rhetorical question as well and needed no reply. At least she gave none. Instead, she hopped down from the piano and went stalking across the bar room before leaping up on the bar itself, next to the gunslinger.

Richard, bemused by all this, played on for a while, though he found himself oddly jealousy that the cat had chosen to spend her time elsewhere in the bar. The top of his piano seemed oddly empty without her. A sudden sense of dislike for the gunslinger swept through him, though he was aware that it was lacking in logic. All the same, Richard felt partly betrayed by the cat—partly envious of the gunslinger for gaining her attention. The gunslinger, for his part, seemed unaware she was curled up on the bar next to him. Or that he was stroking her absent-mindedly, eyes still sweeping the room as he drank whisky from a shot glass.

Richard could not bring himself to question his sudden possessiveness about the fractious feline. It was ridiculous he knew, particularly after such a short time. But the feeling was there none the less.

After a few more songs he decided it was time

for a break anyway. His fingers ached at the knuckles and tips. His back had been hunched at the piano for several hours and throbbed at the base of his spine. His eyes felt heavy, itchy and watery. At least he told himself that this was the case and the reason he got up from the piano, rather than the cat's abandonment of him for the gunslinger's side. But all the same, he needed a break from ivory tickling.

He closed the lid over the keyboard and made his way across the bar room, following the path recently trodden by his feline companion. As he arrived at the bar, he remembered what the cat had said. *'He has a story to tell you might find interesting,"*

'Nothing seems to make a great deal of sense in this place.' Richard decided, *'Guess I may as well hear this gunslingers tale,'* he had mused upon this as he walked over to the bar. Now he was there he was not sure how to start a conversation with the gunslinger. Ordering a coffee from Lyal, he turned to the arid drifter and opted for the simplest opening he could think of and said, "So you like, Hey Jude?"

They talked of nothing much for a minute or three. Then a little while later the gunslinger began to tell his tale.

'And the world moved on… '

CHAPTER SIX
================

A Stranger Rides In…

From the balcony of the saloon, she watches him riding into town. A lone figure riding out of the desert, no more than a shimmer of indistinct black in the heat haze but growing ever more in focus the closer he came. She knew it was a man even though he was still too far out to tell much beyond that.

She was not sure why she watched, but from the moment she saw the figure on the horizon, kicking up dust from the dry ground, she had found herself staring at him from the balcony of her room. As if she was staring at a storm brewing on the horizon. Drawing ever closer.

Perhaps it was simply that travellers were a rare enough sight coming into Lost Springs.

Or maybe it was because travellers coming in from the high desert to the west were all but unheard of. People rode into the high desert, they never rode out of it.

But from the moment she had seen the man she felt a sense of foreboding. She could sense the rider was something to be feared; Feared and something more. She felt cold just looking at him, like someone was walking over her grave. Something was coming to town, something terrible. Yet, for all her apprehension, she found herself almost welcoming it. So she watched his slow progression towards the town.

Out of the heat haze.

Out of the high desert.

Out of a place no living man had a business being.

As he drew closer, the strange unwarranted fear he raised within her grew stronger. From mild anxiety it grew towards a purer form of fear by the time he was passing the first outlying buildings of Lost Springs' only street, his horse never wavering in its slow plodding gait.

Once he was closer, she took time to examine the man—tall, lean framed, yet visibly strong—hidden though he was beneath his heavy dark duster. His head held high, his eyes never wavered in their gaze, staring straight ahead as he rode. His large brimmed hat shaded his eyes, while lack dirty blonde hair, gritty with desert dust, framed his face, which seemed long and drawn and emotionless. There was a menace about him that was impossible to ignore, which had nothing to do with his six shooters occasionally visible when the breeze whipped up the folds of his duster.

Others turned to watch him as he passed along the street. Silence seemed to surround him like a bubble as he rode. The townsfolk stopped, ceasing their chores and conversations, and just stared at the stranger. She could almost taste the wave of fear that came from them as he passed by, a gun wearing stranger riding in from the high desert in the high noon sun; Almost the fairy tale of the west. Someone's death riding in on a pale horse. Fear was gripping the town: The primal fear of the sheep, caught in the presence of a wolf. A coppery taste deep down at the back of people's throats.

She watched intently, as his horse slowed and came to a halt outside the saloon. He seemed to pause motionless on the horse for a long moment. Then his head tilted towards the balcony above him.

He looked straight up at her, and she felt a shiver run down her spine as she looked back into those cold blue eyes. They locked on hers. She felt his stare, a physical gaze like cold steel daggers, delving into her soul. She felt the masks she built against the world being stripped away from her. She knew, in the core of her being, that he saw straight through to the real her that cowered behind those masks, reading all her fears and doubts and weighing them against the world. That stare seemed to last an age as it tore away at her, but was less than a moment, before he looked down once more and climbed from the saddle.

She watched him tie his horse to the post before the water trough and calmly, methodically, stroke the beast while it drank deep from the water. The grey had seemed almost an extension of him as he rode in. Now it seemed much like any other horse, as its rider gave it some little attention and encouraged it to drink its thirst away. She watched him do this with all the fascination of prey for the hunter.

She felt suddenly a flush of warmth and realised she was blushing. She felt an ache deep inside her, one she seldom felt in these latter days of the world. It came as a surprise—desire mixed with fear, lust with a tremble of awe, feelings she had not experienced in years. A heat grew from a flame she thought extinguished by the harsh reality of life. Her breathing had become rapid, and urgent with it. She felt her chest rise and fall as her heart rate rushed faster with that flush.

But the fear was still there, mixed in with the lust. This man was a killer, a life taker, a wolf among the flock. She had seen that much in his eyes, his stare so hard and unyielding. Yet she sensed a justness about him that held the killer in check. She could not tell you how she knew this. The knowledge came from nowhere, with no basis she could explain. It was however simply something she knew to be true, deep in the core of her existence.

She watched him turn from his horse, now tied

to the beam beside the trough and enter the saloon.

She almost tripped over her own feet, as she ran from the outer balcony, through her room, to the inner balcony that overlooked the saloon itself. Her heart pounding now, she struggled to hold herself in check with her shredded willpower. Foreboding settled over her as she could almost feel it like a weight pushing against the world.

As she watched, an unnatural silence settled ominously over the bar. They knew something was coming. Conversations died mid-sentence. The piano player lifted his hands from the keyboard mid-song. The bar rooms occupants seemed to take a collective breath. They had all felt it, that sense of the storm approaching; the air getting heavy, about to break.

As he entered, that sense of unease changed to fear and awe. The collection of strays and itinerants, which formed the bars customers, reacted like a herd. One that collectively felt the predator as it entered the room.

All save one drunken miner at the bar who continued to argue with the barkeeper, ignorant to the fact the barman's attention no longer focused on him. His eyes fixed on the stranger in the doorway who had remained there for a moment, standing in the frame of the swinging doors he had entered through, surveying the room with those cold ice blue eyes.

To her, as she watched from the balcony above, it seemed as if the stranger was taking a moment to make note of each person in the saloon. She felt like he was weighing their souls against some tally of his own making, taking their measure and deciding their dues. She could feel the fear permeating the room—they all could—while he just stood, slowly moving his gaze from one man to the next.

She knew with a strange certainty that they all felt the same intense reactions to his stare as she did. Though it would be a different reaction to her own, she was sure. Theirs was more one of primal fear, the one born when you were faced with the alpha. Her own, though it held fear, held a lusting in equal, if not greater, measure. She realised this with a warm thrill and a renewed ache within her. One she thought long dead. At the last his gaze fell upon her once more and for the briefest of moments, which lasted for an age, she held her breath.

Then, silently, he walked from the swinging doors towards the bar, each pair of eyes in the room following him. The mesmerised trance of quarry at bay. The room collectively held its breath as the swinging doors creaked shut on their hinges behind him.

"Whisky," he said to the barman, frozen in the act of polishing a glass. He threw a handful of coins on the bar. The barman, his face a portrait of apprehension, reached below the counter for a bottle and glass. Pouring it quickly and then leaving the bottle at the side of the glass, he scooped up the coins without a word.

The stranger drank the glass in one, then took hold of the bottle, keeping the glass in hand as he strode to a corner table from which he could watch the whole room. The eyes of the room followed him once more, while that same silence impregnated the atmosphere, save for the random gibberish argument the drunk was having with no one. Reversing the chair, he sat silently facing into the room, idly drinking, but doing so with cold detachment. The room continued to stare back at him.

On the balcony, she felt an intense sense of fascination. He held the room captive, all without drawing a gun or saying more than one word. The primal fears that seemed to emanate from him, infecting the room, she could feel from the balcony. That strange excitement continued to rise within her; someone would die soon. She could feel it. Everyone could feel it. Tension hung in the air, and death, waiting for only the slightest of reasons, hung with it.

Yet for her, the fear was mixed with desire, longing even. Whatever was going to happen, she felt compelled to watch. To be part of it. This was life as well as death. This was a moment on the edge of the abyss, tilting out over a gulf. Life never feels so worth having than when it is threatened. The threat was palatable to everyone.

She felt a sudden shiver that ran the length of her spine. He was looking at her once again, his cold steel eyes locking her in their gaze...

....

Richard could not explain why, to himself or to

anyone else, but he felt drawn into the tale as the Gunslinger told it. Much like he had the night before when Sonny had told his story. He could almost feel the fear and tension within that saloon. He could almost smell the sawdust on the floor. Hear the creaking of the swing doors, though he was looking at the Gunslinger in Esqwiths. He was also in this other bar room, this western saloon, surrounded by everything you would expect in such a place.

He felt engulfed by the tale once he had gotten the Gunslinger to tell it, which had been easier than he expected. Almost as if the Gunslinger was there to tell it to him.

Perhaps he just liked to tell this story. This strange story of an old west which seemed wrong somehow and yet true none the less.

Richard took a drink from the coffee he had ordered and listened on, surprising himself with the knowledge he felt the self-same fear everyone had felt in that western saloon. The same tension, the same holding of breath, waiting for the inevitable.

The Gunslinger continued his tale...

....

It was the drunken miner who broke the spell. Unable to get served by a barman too used to the fool's antics, and, seeing a man drinking alone with a full bottle, he eyed a chance of a drink and stumbled on unsteady legs across the saloon floor. With a smile of crooked teeth beneath an unshaven face, he waved a hand in front of the stranger.

"Hey Mister, what's yar name then? Don't see many like you out here in the back end of nowhere," he tried to say, but the words were slurred with booze and heavily accented. The stranger looked up at the drunk, with an almost weary look in his eye. The rest of the saloon held its breath with one collective inhale.

The stranger poured another glass of whisky and shoved it over the table to the drunk, without saying a word.

The miner suddenly felt fear grip at his heart as he found himself staring into the stranger's cold steel eyes. He wavered for a moment, his hand pausing on its way to pick up the glass, trepidation and that same infectious terror gripping him now, as it had grasped everyone else when the stranger had entered the saloon. That fear alone stayed his hand. But the desire for the whisky, an urge he could not fight, overcame that fear and he grabbed the glass, drinking the shot down in one slug.

"Thank ye stranger," he said simply, and the room relaxed for a moment. Their collective breath let out once more.

"Don't thank me," said a voice like boots on gravel, grating and unyielding, little more than a whisper, but grinding through the silence like fingernails down a chalkboard. The stranger was looking straight at the drunken miner, his gaze steady and hard as iron.

"What you say Mister?" The drunken miner replied, confused and fearful. She could see him shaking from her vantage point on the balcony. These were not the shakes of a drunk; these were the shakes caused by the terror running down his spine.

The Stranger continued to look up into the drunk's eyes. The drunk wanted nothing more than to turn away from that gaze, but could no more do that than he could have turned down the whisky. A moment past and then the stranger spoke again in the same voice of gravel- scraping harshness.

"Do not thank me for that. Whisky will be your death. Even now it's killing you, eating away at your insides. Maybe a year, maybe six months, but you're just a dead man walking now because of it. All I have done is hasten you to your nasty, painful, inalterable demise." There was finality to the words that ran like a cold shiver through everyone in the room. That they were true, that the stranger had foretold the man's death, all those in the room knew with absolute certainty.

From the balcony, she watched the drunk stumble away towards the door. Fear now gripping him stronger than booze for the first time. He fled from the saloon and the stranger...This stranger, this harbinger of a death to come. And for a moment she had a vision, a moment of clarity. This was indeed whom the stranger was.

Death.

Death come riding into town.

And just as suddenly she realised she desired him. Desired death. Welcomed him. Welcomed death to this saloon, in the end of places.

The room slowly returned to life, a few whispered words and the stranger's spell began to be broken. There is only so long the world can hold its breath before it starts to turn blue. The piano player hit a couple of loose cords, then began to play a gentle melody, unlike the normal bawdy music favoured by the regulars, but it seemed to suit the mood of the room. Conversations started up once more. The card game resumed.

From her place on the balcony she watched as the world returned to a semblance of normality, but from her vantage point, it was easy to see that everyone took a glance at the stranger at any point they thought they could get away with without raising suspicion.

She watched them with cold fascination as they slowly tried to return normality to their environment. Her gaze swept from face to face, as she wondered if any of the others had sensed it.

She could see the mark upon them. While they railed against the fear that had gripped them, it still hung in the air around them. He had left his mark upon each and every one of them as his gaze had passed over them. His mark, Death's mark.

It seemed to hang over each of them. Why they could not see it themselves, she could not guess. Fascination, mixed with that selfsame primal fear she could no more explain than ignore. So she watched them. Her hands gripping the wooden balcony so hard that they ached with pain, her knuckles white. The certainty of it all was overwhelming her.

Death had come to town.
Death had come to end it all.
Could they not see?
She felt that same tell-tale shiver once more and

realised his eyes had come to rest upon her again.

His eyes never left hers as he stood, and began to cross the saloon, walking inextricably towards the stairs which lead up to her perch upon the balcony. She watched his progress with a mixture of captivation and dread.

Where he passed, men died.

The man who had been closest to the stranger collapsed on his table, his head turned to the side, a bullet hole in his temple; A Bloodless hole in the middle of a corpse-white face.

The next half jumped from his seat, rope marks around his neck showing him to have been hanged as he collapsed to the floor. The piano player stopped suddenly as the line of his neck was cut by a jealous lover two years in the future. One man seemed to shrivel and age before her till his heart gave out of 40 years hence. Another's face turned black with syphilis as he collapsed on the table. Yet another turned red with fever as he fell then turned once again to drip white as he lay upon the sawdust floor.

One by one the room's occupants succumbed to deaths, which were awaiting them in the future, falling silently to the floor behind him, as the stranger progressed through the saloon. The last man to fall was the barman. As the stranger mounted the steps, his eyes shifted to watch as the barman collapsed on the counter the wounds of a shotgun shredding his face and leaving burn marks from the powder. His eyes moved back to hers as he commenced to climb from the graveyard the saloon had become.

....

Richard's coffee cup was empty. His mind, however, wasn't. He felt engrossed by the gunslinger's tale. He could taste the sawdust on the floor of the saloon. He had felt something akin to fear, or perhaps just plain horror, as each death was described to him. He could feel the fear in the bar, the grim presence of the stranger, the heat of the desert air. The further the story went, the more Richard felt as if the bar around him was becoming the saloon. As if he was seeing through the eyes of the woman on the balcony.

He reached down and found his coffee refilled, and the cat staring up at him with amused eyes. But he hardly noticed her. So deeply engrossed within the tale had he become.

He could feel the echo that same terror the woman on the balcony felt as she looked down at the stranger climbing the steps. And perhaps, somewhere deep within himself the same longing and desire mixed within that fear.

The gunslinger continued his tale.

....

Frozen in place at the top of the stairs, her grip on the balcony unyielding, she was unwilling and unable to flee from this vision of death before her. The self-same detachment and heat she had felt through all this still gripped at her. She wondered at her sanity.

Was she going mad?

Was this all happening?

In desperation, she closed her eyes and wished the vision of death to vanish. But as she opened them once more the carnal house below her had not changed. The room below her was still littered with the dead men, their deaths brought forward to strike them down before their time. The only sounds now were his footfalls on the stairs which creaked under his weight, and the near thundering of her own heartbeat. She watched his progress up the stairs, fear gripping her tightly in a gloved hand. She fought for breath in air so still, it seemed to lose all life and she watched him. This man, this death come to town, coming for her now, and she could not, would not flee.

"Stay back."

She heard the words without recognising them as her own.

"Stay back," she repeated with a desperate edge to her voice. She knew she was saying it, but she knew at the same time it was not what she wanted. She wanted him to climb the stairs. She wanted him with feelings long forgotten and suppressed. There was a longing within her which he had awakened from the moment she had set eyes upon him, a longing which was running roughshod over every other instinct within her. The awe he inspired was as palatable as his existence to her.

She could not turn away.

He shook his head, his face emotionless, cold to the world, and continued to climb the stairs. She wanted to run, more than anything she wanted to run, more than anything but the one thing which kept her in place.

He stopped in front of her, his eyes, his cold, icy eyes burning into hers. She could feel his breath upon her, icy cold and frosting despite the dessert heat. The room itself had dropped in temperature rapidly, like the night air had sucked the heat out of the world, despite the sun still blazing hot outside.

"What... What are you..?" She stammered, wanting to back away from the coldness.

His eyes, icy steal and unblinking, looked into hers. She had known the answer before he gave it. He was death incarnate, the death of the old west, the stranger that rides into town and leaves nothing but cadavers behind him, bleaching in the desert sun.

"You know what I am" he replied as if he had read the recognition in her eyes.

"What,,,,, what do you want here?" she managed to say, the words biting through the choking sensation in her throat. Another question for which she already feared she knew the answer; feared and yet it was a fear, tipped with anticipation for his answer.

He raised one hand in answer, a single finger pointing at her chest.

"I came for you," he replied. His voice still cold, no vestige of emotion within it. She shook visibly as he pointed at her, cold shivers running down her back. Was it her death he sought or something else? What had she done to deserve the attentions of the grim apparition that stood before her? There seemed a timeless moment where she stood and stared back at him while he pointed at her. The last syllable of his 'you' stretching endlessly into the frozen moment.

"I came for you!"

The moment was broken by an eruption of noise from the saloon floor. The silence which had been so invasive was replaced with the sounds of life once more. The piano burst into the middle eight of 'Hey Jude'. There was laughter, of the coarse bawdy type she was so familiar with, coming from the card tables. The harsh words of an argument were easily picked out over the general kerfuffle of the tap room, an argument she had heard more than once between a cattleman and a sheep farmer from over at Dolton's ridge. She could almost pick out the squeaking of the barman's cloth as he cleaned glasses behind the bar. There was a wave of relief that flushed through her, despite the stranger's presence. The barroom was alive. This had all been some strange delusion. She assumed she had just spent too long on the balcony, staring off into the desert sun. It was hardly surprising she was feeling light headed and imagining strange things, she surmised.

Yet before her still stood the strange visage of Death in a duster and rawhide hat.

"They're alive," she said simply, while rejoicing inwardly at the noise of the piano and the bawdy voices filling the silence.

His grim expression did not change, his head merely shaking slowly left to right and back again.

"No," he replied in his monotone gravel grate. "They just don't know they are dead. They are the ghosts of those who once were. They will pass soon enough."

That sense of horror she had just passed off as sunstroke swamped back over her. She pulled her gaze away from him, staring down at the barroom floor below the balcony.

He was telling the truth. She knew that somewhere inside herself before she even looked. The certainty of his words was overwhelming. She stared down at the patrons of the barroom below her, their animated bodies still bearing the scars of their brutal deaths. Bullet holes gaped in chests, a head hung back where a throat had been slit. The pockmarks of pestilence and rot were visible on others. The cadavers seemed unaware of their condition and ignored even the most obvious signs like malformed broken limbs, and necks, occasionally pausing in puzzlement to correct a stray body part.

The town had become one of ghoulish spectres and ghosts.

Her attention switched back to the stranger; An attempt to distract herself from the greater horror below, with the lesser one before her. She focused her attention upon him as completely as she possibly could. Ignoring the sounds of life, which were slowing becoming more like the groans of the dead.

"What,,, what do you want with me?" she stammered.

His cold eyes burned into hers, his face expressionless, icy and hard. He seemed to be weighing something in his mind, as another long hollow moment passed between them before he answered her in that same monotone tombstone cold voice.

"I am the reaper of souls, the bringer of Discordia, the death incarnate of this world. I have ridden upon a pale steed across the four corners, for time uncounted. I am the bringer of endings and despair to all. With you I would break that cycle, with you, I would bring life rather than death, if but once upon this world."

She stared back at him, her gaze as hard as his. Uncomprehending, unable to join the words he had spoken to ones with meaning in the real world. She felt frozen before him, rooted to the spot. Terrified and yet enamoured with the vision before her.

"I don't understand," she said, her mind swimming, raking over the words he had spoken. She was unable to make sense out of them. What was he saying and, what was it he wanted?

Then realisation dawned upon her, breaking over her like a wave of fear and revelation.

Suddenly she could move once more. She backed away but each step she took, he followed.

She continued to back away, her fear now a living thing, but he continued step for step towards her. His face a crag of impassivity. His eyes as cold and heartless as the desert sand at midnight. His cold breath was freezing in the air before him despite the noon heat. The air around him had an unearthly feel, as if the world itself was trying to reject his existence.

She felt the tears before she realised she was crying. The cold line they tracked down her face made her shiver all the more.

"Stay back,,, please stay back." she half whispered still backing away, but already aware there was nowhere to go. The door of her room was open behind her, but she knew that, even if she sped through the door and slammed it shut, it would prove no barrier to this creature. This death, made man, this was a demon made flesh. How could simple wood hope to hold him back?

"Nay," he said, and then paused as if getting himself around a word that proved hard to say. He tried once more, "Nay beloved," the word had an odd stress coming from his lips. Following her footstep for footstep, he said again, "Nay beloved," and continued, "you will submit to my will, you shall become the vessel of my offspring, you shall become mother to my child and bring forth life from death."

At these last words her nerve, which was already in tatters, broke completely, and she turned sharply, fleeing into her room. Behind her he slowly, inevitably, followed. Now trapped within the confines of her own room, her head swam once more. What was happening? It became even more dreamlike to her, though nightmarish would perhaps describe it better.

She now expected to be raped. Which she was, but not the way in which she expected—not brutally, not hard and painfully. There was pain, but not how she expected. Lost in it all, she lost the will to fight. Or perhaps it is truer to say he took it from her.

He clasped her by the arms and pulled her

towards him, firmly but without hurting her. Her resistance fled, the desire which had been there before swam back in its place. Bending his head he kissed her, firmly but with enough tenderness to calm her a little. Though her heart raced so fast she felt it would burst. She was caught between the desire she felt and the fear which threatened to overwhelm her, wanting to flee, to run as far and as fast as she could from the nightmare she was living through. She wanted to vacate her body, to move aside and let it experience everything without her for a while. But she could not push out away from it.

A hand cupped her left breast through her shirt. Hard and firm, her nipple sprung erect under his touch and was pinched between his fingers. His other hand pushed her skirt up and aside, sliding between her legs, caressing her inner thigh before moving up to her vagina and above it to touch her clitoris and push hard against it. She moaned with unexpected pleasure despite herself. She felt flushed and felt herself getting damper, anticipation despite the circumstance, making her more aroused. His body was taut, firm and hard against her, she felt pleasure build up inside herself and he pulled his member free of his trousers and she gasped as he took her, slowly at first, then building up in rhythm and depth, each thrust a little deeper, harder. Each moment she became more entwined with him, and more lost within the act.

That night was dark and full of shadows. Of screams that could have been pain or pleasure. Of heated passions as cold as the grave. Lust that burned like ice. Cold beyond cold, and hot beyond hot.

She remembered none of what passed in that room in the morning. When she woke, he was gone and she felt nothing but yearning for him.

She remembered, slowly, fragments of the night. Their bodies entwined; the cold heat of his skin; the feeling of him inside; the moment their orgasms hit simultaneously. That moment of him being within her and the two of them joined utterly in the most basic, and yet truthful, of ways.

Afterwards, she fell asleep in his arms, weeping gently to herself, though even she didn't know if it was relief, or anguish, or something else. Something less palatable to think about….a yearning.

The town was silent, the desert dust blowing in through the street. Tumbleweed blowing in with it, silent and dead, already being reclaimed by the desert. She rose from her cot and moved slowly to the balcony, clutching a bed sheet over her nakedness. She stared out into the desert as if imagining him riding off into the sun, though he was nowhere to be seen. No one was anywhere to be seen.

The town was dead and empty. The only life here was her own.

Her own, and that of the child she knew was within her. She imagined she could feel the child already growing within her. But she knew that was just her imagination. She knew it grew there nonetheless, of that she was certain, if little else.

The stranger had been death incarnate, but human once, cursed for some unspoken sin by the old gods of the west to walk the earth, reaping souls in penance. Her mind swam with questions. Who had he been? How had he come to be what he was?

But there were no answers.

Growing within her, he had a sort of redemption, bringing life instead of death, the growing child in her womb testament to this. Whether he achieved his redemption, she did not know. She knew not where he had gone, vanished in the dawn.

The town was dead

The corpses were gone

His horse was gone

He was gone.

Tumbleweed rolled across the empty, lifeless street

She sat on the balcony and wept. Not for herself, not for the child growing with her, not for those who had died, but for him.

For her stranger.

Where ever he was.

....

"That is the story of my conception, as my mother tells it. As my mother told it to me," the gunslinger said, finishing his tale and drinking the last of his whisky. Richard felt the hairs on the back of his neck stand up. And he breathed in sharply, only now realising he had held his breath for the last bit of the story. Disbelief washed over him. That feeling of being in the story faded as well. Though slowly, like a movie fading out as the credits rolled.

"Thanks for your story. It was,," Richard struggled for a word, then shook his head and smiled at the gunslinger. "It was definitely interesting."

He went with the most neutral comment he could think of. He felt he should explain how engrossed he had become, how drawn in he had been, but could not find words to explain it, to the gunslinger or to himself.

At the end, he had felt everything she had felt, washing over him: her terror, her exultation, her feelings of guilt, of having been abused and dirtied. And her grief, sorrow and sense of loss when the morning had come. But all that was fading now. Fading with the credits as they rolled.

He could not explain the empathy involved. He could not explain any of it so he went with a neutral comment to hide his astonishment.

There was a flash of anger in the Gunslinger's eyes, but he seemed to relax quickly and smiled back.

"You don't believe me, and I can't say as I blame you, Piano Player. Dare say I would not believe it myself if I was you." He stretched a little and put down the whisky glass on the bar. "Time I was moving on anyways. I'll be through here again no doubt. No matter where I go, I seem to find this bar once in a while. Never strikes me odd at the time." The gunslinger paused for a moment, as if considering this fact for the first time.

"Now that's odd don't you think, I ride for days and in some sleepy little town I wonder in through the doors of this place? Always a different town. Yet I manage to find the same saloon. And it only now occurs to me to wonder how the saloon moves from one town to the next." He smiled for the first time Richard could remember. "Always something new to learn I guess."

"Guess so," Richard replied, finding himself not wishing to wonder too much about how that happened either.

The gunslinger took Richard's hand and gave it a quick shake before nodding farewell. The big man turned and adjusted his hat slightly before walking towards what Richard for a moment saw as saloon-style swing doors at the exit. He paused with his hand on the door and turned back, looking at Richard straight in the eyes, his face impassive once more.

"Can you do me a favour, Piano Player?" he asked.

"Sure," said Richard for want of anything else to say, wondering inwardly what kind of favour this dust-raddled gunslinger would want of him.

"Places like this, places that aren't rightly all it seems—well, seems to me it's just the kind of place you may one day meet that which fathered me in."

Richard felt a lump in his throat all of a sudden, as the gunslinger continued.

"See, if you ever do, you be sure to tell the old bastard I'm gunning for him," he said, before turning and walking out of the bar.

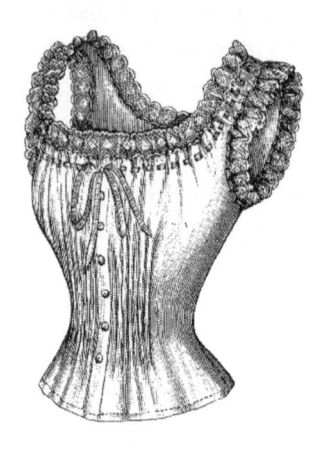

CHAPTER SEVEN

Jolene Followed the Morn

That night Richard awoke in a cold shivering sweat, vivid nightmare images of zombies clothed like cowboys and steel-eyed strangers on pale horses still flickering through his mind.

He lurched upward from the bed, pulled his knees tight to his chest and clasped his arms around them. Clinging tightly, while the grasping tendrils of the dream slipped slowly away into the dark corners of the room.

As he sat there shivering in the chill of the night, his eyes were drawn out into the darkness. Seeing faces in the shadows. Grinning faces of angels and demons in the darkened corners and the cracks in the ceiling. Faces of the dead and the dying, twisted in horrible caricatures of life, half seen, half imagined, and something else.

Something in the darkness, something that seemed to pulse with a deeper darkness, tinged with red, the deepest darkest red that could be imagined. Something which scared him more that the all the ghosting images in the night together.

In those hazed moments of waking, he could not tell truth, from the fictions of his mind. For those few moments he was frozen, as tendrils of terror slowly and ever so begrudgingly, released their grip on his psyche.

As the waking fear slowly gave way to reality, it was replaced with surprise. It had been such a long time since he had suffered any form of a nightmare, other than ones of his wife. Truth told, until her death, he had seldom suffered from nightmares at all. Horror movies and ghost stories had never affected him the way they affected some people. He had always just enjoyed them for what they were. Never feeling drawn into their fictions. His terrors had always been ground in the grimmer fictions of reality.

The gunslinger's tale had, however, been different. To say he was drawn in was too pale a description. Richard had been unable to clear it from his mind for hours afterwards. He found himself dwelling on the tale at the strangest moments as he played his way through the evening in the bar. The weird way the story had felt so real to him. How he had almost experienced the heat of the desert wind, the smell of the sawdust of the saloon floor, that metallic taste of blood and death, how he had seen it all played out before him so much more vividly than if he had truly seen it happen.

Now, as he sat there staring at the wall, he realised it was no surprise it surfaced in his dreams too.

It had been such an intense experience for all he had just been listening to a story being told. He had wondered afterwards if it had been something in the qualities of the gunslingers voice. Something that fired his imagination. He could remember the shiver at the base of his spine he felt as he was told of the stranger entering the saloon. The way he has heard the hush descending on the barroom so he could almost hear the crushing of grit beneath the slate-eyed killer from the high desert.

He experienced it all on a level that made no sense. It was, after all, no more than a story told to him in a bar. But it had pulled him in all the same. Submerging him in the tale, and those echoes of the story stayed with him as he stared at the faces in the dark. The way the shapes in the shadows merged to form them and then stared right back into him.

Some time later, the cat slinked into the room. Joining him on the bed, she nuzzled her head against him insistently until he gave way. Richard found himself curling up on the bed with one arm gently over her as she snuggled into him. The soft vibrations of the cats purr, and her occasional subtle movements as she settled in, drew him back towards sleep. Easing him back to that happy oblivion.

Before long he was deeply asleep once more, and as he slept whatever grip the gunslingers story had upon him slowly melted away into the night.

Despite the nightmare and his broken sleep, Richard awoke the following day feeling more deeply rested than he remembered feeling in months.

The cat had left him some time in the night. Richard found himself musing that she must have left only once she had calmed him down to the point where he had slept. Then found himself smiling at the ridiculousness of ascribing such a philanthropic gesture to a cat, dismissing it from his thoughts.

A quick shower and the mild panic of the daily ritual, known only as the finding clean socks, he was dressed and running down the stairs.

He gave little more than a cursory good morning nod to Lyal as he passed the barman. As ever was polishing glasses behind the bar.

A brief, and surprisingly jolly, "Morning" followed from the Greyman as Richard dodged his dancing mop and bucket. Which were being swung around the bar room floor with the Greyman's normal vigorous enthusiasm for the task as he whistled away to himself.

Sitting at the piano, he uncovered the keyboard and flexed his fingers. A strange feeling of been exactly where he should be took hold of him.

Before he fully realised what he was doing, he felt his fingers finding the keys, trying to pick up the tune uttering from between the cleaners pursed lips. Unfortunately, the swift dance of the mop took the whistler away from him before he could fully catch the tune.

Instead, after the first few keystrokes the notes morphed into the first bars of *'Forever Autumn'* without any real thought on Richards's part.

As the realisation of what he was playing struck him, he faltered for a note or two. Those self-same bad memories being triggered by the tune, but he found himself compelled to continue playing the song. Remembering the cat's suggestion the day before he found himself thinking that 'If it's a form of catharsis, then better to embrace it than push it away.'

By the time he was approaching the final verse, he was singing the words under his breath as he played.

"Through autumns golden gown we'd kick our way...You always loved this time of year... Those fallen leaves lie undisturbed now..."

"Cause you're not here," A feminine voice cut in.

The voice's owner standing before the piano holding a coffee cup with two hands, at arm's length, and offering it out to Richard with a smile. He did not remember seeing her the day before, but he thought it safe to assume she was another member of staff. In fairness, the waitress uniform she was wearing made it not much of an intellectual leap. The uniform itself look like something out of a diner in the fifty's. The woman wearing the uniform, however, did not.

She was short, and thin, waif-like even, with an oddly childlike quality to her face. There was a suggestion of innocence about her, though as her smile broadened it suggested otherwise. She also had short cropped hair which was dyed green and spiked up like foliage around her thin face in a very un-fifties way. That green hair seeming all the brighter because of her pale complexion.

At first, Richard took her for little more than a teenager, before he noticed there was someone older behind her equally bright green eyes. They seemed full of light, lustre and life, much as did she, but also they held of something knowing about them. That and the kind of sadness that comes with having lived through troubled times.

He returned her smile and played out the song, repeating the last line with her twice more before he took his fingers from the keys and accepted the coffee gratefully. His morning caffeine craving had just begun to bite deep.

"Thank you ….." he said leaving the sentence hanging and smiling to enquiring as to her name.

"You're welcome Mr Piano man." She replied, her voice had a light, breezy quality, which brought to mind a soft wind through an orchard. *'Or even the gentle rustling of leaves in autumn,'* Richard thought, before been momentarily disturbed by the idea given what he had just sung.

She had he realised, clearly not picked up his subtly implied hint as to her name. Richard found himself unsurprised, no one in the passing place seemed to follow the normal social patterns of behaviour. They all seemed to have, at the very least, eccentric social skills.

Richard was trying not to judge them for that, but it made introductions awkward all the same.

The only exception had been Sonny who at least seemed normal when it came to conversation. Normal compared to some of the others at least. Though that was a special kind of normal if the story he had told Richard on the night of his arrival had in any way a grain of truth to it. Normal for a man who should be a hundred and twelve but looked forty. Richard was not sure he was entirely coming to terms with that little nugget of information, but then he was not sure he was coming to terms with a great deal of what was happening to him.

"It's Richard….." He replied, leaving a long pause, waiting once more for her to tell him her own name. When she did not take the opportunity after a few seconds, he added, "Richard Barrick." If only to fill the silence.

She looked at him oddly and tilted her head to one side once more. *'Yes, it going to be one of those conversations'*. He thought to himself with a certain degree of resignation.

"Richard ………Richard Barrick," she seemed to linger on the name, trying it for size on her lips. Smiled slightly and continued, "I am most pleasantly pleased to make your acquaintance, Richard ……..Richard Barrick. I am Morning That Brings The Joy Of Delicate Sunlight Through The Leaves Of the Forrest In The Late Spring In The Ever Dale When The Gentle Wind Blows From The

East And Unsettles The Blossoms Which Flutter In The Breeze."

"Morning of delicate…" he tried to repeat, only to be brought up short when she raised her hand and smiled brightly at him.

"Just Morn will do, no one ever remembers it all, and isn't it just dreadful when a person garbles your name." She said. Her smile taking on a slightly mocking lint, she tilted her head slightly again. He was not sure if she was still trying to reach a conclusion of some kind or trying to confuse him further. She seemed to nibble at her own lip for a second, seemingly, trying to formulate a reply.

"And I shall call you Richard because that long pause is just a little weird. I mean who has a pause as a second name? It's just a little pretentious don't you think?" she said after a moment. The oddly quizzical expression on her face made him not at all sure she was joking.

His expression must have betrayed his own bafflement, because she suddenly looked more serious and tilted her head to one side again.

"Was I just rude? My apologies if I was, I can never tell, and I hate it when I am." She said after some consideration. Looking genuinely worried for a brief moment.

Richard smiled back, trying to look reassuring. Feeling both awkward and out of his depth at the same time. There was a genuine note of sincerity in her voice, but he found it hard to shake the feeling she was playfully ribbing him all the same.

Regardless, she continued to smile and continued tilting her head in the same odd fashion every few moments. It was an oddly inhuman mannerism that reminded him of a wading bird he had watched once morning in the Louisesianna levies that was trying to find its way to a fish hiding beneath a submerged log. She seemed expectant, Richard wondered if he was being rude himself.

"Think nothing of it Morn, I'm not easily offended, and just Richard is fine," he said, realising he needed to break the silence. Her smile broadened at this and he added, feeling slightly less awkward. "Oh and thanks again for the coffee Morn, much appreciated."

She winked at him and spun on her heels nimbly and skipped sprightly away. Calling back to him as went. "Your Welcome Richard."

He sipped at his coffee and watched her go, there was something about the sway of her hips and the oddly half skipping gait brightened his morning still further. He took a long drink, then put the coffee down as he realised exactly what he was doing. Knowing full well he was now the one being rude, at the very least, or more honestly, just plain lecherous in his gaze.

He found himself smiling all the same. Surprised at the sudden moment of attraction he was feeling, and at the same time a little pleased, to feel it. It seemed a long time since he had felt that way. Pleased enough that the small moment of guilt he felt afterwards almost slip past him.

Morn was in truth, not the first woman he had found attractive since Carrie's death, and it was not like time had passed since she left the world. However, he always felt a measure of guilt when he did, ridiculous as some would find the idea.

Despite this, those moments of attraction always brightened his days, all the same. There seemed to him something very human about feeling attraction to another person, however fleetingly. It reminded him if only for a brief few moments, that he was not as alone as he felt.

The day wound on, with Richard spending it all behind the piano.

He found his way from one song to another as customers filtered through the door in dribs and drabs. While he paid them little more attention than he had the day before. Happy to just lose himself in his playing. By the middle of the afternoon, however, his fingers were beginning to cramp up, and he had a nagging ache across his shoulders from sitting in the same position for so long.

Other things had also begun to nag at him as the day progressed. The good mood of the morning had started to fade slightly.

For one thing, the cat was noticeably absent, and Richard found himself missing her company as well as the occasional cryptic comments from the top of the piano. He was surprised how quickly he had adjusted his world view to include a talking cat. He was, however, all the more surprised to find her absence pained him. There was a tiny void in his day where a cat shape should be. It seemed ridiculous, all the same, that he had formed an attachment to the beast so quickly, but the cat seemed to know him better than he knew himself. There was something so familiar about the way it talked to him. Its mannerisms and patterns of speech, the choice of words it used.

Too familiar perhaps, though he found it hard to put his finger one why he felt that. He tried to put that strange familiarity out of his mind without success. He was missing the cat, he knew, and that sense of missing seemed to merge with the sense of loss that thoughts of Carrie brought to mind. Which was the strangest thought of all.

As he spent the day caressing the ivories he found himself occasionally watching Lyal, Morn, Sonny, and other staff members, whose names he had yet to learn, as they kept the bar running. It was a distracting form of voyeurism, all be it a very neutral kind.

As another coffee arrived courtesy of one of the other staff he found he was playing '*Love Me Tender*'. The timing of the song was probably a coincidence, in fact, he was sure it was, but having placed the coffee on top of the piano the waitress leant upon it, nodding her head along to the tune.

This one set Richard in mind of a mid-west dinner waitress from deep in the Bible belt. Land of the holy trinity. Elvis, Jesus and Apple pie. She wore a red check shirt tied at the waist and had strawberry blonde hair towered up into a beehive cut. Her smile was as bright as her makeup. Which, in truth, was a little heavily applied. He suspected it was to hide the crow's feet around her eyes. Which seemed a harsh thought to entertain, even as it occurred to him.

She had a way about her that spoke of faded beauty. Which is not to say she was not still an attractive woman, but she had that look. She was, he guessed, a former homecoming queen, trying to hold on to the beauty of youth that had been worn away be the passing of a couple of decades. *'Another living cliché '* he thought to himself.

"Richard." He said, by way of introducing himself, holding out a hand as he finished the last cord.

"Jolene, honey, bless yar, thought I was gonna miss the jukebox, but yar play real nice." She replied, her smile broadening which seemed to make the years fall away for a second. Taking his hand in a slightest of touches.

"Kind of you to say." He replied, taking the coffee and risking a sip while it was still too hot. Burning his lips slightly.

"Ain't no kindness honey, just the truth. Shame the King ain't here to sing along to you. Maybe one day he'll drop in." Jolene said turning away. A wistful note in her voice, which lacked the world worn irony Richard would have expected from her.

As she went off to wait on a table, he watched her go. Wondering to himself if she was one of those Elvis fans who refused to admit the 'King' was dead. He guessed that would fit the cliché well enough if it were the case.

He found himself wondering where the compulsion to see clichés was coming from. Further, he found himself trying to decide if he was thinking in them, or just seeing them in others, or, stranger still, that the bar drew them together.

Morn was a cliché, a strangely attractive youth with an ancient soul. Sonny too, come to that, a worldly black guy of humble position dishing out wisdom to the world, with the glint of mystery about them. No doubt to be played by Morgan Freeman in the movie version... The grey man well he was, if not a cliché, an allegory of some kind perhaps... Now there was the world-weary waitress with a southern bell accent, and a hidden heart of gold, he had no doubt. Oh and she just happened to be a fan of old killer sideburns and swivel hips who's '*mamma always told him'* with doleful eyes and quiffed hair. Just to fit in with the cliché.

It would be the mad chef next…

As these thoughts passed across his consciousness he for a moment wondered to himself which cliché he was. An odd thought if ever there was one. One that led him back to Carrie, who more than once called him out on been '*Just another cliché…*' the ubiquitous tortured artist. Whenever he complained about some gig or other which had gone sour, or had argued with a bandmate over a song's bass line.

Knowing the signs of his own malaise too well he pushed that thought away as he watched Jolene make her way between tables and slap away an over friendly customers hand, just to add a little more to the cliché.

Then he let his fingers find the keys once more, less than surprised to find himself playing another Elvis standard, '*Don't be cruel.*'

Richard had never been a great Elvis fan himself. Though he could see the attraction of the man with the killer sideburns. He considered it a shame he died so young, and indeed how he died. But at the same time, with a certain cynism, he knew it was better for the legend of the man. Much like Jimmy Dean and Monroe, there was a mystic about never growing old that made them icons long after they should have faded away. People latch on to them somehow even after their deaths, cling to the lost icons of a world that had moved on.

Richard wondered passingly if that was the case with Jolene, clutching to the idea of the living Elvis like born again Christians cling to the idea of the living Jesus. She would hardly be the first he had met over the years.

On a Greyhound ride through Tennessee, he had shared a seat with a man called Buck who was utterly convinced the King had not died at all, just retired to run a dinner somewhere. Buck's whole and only motivation for taking up the Grey Dog life had been to find that dinner. While Richard could tell Buck was clearly deluded, he had half admired the man's determination to find that self-same dinner and convince the King to make one last comeback. While wondering what past trauma had driven Buck to retreat into his personal fantasy of a Rhinestone jumpsuited messiah flipping burgers in the mid-west.

It was, to be fair, far from the strangest delusion Richard came across on the back seats of Greyhound buses.

As his fingers finding the opening notes of slowed down version of '*Jailhouse Rock*' Richard looked up for a moment and saw Sonny by the door. For a fleeting second, he was brought back to Sonny's story, and found himself wondering if Elvis ever had just wandered through the Passing Place doors at some time in the past. Then found himself smiling at the idea.

He had a mental image of the king in his Las Vegas heydey, all rhinestones and big collars, standing at the bar ordering a cheeseburger, and found himself laughing.

Richard found it hard to think of the Elvis pre-seventies, though he knew that was just because it was the image that was almost always portrayed in the media. The one that had spawned so many impersonators over the years. Looking around the bar as he thought about seventies Elvis he had a minor epiphany. Suddenly he Realised what it was about the customers that had been bugging him all day. So many of them looks a little out of time.

Even a cursory glance at the patrons had caused Richard to wonder what they were all doing in the same place. Some, looked like they would be more at home in a run-down roadhouse, while others would look less out of place in a Manhattan wine bar or taking tea at the Ritz.

To call them a strangely eclectic group was to be the master of understatement, but it was that odd out of time quality that had been jarring him the most. Some of the patrons looked like they were twenty, forty or even a couple of hundred years behind fashion. While others looked like they had walked off the set of some Hollywood sci-fi flick. As a collected group they just looked wrong, like a Gen Con crowd in a random hotel bar somewhere. Still all costumed up.

These, however, were not costumes. He was sure of that much. They did not have that costume fakeness about them, that no matter how good the costume, it always maintains the lack of a lived-in look about them. Instead, these were just the customers everyday clothes, everyday clothes from different eras.

There were other things about them that jarred with him as well. The strange mix of accents that he could not quite pick out individually, yet were from everywhere. Modes of speech which varied as much as the clothing. Everyone seemed to be speaking English, or at least were understood in English. When he tried to listen closely, he was not so sure it was what everyone was speaking.

He was half sure he had been asked to play some Bach yesterday by someone who had asked him in German. Not the accent, but the language. Yet Richard had understood the request perfectly. Indeed it was not till the customer wondered away after dropping a couple of notes in the tip jar, that Richard had even realised what had happened. In truth, he was not entirely sure, even now, that it had not just been his imagination.

It was all the stranger because Richard had worked enough bars to know that when someone with a strange accent was talking, it stood out above the din. A note of discord in the general bubble of noise, that everyone would hear. He had worked in a Queen's bar once where an accent from the lower east side would cut through the hubbub and cause everyone to stare daggers at the speaker. Admitably, that particular bar had been somewhat more insular than most. A place popular with the Queen's wiseguys. In there, if you were not a local, then you were prospectively a cop or worse you might be connected with some other fraction of the NY underside. Richards own South London accent was ironically the main reason he had been an accepted voice behind the bar. The last time a Brit had pulled a gun in Queen's was probably back in 1783 as far as the locals were concerned, so he was probably safe, or at least not NYPD.

That had been a small bar in Queen's however, here in the Passing Place, Richard realised, everyone had a different accent. Yet weirdly somehow they all merged together so no one voice stood out as wrong. Even if, as he had now realised, they were not even technically all speaking in the same language.

Accents and clothes were one thing, all the same. There was a bigger thing which had been jarring at Richard all day, which he also realised in his epiphany. It was the way some of the patrons did not even look entirely human.

Generally, it was in subtle ways it was true, an odd mannerism, a strange lint to their eyes or cheekbones. In some other cases, however, if Richard did not know it was an impossibility, some were almost certainly not human at all.

Richard realised, he had been trying to rationalise it away. Telling himself that it could be all just part of the craze for body modifications which had swept through the East Coast of late. He knew he had dropped a little out of touch with the latest trends on his Greyhound ride into oblivion. But even before he left New York he had been aware that with tattoos had become all the more mainstream in the last decade. With that the case, the rebels had started needing something new to stand out from the society with. Driven as the fringe always is to find a new way to disassociate from the bland mundanity of it all. What, after all, how can they see you're a rebel if you look like everyone else? As the logic of youth subcultures always had it. If the mainstream had tattoos, if soccer mums had tramp stamps, and even politicians showed off their ink for Vanity Fair, and nose studs did not even cause a second look then it was time to up the ante if you wanted to shock the tired old world.

This was, at least, Richard's theory for the sudden appearance of sub-dermal implants, self-scaring and other forms of bodily mutilation. As a musician, he hung with the same kinds of crowds and came across all kinds. He tried not to judge them for their choices himself, though he was occasionally he was sure it was no more than posturing for the attention it got them, but then in every crowd, there were the ones who lived it and the ones who wanted to be seen to live it.

The difference to Richards view was those who actually lived it did not care about getting a reaction. Like Brando's in *'Rebel without a Cause'* their attitude was not so much I'm a rebel look at me, as what makes you think you have anything I am rebelling against? Which made them more authentic than the *'look at me!'* rebels of the other kind, to Richards mind.

Despite these attempts at rationalisation, Richard was sure that the stranger looking people in the bar were not just a bunch of body mod punks. The oddities about them were, not to put too fine a point on it, just too damn odd. Yet all the same Richard had to look, really look, to see these oddities. Somehow everyone managed to look in place, rather than out of it.

This particular realisation had struck him earlier that afternoon when asked to play '*Sympathy for the Devil.*' The customer making the request sported two distinct, if subtle, horns on their forehead. His teeth too, for that matter, were just a little too sharp. Though what worried Richard most about this observation was that he had chatted with the customer about the song a couple of minutes or more before he noticed.

Afterwards, he had tried once more to put it down to the vogue for body modification. Having horns implanted and teeth filed to points, well that was the sort of thing the rock crowd might do, he had reasoned to himself as he played. While he tried to ignore the part of him saying 'M*embers of the rock crowd don't wear pinstripes suits, and have red carnations in their buttonhole.*'

That customer had bugged him for a while, try as he might to ignore it. To take his mind off the oddities of the customers, he instead focused on watching the staff, whenever he looked up from the keyboard. Finding himself a little fascinated by the differences between them.

Lyal buzzed around like a bumblebee, polishing glasses, mopping the bar top and moving swiftly between customers. His conversations with the bars patrons varying from long and languid when he was at his ease, too terse and short if anyone was waiting to be served. He always seemed busy and always smiling, at least whenever a customer was looking his way. Richard was taken aback when he realised that Lyal's face would often change to a cynical sneer whenever he thought no one was looking in his direction.

Morn, the girl with the impossibly long name, in comparison, seemed to saunter around the barroom, taking drinks and food to tables. Inevitability stopping to chat to customers as she went.

When behind the bar she seemed to have time for everyone and a smile to accompany it. She never seemed to buzz about like Lyal. Instead, she had that same steady saunter either side of the bar. Yet somehow she seemed to get the same amount done. She had a few quirks, though one, in particular, leapt out at Richard. Whenever she had nothing to do, she would start running her hands over the bar top in an almost loving way. She would stroke it like someone else would stroke an animal. Her hands following the grain of the wood in long, languid movements. Yet the whole action appeared perfectly natural when she did it. It had taken a while before Richard realised just how odd a habit it actually was.

He found himself watching Morn more than anyone else as he played. While he would flick his gaze to Sonny, occasionally to see some new customer arrive, or let his eyes follow Jolene as she weaved her way between tables and Lyal's buzzing presence behind the bar. His eyes always went back to the odd little green haired girl as she sauntered about. The strange way she would let her hands would seem to slip over the wooden furniture, so much like a lover's caress, charmed him. Though if he were pushed, he would admit to himself at least it was the sexuality she exhibited as she moved which really fascinated him.

Morn moved with a natural flow, a grace which was hard to put into words. With anyone else he would think it an affectation, yet with her, it seemed more something ingrained within her.

When he caught himself letting his eyes dwell upon her too long, or more truthfully whenever she was looking his way, he would make himself look elsewhere. At the keyboard, or somewhere else in the bar. Occasionally feeling a flush come over him when he did. He felt almost like a school boy with a crush and thought himself ridiculous for feeling so.

The tenth time or so he caught himself watching Morn too closely he turned away and found his eyes following Jolene instead as she walked between tables, tottering slightly on high heels, as she carried a tray in one hand above her head. Finding himself impressed at the waitress's dexterity as she swayed around the barroom. He was still looking when a purring voice near his feet spoke.

'*She is way… too old for you.*'

It was, of course, the cat, who had slinked upon on him unawares. She managed to sound mildly scathing, as she hopped onto a table then over to the piano lid. Prowling along the length of the piano a couple of times before settling in the middle with a loud yawn.

"I wasn't thinking of her in that way," Richard replied, feeling a strange sense of guilt as he pulled his eyes back from Jolene, as the waitress disappeared around a column.

'*Not her, the other one.*' The cat purred in a strange way that sounded like laughter.

Richard's eyes followed his guilt, going straight to Morn, who at that moment was polishing the bar surface with a damp cloth and distractedly talking to a customer. He was a little perplexed by the cat's odd exclamation. Not least because Morn looked to his eyes to be in her late teens, perhaps a young looking woman in her early twenties at most. *'Too young for him,'* would have been the more accurate pronouncement surely...

He felt like saying so, not least because he was also mildly irritated with the cat for making judgements of him.

Though mostly if he, conceded to himself, with being caught in an act of mild voyeurism and called out on it by the feline.

He could not say way, but that it was the cat which caught him doing so. made it all the worse.

Morn glanced his way, smiling, though probably not at him. He was caught once more by surprise at the way her eyes looked so much older than she did. Wiser was perhaps a better description, wiser than any teenager's eyes should ever be.

For a moment his gaze remained locked on her, as he tried to formulate a feeling he could not name into words. Then he snapped his gaze back and focus on the piano once more.

"She's just a kid," he muttered under his breath,

letting his fingers find the last few notes of '*Moon Shadow'*.

'*Hardly, she had old roots that one.*' The cat said with renewed cryptic pretension, before saying with a smiling insistence, '*Play it for me.*'

Richard was tempted to ask her to explain, the first comment. A mild sense of annoyance creeping into his mood. Instead, he replied rather briskly. "Play what?"

'*You know what.*' Came a reply with the merest hint of disapproval.

He sighed to himself, and let his aching fingers find the opening bars of '*Forever Autumn.'*

Put Morn and questions out of his mind for a while and let his fingers play the ivories.

$$T \xrightarrow{\beta} M \xrightarrow{\gamma} Y$$
$$\delta$$

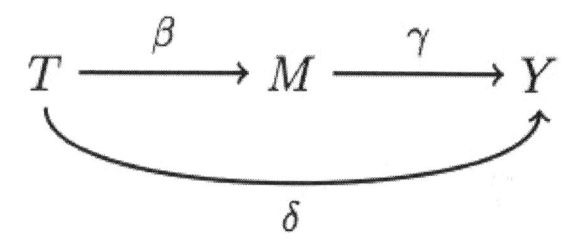

CHAPTER EIGHT

Causality Sandwich

By late afternoon, Richard realised he hadn't had a bite to eat all day. Periodically supplied cups of coffee were no longer enough to stave off the hunger that gnawed at his belly.

'Time to take a break,' he decided, not least to ease the ache in his back and the nagging cramp in his fingers. All of which were becoming increasingly painful.

Decision made, he closed the cover over the keyboard, then stood and grabbed an empty coffee cup from the piano lid, setting off to investigate the kitchen in the hopes of scrounging up some food.

Richard had yet to venture into the kitchen. The furthest he had ventured since arriving was between the piano and the bed in his room, save, that was, for the occasional call of nature or saunter to a seat at the bar. Finding the kitchen wasn't overly difficult all the same. Food appeared in the hands of the waiting staff through the door which was mostly in the wall opposite the bar. *'Leastways when there isn't just a large serving hatch where the door is now'*, a rogue thought nagged at him for a moment before it slipped from his consciousness.

He had started to notice a few oddities about the Passing Place, and that was just one of them.

The barroom, for instance, did not stay the same all the time. It seemed to ebb and flow in some strange, impossible way. The same ebb and flow that seemed to permeate everything in the Passing Place, a disconnection to solidity, a feeling of entropy, of impermanence, that felt like an itch he could not scratch. Yet even while he was noticing it was a realisation that he could not hold the concept in his mind all the same.

He would realise something had changed. A door would be where no door had been previously. But before he could question it the moment had passed, and he would be shaking his head. Sure as sure could be that he was mistaken and that the door in question had always been on that side of the room. A trick of the light, or his memory playing tricks on him, no more than that.

Yet, all the same, it seemed that the bar grew in some way—or shrunk in others—expanding and contracting. As if the bar could grow in size to meet the requirements of the moment. As if the walls were breathing. '*Breathing*' that was the word that kept coming to him, only to be dismissed in the passing of a moment with an equal sense of incredulity.

After a while though even the incredulous starts to ring true and while he knew it was impossible. While he knew he had never seen it actually happening. He had begun to be convinced it was truly happening all the same.

The whole concept was laughable as well as impossible. As laughable and impossible as so many things seemed to be in the Passing Place. Never the less, at the same time, he was becoming convinced it must be happening.

At least for those few moments before it slipped his mind.

The kitchen proved to be smaller than Richard expected, considering the sheer number of meals which flew through the serving door when the bar was busy. Come dinner time the waiting staff would flow through those doors back and forth constantly with plates and trays. Yet what he found seemed more like a farmhouse kitchen, than the working kitchen of a busy bar. He had expected bustling activity, and lines of ovens and grills with chefs and helpers scurrying around like ants.

Every working kitchen Richard had ever been in reminded him of just that: the chaos of an upturned anthill, bustling with activity, everything taking place at break-neck speed while the head chef lorded it over his minions, a general, or perhaps a drill serjeant in charge of nervous foot soldiers in the culinary battleground. All chrome and stainless steel and clouds of steam.

Instead, it was a homey looking place with only two people inside. A large wooden table served as a makeshift worktop in the middle. A single stove with one pan on the hob off to one side. A crowd of little spice pots in a rack beside it. The floral pattern of the tiles on the wall looked like something from the sixties, flower power kitch. Lines of cupboards ran along the walls, with pale blue doors painted with sunflowers. It had a bright sunlit quality to it, clean and wholesome. A kitchen for someone who loved to cook, but without pretensions, the type of person you would see on the cover of a cookbook that used the word '*Homemade*' in the title.

The actual cooking, it appeared, took place at a leisurely pace. The sole preserve of the single chef present.

He was definitely the chef, given his apron and the way he was professionally cutting onions with a large kitchen knife. Richard quietly decided not to let the chef's bowler hat faze him.

Just as he chose to ignore the chef's neatly cropped moustache and horn-rimmed spectacles. Which had the effect of making him look more a bank manager than a chef. He did, at least, the white apron over his pin-striped business suit. Wisely considering the smattering of stains upon it, but even with it, he looked out of place in a kitchen.

Bowler hat aside, however, was the only one doing the cooking which more or less made him the chef by default. Richard decided, therefore, to take it at face value. What was one more oddity in the

Passing Place after all?

To one side of the kitchen, at the sink in front of the large sunlit window, the Grey Man was working his way through an unreasonably large pile of dishes. As ever, the strange man was whistling happily to himself as he worked, his usual monotone façade broken up by a pair of yellow marigold gloves.

Richard wondered, not for the first time, how the Grey Man found joy in such humdrum tasks. There was a permanent air of happiness about him while he worked no matter how mundane the task. For a fleeting second, Richard envied him, though he did not envy doing the mountainous pile of washing up.

"Come in, come in, Mr Piano Player, Let *'the wood back in the hole'* behind you as my blessed mother would have said there's a good man," the chef said loudly. His accent was British, of the Oxbridge kind, and jolly with it. He continued with his ferocious onion chopping, despite looking away from his task to smile at Richard. Dexterous, practised fingers at work with assured speed.

"Could I grab something to eat?" Richard asked as the door swung shut behind him, cringing a little as it slammed back in place. Mostly because the Chef was cutting onions so fast, without looking at his work. He half expected a stray finger to join the pile of chopped onion. Richard had never felt comfortable around people who were preparing food in that way. He'd had too many close calls with his own fingers in the past.

"Of course, my good man, of course, grab yourself a seat, and I shall rustle you up a veritable feast. I can offer you tantalising tastes, satisfying savouries, mouthwatering morsels and gourmet gastronomy from seven worlds, or if you prefer I do for you the best sandwich you will ever taste, and supply it with a reasonably good cup of tea," the chef intoned with dramatic hand gesturing.

So dramatic in fact that Richard was once more passingly worried, this time, because of the way the Chef was waving around his large and very sharp kitchen knife. Which at one point it past a few inches from the back of the Grey Man's head.

The Grey Man himself remained oblivious to this and continued washing dishes and whistling happily the same indeterminate tune to himself, oblivious to how close the blade came to giving him a close shave.

"The best sandwich I will ever taste?" Richard inquired, his voice betraying a little of the strange nervousness he felt. He took a seat at the large oak table that took up most of the centre of the room as advised, and felt his unease passing.

Having lived in New York for several years, Richard considered '*the best sandwich you will ever taste.*' To be a bold claim from anyone and if there was such a thing as a sandwich connoisseur, Richard considered himself to be one. There was a deli down the lower east-side that made subs that Shaggy and his canine life mate would have been proud of. Layers so thick that you would need to dislocate your jaw to get your mouth around it. It took an age just to pick away at the fillings till you could finally take an actual bite of the thing. That was a sandwich of epic proportions, though as far as Richard was concerned, his mum's egg buttie's took a lot of beating as well.

The chef was smiling at him, unaware of the challenge he had set himself in Richards's eyes.

"Most assuredly old boy, I have perfected the art, Lincolnshire pork and apple sausage from the Maple's family farm, the finest Danish back bacon, with most of the fat cut away, but not all, you understand, some is always needed. Then we add the best red onions from the Carcassonne in southern France, fried in good burgundy red wine from Chateau Rouge, the 72 from the south facing vineyard, layered upon a baton of fresh stone oven baked crusty bread, and topped with the finest English mustard from a little farm shop in Sussex, black pepper ground from the mill with three and a half twists, and a pinch, just the merest pinch, of Tabasco sauce." The chef's face seemed to light up with his passion for the subject. He looked at Richard expectantly.

Knowing something was expected of him, and not wanting to offend the chef Richard replied, "That sounds wonderful," while wondering if such a concoction could actually taste anything other than vile. He did not sound overly convinced, even to himself, but the chef just smiled back at him seemingly oblivious.

"Then you shall have one, Mr Piano Player, with my compliments." The chef smiled and continued chopping onions with a vengeance.

Richard suppressed a groan. He had never been overly fond of mustard for one thing, and Tabasco had a habit of turning his stomach. But he had no wish to start alienating the chef by saying so.

A good rule for life, in Richards opinion, was never upset the chef. As a mildly successful musician, he had worked enough kitchens while between gigs over the years. Few musicians hands never knew the feel of soap suds, nor they the smell of industrial washing up liquid, when times got hard. But as a result, he knew only too well the kinds of things that angry kitchen staff could get up to.

'A little extra salt in his soup I think…'

It does not do to upset the men who prepared your food.

So instead of complaining, and partly because he was British and a certain level of rueful acceptance is the norm, he just sat at the table expectantly waiting for the sandwich he was secretly dreading. Watching the chef prepare vegetables and drop them in batches into a large cast iron pot.

Carrots followed the onions, parsnips followed the carrots, and some root vegetable Richard didn't recognise came next, followed by potatoes. A good ten minutes slipped past like this. Richard began to wonder how much longer whatever the chef was preparing would take, before he made the promised carbuncle of a sandwich. Hunger gnawing away at him and he started to feel a tad irritable.

Eventually, with an absent-minded gesture of surprise, which seemed to suggest he had been lost in his work, the chef noticed Richard still sat at the table.

"Oh, I am terribly sorry. I forgot you for a moment there." He waved his knife about a bit in a vague gesture then added. "The sandwich is on the counter behind you," before resuming his chopping.

Richard turned and with a lack of surprise borne only from becoming used to oddities, he saw the sandwich waiting for him on the counter just as the chef had claimed.

It was, he considered, perhaps the hungry and the waiting, but despite his reservations on the subject of mustard and tabasco sauce, it looked extremely appetising. He turned further around and reach over to pick it up.

When he turned back, a mere moment later, there was a cup of tea sitting on the table in front of him. A cup of tea, where there had certainly not been one before.

The chef continued to chop vegetables. Richard suppressed the urge to ask how he made the cup of tea so quickly and seated himself back at the table. He also suppressed the urge to wonder how the chef had managed to do so without missing a beat of his chopping.

It was better not to think about it, he decided. If he started worrying about every little oddity he encountered in the Passing Place, then he would never have time to think of anything else.

"Tuck in, dear boy, tuck in, we're informal here," the chef urged as he began the delicate task of crushing garlic on the chopping board.

With only a moment's hesitation, mostly at the thought of Tabasco sauce, Richard did as the chef suggested. Hesitation soon changed to eating with gusto. He discovered the chef had not, in any way, lied about the nature of sandwich.

His mouth watered with each bite. It was the best thing he had tasted since… Well, as far back as he could remember; perhaps ever. He had to force himself to slow down and take his time. To try and savour each mouthful, despite an urge to cram it all down in huge bites.

The chef carried the pot to the main stove and put it on the heat. On his way back he stopped at the bread bin to grab a small baguette, then raided the fridge for ingredients before he returned to the table and set about making a sandwich.

"Making one for yourself?" Richard asked after swallowing another bite cheerfully, thinking to himself he could hardly blame the chef for doing so. Thinking '*I could live off these*,' to himself in passing before biting down again.

The chef shook his head, pulling an odd face.

"No, no, bless you, but I can't abide Tabasco myself, I am making that one for you," he replied pointing at Richards plate.

Richard was about to decline the second sandwich. Somewhat to the distress of his taste buds. When he realised that was not what the chef had actually said.

"Erm… did you just say you are making this one?" he asked taking another bite of the wonderfulness. That seemed to be the implication of the chef's phrasing, for all it was an insane idea.

The chef managed to look mildly taken aback, raising his eyebrows for a moment, then replied, "Why yes my dear boy, I can hardly not make the sandwich now you have eaten it can I? It would cause all kinds of confusion if I didn't make it. I find causality can be bent somewhat, but it is best not to break it."

Richard swallowed the last of the sandwich and tried to get his mind around what he was being told. It was, however, a twist further than logic permitted.

"So, hang on. Just let me get this straight. You're making the sandwich I've just eaten... after I've eaten it... so as not to break causality?" He sipped the tea, which was, as the chef had previously described, passable.

The chef beamed at him. Giving the impression of an impressed teacher who has just met a gifted student.

"Precisely my boy... well done. Most people get a little flustered about these things, what with them being impossible and all. Between you and me I must admit I find such conversations get a little tiresome after a while. It makes such a nice change to meet someone willing to just accept the obvious." There was a note of the conspiratorial to voice as he said this. Accompanied by a sidelong glance towards the sink where Grey Man was still washing up, and a knowing wink.

"Perhaps... that's because it's impossible," Richard ventured in reply, still sipping the passable tea.

The chef sighed loudly and did a little shrug. "Oh dear... I take it that this is going to be a tiresome conversation after all." He said, raising his eyebrows with an air of resignation.

"No no... please don't feel obliged to explain. I

will happily just believe what you say and enjoy the tea." Richard replied quickly, mostly out of a desire not to offend the chef. As aforementioned he had learned a long time ago that offending a chef is never a good idea.

He had a vague flash of memory regarding the guy in Gino's Pizza who like to add…well, let's just say despite shaving his head, he always found a hair for a disagreeable customer to not quite find in their pizza.

The chef squinted through his spectacles at Richard, before taking them off to polish on his apron, then sighed once more as he put them back on.

"It's okay I am used to explaining this to people," he began, sounding resigned to his fate.

"It's okay I don't….."

The chef raised a hand to stop Richard's protests. "No, Piano Man, I shall, as I must, explain. I have found that it's generally best to do so in the long run."

"Ha," came a sound from the vicinity of the washing up.

Sensing it was a losing battle Richard ceased to protest and took refuge in the tea cup. While being surprised to hear the snorting little laugh that had emanated from the direction of the Grey Man, who had then just continued to wash up. It seemed his only contribution to the conversation was to be a mild derision towards whatever the chef was about to say.

The Chef fixed a stare upon the offending washer- upper, making his displeasure the Grey

Man's interjection clear and then with a shake of his head he turned back to Richard and smiled.

"You see it is my belief that Esqwith is a shared dream, and as I am sure you're aware causality in a dream can run both ways. Indeed in a dream, it doesn't have to run at all, as I am sure you know. However, because this is a shared dream, causality for all intents and purposes exists and must, therefore, be followed you see. But as it's still basically a dream, hence it needn't necessarily be followed in the right order."

The Chef smiled, and Richard found himself nodding, pretending to understand, which utterly failed in convincing the Chef that he did.

"You asked for a sandwich and, as I am the chef, I have to make the sandwich for you. Otherwise, what is the point of me being here after all? My presence here is defined by my task, and my task defines my presence, you see. I am the chef, so I must prepare food, otherwise, who am I? However... however, as you were hungry when you came in, and I had my hands full at the time, it makes more sense for me to make it after you ate. That way you don't have to wait while I finish the chopping for the Beef Alvec stew. The advantage of being in a shared dream. You get to eat while you're hungry, I get to finish chopping the stew before I make your sandwich. Flexible causality, you see. It really is the most wonderful time management tool in the kitchen."

This whole of this explanation was accompanied by waving of hands and nodding. For someone who found explaining this tiresome, the Chef seemed to warm to his subject remarkably quickly.

Richard felt like he was listening to a lecture. More than that, however, it felt like a lecture delivered by an accountant, with all the flair you would expect. But despite himself, he could not help the urge to ask questions.

"Hang on, you said a shared dream?"

"Of course, it's the only explanation which makes any sense. We are all here sharing a dream. Well it's either that, or it's all my dream, and you're all figments of my imagination," the chef replied, chuckling to himself a little.

Richard shook his head, "No, I am real, I know that much."

The chef tilted his head slightly and screwed up his eyes behind his glasses, as if peering closely at Richard and then smiled again.

"Yes… but you would think that would you not. Indeed, my good fellow, you would say that. Even if you're just a figment of my imagination, because I imagine you to believe you exist. It doesn't matter if you think you're real, or even if I think you're real. If you're a figment of my imagination, then you're not, but you wouldn't believe that would you? You can't prove you exist if you don't, and I can't prove you don't exist because my imagination tells me you do. It's a bit of a black hole of logic that one I'm afraid," he said still smiling. Richard tried to follow his argument but could feel the logic turning around on itself as he did so.

"But all in all," the Chef continued, "I believe a shared dream makes much more sense. Or at least it would be preferable if that's true, I think. Of course, I'm just dreaming. So in all likelihood you are imaginary. But I choose to go with the shared dream idea. It's much nicer you see. Believing that I share this world with others rather than populate it with my own imagination." He was still smiling and working away at the sandwich. Which did look to Richard remarkably like the one he had just eaten, he had to admit.

"Okay... say that's true, how do you know your dreaming?" Richard asked, to an extent he was warming to the subject, while not buying into any of it. It was, at least, an attempt to explain what was going on, which made a change from all the cryptic responses he got from Sonny and the others.

"Oh, that's simple. All my life I have wanted to be a chef. And here I am a chef. Indeed I am the Chef in a kitchen that obeys fractal laws of causality. A kitchen in which I can make any dish I have ever heard of, and a fair few I never have. How could this be anything but a dream? And a most wonderful dream at that." The chef said, still smiling, a levity in his voice that was matched with a strange seriousness, that left Richard in no doubt that the chef believed what he was saying to be the truth.

"I see, so you're not a chef?" Richard inquired, feeling he knew the answer to that question already.

"Of course not, I understand fractal causality and how things can happen in the wrong order provided they happen in the wrong order without breaking entirely the laws of cause and effect. How many chefs understand such things? It requires a certain deftness of mind that is not generally present in the culinary world I fear. Not to belittle my fellow providers of gastronomic delights. They are often the most wonderful people. They are, however, normally obsessed with following recipes in the right order. They tend towards a certain linear turn of mind."

"Okay,,, so you're a physicist then?" Richard ventured a guess, while equally sure it was the wrong guess. The creeping suspicion that he already knew the answer was itching away at him. He just didn't want to say the word. It was a word that made him shiver as a rule. A shiver the word brought to most people he suspected, particularly in tax season.

"Ha, those fellows are too locked up in complications of the possible, bound by the relative laws of Einstein and Newton. No, dear boy, I am not so hidebound as they. I am a mathematician of the purest form. I understand numbers and how they work better than any physicist you will ever meet."

Richard groaned inwardly. He dismissed mathematicians for the same logic and went with his first guess after all.

"Accountant?" he ventured.

"Of course, my dear boy. Only accountants can get to grips with effect's happening after cause's, without breaking the laws of cause and effect. You should let me do your tax returns when we wake up. You would be amazed how complex it can be to make a multi-billion dollar company earn zero profits on paper and require a tax rebate, while paying out large premiums to its shareholders. There is an art to creating a web of financial transfers so all the money is earned in the Cayman Islands, despite selling the goods everywhere else in the world. Though, the real trick is to make the government have to pay the accountancy bill, while billing the client for treble hours. Compared to that, making a sandwich after it has been eaten is just a party trick. Fiscal causality is always flexible."

"But it isn't. Effect follows cause. If this was a dream then perhaps not, but in the real world you cannot make a sandwich after someone's eaten it," Richard replied with slight frustration.

The chef smiled the smile of one who believed the argument won, and his case proved.

"Of course not, dear boy. In the real world you can only mess with causality as an accountant. A good set of tax returns makes quantum mathematics look like child's play. But everything else obeys the basic laws of cause and effect its true. As I am sure you will agree, you cannot put the cart before the horse and expect to get anywhere. Well, unless you teach the horse to push, I suppose…" He beamed, convinced no doubt, that his point was proven. "So you see this is, and indeed must, be a shared dream. Else you haven't just eaten this sandwich," he concluded, placing the self-same sandwich on the bench behind Richard. Exactly where he had found the one he had eaten ten minutes earlier.

Richard shrugged, deciding it was simpler to concede the point than argue against it. At the same time he decided he was happier not knowing how the chef managed to make the sandwich out of sequence with cause and effect. If that was indeed what he had done? He had enjoyed the one he had eaten, and the one behind him now, well it was obviously there, he didn't need to look and see the empty space that it didn't take up. Instead, he decided to just accept the chef thought he was making it out of order and move along, *'nothing to see here'*.

His cup of tea finished,

Rising from his seat he made for the door, not looking at the bench behind him. Nothing like happy ignorance. If he didn't look, he did not need to be concerned at the impossibility of it.

"I better get back. Thank you for the sandwich," he said, making his way back out to the bar.

"You're welcome, my boy," came the reply from the chef as he poured the cup of tea Richard had just finished drinking.

Richard found his way back behind the piano, feeling satisfactorily full and better for the sandwich, if not the explanation of it. He sat and glanced around the bar, spotting Sonny as ever present in the shadow of the entrance, even when he wasn't in the doorway. Morn polishing at a ring stain on the bar top someone had unthinkingly left behind. Lyal polishing away at a glass, while standing in a position that allowed him a fair view of Morns backside as she scrubbed, which may or may not have been purely coincidental. Jolene gave the barman a telling eye as she passed, and Lyal turned his gaze elsewhere.

Everyone seemed busy, and the general babble

of the customers filled the air. *'Sharing a dream...'* Well, there were stranger explanations for all this, Richard supposed.

He sighed to himself, flexed his fingers and was about to start playing again when he was tapped on the shoulder.

Turning he found he had been followed out by Grey Man, who was smiling in a mildly disturbing way, which was the best his grey face could manage. It was a face not designed for smiling. Richard thought this and tried to forget thinking it. At least the Grey Man always seemed happy. But maybe that was what bothered him about the monochrome individual, maybe he always looked too happy.

"He's wrong, you know, it's not a shared dream at all," Grey Man said blandly, in an equally monotone voice, before turning to get back to the kitchen and his dishes.

"It's not?" Richard replied quickly, hoping to get a little more out of the strange colourless man.

"Oh no, it's not a shared dream at all. Isn't it obvious? This is heaven," Grey Man said with a hint of cheerful getting through his monotone voice. Happily, he went wandering back to the kitchen, whistling to himself once more.

'Now there's someone with an interesting tale to tell.' said the cat from the top of the piano, which Richard was sure had not been there a moment before.

"Really?" Richard replied, trying to dismiss the feeling that the cat had just appeared from nowhere.

Turning, he watched the kitchen door swing shut behind Grey Man.

'Oh yes, but it can wait, right now I think you should play a tune for me.'

"Any song in particular?"

'You know which,' the cat preened.

"Again?"

The cat looked mildly offended at this protestation.

Richard sighed to himself and wondered absently if either the chef or Grey man was correct. Or if this was all something far more complicated.

He began, with some little reticence, to play the first few bars of Forever Autumn.

CHAPTER NINE

The Girl in the Nighttime

Richard awoke to the distant sound of sobbing, something all too familiar to him. Of late, though, to wake and find the sobs were not his own was a new experience. It was one he found more than a little disturbing. One which also triggered memories within him.

Memories of another time in his life. A time when waking in the night to the sound of another's tears had been all too commonplace.

Memories he had tried hard to bury.

This trigger was all the worse for the femininity of the voice he could hear saying indistinct words between her sobs. A voice that sounded young, lost and impossibly distant. Yet, at the same time, close at hand.

Memories of other nights flooded over him. Nights when had been woken by similar sounds, echoing through the darkness; Those black nights when Carrie was going through her darkest days.

Often she would have surreptitiously climbed from their bed and tiptoed through the apartment so as not to wake him. Finding her way inevitably to the kitchen floor. Leaning up against the cabinets, clinging to her knees, all but naked on the tiled floor.

Sometimes he would wake to hear the crying in the darkness. Waken to perceive faces in the veiled shadows of their bedroom, demonic visages leering out of the darkness, while her weeping would echo in the nighttime like the lament of the damned.

They worst of awakenings and in those bleary-eyed moments, Richard hated her for it.

Not for the weeping, but for hiding it from him. A stupid hate to feel, if ever there was one, and he knew it. He would far rather that she had shaken him awake when she hit a big down in the night, talked to him about it, or even just clung to him.

Let him be there for her.

Let him help her.

A stupid, self-centered want, he knew. Pernicious and nasty, and born of his own need to have some control, rather than any selfless desire to help her. What was worse, he knew that too, which only fed his anger and the tension between them.

Predictably, that tension led to arguments. Terrible arguments that were all the worse because he knew only too well that he started them and always out of his own sense of hurt and rejection.

Even then, he knew all the while, the thing he really wanted more than anything was to help her through those dark periods. He hated himself for that. For putting his own selfish needs and anger first, and always when she needed him the most.

With that ever hateful thing hindsight, he wished he could have put all his own feelings to one side. Then just really been there for her when she needed him. He never could. It was a flaw he had recognised in himself even then.

One that now he could not in any way forgive himself for. That she always forgave him that flaw just made it all the worse.

On those occasions when her sobbing woke him were better than the ones he slept through. If only because he did not feel quite so helpless then. He could at least try to comfort her. Be there when she needed him. That this was always the last thing she wanted or for that matter needed, never occurred to him.

At least until it was too late.

Much too late.

After a bathroom in red…

It became just another flaw, just another mistake, he could not forgive of himself.

On those nights, however, he would find her

encamped in the kitchen of their small apartment. Usually in nothing more than one of his old band t-shirts she chose to sleep in. Sometimes in nothing at all.

She would sit on the cold tiled floor, her knees pulled up to her chest and her back to a cupboard. Sometimes just staring at the wall, others with her head buried into her knees, her long hair sprawling over them.

She would sob until her eyes were red and her face drawn. Shaking in the cold night air. Muttering incoherent sentences of anger and frustration. Pleading with the universe for answers. Answers to questions that had none.

"Why me?"

"Why is this all so wrong?"

"What is the point of all this?"

"Why?"

"Why?"

The endless question "why?".

Always her favourite question. Always with no real definition, leastways that was, none he could understand. One he could never answer because he did not even understand what she was asking.

He was not even sure she did.

"Why?"

Now the selfsame question he had posed to the Universe so often since that fateful night. Yet knowing the reason he asked was no consolation to him at all.

Back then, when it was Carrie asking that question on those cold nights on the kitchen floor he always tried to answer it in the same way. Or to be more honest, deal with it the same way at least.

Tea with lots of sugar and calm words.

It was a legacy of his British upbringing. His mother's answer to any problem. Come off your bike and scrape your knee? "Here, have a nice cup of tea."

Lost your favourite action man to a bully in the playground? "Never mind son, here let's have a nice cup of tea."

Stressing out over your upcoming exams, to the point of cutting yourself? "Don't worry so much son, I'll go put the kettle on."

Your wife committed suicide while you were upstate playing with your band? "Oh dear son, tell you what, go make yourself a nice cup of tea and have a sit-down."

The last conversation never happened. His mother had been long dead by then. But he was more than half sure that would have been her response all the same.

Sometimes they worked, those late night cups of hot sugary tea. Other times, though, it drew out nothing but her anger and led to rages. All too often if all was told, but he felt helpless if he did nothing.

He had wondered since if that was the point of making tea. Not so much to make the other person feel better, but to give yourself something to do. To keep you from feeling helpless, and to buy time for them to find a way to deal with whatever was troubling them.

The worst of it was he often put the kettle on as much to hide his own anger as anything else. He had hated the helplessness he felt. He had tried to swallow it all down, knowing it was something in her that he should help with, be there for her, and put his own issues aside. But he felt powerless and lost.

Unable to help her, he turned that helplessness into rage instead. Deep inside himself resided and inner rage at the helplessness he felt. Yet, knowing it was unfair of him to do so,—wrong of him even—he would try to swallow down the bile of it. Try to find ways of coping. Nothing else he tried was any more successful than making tea, however. So after a while, it became a habit.

Throw the kettle switch, then kneel down beside her and try to be better…for her.

It all came flooding back to him as he awoke to hear that sobbing in the night. It was somewhere beyond his room, out in the corridor perhaps.

Someone alone.

Someone afraid.

Someone crying in the night.

He was struck with the selfsame sense of overwhelming hopelessness, the one he remembered so clearly. Closely followed by a determination to seek out the source of that heart-wrenching sob, partly to do what he could to help. Partly to put those feelings of hopelessness back in their box, before they engulfed him.

He tried to convince himself that he was not just repeating old habits. That this was just simply a case that he could not in good conscience lay in bed while someone close by was suffering.

He was not sure he believed himself.

A part of him, the honest part perhaps, knew it

was as much to do with his memories of failing to be there for Carrie. The guilt he felt at failing to be there in any meaningful way when she wanted him to be. With the knowledge of that failure so strong in his thoughts, he could not just remain laying there in his bed and fail to be there for another lost soul in the darkness.

Pulling on his old jeans for the first time since his arrival at the passing place, he grabbed the first shirt he could find. Pulling it on unbuttoned, he stalked into the corridor seeking the weeper in the night.

The corridor seemed strange to him.

It's lighting for a start, normally bright and cheerful, was dimmed down. A strange hazy quality to it that seemed not so much to push back the shadows but hold them tentatively at bay. He tried to dismiss it, put it down to simply his eyes taking time to adjust as he left the darkness of his room. Yet it still felt wrong all the same.

Other things seemed different as well. He was, for example, sure there were only five doors leading off the landing and one dead end corridor, two doors along each side and one at the opposite end to the stairs. But now it seemed there was a corner by the door at the end. A corner which turned off to the right where there was only a wall before.

He still felt muggy from his unexpected awakening. He managed to half-convince himself it was nothing but sleep still clouding his head. He shook himself, trying to clear away the cobwebs, putting the forgotten corner down to a false memory. It was not like he had never had a reason to go to the end of the corridor after all. His room was the first on the left at the top of the stairs. It was possible he had never even noticed it was there.

Just how much attention do you pay to a corridor you don't need to walk down?

Just his memory playing tricks with him, he was sure. After all, what else could it be? Corridors don't simply appear in the night.

First left at the top of the stairs... There was something about that which was suddenly bugging him. It had not occurred to him before but the first night he arrived Sonny had said, "*There's a spare room up the stairs for you.*" But he had not said which one.

How had he known?

Had he just assumed that was his room and gotten lucky?

No, that wasn't right... He had known it was that room without thinking about it.

How had he known?

More to the point, why had it not occurred to him until now?

Perhaps it was the brandy, perhaps he was just remembering wrong. Maybe Sonny had told him first on the right after all. Yet now he thought about it, he was certain that had not been the case.

He had a moment's flash of memory, remembering the cat waiting for him at the top of the stairs, leading him into the room.

Was that what happened?

It seemed ridiculous as an idea.

He shook himself again, staring towards the corner in the corridor that now lead off to his right, his moment of revelation forgotten once more.

'*Corridors don't just appear,*' he told himself, but then a second thought kicked in '*Yer, but bars don't grow bigger when more customers arrive either.*'

And there is was again. That feeling that nothing was, strictly speaking, impossible in the Passing Place. A notion becoming firmly rooted in Richard's mind now. He reminded himself of the deal he had made with himself to stop questioning the oddities. It was simpler after all just to accept them. A desire for things to make sense did not make them do so. If the world was determined to be strange or just plain ridiculous, well, it was easier to just roll with it for now.

The lights in the corridor seemed a constant at least, spaced equally, and shining with the same… he wanted to think brightness, but brightness was not the word. Yet as he turned the corner into the new passageway he was sure they grew just a little dimmer, and taking on a strange red tinge to the light they gave out.

The 'new' passageway… was it new, had it been there before? Never noticed somehow?

Again, he tried not to think too closely about that.

The sound of sobbing seemed to be no closer as he began to walk down the carpeted floor. Yet he remained certain its source lay ahead of him all the same, though why that was the case he could no more explain than why the redness of the light made his skin crawl. Or the disconnected sense of wrongness he was starting to feel.

He felt himself shudder, though there was no chill in the air.

"Something is wrong here." he heard himself whisper in a voice he was not quite certain was his own.

He was not even certain what he meant by that. Did he mean in the corridor, in the night, or in the whole of the passing place? He was not even sure of his own thoughts.

And red, something about red… Not the colour itself, but something red all the same, the same way the lights were making his skin crawl. It was a feeling that he had had for days now, even before he arrived here, something red in the corner of his eye.

More doors lead off on each side of the corridor, while the décor along with the lighting seemed to grow darker.

Dank was perhaps a better description, he found himself thinking, like something out of a haunted house movie.

There was a smell he associated with decay and damp in the air, musky and cloying. He could taste it as he breathed. He could see the remains of old cobwebs in the corners of the ceiling, clogged with dust, like everything else. All dusty and old somehow, a forgotten place, abandoned. Yet at the same time, he was sure it wasn't. It was more a feeling than anything he saw, an atmosphere of age, decay and wrongness which seemed to be developing around him with each step into the growing darkness.

There was that something else as well, that strange, threatening something, that sense of something red. He found he could not think of it in any way other than that—something red, something visceral, and something bloody. A strange feeling of life and unlife about it. Something potent with the potential for... For what he could not put into thought, not describe beyond the word wrong. Something yet dormant, waiting perhaps... but dreadful all the same.

He tried to shake the strange idea from his mind, to focus on the corridor before him, on seeking the sobbing voice ahead, but it kept coming back to him, that itch he could not scratch or name.

He had taken too many steps as well. He knew that with a back of the mind certainty. The corridor should not have been this long. Could not be this long.

He wanted to turn around, to look behind himself. But he had a sudden pensive feeling, sure somehow that if he did he would see the corridor he had walked down stretching off into the distance.

Stretching far further than he could have walked in so few steps. It nagged at him, a feeling he could not place. This was all wrong; it felt like a dream.

"No, not a dream. It feels like a nightmare," He whispered to himself, not even realising he had voiced the thought aloud.

"*That's because it is,*" purred a voice near his feet.

He looked down to see the cat at his heels. A sense of relief swept over him for a second. He realised, strange though it may be, he felt safer the moment he knew she was there. She looked up at him, meeting his gaze, her eyes mirrors, that reflected what little light there was, making them almost seem to glow in the darkness. Then she added with a tone that spoke of concern.

"*But not yours*,"

"Whose then?" Richard asked, surprised by the uncertainty in his own voice. The feeling of wrongness sweeping back over him.

"*Her's*," the cat purred. Turning her head away from him and looking down the corridor.

He followed her gaze, seeing the source of the weeping for the first time.

It looked like a young girl with her back to him, dressed, much like Alice in the illustrations of Wonderland, in a pale blue petticoat of Edwardian style. Sat with her knees clung to her chest. She was only a few yards further down the corridor, where he was sure she had not been a moment before.

Long dirty blonde hair that seemed lank and lifeless hung down past her shoulders. Her clothing was old, tattered and darkly stained brownish red patches caused by something that could just have been rust, but gave made him think of something less wholesome. Her arms, tightly clinging around her knees, had cuts and scrapes all down them. Ripped stockings socks were visible under the pile of skirt and underskirts crumpled up at her knees, and the heel on her right shoe hung loose.

Then for a fleeting moment she was dressed differently; in a ragged and half ruined school uniform. The modern kind, white blouse and knee length skirt. Her hair, though still dirty and lank, seemed to developed curls within it that tightened up as he watched.

As he came closer to her, he noticed she was holding something, or more correctly had something wedged between her knees. A food tin, he realised, with no label. In her hands, she held a half broken hammer and a rusting screwdriver. The tin was clasped by her legs, as she struggled to open it. Little cuts lined her thighs, where the tins rim had cut into them. He wondered for a fleeting moment why, then realised as she aimed the screwdriver at the tins lid and brought the hammer down upon it, making it jump and cut into her legs once more.

He had a strange feeling that this was something true he was seeing. Or truer perhaps was the right words, strange though the thought seemed to him. That this image was more real than everything else around him.

He shuddered as she brought the hammer down vaingloriously once more, and made the screwdriver bounced off the tin and scrape down her leg.

Then that fleeting glimpse past, the thoughts slipping from Richards mind along with it and the Edwardian Alice was there once more. Ragged in her petticoat dress, he looked like she had been dragged through a hedge backwards, or perhaps, came a musing thought, fallen down a rabbit hole.

Richard edged forward, at a loss for what he could do to help the sobbing girl with her back to him. A strange helplessness, tied to a feeling of otherness he always associated with children. He had never wished to be a father, nor had Carrie ever spoken of having a child. He never had quite felt at ease around them, even when he had been one himself. Faced with a sobbing child kneeling before him in the strangeness of the corridor he was unsure what to do. Comfort her somehow, find out what was wrong perhaps?

Yet in an abstract way, he could not quite name, what he felt most was the need to find a kettle.

"*There, there, child, let's have a nice cup of tea, I am sure it will all be fine...*" his mother's voice whispered in his mind.

He tried to get a grip of himself again, to focus on the present. On the crying child.

He bent down, moving closer but unable to think of anything else to say. He grasped about for words but all he could come up with as *'Hello,'* but as the words reached his lips the cat pulled him up short,

"*I wouldn't if I was you,*" she purred, pushing herself forward until she was between him and the sobbing child. An action that it seemed to him almost a protective gesture.

There was a pulse of redness, in the corner of his eye, that itching feeling of wrongness. He suppressed the urge to turn and look for the source, not least because he felt a flush of anger that rose from deep within him, or perhaps from nowhere. Flashing through him at the same moment as that sense of redness.

"She needs help," he snapped loudly at the cat, then felt his anger suddenly turn inward, a wave of remorse sweeping over him for snapping at the cat.

More than remorse, he realised fleetingly, it felt exactly the same as those times he had snapped at Carrie when he was failing to help her; that same feeling of instant, overwhelming regret and a desire to take back the words. The one that always came the moment it was too late to do so.

The cat slunk away from him. Richard's eyes followed her backing away down the corridor. A wave of confusion rolled over him. It seemed strange that she was reacting so strongly to his moment of sharpness. Normally she would snap back a dismissive comment at him if he was short with her at all. A wave of guilt washed over him again. "Sorry I did not mean to snap..." he began.

Then a shriek filled the corridor where sobbing had been a moment before.

In that sound was contained all the Discordia of loss, of suffering, of grieving. The sound of pain so deep it became all there was, rolling through the corridor like waves crashing on a beach, overwhelming the darkness in its notes of suffering.

It went through him. It went over him, consumed and rejected him.

A terrible aching sound.

A sound that was all fear and rejection.

Looking back, terrified of what he might see Richard found the girl was now standing and had turned to face him. She was no more than a couple of yards away, the sobbing gone. The intense inhuman howling shriek had replaced it. A sound seemed to tear at his soul.

And then there were her eyes. He could not take his own off her's, or where they should be.

Instead of eyes, there were just holes, holes in her face of deathly white, with blue lips.

Two black holes, bloody and torn around the edges, and impossibly, they stared back at him. Wells of the void, empty and somehow deep enough to fall into.

The sight froze Richard in place, fear holding him in a vice, a primal fear that tore into him. As the screaming howl became shrill to the point of pain.

The girl in the Alice dress raised her arms towards him, her palms outstretched. He could not turn his gaze away from her. From the way she seemed to move in awkward jerks, like bad motion stop photograph. Inhuman, dead, a body trying to remember the actions of life, mimicking them but lacking all grace.

Entranced, he watched as she raised her palms up before him. He felt his breath tightening in his chest. His heart racing, he could feel the pulse in his throat. He realised he was shaking, trembling as much from anticipation as fear, his breath freezing in the air.

Those palms, held up to face him looked straight at him. For in the centre of each was an eye embedded into the palm, lidless and mobile, they moved in erratic twitches.

Amidst her piercing shriek, there came another scream.

He became dimly aware it was his own.

A cold shiver ran down his spine as she walked towards him. He found himself staring at those eyes, those impossible eyes, unable to move, or even think of doing so.

A horrid fascination overtook him. There was something base and ancient here. Something that spoke of fear and loneliness. He heard sounds in her screams which could have almost have been a voice, pleading and desperate, but lost within that shriek. As the apparition drew closer, he heard himself screaming again, over and over.

Suddenly, after an endless, timeless moment, he felt a sharp needle like pain in his ankle, snapping him out of whatever had taken such a grip on him.

He looked down swiftly, to see the cat sinking her teeth into his leg. The needling pain brought him to his senses.

"*This is the point where you run,*" she told him in her usual calm and mildly sarcastic tones. There was only the slightest note of urgency to her words, but it was there all the same.

Whatever spell had been upon him, the sudden pain of the cat's teeth had broken it. He found himself fleeing down the corridor in the direction he had come, rushing away from the darkness behind him towards the light of the corner. The whole corridor seemed to shorten as he fled like it was all some strange optical illusion. Each step he took seemed to take him the distance of three. The air seemed to be alive, rushing past him, similar to air fleeing from a pierced balloon.

It felt like he was running out of the nightmare, figuratively and literally: The world becoming more real around him, the lights brighter, the sense of decay receding behind him, the corridor taking on an aspect closer to the reality he knew.

Behind him, he could hear the shrieking becoming more distant. The cat was running ahead of him, helping to draw him forward by her presence alone.

Finally, on reaching the corner, he found he was moving so quickly he could not slow for the turn. Instead, he ran full-faced into the wall. His chest burning and his breathing laboured, hyperventilating.

He collapsed against the wall as the shirking stopped.

Unsteadily he tried to get to his feet, still shaking, but slipped back down once more, his heart thumping hard in his chest. He fought to get his breathing under control, an acid taste in his mouth. The fear which had become so palatable still gripped him. He turned, putting his back to the wall, and pushed himself to his feet against it in a maddened scramble.

Then he found himself staring at the blank wall where the corridor had been.

He stayed there propped against the wall, his heart still pounding away and his breathing slowly levelled out enough to talk, but was still ragged and painful.

"What was that, a dream, a nightmare? Is it time to wake up?" he thought loudly to himself, before he realised he had spoken aloud.

"*All three, but none of them yours. It's time for you to go back to sleep though dear,*" she purred, and then began slinking off toward his room.

Dazed he followed her through the door and laid on the bed without undressing.

He felt cold, colder than he should, his shivering, caused not by the temperature, but the image of the girl with no eyes that seemed burned into his mind. The sense of loss he got from her, that palatable burning grief that was so hauntingly familiar to him.

It felt like ice on his soul.

"Who was she? What was she?" he asked, not noticing the desperate plea in his own voice. It held the need to understand; to be able to rationalise it all, to regain his grip on the real and the solid.

"*A nightmare nothing more. A thing of the darkness between.*" Purred the cat, prowling around him on the bed, protectively.

"She wasn't real?" he asked, still fighting for calm.

"*Of course, she was real. She was still just a nightmare, though. She is gone, she can't harm you now.*"

"That wasn't a nightmare that was something else," he insisted, a wave of indigence sweeping through him. The cat was not telling him the truth, or at least not everything, he was sure of it. More than that he was afraid, genuinely afraid, for the first time since the night he arrived at Esqwith's. No that was not right, it was the first time since, since…

Since…

The thought slipped away.

"*It was a thing of the void, Richard, nothing more, a nightmare given shape by the fears of the dreamer,*" the cat purred, still prowling. If she could feel his fear, she reacted to it by trying to calm him.

But there was a note of belligerence in her tone now. Whatever it was, she was not telling him. She was determined to keep it to herself. He was sure of that much.

"And who's the dreamer?" he snapped, his fear giving anger to his voice. His fear and the need to understand, to be able to make sense of it all.

"*You saw her yourself did you not, for a moment at least, I know you did, no matter how fleeting. But you saw her. She is just a girl nothing more, someone trapped in her own darkness. It's not her fault she just created a need. And in doing so, she gave something from the void something it could use to reach through.*"

He did not understand, not in the slightest. He remembered the other girl, though, the one trying to open the tin of food. He remembered feeling a sense of despair and loneliness from her, whoever she was. He knew that she and the girl with no eyes were linked somehow, but separate all the same. One real one a dream, or her nightmare perhaps… But he did not know how he knew.

"This is insane," he whispered. Shivering all the more. He founding himself huddling on the bed. Trying to make himself smaller, to feel safer. Less vulnerable to everything.

"How?" he asked without knowing what it was he was asking.

"*There are many doors to me. Some of them should never be opened. But sometimes the things outside find them and try to use them to enter me, and through me enter into the real world,*" the cat replied.

Passing Place 201

At least, he thought it was the cat's voice. Yet for a moment that voice seemed different in his head, deeper, hollower, and ancient somehow. The same voice as before but more encompassing, not coming from the cat but from everywhere around him at once.

He tried closing his eyes, but all he could see was the girl in the corridor, the black eyeless holes staring back at him. He felt he could hear that terrible lonely wanting sound of her scream once more, but he felt a heavy tiredness overtaking him. his limbs felt heavy, his eyes struggling to stay open.

A stray through wondered through his mind. "Me, you said enter me?" he said, but not really understanding what he was asking. He felt he was grasping at the idea, more seeking something else to latch on to than anything else. Something, anything, to distract his mind from the echoes of the nightmare thing in the corridor.

"*Relax Richard, you need rest now, sleep.*" She said. It was the cat's voice again, her endlessly calming voice. It lulled at him to relax, but he could not find that calm in himself, torn between the memories of the corridor and trying to understand what had just been said by the cat in that other voice.

"You said.."

"*Pay it no mind. I've asked the grey one to come and tell you a story, would you like that?*"

"What?" he asked, confusion coming over him. Would he like that? Why would he like that? What had she said? What was it about her words?

Something he needed to remember, something he wanted her to explain.

"*The grey one, let him tell you his tale, focus on that. Let everything else slip from your mind, better you forget this, for now at least, we will speak of it again in times to come.*"

"What?.. The grey? Oh yes, Grey Man... I..." What had he been thinking about? What was he trying to remember? He was certain it was important, but what was it?

He heard footsteps coming from beyond the door. For no reason he could put his mind to, he was suddenly afraid again, afraid of something beyond the door.

The handle turned, and Richard drew a deep breath like he was taking on air before diving into a pool. Readying himself in case he did not get a chance to breathe again, the hairs on the back of his neck standing on end, he felt his heart rate going up. Yet could not understand where his fear was coming from.

Grey man entered the room, smiling his ever-present monotone smile.

Richard felt himself relax once more letting out the breath he had been saving.

"*Shush now, yes that's right grey one will tell you his story. Listen to his voice now, Listen to his story, and let everything thing else slip away now...*" the calming voice of the cat continued while the grey man moved to take a chair by the bed.

"Yes, okay, yes..."

Grey Man smiled, resting a hand on Richard's arm. "Let me tell you of who I was before I came to

Heaven, Piano Man," he said in his ever bland monotone voice.

He began to tell a tale, one which Richard found himself listening to while slowly drifting to sleep. An odd blank calmness replacing the feelings of fear and confusion which had gripped him. The world seemed to drain of colour while the tale was told.

Richard began to feel calmer, focusing on the tale. Letting his world become the words, and the story become his only focus. He found himself fighting back sleep only to hear the stories end.

No longer thinking of the things that had been said to him by the cat's other voice, or thing he had seen.

He was lost in the story and the sound of the monotone grey voice that was doing the telling, so bland, so safe, and so grey.

CHAPTER TEN

Rhapsody in Grey

He wears a plain grey suit, of a cut which could only be described as bland. If there is a thing called fashion in this world, the suit defies it. Not out of rebellion, no never that, more simply out of apathy perhaps, though in truth it is a suit that conforms to a norm which never changes. His shirt, of the same dull grey, is unadorned with motif. A grey tie pulled tight to the neck, is worn with an insipidly tight little knot. There is no style about any of his clothes, they are as utilitarian as his haircut, short, lifeless, and grey. He wears grey plastic spectacles, with thick myopic lenses, framing eyes which are dull, lifeless and equally monotone. Even his skin has a colourless dreary pallor, lifeless, pale, without ever being interesting.

To be interesting would be to attract attention. To stand out. To do such would be repugnant to him and his world.

You do not stand out, you conform, you are one of the many and the many are as one.

He is a grey man, one of many who stride through this world.

This world that is as grey, dull and lifeless as he. The vigour of ages past has long since departed. It's landscape is one of concrete and ageing grey stone facings, the crumbling remains of the glories that never were and the ones that shall never be again.

Clouds, as colourless as the streets, hang heavy in a sky that no longer sees the sun. The relentless drizzling rain is, as always, falling, though it never quite works up the energy to become a storm. Such energy would require life and life has drained from this world, where all colours have run to grey.

Within this world of endless monochrome monotony, the Ministry stands paramount.

Behemoth of the state, the directive of lives, keeper of the status quo, housed within a monolith of granite walls. Austere, imposing, it dominates the centre of the city. The hive of everything.

Within those weathered grey walls they reside. The ones who impose order, the ones who sign and stamp, the ones who accept and decline, the ones who control the flow of the world, shaping and controlling the lives of all its denizens. Behind walls which could never claim any architectural style. Just slabs of murky utilitarian grey stone. Beyond windows from which no light ever escapes.

Within, the grey man and the thousands like him work at their grey desks. Faceless gears moving the machinery of the state, the cogs of governance grinding away with their soulless efficiency.

The grey man's desk lay on the thirteenth floor of the monolith. A cubicle formed by partitions, just one cubicle among many, characterless, isolating, without an ounce of human warmth or joy.

The calendar on the cubicle wall is just numbered boxes with no pictures. It hangs there for the sole purpose of keeping track of days which are all the same. No more than a series of identical links in an endless chain of banality.

The monitor, high on the office wall, streams the ministry channel, as is required. Its display is in monochrome. Interference and static, breaking the pictures. A stream of endless statistics and propaganda roll across the screen, interspersed with the trials of traitors, lists of their crimes and still shots of their hangings.

Traitors to the state. Their Heads in sacks to hide their features. There crimes written over them in plain text.

Flickering reports on the war, which they are, as ever, winning.

Then more propaganda, more statistics. Colourless words approved then transmitted, to mean nothing and inform no one.

An endless stream of news as depressing as the

grey skies which never see the sun.

Two trays, one saying 'IN' and the other 'OUT' sit at either side of the grey man's desk.

In the IN tray there is always a stack full of files in dull grey folders which await his attention, a stack which never seems to reduce in size; never waivers in waiting. Each hour a man in grey overalls comes to add more to the IN tray. Then another man comes half an hour later, indistinguishable from the first, to take away the files placed in the OUT tray.

He knows not if they are the same man. Or why the first could not take the OUT files. It may never have occurred to anyone this would save a second trip. It has always been done this way, so it always should be. Change would be an athama within these walls.

The files In the 'OUT' tray have been assessed. Then they have been stamped with grey ink from the grey stamp as complete. Left then by him, to be taken away, to be filed, or acted upon or shredded or perhaps burnt. The grey man does not know where the files go and what is done with them when they get there. Any more than he knows where they come from before they arrive at his desk. They are simple the files, and it is his task to process them. Beyond that he knows nothing of the workings of the ministry he serves.

This lack of knowledge worries at him sometimes. Somewhere inside himself he knows he should know more. However, this worries him less than the truth of his situation. That terrible truth he knows. That truth that gnaws at him, for he does not know what function he is performing. He knows not why he is processing the files. He knows not how they should be processed.

Lurking within him is that fear. Like an emotion of colour buried deep within his grey exterior, buried so deeply he hardly knows of its existence.

It eats at him.

Chews at the shrivelled remains of what he once may have been, before he became what he is.

A simple terror, one he thinks is his alone, the fear of being found out, the fear of being discovered to be a fraud. A lie given flesh, he is a man who does not even know what he does.

Where do the files go?

Where do they come from?

What purpose he have in the great machine of the state?

Why does he sit at his small desk each day?

It is a fear he has lived with a long time. He suspects he has lived with it longer than he can remember. For if there was a time before now— before he worked at this desk—he has long since forgotten it.

Each day is spent appraising reports, reading them without understanding, then stamping them.

The stamp says 'Assessed' with the official florishless font. It is his official ministry stamp.

It stamps in grey.

Once he has finished assessing each report, he writes in the box formed by the stamp. One word or the other, the only comments he ever adds.

Sometimes he writes 'Accept', sometimes he writes 'Decline'.

The decision is arbitrary for his part. The reports are as dull, flaccid and grey as everything else in his world. They contain no clue as to what it is he decides upon. Grey language in grey ink, each report as bland and lifeless as the last.

Each has a name, a monotone picture and a reference number.

Minor details differed: marital status, work assignment, position, rank, and grade, a sequence of dates that tally to nothing, that could be birth or death or first tooth for all he is aware.

There are tables and graphs, lines of number under titles with only initials, CON, PIA, WEL, RES, and dozens of others. No two tables on two reports the same. No key to explain what any of these mean. The hand written reports at the bottom are illegible, or perhaps in some form of shorthand or code.

He is sure he should understand all this, the tables, and the shorthand, what is being requested, or accused, or issued.

Sometimes he thinks that once perhaps he did. But if he did, it is knowledge lost in the monotone of the nothingness of memory, clouded like the grey of the sky.

Was there a time once, before everything ran to grey?

Before meaning was sucked from the fabric of the world?

Before life lost all colour?

He can no longer recall.

Other times he suspects he never knew, that his task has always been nothing but meaningless to him, or just one he was never trained for.

Perhaps it is just meaningless to everyone?

A task without purpose.

Or perhaps it is a task of such meaning he cannot conceive its import.

He is not sure which would be worse.

In former years, now long past, when he was still young, there had been moments of rebellion. Moments when he had railed against his lot. Days when he had written 'Decline' on every report. Others when he had only written 'Accept' for three days straight. Once he had alternated between one and the other throughout the day.

He had been inviting censor, wanting someone to question his methods. To perhaps question his dedication, or his fitness for his task.

At the time he had found it depressing that no such censor ever came.

Greyer years had slouched past since the rebellion of youth, and it has long since vanished.

Fear of his superiors, of the state, of the ever long shadow of the ministry, had long since cowed him.

Whatever small spark of colour was once within him has long since crawled away and died. But he does not mourn its loss, for it was never truly alive to him. There is only grey, in its endless shades, never quite black, and never quite white.

Now his decisions are purely arbitrary. He looks at the picture, or the name, or sometimes just one word in the report, and just chooses.

Accept or decline

A simple choice with the only factor of influence

the choice itself. So each of his day's progress.
Take down a folder.
Pretend to read the report.
Stamp it 'Accessed'.
And then chose.
Accept or decline.
Every day the same.
The same grey world.
The same withering drizzles from the same monotone sky.
The same claustrophobic cubical.
The same grey men in the same grey suits.
The same grey report folders.
Accept
Decline
Accept
Accept
It goes on.
And the inbox is ever refilled.

He will look up from time to time to see the news. Not out of interest, but because he feels the need to be seen to be interested. Everyone else looks up at times to watch. He wonders to himself if they do so for the same reasons as he. If their tasks are as much a mystery to them as is his own. Do they just go through the motions as he does? Perform reverence to the ministry and force down the paranoia that eats away at them, as it does him. Make their choices about files before them they don't understand? Make decisions without knowledge of consequence.

And if they do, do they care?
Does it bother them?

Does it matter to them?
Does it matter to him?
Accept
Decline
Decline
Accept

A glance at the news shows a hanging. As the camera focuses in on the traitors, a bag slips from a head.

He sees a face, a face he recognises. A face that sends a cold shiver raking down his spine.

He knows that face, but knows not from where.

He shakes his head, trying to clear the image from his mind, forces himself to his work and opens the next file.

Decline
Accept
Accept
Decline

He stops, grey ink drying on the page and in that moment a certainty falls upon him.

A certainty as clear as the sky never is.

That face, he knows where he has seen it.

In a report.

One of those endless greys reports that pass across his desk. The reports he reads and accesses.

Reads assess and stamps, as he always did.

Accepts or declines.

Realisation falls upon him, a deluge of thought, soaking through to his marrow—Is this what he does? Is this his task, to assess, to decide, to make judgment on the fate of others?

The thought horrifies him, and he knows at once it is the truth, the nugget of truth that shatters him.

The years of arbitrary decisions.

The grey man in the grey suit.

Choosing life or death

Execute or absolve.

Deciding upon the fates of faceless thousands. he would never know, behind his grey desk with a stroke of his grey pen.

A new thought rushes through his mind, vied on by the last smouldering spark of his once youthful rebellion. He articulates it to himself in silent anger.

'Well damn the ministry, damn the whole colourless world. I shall decline every notice of execution from this day on...'

And for a moment—a second, no more—he feels a burden lift from him. He feels, at last, he can do something, make a difference to his world. It is as if the colour so long missing from his life floods back. And then...

The second realisation strikes him all the harder, draining his pallor from grey to white. For even now, knowing this, knowing the enormity of the task he has performed each day for so many years, he does not know what his decisions mean.

Accept or Decline.

Accept or decline what?

Is it the order of execution?

Or is it the appeal for leniency?

A list of extenuating circumstance?

A List of accusations by the state police?

Accept or decline ……..

He might decline every report, and send

everyone to the noose.

Or accept each and do the same.

And who can he ask?

What protest can he make?

How can he claim he has never understood what he chooses, never knew the decisions he was making for so many years?

There is no recourse; He cannot admit his ignorance, that he has condemned so many in such arbitrary fashion. He cannot ask for an explanation of his role. For whom would he ask? If he does not know what his job entails then who would in the monolithic structure that is the Ministry?

He is just a tiny cog in the machine of state. There is no mechanic to fix the broken parts. He cannot admit to his failings. For his failings would be the failings of the machine. The ministry is never wrong. It is incorruptible. It is omnipresent. It does not have to explain, even to itself.

The machine grinds on as it always has. He has no option or recourse but to continue as he always has and do his job.

Accept…

Decline…

He opens the next file.

It is his own.

……………………………………………

The Grey Man's tale ended.

Richards's world, which had faded into grey, reverted to colour, like a slow fade on the cinema screen. He felt calmer now, though he only had the vaguest of recollections of what had occurred before the tale began.

The Grey Man smiled down at him, gave him a non-committal salute of sorts and moved to leave.

"Was that true?" Richard heard himself whisper, half asleep now. He was not sure he heard the answer. He told himself with a tired thought, that he must remember to ask Grey Man in the morning.

He curled up under the sheets still clothed, one hand gently stroking at the cat, absent-mindedly, who was now curled up beside him.

Somewhere at the back of his mind, there were the memories of things, and the knowledge he had forgotten them, for now at least.

A note of inquiry stirred him in his sleep. The thought that there was something, something the cat had said, a strange turn of phrase that did not quite sound right, or perhaps said more than had been intended. Something he was grasping at, but the more he grasped the further it drifted away from him.

Before long that too was forgotten, and he fell deeper into his sleep.

Sometime later in the night the cat slinked out of his room.

CHAPTER ELEVEN

Parisian Walkways

"So Piano man, do you fancy a stroll and a bite to eat?" Sonny asked Richard, who was in the process of closing the keyboard cover and massaging cramping fingers. His fingertips felt raw, as they did at the end of every night. He was not sure if they felt better than they had the night before. They were at least gradually regaining the calluses a piano player could expect. Despite this, they still felt painfully abused.

The fingers themselves felt tight and clawed. But he hoped that would pass in a few minutes. It was his own fault he knew, he had been playing for hours each day since he first arrived at Esqwiths. He knew that he should probably have taken more care with them, rested them more for a start. But it felt good to be back behind a keyboard again. Even if a day away it would probably be wise, for the sake of his hands.

Behind the keyboard, he found his troubles slipped into a softer focus, as he concentrated on playing. At times he even managed to forget his problems, for a while at least. So he kept on playing even though he knew he should rest his hands sooner rather than later.

Thinking of the pain in his fingers and the need to rest them he realised he was not even sure how long he been at the Passing Place. It must have been five days or perhaps six, certainly no more than seven that much he was sure of. Though now it occurred to him he was not actually that sure at all. The pain in his fingers seemed to suggest it was more than a week or two. Time seemed to just slide by here without taking much notice of the days. He shrugged to himself and decided not to think about it.

Right now at least, he had other concerns. His stomach felt empty, growling at him for the lack of attention he had paid to it. Also, it occurred to him suddenly, he had not left the building since the stormy night of his arrival. A stroll outside in the fresh air followed by some food sounded like the finest idea in the world right at that moment. Even if it was in the dead streets, and dead air, of Hicksville at stupid o'clock in the morning.

Richard turned his head, smiling back at Sonny

Burbank's, who was showing the last of the stragglers the door. An action handled in the courteous, professional, yet never the less very insistent way of club bouncers everywhere. The way that said, *'I am being polite, you do not wish me to be impolite anymore than I wish to be impolite, so if you would be so kind as to politely leave now, we can both be spared any unpleasantness.'*

It is the wise customer that takes note of the smiling 250lb man who is also sober unlike you generally and more than capable of carrying you out the door.

Only the very unwise would wish to endure the kind of unpleasantness on offer, as a rule.

"Sure, I could do with a change of air. Just give me a few minutes to wash up," Richard replied loudly enough for Sonny to hear, before standing up slowly from his stool to avoid cramping his back. Even his ankles hurt from sitting at the piano. Pushing foot pedals all day is not what the human foot was designed for. *'Air nothing,'* he thought to himself, *'I need to stretch my legs, or I'll ache all night.'*

He made for the bathroom and a hot tap to wring his hands under, wondering once more, as he felt the heat entering his tired fingers, just how long he had actually been at Esqwiths.

He tried some basic mental arithmetic, thinking of incidents on individual days when he played this song or that song for a customer; The Gunslinger, the guy with the horns. The woman in the red dress who wanted to hear something from a movie he had never heard of, but surprised himself by knowing the tune. When the chef made him that first impossible sandwich, that night the Grey Man had told him his tale...

Five then, he concluded. Or six if he included the night he arrived. Five days behind the piano, with breaks only to eat at the bar or the kitchen, and the crawling upstairs to sleep. It was little wonder he was starting to feel claustrophobic, now that he thought of it. And little wonder his fingers burned with a deep ache from playing the ivories.

The idea of leaving the bar for a while had not even occurred to him before. Getting out, for a while at least, seemed suddenly a very inviting prospect, now Sonny had suggested it. '*If only,*' he admitted to himself, '*to avoid slipping too deeply into another rut.*'

It would, he knew, be all too easy to bury himself in the piano. Which would be all well and good, but he knew himself too well not to be aware how easily he could slip deeply into an obsession. To escape behind the piano keyboard was no less an escape than six months on greyhound busses and no healthier, he was sure.

As he thought about this he realised, with no small surprise, he was not looking for an escape anymore.

It was not that he did not still want answers.

He still wanted an answer to that impossible question '*Why?*'

Needed an answer...

It was just running away no longer seemed the way to find it.

As this realisation occurred, he fought against it all the same. The thoughts of Carrie, of his desperate need for that answer, of the urge to flee from it all that drove him across the back roads of America.

Staring at his reflection in the mirror. As the hot water ran into the sink below him. He shook his head and tried to bring himself back to the present.

Sharp needles of pain ran through his fingers as he cracked each knuckle under the streaming water. Snapping the pre-arthritic nodules, and added to the general ache but giving him small moments of gratifying relief.

It was an old habit, from days before the cramping got more severe in later years. A habit which had drawn lectures from Carrie on the harm it did his joints more than once. She would chide him while smiling, but he knew the habit angered her all the same. As he knew Carrie only chided him when he was doing something she considered foolish.

He found himself wincing at the memory of his wife's uncharacteristic sternness whenever she told him off. Of how her anger always burned bright and fast, and then was gone. It seemed a strange thing to miss, but he missed it all the same.

He found himself staring into the mirror again as he cracked another finger, imagining her stood behind him, lecture in full swing.

A wave of regret washed over him, and he closed his eyes for a moment. And for a second, fleeting though it was, he could have sworn he could feel the heat of her breath on his neck, causing him to shudder. When he opened his eyes, the smallest beads of tears ran down his cheeks.

He broke his moment of melancholy by dousing his face with cold water and combing back his hair once more. Scragging at the tangled mess it had become over the course of the day as ever.

He had considered cutting it short, or oiling it down, but tethering it back in a ponytail was the simpler compromise. He was used to it being long now. Six months of wandering the back lanes of America had given him a hairstyle that fitted the wanderer. He had not worn it this long since his teenage years.

Feeling slightly better and a little less like a much abused human jukebox, he wondered back out to the bar to find Sonny waiting for him by the door. With, Richard was only slightly surprised to find, the cat prowling around the doorman's ankles.

"She coming too?" Richard asked as he pulled his tuxedo jacket back on. Trying his best not to feel overdressed for a stroll through a midwest hick town at God only knew what hour in the morning in search of food. He was half tempted to head upstairs to change into some of his old travelling clothes, suspecting he would feel a tad less conspicuous that way. But did not want to keep the doorman waiting. Besides which Sonny was dressed in his own tux anyway. So Richard rationalised to himself that, *'If he doesn't feel overdressed then why should I.'*

"Princess here will do as she likes no doubt. But I know she has a fondness for Parisian walkways at this time of night. So I wouldn't be at all surprised if she tags along." Sonny replied with his trademark half serious smile.

Richard raised an eyebrow in enquiry. It seemed a mildly oblique thing to say. The cat had never asked him to play the old Gary Moore standard, but then it was not really something you could play on the piano. He shrugged it off as just another of Sonny's ever cryptic replies. He was learning to let such things slide by, rather than question each one. He assumed, as ever, that he was missing some minor nuance of the doorman's humour.

Shrugging his shoulders, he walked across the bar room floor and joined the two of them in the doorway.

He looked out into a crisp autumn night and a street that he did not recognise. He stared silently for a moment before stating what was now became obvious to him, more to himself than anyone else.

"This isn't Providence Nebraska is it?"

The conversation with the gunslinger a few days before came to mind, along with a whole lot of other things over the last few days which had struck him as odd in the moment but been dismissed as impossible.

The odd way no one in the really bar fitted, or rather did fit but should not have done. The things he had shrugged that off as just more strangeness. Ignoring what was obvious because it was insane. All the same, somewhere in the back of his mind, he had registered the fluidity the bars location. The door could not always open out into Hicksville nowhere. The strange cast of customers could not all come from a mid-west desert town. Rediculous a notion that it may be. This was, however, the first time he was truly confronted with the truth of it.

Not for the first time in recent memory he found himself questioning his own sanity, just a little.

In truth, his mind was swimming with the possibilities that this realisation suggested. He found himself unable to dismiss them so easily now they were so obviously in front of him. The Passing Place was not tied to one location. Its door was, it seemed, a doorway to where ever Esqwith's just happened to be at any given time, which could, he realised, be just about anywhere.

As an idea Richard needed to adjust to slowly, an adjustment he found hard to contemplate fully so he tried to let it slide away from the fount of his mind even now, determining instead to focus on the present.

"Location Relative Richard, have you not grasped that yet?" came Sonny's half mocking rejoinder from behind him, echoing his thoughts. There was though, a chuckle in the doorman's voice. He gave Richard a gentle, if firm, nudge in the back to get him moving through the doorway. "We aren't in Kansas anymore either Toto," he said still grinning and stepped out into the night behind the piano player.

Richard breathed in deeply, filling his lungs with the cold night air. He felt an unexpected chill in the air, colder than the expected desert night. It was, though, a welcome change to the cloying warmth of the barroom. Yet it made him feel slightly light headed at the same time. Though that may have not been the air... Suspecting that the door did not always lead to the same place was one thing, knowing that was the case was different. He took another deep breath and asked a question which was no doubt expected of him, if not obligatory at this point.

"So if we aren't in Nebraska, where are we?"

He was still looking around while he asked. He got the impression wherever they were it was still early evening, far too early in fact for the bar to be shut for the night, though his internal body clock said differently. He thought about this for a moment. The obvious answer, he knew, was that the bar was in a different time zone. Which made sense to him, and he found himself smiling at the idea. He guessed if you could fit your head around one impossible idea, then all kinds of possibilities became merely plausible, if not for that matter obvious.

All the same, though, it was disconcerting to face directly.

"At a rough guess, I would say we are on the Rue de Monttessuy in Paris. The one in France that is, not the one in Texas. Of course, I am only guessing. We could be anywhere I suppose. But that street sign above your head is a bit of a clue. Not to mention the mountain of scrap iron you can see up the far end of the street," Sonny replied, his habitual smile coming through in his voice.

The doorman was pointing down the street a ways and Richard followed with his eyes. It was, he had to admit, a little surprising to see the Eiffel Tower dominating the skyline. But it certainly helped put a pin in the map.

"So anyway, my own question is not where so much, as when we are," Sonny continued. Richard suspected, as he often did when talking to Sonny, there was a hint of sarcasm in his tone. But it was hard to be sure with the doorman, sometimes it seemed he was mocking when in fact he was just explaining something as simple as he could.

"You see my friend, I have been aching to see Jose's Baker at the Folies Bergère for years. Missed her by several months last time I was here, which was a damn shame, I don't mind telling you. A damn shame..."

The name meant nothing to Richard though he would have hazard guessed it was a show or perhaps a movie or something. While drifting he had fallen out of touch with new releases and what not over the last year. He had more or less ignored the posters in bus terminals he had seen. Going to the movies alone had never been his idea of a good time. As this thought crossed his mind, it caused the familiar ache in the pit of his stomach.

Carrie had loved both the movies and going to shows. She would joyously drag him along to them whenever she could persuade him to go.

In truth, he seldom had needed much persuading, even if he would agree to go just because it pleased her. It was even something of a game between them. He would look none too interested in whatever had taken her fancy and she would gently nag at him to go until he agreed. The more he wanted to go himself, the more he would put up a faux defence. Mainly because he loved to see that triumphant look of victory in her eyes when he finally caved. Which he always did, even though he was sure she knew, as well as he did, that he would in the end. He enjoyed watching movies with her too much, and dissecting the plot afterwards, arguing over minor points or revelling in the shared joy of the big screen.

For a moment he was lost in the memories again, until the cat brushed past his leg and gave a sharp yowl, dragging him back to the moment, before she went stalking off down the street towards the tower.

Sonny started after her at a gentle pace and called back over his shoulder for Richard to move himself and, after a short lurching run to catch up with the doorman, they all walked in silence down the Rue de Monttessuy in the Paris night.

They emerged on the broad tree-lined avenue of de la Bourdonnais where they paused for a moment, as all tourists often do the first time, to take in the full grandeur of the Eiffel Tower lit up in the Parisian night.

"Amazing what you can do with enough scrap iron and the will to show off, isn't it?" Sonny intoned gleefully, before leaving Richard staring up at the tower while he rummaged about in a waste bin at the side of the avenue.

Richard, slightly in awe of the tower, realised he had gone after a moment and was surprised to see the doorman come back holding a newspaper and sporting a broad grin.

"Sixth of November, Nineteen twenty-six. We, my friend, are in luck," Sonny said, holding up the front page of the abandoned paper. Then laughed slightly as if he was about to make a joke, something Richard had noticed was a habit the doorman enjoyed.

"Year after Lustig sold it for scrap," he said waving the newspaper at the tower.

"What?" said Richard, taken off guard he was not sure whether he was questioning the date or the randomness of the fact Sonny had alluded to.

"Victor Lustig, he was, or is right now I guess, a con artist. Clever bastard, even for one of his ilk, too. Story is he convinced some idiot to buy the tower for scrap. Got to admire his gall, doing that, don't you? He had an interesting career I'm told, even for a con artist. Real character he was, is, whatever…. I heard told that this one time he conned Al Capone out of five grand? Didn't even do it for the money as such. Just did it for the bragging rights, Y'know. Imagine the kind of stones you gotta have to do that.." Sonny said with a note of admiration in his voice.

"Capone… The Al Capone, as in the Chicago mob Capone?"

"You know of another Alfonso Capone worth mention of?"

"Well no, can't say I do," Richard replied, his mind reeling a little, not over the exploits of Victor Lustig as such, but at being in Paris, France, apparently years before he was born.

'Anywhere and perhaps anywhen.' the thought rushed passed his conscious mind, a tiny thought that was duly suppressed. He was struggling enough as it was, without considering the connotations of that thought right then.

"Well yes, that Al Capone," Sonny said taking back up his tale, oblivious to the confusion racing through his friend's mind. "Now, as I heard it told, Lustig took him for five grand in some short con scam or other, rigged it special to hook in the man himself. And then, which is the best part, he damn well shakes the son of a bitch by the hand. Hell way I heard it, Capone even thanked Lustig for his honesty. Takes some special kind of guts to pull that off, y'have to admit. You just gotta admire a man like that."

"Capone?" Richard, still a little bewildered, asked. *'Anywhere, anywhen'* was still pushing at the back of his mind, making it hard to focus on the conversation. Sonny gave him a sharp look, a tinge of anger even seemed to cross his expression for a moment, then it softened suddenly as if he realised what the piano player was trying to come to terms with.

"Sorry, my friend. All coming a bit fast, I know. I was talking about admiring Lustig that's all. Take my advice man, and don't dwell on it tonight. I can guess what you're trying to get your head around. Just enjoy the Parisian air." Sonny raised his hands in mock salute to the night air, took a deep breath, grinning broadly, then started walking towards the banks of the Seine. Calling back over his shoulder as he did so, "Hell Piano-man, it's Nineteen Twenty Six, and Paris is in love with Jazz. All things black and all things American. And we my friend, we are off to see the show."

"What? Erm," Richard tried to ask while jogging to catch up, He felt like he was being swept along in some mad adventure, without a guide book. Pulling level he slowed enough to ask. "What show?"

Sonny's grin, if anything, got wider, and he clapped Richard on the back with enough force to send him lurching forward, spluttering slightly.

"Man, we are off to see Miss Josephine Baker dance at the Folies Bergère, and right in her prime, I may add. God damn, but that's so cool!"

"It is? I mean, we are?" Richard replied as he found himself having to keep up the half jog to stay level with the big bouncer who was trotting through the Parisian night, following the embankment along the Seine.

Sonny shook his head in mocking despair, half laughing as he did so.

"Guess it is too much to expect a musician to know something about jazz..." he mocked with some amusement, "My friend, this is Paris in the twenties. The city that fell in love with jazz. Came through the war and those grim years, and reinvented itself the way only Paris can. Black American music is the thing here now. They 'all here, before the Cotton Club back home was even an idea. The Duke, Louie, Earl Hines, all of them. And, well, let's just say that Josey Baker is the hottest ticket in town."

"And we have tickets?" Richard asked, still more than a little bemused, but suddenly just happy to go along with the insanity of it all. There was something about the moonlit waters of the Seine which had a magical quality. Perhaps that was all this was, magic. '*If so,*' he mused to himself, '*it's a shame I don't believe in it.'*

As he hurried along in the wake of the doorman, Richard noticed the cat sitting on a bench ahead of them. Preening itself in the self-absorbed way that only cats can, before looking back at them, as if it was wondering what had taken them so long to catch up.

"Providence will provide I am sure," Sonny said as they reached the bench and he leant down to tickle the cat's ear. The cat purred gratefully and shook itself as it stood up revealing the envelope she had been sitting upon. Smiling, Sonny retrieved the envelope, opened it and took out a pair of tickets, his eyes lighting up.

"Thank you providence," Sonny said, kissing the tickets. The cat hissed at him and flicked her tail in disgust. Sonny smiled down unperturbed and stroked her gently.

"I'm only joking, princess. Thank you, obviously, thank you so very damn much." He consoled the cat and she nudged her head against him, purring once more before she leapt down from the bench, resuming her walk along the riverside. Flicking herself gracefully up onto the top of a railing, she strolled along with the selfsame grace, as if it was not only an inch wide and cylindrical.

"This another of those things Esqwith provides?" Richard asked as the pair started walking once more. "Tickets that mysteriously turn up when they're wanted?"

Sonny laughed happily, still sporting a big child-like grin. "It's been known to happen, but I think in this case it's more that she knows how annoyed I was to miss the show last time we passed through. I sulked for a month, I am none too proud to admit. I think Esqwith doesn't want a repeat performance."

Richard struggled with the concept of a twenty stone bouncer sulking, then returned the smile, as a stray thought occurring to him that caused him to ask, "Don't suppose Hyde Park and the Stones in sixty-nine is ever somewhere we might pass through?"

"They were better at Woodstock," the bouncer said with an oddly dismissive tone.

Richard shook his head, mildly disappointed, though he could not say why. "The Stones didn't play Woodstock."

"Your Woodstock perhaps, they did the one I was at last month with the princess, blew the rest of the acts away they did," Sonny retorted. *'Anywhere, anywhen'* went the voice at the back of Richards mind once more. An even more complicated thought dragging along behind it.

"There was only one Woodstock."

"You're right, there is only one Woodstock in every reality, and never with the same bill twice." The doorman smiled at him. Richard was not entirely sure if it was a joke or not. Yet, all the same, he had the feeling that the doorman was telling the truth, at least as far as Sonny believed it at any rate.

"*Anywhere, anywhen*," the voice said again. Only this time rather than at the back of his mind it was a whisper half under his breath; A whisper betraying the mixed emotions that were finding a voice within him.

Sonny said nothing for a moment, giving Richard half a look. A look part questioning, part worried. Then he broke the sudden tension with a wide grin before breaking into a stroll once more.

"Richard my good friend, we are in Paris, in the moonlight, with tickets for the Folies Bergère," he said loudly, before raising his arms and taking a deep breath and laughing loudly. "There are days it is good to be alive, and this is one of them."

Then for a moment his laughter stopped and he looked straight at Richard, seeing his pained expression.

"Later for questions. Let's go enjoy ourselves for a while," the doorman said with a finality to his voice.

....

It was later, and they were sitting in a small bistro off the Rue Marr.

Sonny's face was lit up with a boyish grin that would not go away. Indeed, had not, since they had taken their seats at the show earlier that evening.

Miss Baker had, Richard was forced to admit, certainly been something. Though, if he was truthful, he was not sure what that something was. He wondered if it was because it was something out of his time. If perhaps the jaded sensibilities of being a twenty-first-century guy living in America led him to a different appreciation of such things. At least compared to someone from the nineteen twenties. Richard, even in England, had grown up with too many rock videos and cable TV channels, that made what was once the erotic seem everyday fare.

Sonny had enjoyed every second of it however and had spent most of the meal afterwards filling Richard in on Miss Baker's life story. So much so that it was soon obvious to the piano player that Sonny had a special place in his heart for her.

That much, at least, Richard could understand. She was certainly a woman with qualities. There was something of the wild about her. According to Sonny, it was the spirit of jazz. A Sonny who had warmed to his subject through the first two courses of dinner. Gesticulating with enthusiasm on the matter between mouth fills. He only started to run dry when they ordered brandy for a nightcap.

Richard for his part had listened distractedly to Sonny's illuminations of the life of Miss Baker. The earlier conversation about '*anywhere and anywhen*' kept coming back to him. Sonny seemed not to mind, though it was obvious he could tell that Richard was not really listening. In part, the doorman was talking to fill the void in conversation which had developed between them. Finally, however, as the wine waiter poured two large brandy's, a silence dropped between them which hung in the air as they both considered their drinks.

'*Anywhere, anywhen,*' thought Richard for the hundredth time that evening. He wanted to ask so many questions, but at the same time feared any answers he might receive.

'*Could he go back?*
Could he save her?

Could he change the past?'

The thoughts cascaded through his consciousness.

'Would she want to be saved?' Came painful second thoughts, crashing down upon him over the course of the night. He had lived so long with grief that hope was somehow the most terrifying of thought of all.

The silence between them drew on.

Sonny seemed aware of Richard's inner turmoil but was keeping his own council, though his own expression grew more troubled with each passing moment.

Eventually, the tension grew until finally Sonny spoke again.

"You lost someone!" It was a statement, not a question. There was a narrow look in the doorman's eyes that displayed a level of insight in his words as they cut through the silence.

Richard took a sip of his brandy to disguise the twinge of grief he felt, then smiled weakly back at his friend. Saying simply "My wife."

Sonny breathed in deeply and shaking his head absently. "Suicide!" he exclaimed, again a statement, not a question. It caused Richard to look askance at the doorman, wondering to himself, *'How did he know?'*

Richard felt an unreasonable anger welling up inside himself. So much had happened in the last few days he did not understand. So much he would have considered impossible or just plain insane. Now this man, who claimed friendship with him, knew things that were inexorably personal. Things he had not chosen to share. Things he did not want to share.

Not his grief.

Not with this man, not with anyone.

It was too private a thing, too personal. How could he know? How did he know? What else did he know, come to that?

Was his life an open book, something talked about in the bar? Was he a joke to them, his new friends, or someone to pity?

He did not want pity. He did not want knowing looks and sympathy. He felt that kernel of rage growing within him, boiling inside and twisting like a knot in his stomach. His anger must have shown, for Sonny raised his hands, palms open, in the same gesture he always used to pacify a troubled customer. A gesture which cut through Richards's anger.

"A guess, Richard. Just a guess," the doorman said shaking his head. His tone placating if troubled, then he released a heavy sigh.

"You remember when I told you my story? How I made a deal with God about the taking of my own life? I saw your eyes tighten. I saw the discomfort it gave you. It obviously pained you to hear someone talk about suicide. From there it wasn't much of a leap all things considered, but it's just a guess. I've told no one else my suspicions. It's your business not mine."

"Yes...." said Richard relaxing, the anger draining away. He could see the concern in the doorman's eyes was the concern of a friend rather than pity. He found himself suddenly wanting to talk about it all. "She… She took her own life. She was troubled, depressed… I…" he could feel the tears welling up behind his eyes.

"It's okay my friend. You don't need to talk about it, not now, not ever if you would rather not. I knew there was someone when I saw your reaction that's all." Sonny kept his voice calm and low. Openness about him that succeeded in putting Richard more at his ease.

"I wasn't planning on asking. There are some things best left, well, just best left, unless the other person brings them up, I guess. Not saying I wasn't curious. The good Lord gave me that vice, God knows, but, curiosity aside, I have no right to know. If you wanted me too, or someone to talk to, you would have told me yourself. And if you ever need a listener, I am happy to listen, but if not? Well, it's your business my friend, not mine."

Richard managed to fight back the tears. Anger replaced with a sense of gratitude, he half whispered a reply, "Thank you, Sonny."

Sonny sighed, shaking his head once more. His hands raised palm open again, he gave Richard a level look.

"I mentioned it only because I could see you are thinking about the possibilities of the things that came up earlier. Possibilities that, well how to say this… best to say it's a blind alley my friend, but you're not the first to dwell on them."

"Yer?" Richard inquired, somewhat obviously, knowing he was looking for a distraction from the thoughts in his own head. Hoping selfishly that Sonny would move the conversation on, and let him hide his own troubles once more.

"Yer…" Sonny said, clearly knowing he was being led, but happen to talk, if only to give the piano player time to collect his thoughts.

"When I worked all this out for the first time I wanted to save my father, go back and find him. Talk to him, send him home to my mother and me. Stop whatever killed him from ever happening. Hell if he had gotten sick then I could bring the cure right? Even if they found it fifty years after he died. Hell, go back and save his life with some golden bullet miracle pill. If he was run down by a car, then I could go back and slash the cars tyres the night before. If it was a fight, well I am damn sure I could beat the good lord's mercy out of his attackers. You understand?"

"All those possibilities, all those different days to the one when he died. I had it all figured out. I spent days thinking about it. Weeks perhaps, I don't know for sure. Thinking of how my mother's face would light up on the day when he walked through the door. Thinking of the childhood, I never got. A childhood spent with my father. A different life."

"Hell, if it wouldn't have changed everything. The whole misbegotten story of my youth. All the things that led me to that death cell. The mud and the blood of the war. Burying my mother in a pauper's grave. All of it, if I just changed that one thing… Saved him…"

The pain in Sonny's voice as he said all this cut into Richards malaise. The deep-seated desire behind these thoughts, something he understood only too well. Then the big doorman sighed and took a mouth full of his brandy, levelling his gaze once more.

"But it doesn't work that way. We can't change the past that way. We can't alter the course of our lives have taken, or that which led us to here. God knows I wish at times it did work that way, but it doesn't."

"Why not?" came the plea from Richard, his own pain, and a residual of his anger, in his voice. He had felt like a man that had been offered salvation. Now he felt like Sonny was snatching it away. He could feel himself welling up as much with frustration as anything else.

Sonny closed his eyes for a moment, and Richard realised the big man was holding back tears of his own. Then the doorman smiled a smile full of sympathy for the piano player, which then became a grimace, and he took another long drink of brandy, shrugging his big shoulders and shaking his head.

"Why Not?" Richard asked again, angry now, at the universe, at time, at fate, at everything and anything. But more than that he knew, unreasonably, at the man in front of him. The man who was always so full of answers and yet no answers at all.

As a professional doorman, Sonny was a man used to dealing with irrational anger in others. He carefully put down his glass and smiled weakly at his friend the piano player. His hands once more held palm open, whatever grief he was feeling himself having spoken of his father, choked down.

"Richard," he began, then paused to take a

breath and collect himself a little more... "Richard, I could give you a wonderfully long-winded explanation about quantum mechanics, paradoxes, butterfly wings and lord knows what else. But in the end, it would just be so much hokum."

Richard forced himself to breathe slowly, forcing himself to feel calm and relaxed. Trying to ease his unreasonable anger away.

"Why is that Sonny?" he asked, his voice even, almost a study in self-control, though he could hear the cracks within it.

Sonny gave one more heavy sigh and frowned deeply and offered Richard the bottle of brandy.

"Because my friend I am not a physicist. I'm a club doorman, plain and simple. I no more understand all that stuff than you do..." he replied.

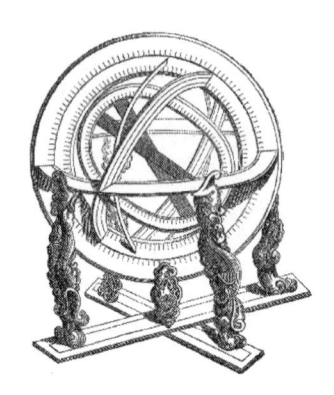

CHAPTER TWELVE

World Tree in the Garden

"Have you seen Morn?" Richard asked.

"About this high, green hair, works tables and the bar. Yes, of course, I 've seen her," the ever literal-minded barman replied.

"I meant this morning Lyal. Specifically, have you seen her this morning?"

"Oh I see. Yes, I've seen her this morning."

"And... do you have any idea where she is at all?" Richard prodded.

Conversations with Lyal had a habit of going like

this. It was exasperating at times, but Richard was getting used to them. Though it reminded him of something, his mother used to refer to as '*drawing teeth*.' when she talked to him in his taciturn teenage years. Talking to Lyal was, if nothing else, giving him a whole new appreciation of why he had frustrated his mother so much in those distant days of his pimpled youth.

"I think she's with her tree," Lyal replied after a moment's thoughtful pause in his relentless glass polishing. Then resumed his task once more, presumably assuming, somewhat incorrectly, that with this information Richard was now fully informed. Thus turned his back and commenced restocking the fridge.

Frustrated, and more than a little irritated by the barman, Richard headed across the bar room floor towards the kitchen. He desired a strong coffee, something which conversations with Lyal tended to inspire. In truth, he would not have minded the chance of a bit of breakfast, too. On his way, he sidestepped Grey Man's mop bucket without really looking.

'*With her tree*,' he bemoaned inwardly. If anyone else but Lyal had said that, he would assume they were using a metaphor. However, Richard suspected that Lyal would not understand a metaphor if it was standing over him holding a sign saying. '*I am representative or symbolic of something else.*'

Wrapped up in his own annoyance at the barman's overly literal mode of conversation, and a general feeling of frustration after the night in Paris, he almost walked straight into Grey Man who was uncharacteristically stood still, leaning on his mop.

"Sorry Grey," he blurted out, pulling himself up short, irrationally irritated that the man was in his way, but chiding himself for blaming the grey man for his own lack of awareness.

"Hum…," the monochrome one-half replied. He seemed too intent on watching the second hand of a large wall clock, Richard had never noticed before, slowly tick by, to have noticed anything.

"I said 'sorry'."

The grey man turned to him and gifted him a large smile, nodded and then returned to his strange fascination with clock-watching, a pass time which Richard had noticed before with the clock in the kitchen. Like most mundane things, the grey man seemed to take pleasure in the activity. For a moment Richard thought of asking the grey man about it. The flickering memory of a story half-remembered coming back to mind, and he wondered, in passing, how much of it was true.

The clock ticked past the minute, and Grey sighed a little to himself and resumed his mopping, so Richard decided to let the matter lay a little longer, asking instead the question he had started his day with, "Have you seen Morn?"

"Yes, she's with her tree. Out back," Grey replied, waving a hand vaguely in the direction of the kitchen. He waltzed away with his mop, whistling to himself, as ever, in his own happy little world.

"Out back… there's a back?" Richard found himself muttering under his breath, though he did at least feel a little more informed than before. He shrugged and watched the mop and its owner dance away for a few seconds, then resumed his journey to the kitchen.

Richard had woken with an urge to talk to someone. At least that was, to be more precise, someone other than Sonny, in the vain hope of getting some answers to the questions that were burning in his mind.

The doorman's cryptic comments and his claims of being nothing more than a simple club bouncer at a slightly odd bar had grated with Richard, which was not to say he did not believe them exactly. Certainly, Sonny seemed nothing but genuine. All the same, however, Richard had gone to sleep dwelling on those '*Anywhere's and anywhen's.*' Those, and Carrie.

Always, as ever, Carrie.

The sudden renewal of hope was, he had decided, a terrible thing. How could he move on if there was a chance he could still save her? If he could go back and stay her hand, just that one night, that one moment. It was a desperate thing, a desperate hope that replaced despair, and yet he somehow felt all the worse for it.

Sleep had done nothing to dampen those questions.

Those '*Anywhere's and anywhen's*'.

Nor had Sonny's insistence on the limitations of them.

If anything, that insistence had made them all the worse. Even though Sonny had claimed that he could not explain how it all worked. Richard still suspected the doorman knew more than he was admitting to, but he also was sure that the doorman would play such knowledge close to his chest.

'*I'm a club doorman, plain and simple….*' "My ass you are…" he had found himself muttering when he was alone in his room after they returned from Paris.

While he found it hard to hold a grudge against the congenial doorman. Sonny gave him someone to focus his frustrations upon, even while he knew they were unfair, but the desperate new spark of hope led him to nothing so rational. He needed to know more, needed an explanation that he could find peace with, but knew that it would not be forthcoming, not from Sonny at any rate.

They had left the restaurant in silence for the most part, after the doorman pronouncement of simplicity. That silence had only grown as they returned to the Rue de Monttessuy and the doorway to the other place that was Esqwith's. A simple exchange of 'goodnights' had been the only words they had said to each other after that.

This left Richard laying awake in the night, staring at the demonic faces that loomed out at him from the shadows of his imagination, and thinking about '*Anywhere, and anywhen.*' While he sought the sleep, he could not find. And the problem of whom he could talk to about them.

Lyal he immediately ruled out, if only because of the sheer frustration it would doubtless bring. The chance of getting a straight answer to a complex question from the strangely literal-minded barman seemed remote, to say the least.

Passing Place 245

Besides, there was something about Lyal that set Richard on edge. The way the barman's smile slipped from his lips the moment someone's back was turned, and the cynical sneer that replaced it. Which gave lie to the impression of a simple nature. There was something just not right about him. Richard suspected that his curiously literal mind was also something of an affectation, used to disguise something more disdainful, cynical and nasty in his nature. There was something about him of the mocker, and it set Richards teeth on edge at times. Though he could not pin down exactly why.

No, he knew somehow that he could not ask Lyal.

The limited conversations he had enjoyed with Grey Man left him doubting that the monochrome cleaner would amount to a mine of information. He seemed to have his own wildly unlikely ideas about the Passing Place. His professed belief that this was all some form of afterlife suggested he would be of little help in trying to get a handle Richards questions.

Likewise the Chef, for all his strange ability to make sandwiches appear out of thin air, also seemed convinced of his own theories. Theories which were stranger in some ways than those of Grey Man's. A shared dream was a fine explanation for the Passing Place, Richard thought, but he did not believe it was any truer than Grey Man's heaven. If anything as an idea it fitted too neatly against possible objections. '*It's all a dream...*' It was just too simple an explanation. A cheap pulp writers get out clause for things getting strange. Besides which the Chef had a way of tieing logic in knots that would have put the one tied by Gordias to shame.

Beyond the doorman, the bartender, the cleaner and the chef, the only members of the staff Richard had spoken to at length were Morn and Jolene. A realisation which had come to him as he showered. He was a little perturbed to realise he had been quite so insular. He used to be gregarious in nature before Carrie's suicide. Since her death, he had withdrawn further into himself, which he knew. All the same, he found it disturbing just how little he had spoken with anyone, and how little he knew about them all.

He realised, apart from Sonny, the one he had spoken to most was the cat, and he felt certain somehow that the cat would be less than forthcoming with any real information. They why he was sure of that, he could not nail down either. There was something about the feline which spoke of mysteries all the same, and secrets held close. When he thought about it hard enough, he seemed to recall her talking in more than one voice, and saying things that did not entirely make sense to him. But for the life of him he could not remember when that happened, the whole idea seemed to slip away when he stopped thinking about it.

Also, Richard was not entirely comfortable with thinking of her as a person, for all she was certainly more than a normal feline. Come to that. However, he was still not entirely sure he had not only imagined her talking to him. He wondered, in the darkest part of the night, if her voice was just a projection of his own subconscious, and what it said about him that his subconscious had more than one voice…

So, the cat ruled out, on grounds of possible insanity, he was left with the two waitresses. Which did not help much.

The odd snippets of conversation he had enjoyed with Jolene left him suspecting she was unlikely to be illuminating on the subject of The Passing Place. Nice enough though she was, she did not seem the type to go in for metaphysical thought. Not that he would describe her as shallow, but she was as down to earth as a waitress from the midwest could possibly be. Homespun was the word that came to mind most when he thought of her.

Which left Morn as his only real option, odd though she was. Or, perhaps, because she was odd to start with. She had her own way of looking at things which were not quite on the same page as everyone else. If there were rules to talking about all this, she was the one most likely in his opinion to ignore them.

A sly bit of him, that he tried to ignore, also said she was the one he found himself attracted to and so he wanted an excuse to talk to her. Though he would deny this, even to himself. It was something he was not ready to admit feeling for anyone, Carrie still loomed too large in my psyche.

Thinking all this once more, he made for the kitchen, while also wondering at the ridiculousness of trying to find where the mysterious 'out back' of a pan-dimensional time travelling bar and grill actually was located, with little real information apart from it had a tree within it. But then how hard could it be to find the back door?

Anyway, coffee and toast seemed to be called for.

Well, the coffee certainly.

The kitchen was its normal organised chaos. Chef was busily making pancakes, while stirring maple syrup. He looked up as Richard entered and, smiling happily, he pointed over to the table where a coffee and two slices of freshly toasted bread lay waiting.

Richard did not question their appearance ahead of his arrival. Instead, he merely sat and added sugar to the coffee. While he watched the chef flipping pancakes.

The coffee was, as ever, perfect, while the toast was made from freshly baked bread and homemade butter. Probably from the finest grain in Nebraska. Richard was on the last slice when the Chef turned around and coughed slightly to attract his attention, looking ever so slightly perturbed.

"Oh sorry, I keep forgetting don't I?" Richard replied, before carefully adding in words well chosen, "Any chance of a cup of coffee and some toast?"

The Chef relaxed

"Thank you, Mr Piano Player." The chef beamed at him and flicked on the kettle before returning to his pancakes. No doubt he would make the toast later when he found the time.

Getting the hang of none sequential causality in the kitchen was taking Richard some time. Nothing, however, was more likely to irritate the chef than people forgetting to ask for what they were eating. Richard had forgotten the day before, and the chef had come out of the kitchen in a mild panic, desperate to find out what he had not cooked.

Apparently, the factual nature of causality was causing a loopback surge, which was, in turn, causing the leek and potato soup to boil backwards.

Richard had not asked how exactly something boiled backwards but did own up to having an omelette earlier and forgetting to ask for it. Which seemed to inspire a sudden calm on the chef's bright red features, followed by a stern look that spoke volumes, before he returned to the kitchen in search of eggs and milk.

"Don't suppose you know where Morn is?" Richard asked, as he finished the toast and washed it down with the last of the coffee.

The chef looked up from taking fresh bread out of the oven, smiling cheerfully. "The delightful girl is probably out back with her tree. It's one of her days I believe."

Richard let the *'one of her days'* pass, not entirely sure he wanted to know what *'one of her days'* was referring to, or, for that matter, how the chef would know. He rather hoped it was not what sprang to mind.

Lamenting the lack of more coffee and feeling that he really needed another one to cope with the coming conversation Richard asked, "So how do I get out back?"

"Generally, you would use the back door, my

friend. It's the easiest way as a rule," replied the chef, pointing vaguely at a bunch of cupboards that lined the wall beside the fridge.

"Erm..." Richard had images of some vague Lewis Carol inspired climb through the storage cupboards. But his obvious indecision caused the chef to look behind him to where he had pointed. He turned back smiling.

"Oh, I do apologise my good chap. Was forgetting myself there," the chef said, causing Richard's gaze to return to the chef who was now pouring the coffee.

There was a momentary whooshing sound, as if something had shifted and air had rushed in to fill a void. Richard closed his eyes and counted to five, already sure that there would now be a door when the cupboards had been, but not quite prepared to see the building change before his eyes.

When he looked, he was rewarded with the door he had admittedly now expected to see. It was painted dark green and had little-frosted windows through which sunlight streamed. Indeed, it was exactly the kind of door you would expect to see in a cottage kitchen in the home counties.

"Let me guess, it's only there when it's needed," he said as he got up from the table, a smidgen of dry humour about his voice. Appearing, disappearing doors was just another of those things he was learning to accept at face value. There seemed little point in denying their existence in a kitchen where food arrived before it was prepared. Or in a building where corridors appeared in the night.

Thinking of corridors appearing in the night gave him an unexpected shiver, he could not think why.

The chef shrugged, "No it's always there. The 'there' changes sometimes, but it is definably always there. Besides, it didn't seem right to send you through the root cellar. You can never be too sure where it is and what's down there, after all."

Richard felt a momentary urge to ask what the chef meant with the oddly ominous *'never be too sure what's down there'*, but decided to let it slide. Occasionally it was simpler just to go with these things, or perhaps better not to know. Instead, he thanked the chef for the coffee and went out into Esqwith's backyard via the green door.

Richard was not sure what to expect from the backyard, as much as he might have liked to imagine a large square of grass, hemmed in by a white picket fence with a large beach tree growing at its centre, a garden bathed in sunlight and a crazy pathing leading to it from the door. He thought it somehow unlikely, given it was the backyard of a time and dimension travelling bar and grill which coincidentally may or may not itself be alive.

He was surprised, therefore, when it turned out to be exactly that, with flower beds.

The disturbing part was not the garden that formed the back yard. The garden in of itself was a delight in its own way. The grass, freshly trimmed, was lush and green, the kind of lawn you only saw in the movies and never expected to see in real life outside of a putting green. The flower beds which followed the fence line were full of blooms, a grand display of roses and marigolds, with a bed of sunflowers up against the fence at the edge. Indeed, even the tree, which admittedly seemed a little large for a garden, did not look completely out of place. Instead, it merely looked like it had been allowed to prosper uncontrollably over many years.

The disturbing part lay beyond the fence. Or, rather, in the lack of anything beyond the fence.

There was just that, nothing.

The sunlight that bathed the garden came from no sun.

The light, gentle breeze, which was making the branches sway, came from nowhere.

At least, from nowhere he could see. Even had this been a garden on a cliff top, there would have been something beyond it.

There was nothing.

There was no sky.

Just an empty void.

Yet for all it was just an empty darkness that lay beyond the fence it seemed to swirl and move all the same. Spirals of deepest purple flowed like ink in the blackness. It was disturbing, wrong and yet Richard stood in the doorway for a long moment watching it, mesmerised by the emptiness of the 'not sky.'

Occasionally a spark of silver would appear in the dark, before running like mercury into one of the swirls then disappearing. As he watched, he saw other points of light in the void that came and went. But they were not stars or anything as simple as that. There were too few of them for a start. This was not space he was looking out upon. This was not a universe of possibility he saw. If anything it was the exact opposite of that. It was an emptiness. Utter and complete. An absence. A void.

It fascinated him and repelled him in equal measure. He tried to make reason of it, but his mind fled from making any sense of it all. It was simpler to just try and accept it, all the while trying hard to ignore the feeling of vertigo that was sweeping over him.

He felt his stomach churning as he tried to find some reason in what he saw. He was not sure how long he stood there watching. It seemed to be an age, as if looking out into the void took away all sense of time. He wondered if perhaps that was so. Was there time in the void? In this darkness beyond the garden?

There seemed nothing else so why would there be time?

Just a deep endless nothing, devoid of anything. It was such an alien idea. It was not a place that was part of the universe as Richard understood it. It was the place beyond that, or perhaps before the universe. Or perhaps in-between, the gap between existence and non-existence. It seemed to call to him at the same time as it pushed him away. He felt the urge to vent himself as his stomach turned. The universe was everything, how could you have something beyond everything…

He felt cold just looking at it. Cold and empty, as if he was reflecting the cold and emptiness he could see beyond the white picket fence. But even cold requires heat to exist, required something to be an absence of, rather than an absence of everything. He felt a pull from it all the same, like a longing, desire, a wish to fall into the nothing. He found himself stepping towards it. Wanting to be one with the nothing, something red seemed to be out in the blackness for a fleeting moment, calling to him, urging him towards it, then…

"Hi there, Richard. What you doing out here?" Morns perky voice broke him out of his chilling fascination with the void and the strange compulsion he had felt vanished.

He looked up and saw her sitting on a low branch of the tree, leaning with her back against the thick trunk. An open book sat on her lap. She looked for all the world as comfortable as it was possible to be.

Thankfully for Richard, the thick foliage of the tree blocked out the sight of the emptiness beyond the garden.

"I was looking for you," he said, trying to smile, his mind still swimming. He left the doorway and started walking towards her, doing all he could to keep the tree at the centre of his view.

He felt slightly disturbed as he walked. He could feel the heat of a sun, which he knew was not there, on his face. Knowing there was no sun did not lessen the feel of the sunlight, that warmth of it that penetrated his skin. It felt good, at least for those moments he could ignore the lack of a blue sky and a big yellow sun giving out heat.

"Oh, well now you've found me," said the perky young woman smiling down at him.

"Yes, I was hoping we could talk," he said still

feeling ill at ease.

"Well we're talking," she replied smiling. Putting her book down, she twisted about, hooking her legs around the branch, she hung upside down from the tree, bring her visage level with his, allowing them to talk face to face.

It was, however, somewhat disconcerting, as one of them was upside down. "So what do you want to talk about?" the green hair girl asked.

"Well, I was hoping I could ask you about this place," he said coming to a halt in front of her.

"My garden?" she asked with a gleam in her green eyes.

"No, the whole place. Esqwith's, all of it. Erm, did you say '*your garden*'?"

"Well, yes it's mine, sort of. She put it here for me so Father Beech would have somewhere to grow in safety," Morn said, gently rocking back and forth in a manner that was slightly disturbing. She was obviously agile, but all the same, Richard had the impression that she could fall at any moment. He found it a little unsettling.

"She? You mean Esqwith?" He was not sure if the idea of feminising the bar in that way made sense to him. Much in the same way he was never quite sure how people managed to call a car she or the French managed to give everything a feminine or masculine gender. People were he's or she's. Not objects and things, in his opinion. It always seemed a slightly silly idea to him.

Morn just smiled at him, then with a singular movement which defied gravity she swung herself down from the branch, somersaulted and landed square on her feet. A perfect dismount if ever there was one. Olympic judges would have given her straight sixes he was sure. This left her standing a few feet from him. The broad grin still on her lips. Resting on hand on the trunk of the broad beach tree with the tenderness of a lover.

"Of course, she's a she, how could she not be? But that's not your question is it?" she asked smiling brightly, so the green flecks in her eyes sparkled slightly in a way which seemed infectious. Richard returned the smile, though he already had the feeling he was losing ground with the conversation. So he took a moment to get his bearings a little and find a way to get it back on track. Grasping for something to say.

"Well no, I guess not… This is quite a tree… remarkable even… big tree like this growing here of all places…" he groped.

"That's kind of you to say, Mr Richard, the piano man. Father Beach is very fond of compliments." She replied beaming at him, obviously please he had said something nice about her tree, excessively so he thought. Then in a slightly conspiratorial tone she added, "A little too fond of them sometimes, I am sure he shows off a little too much just to get them on occasion."

Tilting her head to one side, she smiled back at him. He got the impression she was trying to look around what he was saying. It seemed a ridiculous idea and yet it fit in his mind all the same. Just as he was sure she knew he was stalling to get his bearings a little with the conversation. The idea of a tree showing off was not helping him either. He wondered for a moment how a tree would do such a thing. Make its leaves extra green perhaps ... He continued trying to get back on track anyway.

"I mean, it's strange to find anything growing here... in this place... it's unusual, to say the least."

"In a garden?" she inquired, looking genuinely surprised.

"In this garden, I mean how is there even a garden here?" he said feeling slightly frustrated that the conversation was getting away from him again and for some reason, he was getting the impression the truck of the tree was standing a little straighter and more impressively broad than before...

"Why would there not be?" she asked with the same mild surprise in her voice, as if he was asking ridiculous questions.

"You know what I mean? Here?"

"So you're asking why there is a here in the first place. That's a very Zen question don't you think? Like, why are we here? Or why soup?"

He was about to protest when she gave him a hard look and took on a serious visage, which looked altogether wrong for her normally perky, smiley self.

"Because we are. Beyond that, it's all superstitious mumbo jumbo in the end. Gods and creation and what not it's all hokum. We are here because we are here, and there is a garden because Esqwith has a garden. If Esqwith wants a garden, she can have one don't you think. Don't see how anyone is going to tell her she can't have one, can you? There is a tree in the garden because Esqwith let him take root here, which was very kind of her given the circumstances. But it is because it is and that's all there is to it. If it weren't, then, it wouldn't be here to wonder why it is. It's simple when you think of it like that, don't you agree? What's the point of being complicated about something simple, with all that gods and stuff? Trees don't worry about why they are. They just worry about growing, and sometimes acorns, but that's oaks for you, always worrying about their acorns."

"Acorns?"

"Yes, but like I said oaks are a worrisome lot. It's all that *'from tiny acorns mighty oaks do grow'* poetical stuff. It makes them worry if an acorn doesn't grow mighty that it's failing somehow. Trees should know better than to listen to poets, I know, but oaks are so very suggestible."

He tried to get his head around everything she had said, but the idea of suggestible and worrisome oaks kept clinging to him. He shook his head a moment to get back on track.

"But? I mean, why is any of this here? Who is Esqwith?"

"Oh, so that's your question. Who is Esqwith?"

"Yes," he said feeling he was, at last, getting somewhere.

"Oh, that's simple then. I don't know," she said brightly and did a backwards cartwheel for no apparent reason.

"You don't know? How can you not know? If you don't know, how can you say he let this tree take root here?" he snapped angrily, all his frustration boiling over at once, then he regretted the strength of his words immediately with the look that crossed Morn's face.

"He Richard, he, Father Beach is a he, not an it. And as for Esqwith, she isn't a he, at least I am fairly convinced she isn't. If she is anything, then she is definitely a she. Because nothing this powerful and caring could be a he, it stands to reason after all. And I will thank you to watch your tone. You're upsetting Father Beach. He is a sensitive old fool at times, but I cannot say I blame him when you come here and start raising your voice like that, disturbing the peace of our garden."

The anger in her words added a sinister tone to her voice he was not prepared for. More than that, as she had spoken he had felt a wind stirring up in the dead air, the tree branches started to sway, and the few leaves on the ground started to stir up as well, flowing in odd patterns around her feet. Her green eyes seemed aglow with rage, illuminated from within almost. He felt the hairs on the back of his neck standing on end like a storm was brewing out of the dead air. The tree too seemed to twist suddenly in the wind and take on a less welcoming aspect. A wave of fear swept over him, an upsurge he was not entirely sure was irrational.

He raised his hands in a gesture of surrender, trying to placate here sudden rage. It seemed so unlike her; she was so happy go lucky all the time. But then he supposed he had come to her place and subsequently got in her face. A wash of guilt went through him.

"I'm sorry. I didn't mean to offend you, or your

tree," he said, the last words he knew seeming foolish even as he said them. She still looked angry so he added while feeling foolish doing so, "He really is a nice tree, I did not mean to upset him." He was not sure why he said it. It just seemed the right thing to say. Once he had said it, the wind began to drop almost as quickly as it had appeared.

"Well if you're sure you're sorry, then I guess we can forgive you just this once," she replied, a slight aloofness to her tone. She was, it seemed, rising above her anger and wanted to make sure he knew it. Demonstrating that she was the bigger person here. Willing to accept his apology, but only because she was being gracious.

Then the anger seemed to drain from her, the odd glow vanishing from her eyes with the wind and the smile returning to her face.

"It's just all this, is so…." he grasped.

"You apologised, don't make it meaningless by offering excuses…" she chided.

"Sorry, I'm sorry…"

"You said…" she replied still angry for a second. Then suddenly it seemed forgotten, she was smiling, stretching up to the lowest branch and in a smooth movement pulling herself back up, swinging around and raising herself into a handstand on the bow of the tree, before flipping once more to come to rest sat on the branch.

He was not entirely sure the laws of gravity should have actually allowed her to do that.

He sighed to himself and sat down on the grass. Without really thinking about it, he found himself leaning back against the tree. The two of them fell into an odd silence, the kind you need to let the conversation settle back down after it has become an argument.

He found himself relaxing in the shade of the tree, the warm air and the bright sunless sunshine feeling pleasant. Still, there were things missing from the garden, which he found it hard to put his finger on. Apart from the sun which was obviously absent. But all the same, he felt increasingly relaxed as tension eased from him.

Richard could feel something else as well. Another presence perhaps. At least, that was the best way he could describe it to himself. An old soul close by. As he pondered, he wondered for a moment if it was Esqwith herself, though that did not seem quite right. It was something other than the Passing Place itself.

Then he wondered why he accepted the idea of Esqwith being female so easily now it had been put to him.

There was, he realised, something masculine about the presence he felt. That was how he knew it was not the bar. Yet, all the same, he could not quite put his finger on it beyond that feeling of maleness.

Then it came to him suddenly that it was the tree itself, the ancient breathing living thing he was leant against. He could almost feel the flow of the sap in the living wood, a pulse, dull and slow, like a heartbeat. A pulse which thumped less than once a minute, but was more the throb of sheer life force than any heart.

He was suddenly aware that he could feel the

leaves breathing in the air. Sucking it in then letting out oxygen, were lungs of a metabolism both alien to him and yet as natural as could be imagined, a creature so ancient it was a world in of itself. He felt an odd peace coming over him, a oneness with the ancient tree.

Richard remembered the old Nordic myth of Yggdrasil. The world tree. A concept that went beyond Norse mythology indeed lingered deep in many religions. The heart of the world itself. The wellspring of life. More than just an aspect of nature…The world itself.

That was what the tree made him think of. That's what he felt. This tree was alive in a way beyond any normal tree he had ever encountered. It was not just alive, it was life.

The peace that fell over him for a while lasted until something else occurred to him, the thing that was missing from the garden. Everything seemed so natural, so right and yet so obviously was not. With that realisation, the moment of peacefulness fled in the face of the unnatural nature of the garden. *Unnatural* that was the word that came to him, along with the sudden knowledge of what it was that was missing.

Insects.

There were none. No bees, no flies, not even any biting insects in the shade. For all the flowers and the grass, nothing crawled or flew around the garden. It was an oasis of life but sterile at the same time, and he knew for certain for a fleeting second that nothing there was real. How could it be, sat here in the void?

The thought disturbed him. The oneness he briefly felt fled. He found himself staring up at the sky once more. Watching the darkness, the absence of anything, it was hard to comprehend.

This was not a night sky full of cloud. This was an utter absence. And yet, all the same, there were still colours in the blackness even now, as he watched it closely. Swirls of deepest purple, or darkest red. Occasional explosions of dark green that appeared, expanded, and petered away into the dark. He had an impression of chaos complete, utter and all consuming- held within an absence of everything.

Richard grasped once again towards the concept, the idea, this was what lay beyond the universe, or perhaps before the universe. The emptiness of the void, before the universe exploded out from the big bang, filling nothing with everything. He found the idea insane, felt himself slipping into a weird state of mind, as he tried to comprehend the thoughts that lay just beyond his grasp.

Was this where Esqwith was, what she was, a thing outside, beyond the universe? A thing of the void, touching the real world in fleeting caresses but never being part of it. It seemed ludicrous. Impossible to believe.

Yet impossible to deny all the same.

The idea upset him, terrified him. He felt his mind swimming. He was hit with sudden nausea once more, his stomach lurching, and that same strange pull towards the darkness beyond the picket fence, when Morn spoke again, interrupting his chain of thought.

"Shall I tell you a story Richard, one of the old tales of my people perhaps?" she said with a hint of mystery to her question that was palatable to him.

The sing-song quality of her voice also snapped him back from whatever strange place his mind had gone. The concepts and ideas he had been grasping at slipped away once more, and he found himself back rooted firmly to the ground.

"Sure," he said, blinking his eyes which suddenly seemed to be watering. He felt a little unsteady, like a man pulled back from a cliff edge. Yet one that had forgotten the cliff existed a moment later.

'*A story… Well, why not?*' He thought to himself still feeling a little shaken.

Somehow unsurprised at Morn's offer. Everyone seemed to want to tell stories in the Passing Place, after all. "Why not?" he added verbally smiling at her, then laying back against the tree, closing his eyes to block out the disturbing view.

"This is an old tale. A tale of the world before, and a tale of the world now, It is a truth and not a truth. But true all the same," said Morn, her voice taking on an oddly bard like quality.

CHAPTER THIRTEEN

The Wolf King of Winter

Once in the land of endless winter, in a cave high in the mountains of Mourning, there slept the king of the wolves, dreaming the dreams of his kin: dreams of flesh, dreams of blood, dreams of the hunt, dreams of the taste of prey on the air. His dreams were ever thus, the dreams of his kith and kin.

Wolf dreams.

The long winters of the world moved on, slow and cold, as the wolf king slept.

Always winter never spring.

Then one dark night on the eve of old years, a strange thing occurred, a thing that had never happened before. A new dream crossed the mind of the sleeping king. A dream of a golden child, bright and beautiful, a new life in the world of winter. And the wolf king's slumbers became uneasy.

In the wolf king's dream the child came before him saying thus:

"I am the new spring dawning, the return of life to the world. Will you welcome me oh king of the wolf folk? Will you join me for the last feast of winters passing? Will you welcome the dawning of new days?"

The wolf king stirred uneasy in his dreaming and knew a strange fear he had never known before, so long had he slept within his caves, through all the endless wintering of the world.....

"What is this spring of which you speak child?" the wolf king snarled in his dream, but the golden child was gone once more......

Unease remained and in it woke the wolf king.

In fear, in anger, in a rage he could not name.

The wolf king of winter howled in the darkness against the coming spring.

The wolf king gathered his pack: the alphas with their glistening teeth, the young males full of raw hungers, the queens and ladies of the wolf kings court, as vicious and deadly as any male, even the cubs, playful as they are in there snapping of bright new teeth.

The wolf king's great howl echoing through the

mountains drew them all to him.

The great pack, the pack of all packs gathered, and he did speak to them of his dream.

"We must seek out this golden child, this creature called the new spring, and we must rend the flesh from its bones, suck deep upon its marrow, that we shall sleep once more in our winter. Go forth with tooth and claw, go forth with the guile and cunning, go forth with the fury of the howl, seek him, find him and devour" ....

And so, the great pack set forth to search for the golden child of the new spring. They hunted in the high places, delved deep in the ravines, sought him in the valleys and across the glaciers, And all the while the great howls filled the air, taking word back through the echoes to the wolf king's lair, where he awaited word of the golden child called Spring Dawning.

And the wolf king waited in his lair for the night air to bring him word. As he waited fear grew in his bowels, and more voices fell each night from the great howling, till the echoes slowly fled the Mountains of Mourning in the world of winter and his pack seemed to dwindle, to vanish from the night, and his dreams were again uneasy.....

Once more the golden child appeared in the wolf king's dreams. Once more he spoke unto him.

"*Hear me king of wolves, for I am Spring come to bring forth new life and the end of winter, join me in the final feasting of the long dark. Send not your people to slay me, Wolf King. I am the renewal of life to all who come unto me,*"

In the dream the child opened forth its arms and

there was the brightest of lights, which dazzled the wolf king and drove him fleeing in his dream......

The wolf king howled for his pack once more, but none answered his call. The mountains stayed silent of all but the echoes of his howl, slowly dwindling away.....

As morning came, the wolf king determined to seek out the golden child himself, to rend it with teeth and claw, to eat of its flesh and lap of its blood.

"If there is a feasting to be had, then let it be mine," he howled out across in his mountains.

So off he set, crossing the howling peaks, the jagged teeth of stone. Through fields of snow, laid thick for countless days. Past caves where the echoes of the lost ones still sounded. Across ice bridges, over yawning chasms, across the frozen desserts and the flowing ice; down, always down, out of the mountains, following the glaciers with their gnashing teeth that bite so deep. Under grey skies, the cold wind his only companion.

So stalked the king of the wolves and his hunger grew.

Time passed as it is oft to do and his journey aft long did take him beyond his mountain land. But his howl yet remained unanswered and within him his fear grew, while the air itself around him grew restless, with scents not old but new.

Ice, turned water, snow gave way to dew. While new sounds filled his ears, of water running free, the dripping of the melt, and his fears grew greater still.

When at last he came upon a great plain, an

expanse of melting snow, from which shoots of colour reached out from frozen ground. Little shoots of green that broke the icy white. All around him, new life, bursting slowly through.

The wolf king's winter was dying slowly, and he knew not what he should do.

In the last he came upon them, his lost abandoned pack, lazing on green carpets of freshly grown grass. He howled his rage upon them, but they answered not his call.

Then in the sky, he saw him, the golden child from his dreams. Bright was the golden glow about him. He hung in the sky and warmth flowed from him, melting snow and ice alike.

The wolf king saw his folly: The child within his dream, the ending of winter, the coming of the spring, the golden child before him, was the great and golden sun.

The wolf king howled his fury, gnashed in hatred with his teeth, padded in great circles of hunger, raging at the sky

He leapt a biting, high into the sky, his great jaws snapping, howling at the sun.

But no matter how high he lept. He snapped only at the air. While the sun shone down upon him, So bright was its glare.

His enemy did not taunt him, only bathed him in its glow, but the wolf King was not placated, his rage did only grow.

He leapt higher still, snapping with his jaws, but always only fall back, crashing to the valley floor.

He howled in rage and frustration, then beat a hasty retreat, returned unto the mountains. Once more in winters sleep.

And in his dream he plots one day to eat his foe the sun.

He sleeps now, ever still, till the last feasting be done.

CHAPTER FOURTEEN

Existential Meanderings of Gaia

As the tale came to an end the strangeness of her voice while she told it faded away. In the end, she smiled down at him from the brow of the tree, where she still sat. Her eyes which had been distant for the telling seemed to focus back upon him. She had a strange look on her face, as if she had forgotten he was even there for a few moments while she told the tale.

In truth, the incongruity of her little tale made scant sense to him, yet it had a genuineness about it all the same. For all its mythical nature, it seemed to hold truths within it, like all myths, no matter how strange. It had seemed to Richard it was built on a grain of truth no matter how small, though he would be damned before he could figure out what that truth may be.

Myths had always held a fascination for Richard, those weird stories told in every culture. Attempts to give meaning to the world far from understood and the darkness the shadows held. An idea which had resonances for Richard himself and the faces seen in the dark.

Why, he asked himself, should this strange tale which Morn's people told be any different?

It certainly had all the aspects of the mythic, perhaps even echoes of some old Norse legends. Richard vaguely remembered something about a wolf in those too,. Fenris? Fenrir? He could not remember precisely, though one, he suspected, was the anglicised version of the other. The great wolf who slept in the darkest of caves until it would wake to devour Odin in the Ragnarok or something like that. Wasn't Odin a sun god allegory in the oldest tales, driving back the ice giants before he fathered the gods of Asgard? He could not remember exactly, but Norse myth more than most was multilayered he knew, older myths blending into newer ones. Even now the old myths blended with comic book tales and movies, finding new forms that held within them a grain the oldest of tales. He found himself wondering if the myth of Morn's people was some offshoot of those, and for a fleeting moment, he pondered further, if perhaps it was one of the roots.

He found himself wondering once more about

the strange green haired girl who looked so young, yet had such old eyes, with her strange ways of talking, and stranger still ways of thinking. Where was she from? When it came to it, who was she?

He pondered all this in the silence that felt between them after Morn told her tale. A few moments past of her staring, slightly expectantly at him, before he realised he was being somewhat rude and his English good manners asserted themselves.

"Thank you Morn," he said simply, not quite sure what else to say.

"You're welcome, Richard, Piano Man..." she replied. Leaving the kind of pause which says there is more to say.

He watched her eyes, trying to fathom for a moment what made her tell him that particular story in the first place. He had gotten the impression when she suggested telling him the tale that it was one she thought would mean something to him. Yet if that was so, he could not grasp what that was supposed to mean.

The pause she left hanging just reinforced that impression. He thought for a moment he should just ask her about it, but was not sure what to say, so the pause stayed hanging, while she tilted her head to one side in that odd way she had.

The strange tilt of the head, which seemed to punctuate his conversations with the green haired girl, always made him think she was trying to observe him from a different angle. The way you might look at a piece of modern art in a gallery and try and work out what the sculptor actually had in mind when he made it. In some desperate attempt to see past the first impression you had of a shapeless carbuncle, to the artistic merit underneath.

Richard, in all honesty, had little time for modern art. Carrie, however, used to drag him to galleries all the time. As it was in part a recompense for dragging her to small time gigs with crappy New York bands, he seldom complained, besides which she always managed to see the strangest things in works of art. She always looked at things with different eyes to his own, and would make the strangest of observations.

The momentary thoughts of Carrie must have shown on his face, As Morn's smile dropped away to be replaced with one of concern. Her face taking on a look of seriousness once more, though thankfully holding none of the anger it had held earlier.

Though something about that look of concern and worry seemed unnatural in a face that was normally filled with such an easy smile.

"None of us have answers to all your questions, Richard." She said, at last, breaking his chain of recollection.

"Esqwith, well she just is, like the stream in the Forest, the wind in the leaves, or a glade you come across in the dark woods where the sunlight bursts through. She just is… it's not something you can question… But I think what you need to understand is what she is, at heart, is also a place of refuge. For all of us here."

"She's a place where you can take the time you

Passing Place 275

need. A place you can rest as you pass through. She's also a place for stories around the campfire. A place to touch the ground for a while. Rest up and put your troubles on one side. You see?"

He nodded, though he didn't see at all. Not to any degree that helped anyway. His face, he had no doubt, gave him away, and Morn gave him a weak smile of consolement before she continued.

"Ever culture, in every world has stories. We all tell them, it's how we learn about the world. How we explain the world to our children. How we gain understanding, do you see? No matter what other differences people have, they all tell stories. Sometimes to explain the world, sometimes to explain themselves, and Esqwith, well, whatever else she is, she is a place for telling them."

"Perhaps she's the best place to tell them. Perhaps she just likes to hear them, and created herself as a place for people to sit and tell them. Who knows? It makes as much sense and any other theory I have heard, and she isn't telling anyone."

"I don't know why this is, or what Esqwith is. I just know that when I needed a refugee she was here. She offered a place for me and Father Beach when we needed one. For which we are both grateful, will always be grateful."

"And Esqwith offered this to you? This refuge?" he asked. It was far from the first question that had occurred to him as she spoke. But he latched on to it anyway. Not entirely sure how he felt about what she had said, he could see it had a grain of truth to it. The same kind of grain of truth a myth might hold. But there had to be more to it all. He was sure of it, but if Morn had actually spoken to Esqwith, that might explain so much…

"Of course not," she said laughing not entirely without mockery, the seriousness falling away and her smile returning. "It was the cat who found us of course. It's always the cat, Richard, you know that by now I am sure."

"That's not an answer, I mean cats don't talk do they?" he replied a slight note of discord to his voice. He was not angry as such, just confused, more confused that he had been to start with, in all honesty. From the look of concern which crossed Morn's brow, she knew that and took no offence at his words.

"Now that's a strange thing to say, Richard. You know it's not true, you have heard her after all." She chided, before adding with a half-smile, "It's like like telling me trees don't have feelings,"

"They…" he started, only to stop himself as a whisker of a dark look crossed her face.

"I would be careful with the words you choose just now, Piano Man. We may be offended." The blaze of green was in her eyes once more for a fleeting second. She swung down to the ground, landing heavily as if to stamp her feet at him with a bout of petulance.

"Sorry, I mean, it's just…" He struggled to find the right words, not wishing to upset her further. It did not matter that he knew trees were just trees, she felt differently, he knew that now. He edged his next words carefully. "See, where I come from, trees really are just trees you know. I mean there are people who say they have feelings, hippies and the like, and I used to send money to save the rainforest." He added the last as her anger seemed to be growing. He felt the conversation getting beyond him once again. But vainly he tried to rally.

"I supported the campaign to save the redwoods as well... I mean, I like trees, you know... They're important to the world and everything. It's just, well, *feelings*, no one really thinks they have feelings. They're just trees."

"They are never just trees, Richard, never. They are the focal points for the life force which binds the world spirit together. They tie life to the world, your world, my world, to all worlds. They feel in ways beyond your imagining. They are the very heart of Gaia. The heart of the world. They are never, ever, just trees." There was a fury behind her words, a fury and an intense belief that he found impossible to counter. True or not, she believed it was true, with all the violent passion she could muster.

In truth, he found himself intimidated by her fury.

"Okay, okay, time out. I don't understand this, but I believe you do," he said, not sure if he should just walk away before he made things worse. But his desire to understand more about the Passing Place, and about the woman before him, was stronger than the desire to walk away.

"You're right, you don't," she snapped, in no way placated.

"Okay, look, trees have feelings beyond the ken of mortal man. I can get that. I can understand that you believe that. I can get on board with what you're saying. It Gaia, the world, everything, the life force of the planet," he said quoting some old hippie nonsense he heard somewhere once. In the vain hope that he could get the conversation back under control. Morn continued to sieve at him however, so he changed tack completely and asked. "But I can hear the cat talk. I mean, how's that work? How does a cat talk?"

"*I find, generally, I use words,*" a new voice, dripping with sarcasm, said at his feet.

Morn laughed, her laugh like a running stream in the forest. All her anger flowing away with that laugh, and she became once more her happy go lucky self.

"She has you there," she said and started to giggle.

Richard, however, felt his own anger rising once more. He was not sure if it was the sarcastic nature of the cat or the way Morn was now laughing at him, but his frustration with the lack of straight answers boiled over. Suppressing the urge to make an angry retort he turned to stalk off towards the kitchen door. He felt tired as well as angry, and bear headed he stopped half way, having lost the battle with his own will. He turned to snap back some snide remark, but as he did so he took in the emptiness of the sky once more, and felt a sense of awe and fear come over him.

Then he saw it, hanging in the emptiness of the void, a single red star. Which he knew on some base level could not be a star. Whatever it was however, it seemed to grow before his eyes. There was something mesmerising about it, the way it seemed to pulse and wane, yet continue to grow.

"What is that?" he asked, almost absently, not quite registering the fear it inspired within him. He could feel a sense of wrongness about it. A wrongness greater than the wrongness of the void itself. Though he lacked any point of reference from which to explain why it felt so. It made the great emptiness of the void all the worse for hanging within it.

It felt the same way the dream of the corridor had felt--real and unreal at the same time, yet he had just dreamed that, he was sure. The corridor had not been real, just a bad dream, a nightmare…

"*'That's because it is, But not yours*," the cat's words came back to him. A shiver running down the back of his neck as he thought of the words. The Crimson bleed in the sky drew out the memory. That same sickening feeling in the pit of his stomach he had felt that night clawed at his guts.

"But that was a dream…" he heard himself whisper.

The thing in the void was no dream. He was certain of that much. Certain too that it terrified him, and yet while strange seemed so familiar to him now. He had seen it before, out of the corner of his eye, so many times, it seemed to haunt him.

He could taste something metallic in the air, like burnt iron. The hairs on the back of his neck felt ridged, as if there was a static charge in the air. There was something about the way the colours in the blackness of the void seemed to swirl around the "not" star, as if they were being drawn into it as it grew.

Consumed by it, if you could consume the void.

It was becoming, he thought, while not understanding the thought at all. Yet that's exactly what it was doing, becoming, and in doing so it threatened to overwhelm his thoughts, his everything. It was growing, and would consume him and everything else. Yet he could not pull his gaze from it.

Morn came alongside him. Out of the corner of his eye, he could see her face mirrored his. She could feel it, too: The sense of dread. It was like the way hot days become muggy and ever more humid as a storm approaches. The air becomes charged with the expectation of a storm. A storm which promised violence and terror. Primal powers unleashed, chaos at its absolute.

Morn opened her mouth about to speak. But her words were lost to her, much like his own. His too, he could not speak, his throat dry to the point of arid. He knew then he had felt it before, this presence in the void. Even before when he first gazed upon it, the menace it held, this something in the darkness.

This something…

Red…

Time seemed to have no meaning, nothing seemed to have meaning. He opened his mouth to scream, but no sound came.

Then the cat spoke to them…

"*It's a bad thing, but now is not the time. It would be better to not notice It right now,*" she said, before she stalked off towards the kitchen door.

Richard and Morn remained, staring up at the strange red glow in the blackness. Though somehow after the cat's words it seemed to lose its grip upon them.

Moments past, which could have been ice ages.

Then it seemed to fade before them, becoming indistinct, though Richard knew it was still there.

Yet at the same time, he became sure it wasn't. It was like a mirage in reverse, a real thing becoming indistinct. Slipping away, its grip on his soul released once more.

A moment more passed.

"Why are we standing here?" Morn asked, sounding slightly bewildered.

"I don't know," said Richard, who was wondering much the same. Looking for a moment at the inky blackness of the void, which made him feel slightly uneasy, so he turned away from it. He shrugged his shoulders, puzzled and headed back towards the kitchen door. A dry feeling in his mouth that made him feel the urge for a drink, coffee, or something stronger, yes definitely something stronger…

Morn followed him out of the garden a moment afterwards, but not before waving goodbye to her tree…

CHAPTER FIFTHTEEN

Pretensions Afterhours

It was somewhere between late and early, past midnight and still hours from morning. The customers were all gone for the evening, and the bar closed up save for one table in the centre of the room around which they sat.

Richard had worked in bars most of his adult life, playing one gig or another, or waiting tables, or the bar. It was second nature to him, and there was nothing more natural than an after-hours drink with the doors closed. Even here, in Esqwith's Passing Place with the strange collection of oddities that made up its staff, it seemed a perfectly normal concept to him.

He was drinking Jack, neat over ice.

In keeping with the odd collection of individuals around the table was an equally odd collection of drinks.

Sonny was drinking his favourite brandy, out of the right kind of glass, of course, feet up on a spare chair, taking his time and savouring the taste.

Morn sat cross-legged on a bar stool, perched precariously upon it, yet seeming completely comfortable all the same. She was drinking a bright blue high energy drink through a straw. For all it was a soft drink, it seemed to be making her happily drunk all the same, as if sugar had the same effect on her metabolism as alcohol would on anyone else. She swayed a little every now and again, without ever seeming in danger of falling from her perch, and occasionally got into a fit of giggles.

Jolene, the Southern Bell dinner waitress, was drinking a thick vanilla milkshake, with two added shots of Southern Comfort, occasionally injecting her southern drawl into the conversation and words like ' Y'all and 'gonna get'. Added to which she was occasionally winking in an outrageously provocative manner at Grey Man for some reason best known to herself.

Lyal had drunk a couple of beers before making his excuses and disappearing upstairs. It was not till after he left that Richard had noticed the strange frosting on the bottles where his fingers had been.

The cat was curled up on a seat, with a bowl of double cream before her which she occasionally spent a minute or two lapping before curling up once more. She seemed happy to just listen to them talk. Perfectly content, in her feline way, to allow them to take up the room, as long as they did not disturb her.

And finally, oddest of the lot, Grey Man, oblivious to Jolene's flirtations, sat nursing a banana daiquiri, with a slice of orange and a small pink paper umbrella in it. The little burst of colour at odds to his grey demeanour. As ever, he seemed to have a wide smile on his face, as well as an intense fascination with the way the colours swirled in his drink. After hearing the Grey man's tale, Richard had a small incline of what it was he found so fascinating. He found he almost envied grey that sense of wonder.

They had talked a lot, such late night staff lock-in's always led to conversations. They were the usual conversations he would have expected anywhere, for all they had the odd little twists he was coming to expect in the Passing Place. They talked about the odd things customers had done in the bar, or just some of the odd customer's come to that. It was fairly normal fair for such occasions, though odd customers in Esqwith's were a whole new kind of odd.

He wanted to turn the conversations to other things. After the strange talk he had shared with Morn in the garden, he still had so many questions. Though he was now coming to suspect, no one had the answers.

Sonny's protestations in Paris, of being just a doorman, had never really rung true to him at the time. Indeed, their relationship had been a little strained since at first. But later in the cold light of day he had accepted that Sonny was probably being nothing but honest. Despite this, he had found it difficult to fall back into the easy friendship they had shared. A nagging seed of doubt still hung within him.

Morn, however, was a different situation. He found her company confusing at the best of times. Her odd speech patterns and strange way of thinking was not exactly normal and made her hard to follow. If he did not know better, he would have suspected she was not entirely human, come to that. Certainly, she seemed to have some kind of strange overt connection to her tree. Something beyond a mere fascination with nature. Yet he had found himself believing her, when she said she did not understand any more than he did. He envied the ways she seemed to have an easier time in reconciling that all the same. He wondered if perhaps she did not care overly how she had found refuge from whatever she had fled. Only that she had found that refuge, something which he could at least understand.

Certainly, she seemed happy just to be at The Passing Place. He wished he could take so easy a view himself, but the desire to understand it all was all but overwhelming at times. Yet beyond the cook's strange ideas and Grey Man's conviction that this was all some form of heaven, no one seems to have any real explanations at all.

Except, that was, possibly the cat, but how much faith could he put in the words of a small feline. He was having a hard enough time accepting that she could talk as it was, though no one else seemed to struggle much with that concept. Thinking of her as being the font of all wisdom, well that was a stretch too far.

Besides which, he had a niggling feeling that she was not telling him much. Or worse, that things she told him had a habit of melting out of his mind, which was a far from the most pleasant of feelings. Least, for those few moments he could cling to the thought he was forgetting. They never stayed long though. Once he stopped trying to think about something important the cat may have said he found he forgot it entirely. Remembering only there was something he had forgotten.

The worse of which was he knew he was doing so, yet oddly found he accepted it all the same, rather than bearing malice against the cat. He had the strange feeling she was protecting him by making him forget. A concept about which he was not sure how he felt…

"… then he just asked for the dessert menu…" Jolene said, cutting through his self-reflection. He realised, suddenly, everyone but him was laughing, including the cat.

He sighed to himself and made a stab at pretending to laugh, which must have come across as false given the look of annoyance it gained from the waitress. Not wishing to cause offence, he apologised by saying he was miles away and took a sip of his Jack.

"Tell us a story Richard," Morn said to break the momentary tension he had brought to the room.

He shook his head. "I've barely been here five minutes, and not sure I have any."

"Tell us one about you then," Jolene suggested. For a second he thought he saw the slightest touch of vindictiveness in her eye. But he put that down to his baseline paranoia in social gatherings.

"I… I'm not sure…"

"Hell, we don't bite man…" Sonny reassured him. Smiling over his brandy glass as he swirled it.

"I'm just not sure I know any funny stories," he replied with a certain amount of honesty.

"Oh I am sure you could manage…" purred the cat. He wondered if others heard the contribution she made. He knew now others heard her speak at times, but not if they all heard her at once. *"And I for one have been known to bite occasionally,"* she added with a lazy yawn.

Sonny laughed and, as one, they all looked at him with the same kind of knowing looks. Which Richard guessed answered that question.

He took another drink and tried to think of an excuse to get him out of it. He had never been overly fond of telling stories. He never knew where to start, or when to finish. His tendency was to ramble a bit once he started then lose his own thread. He lacked any sense of comic timing for one thing, which always seemed to come so naturally to everyone else.

The moment, however, dragged out, the unfilled silence was begging for someone to fill it. He got the feeling it would have to be him, due in no small part to the expectant looks they were all giving him.

He sighed to himself, fishing about for some story to tell. Band stories were the ones which he knew best. You did not hang around with musicians for long without picking up a few stories worth telling, but generally, only other musicians would understand them. He racked his mind, until a story occurred to him, then found himself smiling as he remembered it.

"Okay, where to start... So a couple or three years back I got a gig playing with this crappy little indie band from the Jersey shore. Asbury Park oddly enough but they were no E-Street band. Anyways the lead singer was a bit on the pretentious side..."

"*Musicians always are.*" The cat purred, her eyes betraying a hint of sarcasm. Morn sniggered light-heartedly, which he took as further confirmation that the others could hear the cats occasionally caustic comments.

He locked eyes with the cat momentarily, then had an odd wave of grief from nowhere. Ridiculous though it seemed, it was the look she was returning him and the words she had chosen. They suddenly reminded him of Carrie, who was always a little dismissive of his musician friends.

He took a drink to hide his unease and topped up his glass before continuing.

"Anyway, the band had started out been called Desolate Stallion..."

"*Pre-tent-ious...*" sneered the cat, though a little playfully it has to be said.

"Well yes, they were, the lead singer in particular as I said. But the sound was good, and they had a few gigs lined up and down the Jersey coast, so it was a paying gig, which made a change at the time. Their old keyboard had left for LA and taken their old name with them. So they were busy trying to find a new one when I joined them."

"Taken their name?" Jolene asked, before slurping away at her alcoholic milkshake, through the over colourful straw.

"Musicians the world over are all the same... They will agonise about a band name more than they will ever agonise about playing the right cords" Sonny chortled, with all the sincerity he could muster, reminding Richard that the doorman had spent a lot of time around the jazz scene in the early twenties... a strange concept he was still coming to terms with.

"You have that right." Purred a voice.

Morn laughed. "I knew this bard once who... never mind." She suddenly looked flushed for a second, then hiccupped. Richard was sure for some reason the flush was Inspired by memories of the bard in question, however.

Richard coughed loudly. "Er, guys, musician here."

They all laughed, but he could feel the warmth in their laughter. It was not directed at him, but with him, and in a moment he found himself laughing along with them.

After a moment or two more had passed Sonny raised his hands. "Sorry man you were saying."

Richard smiled back and continued his story.

"Okay. So anyway there we were, all sitting around in this Jersey bar, can't remember the name of the town. But it was 'Big Mike's Bar'. Or something like that. Never met Mike, but you can probably assume the Hawaiian shirt and gold rings." He said with a smirk on his lips.

"Lyal would be horrified," laughed Jolene, which brought a few more giggles all-round.

"Anyway, so their old ivory tickler had swanned off to LA on a mission to become something big in soundtracks, as I said, and taken '*Desolate Stallion*' with him. He'd bought a domain name, had the Facebook account and all that stuff. And the split was about as amicable as you can get when two people want to kill each other over a girlfriend neither of them had… Can't say I remember the girl's name, but I'd lay pounds to pennies neither could they after a week…"

"That does not make sense, why fight over a girl they could not remember?" Grey Man asked sounding genuinely puzzled.

"Cause it ain't about the girl with some guys, it's about not letting the other guy have her," Sonny said sardonically, a grim expressing crossing his face for a moment. Richard was reminded again of the doorman's story, and how he had come to grief far worse than losing a gig because of a man who would not let go.

"Doesn't she have a say in it at all?" Jolene said in the kind of tone which expressed her opinion more than her words ever could.

"Only say that matters…" Morn growled in support.

"I agree.." Richard said quickly, both because he did and because he did not want to be the cause of another argument.

'*You better...*' said a feline voice.

"Still makes no sense..." Grey Man muttered looking more confused than ever.

"Oh, Honey, men are just idiots, don't you worry Y'all about it..." Jolene said, smiling at the monochrome one, in a way which Richard was sure would add to the man's confusion.

Richard, deciding that digression was the better part of valour, waited for the general hub-bubble to calm down before he continued his story. Not wanting to add fuel to the fire he passed on the opportunity to explain further about the argument between the ex-keyboard player and the singer, and moved on.

"Anyway, this all left the band with the problem of what to call itself..."

"New names can't be that tricky," Grey said in such a matter of fact fashion it brought unintended laughter from everyone, which eased the tension away.

"Yer well, the name would not have been that bad if it wasn't for all the flyers they'd had designed for the tour. Before you ask, if there is one thing musicians hate more than pick new names it paying people to design new flyers. No one ever wants to spend the cash. Which was the source of the problem. They'd had the fliers all made up, posters too. And the artist said he would change the name for free, make a sticker to go over the poster but any more than that was going to cost them. Which made picking a new name all the harder."

"I don't see why?" Morn asked with genuine puzzlement.

"Well, the problem was, there are only so many names you could come up with that fit the poster. And believe me, we tried to come up with them all. *'Abandoned Pony', 'Forsaken Mount', 'Bleak Mare'* all sorts. God, we were at it for hours. The drummer even brought a thesaurus, though he was a drummer, so I am surprised he knew how to use it."

Sonny laughed at this, though the others looked bemused. The doorman coughed. "Sorry, drummer jokes, they always get me, I know too many of them."

"Drummer jokes?" Morn inquired.

"Yer you know. What do you call an idiot who hangs around with musicians all day?" Sonny began.

"A drummer," Richard finished, laughing.

"What do you call a drummer who breaks up with his girlfriend?" Sonny asked.

"Homeless," Richard said still smiling. The others meanwhile, were looking on bemused.

"How do you know when the stage is level?" Sonny chortled.

'*The drool is coming out of both sides of his mouth at the same time,*' the cat purred. They all looked at her with a modicum of disbelief.

'*What, I can't tell bad jokes too?*' She bemoaned, then commenced a long drawn out yawn that became a stretch.

There was more laughter and Morn did a turn at the bar and brought them all refills. Once she returned and resettled in her seat she asked Richard to finish the story.

"Okay, okay, so we had all these names, and none of them was much good. Then Carrie turned up to meet me, and not in the best of moods I should add, this was since I was supposed to meet her from college an hour before, but I'd lost track of time. She was a little put out."

"Carrie?" Jolene asked smiling.

"My wife." He replied.

"You're married?" asked the waitress.

"I was, she's... she passed away." The question had caught him off guard. He had not really been thinking about it when he said her name. It was a story with Carrie in it. Something he had not even considered that when he started to tell it. A wave of grief swept through him as it always did. It was less painful than he expected all the same. He was almost surprised how little it hurt to mention her name. He wondered fleetingly if the congenial atmosphere made it more natural somehow to talk about her. The wave of guilt that followed was mild and irrational, as he knew. After all, he had a right to enjoy himself without feeling he was betraying her memory. All the same, it made him momentarily uncomfortable.

"I am sorry for your loss," the Southern Belle said with a heartfelt smile and a tone which suggested she meant every word. Others too showed genuine compassion, except the Grey Man who seemed to be trying hard to understand all the same. A passing thought occurred to Richard that perhaps the Grey really did not understand love and loss in that way. He did not know whether to pity him for that, or think him lucky.

"It's okay." He stumbled, taking a drink to hide his embarrassment. He was always uncomfortable with strangers offering sympathy for Carrie's death. It was the expected thing to do he knew, he did it himself. But it always had a hint of obligation to it that made it seem an empty gesture. For all the warmth of his friend's words.

"Anyway," he continued, "so Carrie came into the bar and listened to us all arguing for five minutes before she pointed out that the horse in the artwork looked more nervous than anything else, rather than desolate or any of the other words we had come up with. 'A tremulous equine if ever there was one.' She said in fact."

"Let me guess, that's what they called the band?" Sonny hazarded.

Richard smiled and raised his glass in a toast to the doorman. "Yep, '*Tremulous Equine*' a bloody ridiculous name for a ridiculous band. The lead singer loved it."

"*Like I said Lex was pretentious*" the cat purred. Stretching on the table top.

"That's what Carrie always said. That Lex was the most pretension musician she had ever met, and that's out of a great many pretensions." Richard said laughing.

They all laughed, and in the warmth of the laughter, Richard forgot the feelings of guilt and sorrow, remembering instead, his wife's contribution to Rock and Roll history. Not that there was a great deal of history made. The band had lasted six months before he and two other members split. He could not exactly remember the reason why, though if pushed he suspected it was because of the endless arguments between the drummer, who could not take a joke, and the lead singer, who kept making them.

It was much later, once the bar had been cleared and they had all made their own way to their respective beds that Richard was lying awake staring at the ceiling, and it occurred to him that the cat had said *'Lex'*.

It was a disturbing revelation. He tried to think back over the conversation and remember if he had told them the singer's name at any point. He was sure he had not. Yet the cat had known it all the same. Lex Uthar, a pretentious name made up by a guy called Tony who thought it was cool. But she had said it, known it. How could she possibly have known it?

The thought was troubling in its absurdity,

He must have mentioned the singer's name at some point in the conversation, he reconciled. Otherwise, how would the cat know it?

Troubled, and trying to square a circle, he drifted off to sleep.

CHAPTER SIXTEEN

Dylan on the Keyboard

'Now there is an oddly interesting thing to see' the cat purred from the top of the piano.

Richard looked up and followed the feline's gaze to look quizzically in the direction of the bar, in part just to see what had caused her to break a two-hour long silence. He was, therefore, mildly disappointed to see there was little which he could consider unusual. Though what could be considered unusual in Esqwith's was, as ever, relative to its own peculiar version of normality.

"I don't see anything special," Richard replied anyway, while playing the last few bars of '*Just like a woman'* before rolling into another Dylan standard. He had been playing Dylan songs for the last hour or so, for no particular reason, at least none he could name. Mostly it was just because he felt like doing so, though he was starting to suspect it was a dislike of Zimmerman's American folk musings that was causing the cat to be unusually silent for so long. She had started to give him the occasionally bored look bordering on distaste whenever he started yet another of Dylan's back catalogue.

The cat wrinkled its nose at him with mild indifference and stretched herself archly before settling down onto her front legs. She remained staring lazily towards the bar. This may have been just to avoid looking at him, or, for that matter, another register of complaint about his choice of music. Or just her way of directing his attention to the bar because she wanted him to see something. But the most likely reason was, she was in a huff.

Richard was becoming accustomed to applying such mild moodiness to the cat's behaviour. He was sure she expected him to understand everything she said and thought without explanation. Therefore she took great offence if he did not. It was an irritating habit he had noticed in the feline.

'*You're just not looking correctly dear, but I am sure it will come to you,*' she purred. He was not sure when she started using that particular term of affection towards him. Not that he had dwelt upon it over much, but when he first realised she was doing so, he had become a little perturbed. The last person to call him 'Dear' had been Carrie.

Once he got used to the cat doing so, however, he was surprised how little grief it inspired. It felt right in some way that the cat called him '*Dear*', though he could not explain why.

What he found more surprising when he thought about it was how easily he had come to accept the cat as a person.

Shrugging his shoulders, and trying to avoid being obvious, he kept half an eye on the bar while he played.

He was, however, mildly annoyed by the smugness of the cat's tone and he still could not see much out of the ordinary for Esqwith's.

There was a business man on the end stool trying to strike up a conversation with Morn unsuccessfully. True he had ice blue hair, and his suit was of a bizarrely angular cut, but that hardly counted for odd in The Passing Place. The vacant stool next to him had been co-opted for his briefcase, which again was hardly unusual, though it was perhaps a little rude of him.

A couple occupied the next two stools, more interested in each other than their drinks. One of them was dressed like a nineteen twenty's society girl, complete with a pale blue cloche hat. While her partner wore a sixties style mini skirted dress that was straight out of Mary Quant's studio. They were happily engrossed in each other to the point where they were ignoring their surroundings completely. Twenties Girl was slipping an absent-minded hand across Sixties Girl's knee in a way which would have scandalised society in her time.

Richard was polite enough to snap his gaze back to the piano keys when he noticed, rather than become a voyeur. Instead, he focused on playing another song from Dylan's back catalogue.

After the opening bars, he flicked his gaze back up and focused on the other customers at the bar. There was a man in the heavy fur coat, so heavy that he must have been far too warm. But odd choices in garments were hardly strange in the bar. A heavy fur coat was almost mundane.

Another stool or two down along the bar sat a regular, the little emo girl, in gothic regalia, with the killer curly eye shadow and a passion for Egyptian costume jewellery. She was drinking something fruity with a pink paper umbrella in it, which seemed altogether too cheery for who she was, though he could not tell you why he thought that. She came in for an hour or so every few days, smiled a lot and always seemed to know everyone by name. She always seemed perky and was happy to say hello to everybody. Oddly, though, for some reason she made elderly customers look very nervous.

Further along, a couple of Asian gentlemen were having a Saki drinking contest with rules that seemed to involve quoting anime classics badly. One of them had a Godzilla lives backpack leaning against the bar. They seemed to be yapping excitedly to themselves in-between shots, but loud though they were they did not seem to be disturbing anyone over much. At least no more than the nun in the blue habit with the guitar case, who was disagreeing with Lyal about something or other while drinking stout from a straight glass.

Richard sighed to himself, nothing unusual there, he thought and started to sing quietly along to his own accompaniment, coming in somewhere near the middle of the song he was playing.

"-- ain't my cup of meat."

"Everybody's out the trees, feeding pigeons all under the limb."

"But when Quinn the Eskimo get here..."

Then the proverbial penny dropped.

Richard shot his gaze back to the bar, in the middle of which, between Goth girl and the four decades displaced couple, stood an Inuit in full traditional dressed.

It was the man he had mistakenly thought was wearing a fur coat he had only half noticed earlier. A large harpoon was leaning against the bar. It was the heavy seal fur that formed his hood that made him seem just a heavily overdressed customer originally, perhaps someone who had just arrived from the middle of a hard winter somewhere. Richard was not sure how he had missed the harpoon at first glance.

'The pigeon's gonna run to him' the cat purred, filling in the next line, then with all due sarcasm she inquired, *'Caught up, at last, did we?'* She flicked her tail by way of exclamation.

"Okay... So there is an Inuit in the bar. I am not sure if that counts as odd though around here," Richard replied, while deciding at the same time not to continuing singing along to the tune. He did not feel entirely comfortable doing so, and was suddenly unsure how he came to be playing that song in the first place.

'*Purrrhaps, but what's remarkable is how he is adding ice to his drink, wouldn't you say,.*' the cat purred. Something in her tone reminded him of a teacher conversing with a slow student, which he found irritating, partly because it was another reminder of someone else who used to remind him of the same thing.

Richard, his attention drawn to him, watched as the Inuit chipped at the ice frosting his harpoon. Using what looked like a claw or tooth of some kind, way too big to have been easily parted from its previous owner. Richard's first guess would have been a polar bear, but it seemed too long for that. 'Walrus perhaps' he mused.

The fragments of ice had the occasional opaque reddish tint to them. With each blow of the tooth claw thing, a few shards would drop into the glass below, or scatter upon the bar around it.

Morn was giving the Inuit a withering look whenever the ice hit the wood of the bar. She would probably have been more forgiving of his mild eccentricity if the ice bucket had not been in such easy reach.

"Hum… Well that is unusual I guess," Richard replied trying to sound dismissive. Though the truth was he felt unduly fascinated by the bloody ice.

'*He has a tale to tell you, and purrrhaps it has a lesson for you. I think you should take a break and join him for a drink,*' the cat said, with a tone that had a suggestion of mild instance, then she added almost as an afterthought, '*You may want to add your own ice though.*'

Richard played the last couple of bars and

closed the piano lid. He had come to realise that when the cat told him someone had a tale to tell, it was more of an instruction than a suggestion. An order even.

Sure he could ignore her, but she would be huffy with him for hours if he did, and there are few creatures in all creation as capable of a good huff as a cat.

Also because of whatever strange link she had to the ever elusive Esqwith, she always knew when there was something the bar wanted him to do. Or perhaps it was simply that she herself wanted to steer him into certain conversations. What the cat or Esqwith's motive could be for doing so was beyond Richard. Any more than he could understand why he was there in the first place.

Morn's idea that the bar was a place of stories and for stories had struck him as a polite fiction, though he had no doubt she believed it so. It did not make any more sense than anything else he had been told. Yet it didn't make any less sense either. And at the same time, if he was honest, he was starting to believe that stores were somehow at the core of it all. It irked him that he did not understand, all the more because he was sure there must be something to understand in the first place. Morns blind acceptance and fatalism was something he could not blindly accept.

Equally, he didn't like being herded into a conversation either. It stirred up a stubborn side of him, one that wanted to stamp its feet and refuse to blindly follow instructions. That kernel of punk rebellion which had driven him to cross the pond seeking the dream of the New York indie scene nagged at him still on occasion.

Despite this, he had arrived at the conclusion that when the cat wanted him to go listen to someone, it was simpler just to go along with the strange diversions than argue against doing so.

Perhaps there was a point to it all. One he was missing, that was for certain. It was, however, hardly the first time in his life he had felt a little lost and driven by the behest of others.

He decided that he may as well take a break all the same. And he lost nothing by listening to a story if one happened to be told. So he closed the piano lid and arose from his stool, feeling his back cramp slightly and the familiar ache in his fingers.

'Besides that's probably enough Dylan for a while' he thought to himself in a voice that seemed remarkably similar to that of the cat.

It occurred to him for a moment, as he made his way to the bar, that it was just as possible the reason for her suggestion was motived by a desire to stop him playing Dylan songs for a while. That said though the coincidence that he had been playing the Mighty Quin at the time seemed mildly unlikely all the same.

Nodding to Morn for a drink, he seated himself next to the Inuit and said hello. The strange man looked at him for a long moment saying nothing. There was none of the usual idle chatter, which led inevitably to a story. Instead, after a short time, the man began to speak.

Richard knew with an odd certainty that he was not hearing the man speak English. He knew that he understood what was being said only because of the magic of Esqwith's. Something ingrained within the walls of the place, making him hear the tale in words he understood. It was disconcerting all the same, yet less so than he had a right to expect.

The language had all the wrong patterns, more like a chant than a spoken tongue. Something in the way it was spoken reminded him of reading Beowulf in high school, the ancient Anglo-Saxon saga poem, which had been half sung half spoken by the skalds of old. He remembered how even in its translations the tone seemed all wrong for English. The Inuit's chant like tale had the same oddities of structure. It was not meant to be understood in English. Yet he understood it all the same for all its quirks.

He felt that selfsame strangeness come over him as the tale was told. Just as the gunslinger's tale had tasted of sawdust and desert air. Or Grey man's made the world fall into monotone. But he accepted it without trying to fight it this time. Allowing himself to slip into the tale.

So as the Inuit told his story Richard found himself lost himself in a world of ice, wind, and snow.

He felt the air cool around him, and listened.

CHAPTER SEVENTEEN

Weaver of Tears

The cross carriers came
Taught us of the good man who died for us
The priests of the Christ God
They talk to us of the father, of the son, of the spirit
They talk of they who are three but one
They read from their book of stories
Of the water that became wine
Of the bush that burned but did not burn
Of the loaves and fishes that feed the many
Of things that could not be but were

They tell us our beliefs are nothing
Superstitions of fools
Things that cannot be and aren't
The priests of the Christ God tell us of salvation
That we must put the old ways aside
Cling not to them
But the preachers of Rome do not know the great white as we do
So my people hold to the old ways and the new
Honouring both
Finding the path between

On the seventh day, we go to the church of the cross
We sing their songs
We pray their prayers
Venerate the Christ who died
He who returned
But at night we gather in the round house
Breathe the shaman's smoke
Chant to the spirits of the great white for their protection

The Cross men's bible say.
'*You will know no god but me*',
But the spirits are not gods
They are the wind
They are the ice
They are the Anirniit
Their wrath is great
We must placate Sedan, the whale
For we hunt her children with our harpoons and nets
Least she will take her children and hide them from us
For the people will starve without fish and seals
We must placate Anguta, who is death

He who will take us to the underworld
Lest we keep our peace with him in song and chant
We must placate Agloolik of the sharp ice teeth
Lest she bites our boats and sinks them
Offer smoke up to Aningan the moon spirit
When he chases away his brother the sun
The people venerated the spirits of the great white
As we have since the first days
The shamans teach of the spirits around us
Those who live with us
Watch us
Ever hungry
Their anger is mighty
The people fear them
The shaman teaches us of our people
The spirits who live in the frozen land
The great white is harsh
Our people survive
We listen well to the stories
We know the truth that dwells within them

When I was young
A child of the people
The shamans told of Agnooka
Mistress of Ice
She who lives in her frozen home
Far to the north
Holding back glaciers formed of her tears
Weaving them into diamonds
Least they roll over the world
Sacrifice of last great chief of the people
She was his daughter
Most beautiful among us
Offered to the great white
To hold back the rivers of ice
His daughter for the sake of the world
She is honoured still by my people

Sacrificed so they could prosper
She grows bitter
Angry each winter
The ice grows
Till she forgives the people again
Her anger thaws
The people must forget her not
We must remember her in song and praise
Least one day her anger will consume the world
Agnooka of the ice
Weaver of tears
Beautiful as fresh snow
Cruel as hail
Forgiving as summer
Sacrifice of the people

The shaman tells her tale
In chant and song
In the smoking fires of their yurts
The old women of the tribes tell of her also
The tales are different
Told for women in the mid-winter nights
A story of perfidy and arrogance of men
A warning against fathers
A warning against husbands
A warning against love struck boys
A tale well told
Passed from mother to daughter
Men folk cannot know
But I know
How the tale is told

Another daughter of the people
Like unto the world as brief summer
Eyes of grey blue like a coming storm sky
Eyes of promised tempests
Hair was light where the people's was dark

Skin was pale as the sea ice
Alilean of the grey-blue eyes
And I did love her

I wished to meet her in the wedding hut
When the people feast summers mid
But no great hunter I
Nor fishermen of bountiful skill
No wealth in skins
No sledge or Huskies
My worth was short of others suitors

As children
We ran together on the ice
Fought children's wars with balls of snow
Learned together of the world
In the schools of the cross men
Learned together lessons of the land
From the elders of the people
In the schools which have no walls
Where books are spoken
We laughed and had joy between us
For the years of the child
Closeness born of youthful joy
Between us then there was
The years of the child slipped past
In time I longed for her in other ways
Ways not those of childhood
Closeness between us slipped away
Feelings which I could not name
Within me grew
A distance born of fear between us
I grew distant
Knowledge of my lacking
Pushed her away
As I grew to want her closer
I wished to speak of marriage

Of the joys of husband and wife
Of children to come and a long life shared
But I dare not
While others courted her with wealth and words
Words I could not speak
In fear of my own foolishness
Her eyes haunted me
The ghost of friendship
Eyes with anger kept me silent
Glances that once were full of laughter
Stares of longing and regret

Childhood passes
Responsibilities come
In the great white no man supports one who does not support himself
Saving the elders who have earned respect from the people in their long lives
A man must fish, hunt or buy from those that do with other tasks
Parents smile and push children from the door
The years of being cared for pass
The cross men marked the passage from boy to man
Confirmation, acceptance and rebaptism into the Christ man's church
The shamans mark that passage it in the questing hut
On a summer night while the sun burned low
Into the darkness of the shaman's yurt I go

The smoke inside is heavy
Your mind swims seeking the spirits for guidance
Tremble in fear did I before the hut
Inside fear becomes acceptance, longing
Stripped to the waist in the heat of the hut
I knelt and inhaled deeply

Of the Grey green smoke billowing
Shadows dancing in the firelight
More shadows than there should have been
Dancing on those walls
The shadows of the spirits with us
The shaman chant the words of ritual
Half lost words, meaning nothing and all
The language of the people in times long past
When we walked closer to the spirits
He paints my face from the bowl I helped him prepare
Seal grease mixed with blood
A hare snared with wolf gut string
Ocean and land bound together in the shaman's bowl
With my spit and semen
He paints the spirals of life on my flesh
The waves of the sea on my forehead
The three lines of the land across my chest
The squalls of the wind on each arm
He pulls the Christian talisman from my neck
This is the place of the spirits
The great white
One who died on a cross in a hot land can help you here
The old ways are strong here
The new religion has no meaning
Still, he chants the old words
My head swimming from the smoke
From a second bowl he feeds me
Powders ground into greasy fish guts
Hard to swallow
It burns my throat
My guts churning within
The shadows on the walls take form
Dance and weave in the firelight
The words he chants are joined by shadow words

Other voices
Echoes grow deep
Within those walls
Awareness passes
I forget once more

The shaman walked around me
Circling slowly
Shaking medicine bag and rattle stick
Pushing my head over fire
I breathe deeply of the smoke
He circles again
The world shrinking
Becoming the smoke around me
Choking, cloying water to my eyes
His chants go on
His voice is as far from me as
Names to bring the spirits close
To guide the boy to manhood
Anguta,,,,,,
Sedna,,,,,,,,
Akna,,,,,,,
Agloolik,,,,,,
Pinga,,,,,,
Aningan,,,,,,,,
Qailertrtang,,,,,
Agnooka,,,,,,, Weaver of Tears
Her name fills my mind
I call out her name, and know not why
The voice is not mine
The words of the shaman lost to her calling
A new voice filled the air
"Come to me,"

Across leagues of ice and snow
I see a path
To prove my love

Find wealth to spare
The Weaver of Tears
Agnooka
To steal her diamonds
Grant me fame
Grant me wealth
To win she whom I love
With blue-grey eyes of storms
To bring her a single diamond
Prove my devotion
It was clear to me
As nothing else has ever been
Clear in the smoke
To win my heart's desire
I had but listen to the weaver of tears
I heard her again
The world spun around me
"Come to me child of the snow."
Echoed through my mind
My eyes lose focus
I fall into blackness
She speaks to me once more
"Come to me, come north to my bosom."
As I slipped into a void of the starless night
I black out as my stomach purges me

Tough grass of summer is dying under foot
Carabobo turning south as the long days fade
Wind had turned with them
Blowing cold once more
Signs of summer end swift approaching
The great white returning to the land
I set out
North was my only direction
Across the tundra where falls the snow
Already too late
Summer is passing

Winter comes with frozen teeth
But north I went all the same
North to the ice maiden's realm
North to she who is the weaver of tears
Overlooking the village I pause
Looking to my wake
I see her
Watching me depart
Stares as I go
My heart's desire
Blue grey pools where I desire to lose myself
Indecision strikes me then
I would to rush back to her
Tell her of my heart
Tell her of my desires
Tell her of my Love
I almost faltered then
Ran to her

Then comes Kaleb the seal hunter
To stand at her side
Kaleb The Tall
Kaleb the strong
Kaleb The Handsome
Kaleb who was always there
Kaleb of the easy laugh
Kaleb of the winning smile
Hateful Kaleb
Kaleb who mocked me so
Kaleb who left me tongue-tied
Kaleb with his wits so quick
I knew then if I returned, she would laugh
While Kaleb would mock me still
Make me the fool I was
Knowing this as certain
I found my determination
Shaman's ritual had shown me the way

Passing Place 315

I would go north
I turned my back upon them
I walked on towards the white horizon

All I owned upon my back
Seal skin tent oiled with fat
Seal Oil to burn for heat
Leather wrapped salt cured meats
Winter clothing tied for carrying
Summers long days faded fast
Cold dark nights
The weakening days gathered little warmth
Three days north the first snow fell
Winters blanket on the ground once more
Each ever lengthening night the aurora danced
Lights across the heavens guiding my way
Snow got deeper
The world got colder
Days turned to weeks
Legs felt heavier with each step
But when I wearied I remembered her eyes
Found more strength within me
But at nights another called to me
Haunting my dreams
A voice I had never known
'Come to me'
I would wake cold
Fearful of the darkness
The walk north all consuming
Each step a task in itself
Each day less progress through the snow
Blue grey eyes began to fade in memory
Becoming grey and dull
Each step takes all I have
Leaving nothing for desire
Leaving nothing for longing
I longed instead for the whisperer in my dreams

For journey's end

A great blizzard comes to me from clear skies
Still I walked on
Laboured snowshoe steps
Wrapped my eyes with heavy gauss
Least I be blinded by the whiteness
The great wind howled for three days and nights
Qailewrtetang the weather spirit pushed me back
The spirits sought to test me
Conspiring to halt my quest
To break me from my purpose
I drew strength from this
The spirits aligned to prevent my quest
Only drew anger and will within me
I dug deep into the snow
To wait out the blizzard beneath it

Four days of storm
I woke to clear skies
No more of the ceaseless howling wind
I dug myself out of the white
I faced a new test
Ursa, in all its power stood before me
A great bear of the white
Roaring with fury
Roaring with hatred
Back I stumble
Towards my hole
Seeking sanctuary
I grasped for my harpoon
It's long barbed head too fragile
The shaft of the spear a twig before the beast
I clung tightly to it
Holding it before me in desperation
In terror
I knew this was my death

Nanook the master of bears had brought one of his children down on me
To do what the blizzard could not
The master of bears is ever harsh in his judgements
My people know this
It is in our stories
The bear is an almost a man
We respect them
We respect their master
We hang their hides in our igloo
Keep them for days there to honour Nanuk the great white bear
It is he who decided the hunt
We offer the Bear Spirit weapons
We offer The Bear Spirit our hunting tools
For its sacrifice to us
And the spirits of the bears would tell their own
How the people honoured them
Foolish the hunter who treats badly his kill
For Nanook would send one to slay the hunter who had dishonoured his children

The beast came forward
It's maw barking out roars as it did
Larger than any I had seen before
Perhaps Nanuk himself
I braced my harpoon in the snow behind me
A needle against a man
The bear raised itself before me
Ten feet above me
It screamed of my death
It's shadow upon me blocking out the sun
My moment of death upon me
Then words came out of the air
'No, this one is mine, leave him'
The same voice from my vision

The voice of the weaver of tears
The Ice Maiden
Believe me now when I tell you I heard them
As clear as the call of a wolf across the tundra
The bear roared
Defiant and angry
I heard the voice again
'Leave him, he is mine.'
It fell to its feet
Cowered and turned
One pleading roar over its shoulder
Then walked away into the white
I walked once more
North, always north

More days of snow
Wind and ice
Northward
The days slipped by
Without number or mark
The lights in the sky dancing each night
Fuel spent
Food gone
I walked on
Numb from the cold, north always north
A wreck of a man
Mind and vision lost in the whiteness of the world
I walked on.
Convinced I had died beneath the claws of the great bear
Died in the snow
Buried by the blizzard
A ghost of myself
Condemned to walk the white wasteland
Ever going north
Never reaching his goal
The Church of The Christ preach of hell

A place of fire and brimstone
I think they are wrong
Hell is frozen waste
Through which I walk each day
No respite
No release
One foot after another
A slow trudge
Always north
I know not for how many days
Starved
Half blind
I at last came upon it
Where the Aurora meets the ground
The home of The Ice Maiden

A wall of ice raised high above me
A glacier the like of which I had never seen
Larger than any other
It stood unmoving
A towering cliff hundreds of feet high
From first sight a day to reach its base
Each hour it grew upon the horizon
It filled my vision
An icy wall which would march across the world
Would but the maiden but let it
Covering all beneath in its wake

At its base, a door
Ice itself clear and faultless
Barely discernible
The entrance to her home
I stumbled on the final few yards
I hammer upon the door with the shaft of my spear
Hope one within would take pity upon me
As I raise it to strike the door did open
Slow as the glacier

With equal slowness I moved forward
Unable to form a thought
I walked north
Out of the cold

Beyond the doors
Carved into the ice
The Ice Maiden's home
Shadows danced as the blue flames flicker
Warmth around me
A place of magic
The voice speaks to me
"You have come, at last,"
The voice from my visions
I looked around me for the speaker
But see her not
The snow still blinds
Then I saw her
As I knew she would be
A daughter of the people
Black haired
Dark-eyed
Soft-featured
Smiling
She had stepped out from behind a statue of herself
" But tell me, do you come to rob me, or to love me?"
Asked she
Her voice was like a late spring stream
Feeding from the ice
Clear and cold
I say nothing
Incoherent
Mind was dulled by the cold
She quiets me
Her voice rippled over me once more

"It matters not, you are here now."
"A bargain now I strike with you."
"Twenty midwinter nights you must share my bed."
"Warm me with your soul."
"And I shall cry you a diamond."
"As large as your heart."
"To take back to your blue-grey eyes."

How she knew what I had come for
Of the woman I loved
Of my desire and hopes
I know not
But she knew all
The shaper of tears knew my heart
I knew no resistance to her offer
A shell of myself
A frozen fool
Wondered too long in the ice
I agreed
Twenty nights did not seem long

Twenty midwinter nights
The nights which last for days on end
When the sun does not rise
I agreed
Knowing not what I was agreeing to
All gods and spirits are tricksters at heart
Even the God of the cross
A trickster magician making wine into water
Returning from the dead
Trickery played upon foolish men
Twenty midwinter nights
No lie in her words
Only my misunderstanding
I agreed
Gave my word
Gave word to one such as she

Your word a bond on your soul
Twenty nights that come but once a year
Twenty years to repay my oath
Words given in oath
Sacred to my people
So I kept mine
In doing so I was to learn the tale
As the woman of the people tell it

The true tale of The Ice Maiden
A sacrifice unwilling
Given up by a father
She refused to marry one not of her heart
For her love was another maiden of the people
Her tale is one of punishment
Of the perfidy of men
When the gods demanded a sacrifice of the people
Her father gave of her
Rather than himself
And slew the one she loved
Turning her into the fire at the heart of the sun
It is for her the ice maiden weeps
For all the power of ice
It cannot be close to the sun
As the sun cannot come close to the ice
For fear of melting
She is of the people
She turns her tears to diamonds
Least let them grow the glacier
Thus destroy the world
For all her anger
For all her rage
She does not punish the people of the great white
But, at times, she calls one to her
To keep her company
In the long years of her loneliness
Lest it become too much

And the tears flow too quickly

It was this role then fulfilled
My own sacrifice for my people
Consort of The Ice Maiden
For twenty midwinter nights
I would not give lie to this
Claim that it was a captivity
For she was beautiful
For she was wise
It was not love between us.
Just the filling of the void
Left by the one she loved
But we laughed
We loved
Brought some joy
For those long twenty midwinter nights
I forgot Alilean of the grey blue eyes
But memories of her would return
To haunt my dreams each spring
My heart would yearn to return
I would feel the cold once more

Twenty years
On the day that marks midsummer
I stood upon the rise
Overlooking the village of my people
I held no bitterness in the parting
My oath kept she kept hers
She cried me a diamond
I think she cried not for my leaving
But for her lost love
She who became one with the heart of the sun
The true tale of the ice maiden
The story as told by the women of my people
Darker than the men's version of the tale
There are those who would not believe my tale true

Prescribe it to madness
Twenty years in the wilds
I believe it is the truth
What others believe is of no merit to I
Twenty years and one had passed since I last stood upon that rise
In my hand I held the ice diamond
A prize hard won
Melting slowly in the summer's heat
I believe now I always knew deep down that it would
Somewhere deep inside
We can tell ourselves no lies
.
I felt no sorrow in its melting
Gladness filled me
Home at last
Seeing once more the village of my youth
I felt a calm I had never known
I saw it all before me
A glimpse of she who I had left behind
My heart leapt
A young girl standing alone
Turning to look at me
Her eyes blue-grey
Her hair light of colour
I drop the last few melting drops of ice
I run to meet her
My heart light
Beating fast
She had not aged
Not one day since my leaving
As I got closer I saw she had tears in her eyes
I thought they were for me
Tears of joy at my return
Then I drew close
I realised my mistake

The differences were subtle
A rounding of the face
Eyebrows that were darker
It was not her
Alilean of the grey blue eyes
I stop
Stood staring at this girl
With tears running down her cheeks
" Why do you cry?" I ask
Words choking in my throat
"My mother lays dying," She says
I asked her to take me to her mother.
Telling her I was an old friend

Alilean of the grey blue eyes
Lay dying in her bed
No dimming of those eyes
The lines of age had not hidden her beauty
I knelt beside her and cried
"You,"
she says to me
"You come at last,"
"I thought you long dead,"
"I waited,"
"Three years I wait for you,"
"Each year Kaleb asked for my hand
"I said no,"
"Not till I had spoken to you."
"But you never came."
She says all this to me
"I am here now."
I replied between my tears
"Much good you are now old friend."
She half laughed still a smile in her eyes
"I would have married you,"
"But you stopped talking to me."

"And you went away."
"Why did you leave,"
"I loved you"
"You walked away?"
She says to me
"I wanted to marry you."
"I loved you also,"
I told her
"But you did not ask me?"
She says on to me
Coughing hard
A rag spotted with blood

Later that night
I sat with her while she died
And thought of diamonds
Melting in the sun

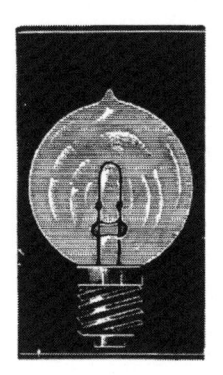

CHAPTER EIGHTEEN

Faces in the Dark

Sleep was being hard come by.

The battle of wits between a busy mind and exhaustion was one that exhaustion was not equipped for. Not for the first time.

Richard remained unsure what to make of the story the Inuit had told him. It was, he knew, a kind of fairy tale, or some old mythic saga. He could grasp that obvious moral of the tale itself. Nothing was plainer. That was not the question keeping him awake. Instead, the question he could not shift from his consciousness was another of those never-ending why's?

Why it had been a story he needed to hear? Ridiculous question that was, but if there was a reason it escaped him.

That he was sure that the story had been told for him to hear, was perhaps that was his ego talking. He knew how very egocentric of him it was, even to consider the possibility. Sure the cat had encouraged him to listen to that particular story with her cryptic and occasionally not so cryptic prodding. But that did not mean it was told just for him, and because of him. Yet he could not shift the feeling there was more than a grain of truth to that idea.

And if that was the case?

Well, that opened up a whole different raft of questions.

It was not the first time he had lain on his bed, unable to sleep and considering such things. There always seemed to be a reason behind him hearing a story. A reason why it was being told to him in particular. Trying to get a grasp on whatever lesson he was supposed to learn was becoming a habit.

Though he was unsure if it was a good habit to get into or not.

If anything, seeking reasons behind the stories was the most fruitless of exercises. It left him feeling the self-same sense of abstract confusion every time. As a result, he would find himself lying in the dark, thinking about the tale he had heard most recently, trying to equate it to himself, trying to make sense of it all.

Generally, he found himself failing to do so.

Yet he lay there, trying to find elusive explanations and staring at the ceiling in the dark. While trying not to see the faces in the shadows and the random patterns in the plaster on the ceiling which took on demonic aspect.

That too was a losing battle.

Richard had suffered from Pareidolia most of his life to one extent or another. Even with the knowledge that it was nothing but a trick of the mind, it still had the ability to freak him out in the best of circumstances. The strangeness of The Passing Place was not making for the best of circumstances.

As a sufferer from the condition he could understand why people ascribed spiritual significance to the phenomenon, though he himself tried to take a rational approach to his affliction. It was not always easy to do so. The more active his mind the worse it was.

This particular night it was worse than usual.

Science claims to have explained Pareidolia. The men in white coats believed it is nothing more than people's brains recognising patterns in randomness, before ascribing significance to them subconsciously. Filling in the blank spaces with what the mind expects to see, rather than what is there.

Carl Sagan, went further, claiming it was a leftover survival mechanism, a product of instinct and evolution. Clearly, the ability to pick out shapes in the darkness would have been something vital to early humans. As an idea that made perfect rational sense to Richard. Yet despite this, he was not convinced it was really the leftover thoughts of his inner cave man. It was too neat an explanation, too simple and tied up with a bow. Perhaps it was because the entirety of the Rorschach ink blot system was based on the same logic, the recognition of patterns by the under mind. Something everyone does it to an extent. Sufferers of Pareidolia just did it in overdrive. If Rorschach was a window to the inner self, then so was Pareidolia. There had, in Richards opinion, to be more to it than a simple throwback survival mechanism, an evolutionary dead end, long redundant in modern man.

Richard had read into the subject in his teenage years when he first began to understand his own issues with it. Science claimed to explain it all, but all the same, knowing it was no more than a trick of the brain did not make it any less scary at times when it caught him unawares.

What Richard could understand, was why there was so much fake science based upon Pareidolia. He had read as much into the foe-science as the real stuff. There were, for example, the claims by fringe religious groups that what people were actually seeing was angels.

As an idea, it had fascinated him for a short time. It did not matter how much science claimed to explain it all, it was, he realised later in life, human nature to seek other explanations. More comforting ones than hard facts.

Those who claimed to be mystics, and he had no doubt some truly believed they were, had been claiming this explanation for centuries. While Richard never truly believed the mystical mumbo jumbo, the idea had still appealed to his teenage self.

Indeed, that teenage self still had a little sway over his older 'wiser' self, if he was honest. He guessed a part of everyone never really leaves the fascinations of their adolescence.

That aside Richard would never have claimed any particular spirituality. He had lapsed from the Church of England long before coming to America. His parents had given up taking him to Sunday school by the time he was twelve. He came to suspect when he was older that they only took him to get a few hours to their selves each Sunday in any case, rather than through their own long laxed religious convictions.

He knew that was a cynical view to take, but neither of his parents had been adamant churchgoers themselves. A few hours free on a Sunday to stop being parents of a pre-teen boy made perfect sense to him by the time he reached adulthood. He knew he had never been a child to hide away. He was always rushing about or messing with his father's music collection. Bungling from one disruption to another, while claiming all the same he was bored.

Richard had only been in a church once since coming to The States as a nineteen-year-old.

While he had always been respectful enough of his friends to never say so out loud, he quietly felt mockingly of the religious right that seemed to make up so much of his adopted home. He struggled to understand how otherwise intelligent people could be so taken in by religion. Even the most liberal among his American friends seemed to have one eye for the Lord. He assumed it was because he had grown up in more secular British society. He regarded religion as no more than a crutch people leant upon. Yet for all that, he could understand the attraction to seek out the Lord to an extent despite his cynicism.

His Anglicanism had driven him to seek out a church the night after Carrie had died. It was far more to rage than anything religious. With a bottle of Jack, tucked in a brown paper bag, in one hand he had spent an hour staring at a crucifix alone one night in a Queens Chapel. Swigging at the bottle between venomous exclamations about the parentage of the figure on the cross.

Church offered no more solace than the bottle that night, not that he had expected much. But then Richard could not understand people who found that solace in religion.

That was, at least, until he spent another sleepless night staring up at the ceiling, seeing angels and demons in the shadows. Then he could understand why it was a comfort to believe. He had wished on more than one occasion that he did, that he could just accept God existed and had a plan. While at the same time the idea terrified him, for reasons he could not explain, even to himself.

Over the years, he had taught himself to just accept the images he saw, accept they were both there and not there at the same time. To allow them to wash over him, and just be part of the background of the night.

His teenage researches had helped with that. He had read somewhere back in those hormone-fueled days that Da Vinci believed Pareidolia was a gift that an artist should cherish. As the pretentious youth Richard had been, he latched on this and made himself seek out those faces in the shadows all the more-- to focus upon them, and let himself be drawn in.

It had become such a habit after a few years that it was now all but impossible to break. If anything it had become a habit that comforted him when he could not sleep. He would try to make the faces more distinct by staring all the harder at them, telling himself that you are never alone if you can see faces in the dark.

Tonight, however, he felt alone, and the faces offered no comfort. Instead, they seemed to twist into the most demonic of aspects.

He wondered abstractly if this was a symptom of his subconscious, the inner confusion he felt manifesting in what he was seeing. It was true that he was struggling to make sense of things: The Passing Place, the strange laws that seemed to bend around what should have been impossible. The strange inhabitants of the bar, both customers, staff--and come to that the cat. And most of all the stories he had been told. If there were lessons within them, he was failing to see them.

That was the real problem, he had decided.

He wanted to see lessons in the stories. He wanted them to explain things, to make him feel better, to make him feel whole again. He had come to The Passing Place a broken man. This was the last stop on his grand tour of America. His grand tour in search of meaning. His grand tour in search of an answer to that damnable question that had no answer.

The question "why?"

He had begun to hope that the answer lay within the stories. That somehow the cat was trying to show him a truth of some kind, an answer to that question. Trying to help him. Insane though the idea seemed at times, he felt it was true all the same. But feeling that, knowing it even, did not make the answer any easier to come by. Neither did it make the meanings hidden within the stories easier to comprehend.

It seemed all the worse because for the first time in a long time he could think clearly.

He was no longer drowning his feelings in the well of America, hiding them behind the need to keep constantly moving. Keeping on the road, always focused on where he was going next.

Find the next bus. Find the next small town. Find the next flakey roadside attraction to wonder distractedly through. Seeing the west coast, the east coast, the Bible belt with its endless small towns and tall churches. The deserts of the west, the redwood forests, the great lakes. The length and breadth of America. Seeking an answer by looking in all the wrong places.

Seeking an answer, by not seeking it, just as hard as he could.

Now he could think, now he had time to find an

answer to that question.

That insufferable "why?".

A question he knew had no answer, for there was no answer to be found. Richard knew only too well that the only person who could have answered that question had long since left his world.

Yet even while he now found himself thinking of Carrie, in The Passing Place he could forget her at times. Forget her more completely than he had ever managed by burying himself in the road. Here in this strange, magical place. Carrie could become nothing more than a spark of a memory, someone he knew he could never forget. But he did not need to remember constantly all the same.

While he was playing his piano, and he had come to think of it as his piano, the music took his mind away from the memories for a while.

Playing had always had that ability to take him out of himself, losing his problems in the notes and chords. More so than ever it seemed here. At times his mind was completely taken up following the tune. Even when he was playing that damn song.

Her song.

'Forever Autumn' flowed out of his keyboard, and the words slipped out of his mouth as he sang them. Yet Carrie would still be little more than a passing thought, a moment of regret, of a dull memory of grief.

At night, though, when he lay in his room staring at the faces on the ceiling, he lay not dwelling upon Carrie herself but a new fear, the fear of forgetting.

It seemed wrong to him, indecent even, that he could put her out of his mind. Worse still, do so without even realising. Just let her slip to some forgotten pocket of his mind and get on with his life.

If only for a few moments.

Was he forgetting her?

He knew with a strange certainty that he was not. She was as alive in his memory as she had ever been. Dulled in the light of the day, but never at night. But all the same, he could feel how easy it would be to let her slip away, and part of him longed to do so.

And yet...

The bed was as empty as it ever was. The hole in his life still there. Alone in that bed the distractions of the day were lost to him. Her absence, that yearning gulf of an absence, was there as it always was, waiting for him to find it once more.

The lacking, that was the thing, the lack of her, whence she should be.

How could all these stories bridge that gulf? Answer the question? Explain the why, that numbing why?

If these stories were supposed to help him, to ease his memories, to make him whole once more, then they were failing when he lay in bed at night, or he was failing to understand whatever lessons they contained.

This particular night was worse than others had been of late. He knew why. He wished it was as simple as him being less tired than he thought he was when he had climbed the stairs to bed. But he knew that was not that case. It was far simpler than that, and yet so much more complicated. He knew exactly why it was worse.

Why Carrie was so much on his mind.

Why sleep was elusive.

Why the faces in the dark were all his demons.

It had been a normal day. Well, normal within the confines of what passed for normal in The Passing Place.

Richard had been playing a melody of obscure indie bands from the eighties, *Strawberry Switchblade*, and *Men Without Hats,* pouring out of the piano. He doubted anyone in the bar had heard of them. That was part of the joy perhaps. Here in the Passing Place he could play anything. No one would raise an eyebrow if he went from Bach to ELO or started the middle eight of *Like A Hurricane*. It was a freedom no musician ever really feels in a day job.

His gaze was slipping over the bar room, as it generally did when the music flowed. He liked to take in the room. The strange customers, all so out of place, yet all in place at the same time. Any one of them would look wrong elsewhere The strange clothing, their odd ways of talking, the occasional extra limb. People out of time and place. People who would never meet in any other place. Or, for that matter, may not even exist beyond the bounds of this bubble of reality.

It was impossible, he knew. But then if every day is full of the impossible, then it becomes normal after a time. He had begun to accept that. He no longer looked with disbelief at those who crossed the threshold. Instead, he looked with wonder.

He was looking with wonder when he saw her.

She was standing at one of the high tables, drinking of all things, tea from a china cup. A full silver service had been, despite all unlikelihood, laid out on the table. It was a strange thing to be drinking in a bar, and a strange way to be partaking of it; an oddity which peeked his interest.

She was dressed in clothes which belonged in the late Victorian era. Yet, at the same time, a Victorian era that never existed. Like some steampunk fantasy of a time when steam was the all-consuming powerhouse of a technology that never existed.

Her dress was corseted in browns and cream, leather and lace webbed over it, with a dozen pouches. Small bottles of glass and earthenware holstered like bullets on small belts. A red silk scarf around her neck and a large top hat made from brown leather sat at an oblique angle on her head. A style of clothing that almost existed but never did, except at geek conventions. Yet these were clothes worn in the way a costume never is.

When she raised her arm to drop sugar lumps into the tea from a silver bowl, he could see a strange contraption mounted on a leather wristband under the sleeve of her dress. It took him a moment to realise it was a small gun, a derringer or something similar. He guessed whatever it was, it was spring loaded in some way to slide free when she needed it.

The strangest thing, the thing which held his attention for longer than a passing glance, was her face. Her skin had the light bronze of the Pacific islands. Her features a mix of European and

Polynesian. Around her left eye she had a tattooed design, spirals working their way outwards in ever increasing crescents, before the last spiral trailed off around her cheek and back towards her ear to spiral down once more.

It was obviously a native tattoo, one native to her people, or at least one of her parents' people, he suspected. Her complexion and tattoo sat strangely with her costume. It combined to make her all the more exotic. She was also beautiful with it.

Light grey eyes in a tan face, eyes with a spark of mischief about them, and a note of cynicism which he found attractive. He found his gaze lingering upon her.

Morn slid past carrying a coffee for him, white foam forming spirals on the top in the dark liquid. The symmetry appealed to him in his distraction.

"Do you know who she is?" he had asked Morn without thinking about why he was asking. A simple enough question, but one with connotations that were lost to him at that moment:

Those being his reason for asking, which were subconscious to him at the time but there all the same.

Morn had followed his gaze, which had not left the body of his question.

"Her? Maybe," Morn had replied and continued her journey to the bar.

"Maybe?"

Richard found himself irritated by Morn's reply.

He muttered something under his breath. *"Cryptic as bloody ever."* Or some such oath. His gaze did not leave the woman. He watched as she drank her tea, the way she lifted her arm to bring the cup to her mouth. The way the corset shaped her waist. He found himself wondering if without it the same smooth curves would be there.

For the briefest of moments he wanted to go over to her. Talk to her, perhaps get to know her a little. He was intrigued, more than intrigued, he was attracted to her. Not in the oblique way he felt attracted to Morn on occasion, but a more intense kind of longing. Attracted to her sense of mystery as much as the way she looked. But there was certainly nothing about the way she looked which he did not find alluring. He had the briefest flicker of a fantasy, a moment of eroticism with-in his own thoughts.

And that was it.

Just a moment, a passing fleeting moment of attraction on which he felt the desire to act, as he came to the end of his tune.

He half rose from his stool, and almost, just almost, went over to her table on the off chance of talking to her. A simple human action. A simple human attraction.

And then it struck him.

He had forgotten her.

Carrie.

For that briefest of instances she was no longer in his mind. She was forgotten, gone. That weight that he had carried. That maddening desire to know the answer to "why?" that had driven him for so long. The grief that clawed at him. The loss, the lack, the empty place in the world. All of it gone.

Just for a moment, a second, a fleeting instance.

And then it all came flying back.

The grief, the hurt, the loss. All back in full technicolour.

He had sat back down.

Horrified with himself. Horrified that he allowed himself to forget her.

For a long while he just sat, looking at nothing, doing nothing. Lost in his own internal narrative.

"Shouldn't you be playing something, Honey?" Jolene had said as she bumped into the piano while avoiding some customers wondering hands, which she always seemed to be doing whether the hands were wondering or not.

Her words shook him his malaise and he started to play, though he had no idea what he was playing. Some dirge or ballad lost in time, dragged up from the recesses of his memory. Keeping His eyes rooted on the keyboard.

When he finally looked up, the steampunk woman was gone, the tea tray cleared away. All signs of her brief existence in the bar room gone with her.

But the memory remained, and with it the betrayal he felt he had committed.

So now he was laying in the dark, unable to sleep, thinking about everything. Trying to find answers, trying to decrypt the stories, hoping they would help with his pain. Help with his own anger at himself, for all he knew it was ridiculous. It was over a year since she passed. Since she had taken her life in the bathroom of their apartment.

He had a right to move on. He had a right to find

someone else attractive. He knew that. All that.

Yet he did not want to. He did not want to forget, to move on. He wanted to remember, he knew that too.

So he lay in the dark, seeking answers he could not find, hidden in stories he could not understand.

Watching the faces in the shadows.

And every face was Carrie's.

CHAPTER NINETEEN

Demonic Home and Garden

"You look down Piano man." Lyal said after pouring Richard his third double jack.

It was not the most intuitive of statements. Richard was not one to drink through the day while he was working. The fact he had been sitting at the bar drinking double bourbons on his break was a sure sign of his bleak mood. As was the way his break had slipped into its second hour, Richard seldom took more than the time for a sandwich and a cup of coffee or tea on his break.

He gave Lyal a cynical look, wondering if the literal barman was having a joke at his expense. Then he decided that was probably just a symptom of his malaise.

"Didn't get enough sleep last night," Richard replied, which was an honest enough answer without going into any actual details. He did not want to think of details. Hence the reason he was drinking at what was probably two in the afternoon somewhere. Wherever the somewhere they were was.

"Insomnia is a terrible affliction when you want a night's sleep," Lyal said with no sense of irony, picking up a glass to polish with the bar towel he kept on a hook on his belt. "Now me, I have never suffered from it myself. Sleep the sleep of the unjust I do," he continued.

Richard looked the barman in the eye, trying to figure out if he heard the last part correctly or if there had been a tinge of humour to the words. They nagged at him for all he wanted to ignore them and drink quietly in his own company.

He sighed and asked the question all the same. "The unjust?" then regretted asking almost immediately.

"Well, I can hardly sleep the sleep of the just can I? It would go against my basic character if I did," the barman said plainly, continuing to polish the glass, straight faced as ever.

There was something wrong about Lyal. Richard had sensed it more than once. A nasty streak at times that was kept hidden for the most part. The piano player had occasionally glimpsed it all the same when the barman did not know he was looking in his direction—the odd sneer that crossed his lips when he turned away from a customer. The odd remark which was snide or cynical in a way only someone being completely literal could be without causing offence. There were other things as well which tended to set Richard on edge around him.

Years ago he had read something in a comic book which stuck with him. *'The devil never lies, it's a point of pride with him.'* Richard did not know if the writer took that from elsewhere or if the idea was his own invention, but it sounded right. The devil never lied; he just told you the bits of the truth he wanted you to know. If he promised you that you would get a chance to get your heart's desire by doing what he wanted you to do, then it was the truth. What the devil just would not tell you was when that chance would be. He would just get from the deal what he wanted and walk away.

That was Lyal, Richard thought. An honest devil, who just told you what he wanted you to know. Tell you nothing but the truth, but edit out anything that he did not wish to mention. He knew it was unfair of him to think of the barman in these terms. But all the same something was not quite right about him, not that he ever did anything overtly nasty towards Richard, or anyone else come to that. Richard just found him hard to settle with when compared to everyone else in the bar. Like an itch of doubt he could not scratch.

Unsure how to answer the barman's odd statement, Richard just smiled instead and took another drink, trying not to think of the faces in the night. Hoping more than expecting, that Lyal would wonder off to serve customers, but the bar was unusually quiet for the time of day.

"Another?" Lyal asked him as the piano player drained the last dregs of the tumbler.

"I shouldn't, but yer go ahead," Richard replied pushing the empty glass across the bar. He was starting to feel the warm glow of the alcohol. It was doing little to break his mood all the same.

"Seems to me you need to talk more than you need to drink," Lyal said, pouring another double, with the same odd insightfulness, which seemed to both be correct and wrong at the same time.

'*Perhaps it's the tone of his voice,*' Richard thought. It was always oddly flat, deadpan perhaps. It was as if Lyal never knew if he was supposed to be funny or not.

"Not sure if it's something I can talk about, Lyal. Just something I am trying to forget," he told him, accepting the tumbler back and nursing it for a while.

"I see," the barman said, though Richard was more than half sure he didn't. Lyal then wondered off to serve a customer, leaving Richard to his own devices for a while. He sat looking at the Jack in the glass, letting it swirl around. He did not feel much like drinking anymore. But the piano had no lure either. So he stayed at the bar trying to lift his mood.

Despite knowing full well that the drink was a depressant if you were down already, he played with the glass for a while, then gave into temptation and began to drink once more. Thinking of Carrie, and their life together, he was unable to move past the hole he had sunk into, the same hole he had been in when he first arrived at Esqwith's.

"Perhaps you would like to listen then. I heard a funny story a few days ago that might make you smile," Lyal said, wandering back with another glass to polish. A good ten minutes had past but the barman seemed not to have noticed, continuing their conversation as if the time had not passed. Either way, it made Richard feel that same unease again. He was somewhat taken aback as well.

The idea of Lyal telling a funny story struck him as an odd one. For Lyal, with his literal mind, to even know when something was funny seemed a bizarre concept. He found himself staring at Lyal with something akin to disbelief.

Lyal just stared back, his face lacking any real emotion. Perhaps it was his own odd mood, or perhaps it was simply a perverse curiosity, but Richard found himself feeling genuinely interested to hear what Lyal consider to be a funny story.

"What the hell, go on then," he said, expecting some short joke or other.

Lyal, to Richard's surprise, suddenly took on all the mannerisms of a showman.

He carefully put down the glass he was always perpetually polishing when not serving and then hooked the cloth back to his belt. Rubbing his hands as if in anticipation, he took a step towards the bar itself, coming closer as if to whisper the story with the aspect of a conspirator. All edged little actions of stagecraft, to build up atmosphere, tricks Richard knew well from the circuit.

Lyal then began in his ever bland deadpan voice to tell his tale. Richard listened with a degree of fascination, mostly at how Lyal failed to put the stresses on the right words, seemingly oblivious to which bits were funny and which were not. All the same, Richard found himself carried along by the simple joy of a silly tale.

"Once, upon a hill, far from the maddening crowd, there was a small house."

"Built of red brick with a roof of black tiles, it had been, for some time, under siege from twisting vines and ivy. A siege which the house was losing, much to the irritation of the houses only resident."

"No matter how often or indeed how far she cut back the ivy, it would grow back twice as thick in a matter of days. This was, as I am sure you will understand, a matter of some frustration to her."

"She had inherited the house from an uncle she had never met. One who had nevertheless willed it to her, though under the strict understanding she must live in the house for a year and a day."

"She followed the bequest rigorously, not least because she feared that she would be cheated out of her inheritance if she did otherwise, holding to that age old simple truth that no lawyer less than thirty fathoms under the sea could be trusted."

"So she had moved from the bright lights of the city, where she had engaged in an active, if somewhat complicated social life, to the small house in the country and set about living a sedate, one might even say dull, life within it."

"This, it has to be said, she quickly found bored her rigid. She soon discovered within herself a longing for the complicated and engaging social life she had enjoyed previously."

"Life in the little cottage was certainly undertaken at a more sedate pace than she was used to. However, this was only true if you discounted the daily chore of hacking away at the rapacious ivy."

"Each day she cut it back, and each morning woke to find it was more uncontrollably overgrown than ever. After a while, she began to suspect some form of magic or another trickery was behind the climbing plants insidious vitality."

"She was, as it happened, not far wrong."

"The uncle had for all his absence from his niece's young life, been nothing but true in his bequest. Indeed, he had purposely sought out a travelling lawyer to write his will, because he wished to do well by the niece he had never laid eyes upon, feeling somewhat obliged to her as she was his only living relative that he did not actively despise. This could, in all truth, have been purely because he had never met her."

"A kindly uncle he might be, he was also a man given to be cantankerous at times."

"The stipulation that she must live in the cottage a year and a day, however, was not his own. It was one advised by the lawyer in question."

"'A guarantee, as it were, that your kind bequest will not be squandered by your niece,'" the lawyer had told him."

"The uncle, who was a simple country boy at

heart, had never heard the old joke about lawyers and the bottom of the sea. This being the first time in his sheltered life he had used a lawyer, he was not as mistrustful as he might have been, of *'Black Hearted Samuel B Starred, Travelling Lawyer & Horticultural Black Magician'* as the sign on the cart had proclaimed him to be. Thinking it no more than an interesting advertising technique."

"Some may call that naïve of the uncle. But then where would the world be without naivety and interesting advertising?"

"So the clause about living in the house a year and a day was placed in the will. The uncle never thought to ask what happened if the clause was defaulted on and, it should be stressed, did not read the fine print."

"He was also most pleased with the '*Free potted plant with every will'* offer, which was a special for the week."

"Following the uncle's unexpected death a few days later-- reported in the tabloids as '*Man mauled to death by spider plant'* and the recipient of the bequest being made aware of her good fortune by mail, the aforementioned Black Hearted Samuel B Starred planted the insidious climbing ivy. Then cast a dark spell, imbuing it with the soul of a Geist of the lower hells."

"A Geist, in case you are unaware, is a demonic force, used by magicians of the black kind to let loose troubles upon the world. A favourite among the users of demonic forces as it is a formless spirit bound easily to black bladed rune swords or perhaps the crown of a mad king or, for that matter, a 1958 Plymouth Fury's, among other things."

"This particular Geist, whom's name is not only unpronounceable but almost certainly unspellable, had, for example, once processed a toga worn by the first senator to stab Caesar in the back. He had also been the mitre worn by three successive black cardinals in the time of the Spanish Inquisition, fun times for a demonic entity. He had also spent time being one of the '*legion*' of which they often are heard to say "W*e Are*" in ominous tones."

He had indeed been party to many foul acts. He was, therefore, a little put out to find himself contracted out to possess a climbing ivy plant."

"Horticultural black magicians were not something the Geist was used to working with. Neither, for that matter, were lawyers. '*A curse on them all*,' as he was heard to say and as a demonic entity, he knew a lot about curses.

"He, in short, wished he had read the small print."

"Here, then, are the principals of our little drama."

"A young woman of several frustrations, not least with her shears, whom by fortune is also a descendant blessed with a bequest from a kindly uncle recently deceased."

"A kindly uncle, whom, if he were still alive, would be at a loss to understand how a spider plant acted like a rather nasty version of its namesake."

"Samuel the black-hearted lawyer with a more than a passing interest in gardening and black magic, which it should be noted are two things more often linked than you would imagine… How else do you explain how some people get such wonderful lawns?"

"And lastly, a Geist demon trapped in an ivy plant."

"Perhaps this is not the most likely cast, I shall grant you, but this is a tale most unlikely. At least, that is the excuse I am using…"

"And so the drama continues, with what we will laughingly call the plot."

"Oh, and before you ask, the girl's name is not ivy, nor is it any other plant based first name, but as she is our heroine we had best, one supposes, give her a name, perhaps, therefore, we shall call her Emmy Lou."

"The lawyer had taken to watching Emmy's stressful attempts at ivy trimming remotely, using magic's known to him, which looked like normal daffodils to anyone else. He took no small delight when Emmy Lou threw down her shears each day in disgust, much to the relief of the frustrated demon ivy."

"The lawyer was, you see, along with his other numerous faults, also something of a voyeur. A man possessed of a desire to watch young women in her frustrations of every kind from afar. In this case, under the thin justification of wishing to know when she fled the house so he could make use of the clause and take it for himself."

"He had, therefore, sent the young maiden several potted plants by Interflora. He was, it has to be said, somewhat pleased with himself, because by happenstance she placed the plants around the house in convenient locations, allowing him to view

Passing Place 353

everything, and he took his chance to do so."

"Even by the standards of his profession, he was a man of few redeeming qualities, as I am sure you can gather."

"He even had the temerity to be mildly annoyed that the one she had placed in the bathroom was pointed away from the shower, which was already beginning to wilt from the steam. Frankly, it played merry hell with the reception. And the mirror it was pointing at kept steaming up as well, which was a shame for him, but not for standards of decency, as Emmy was in the habit of taking a lot of hot showers after a hard day's shearing."

"I ramble somewhat, but let it be explained the lawyer was quite taken with young Miss Emmy Lou, not to the extent that he would not cheat her out of her bequest, of course. But enough to plan to offer comfort to her afterwards, though the comforts he had in mind were of a lascivious kind and more to do with his wants than her needs. He did, however, have the odd happy few moments considering these things while indulging his inner voyeur. He was a man of many a bad habit as I have said."

"For his plans to grasp her assets, however, the ivy needed to grow faster, and outpace her shears."

"The demon, it should be said, agreed with the lawyer. It needed to end the daily cycle of growth than be hacked at by a young woman with so much energy to spare in pursuit of venting her frustrations."

"Admittedly, being a fast growing ivy plant was not the worst possession job he had ever had. There was that time in Sardinia when he was forced to process a vase for twenty years. That had been extremely dull. In his professional opinion, black magic and pottery did not work well in combination. It is very difficult to terrify people by wilting flowers overnight. And occasionally making people bump into you when they are trying to be stealthy."

"However, that said, being chopped at by shears all day was annoying, to say the least, added to which plants are fueled by sunlight. So trying to grow overnight was somewhat exhausting. He would be better off being a mushroom, he was sure."

"The Geist had tried to distract himself with remembering being a black cardinal's mitre and the sights he had seen non-corporeally in the days of the inquisition. He'd had a high time with all that lovely temptation and putting ideas in the clergy's heads, though he had to admit they hadn't needed much in the way of encouraging when it came to torturing witches for confession."

"Those guys had really had something against witches… Hot pokers mostly."

"His memories of less enlightened times led him to dream of all those interesting ways they tied up victims. He also dreamt of his creepers being the ropes. That would be a proper haunting he thought; far more fun than mere growing."

"As he dreamed this one day, the lawyer in his haste to speed up the coming transaction, cast a more powerful growth spell…"

"Sometimes a plot takes a twist, sometimes such twists are easily read in advance. Others are somewhat more unexpected and twisty. However, no complexity of plot for this tale, I fear. If you have been paying attention, you can probably take a wild stab at what happened next."

"Ivy grows, this is what it does, and even with a sentience of the demonic kind guiding it, grow is all it can really do."

"As the lawyer cast his spell regardless, the ivy began to grow with increasing rapidity, and unknowingly, within the little house Emmy Lou took her daily long hot shower, once again obscuring the mirror with steam, much to his disgruntlement of the lawyer."

"It was a long hot steamy shower, and it was blissful up to a point. The point in question been when the creepers that had wound through the house pushed open the door and began to move through the hot moist steamy atmosphere of the bathroom. To be more exact, it was the moment they pulled back the shower curtain, bringing to an end the blissful showering."

"There was a scream, of course. A cry of disbelief, anguish, and generally more than a little distress as separate demonic creepers of one huge processed ivy plant wrapped themselves around ankles and wrists. They only increased along neck and thighs, pulling, tugging, and otherwise dragging, their unwilling victim out of the shower and onto the bathroom floor."

"Naked and quite firmly secured."

"Emmy Lou had never seen '*The Evil Dead*', which may perhaps have been a blessing as the tendrils of the demonic ivy wound themselves tightly around and up her legs."

"A small blessing it is true."

"The lawyer, who had seen said movie, was currently busy cursing his bathroom daffodil which had finally wilted completely from the steam."

"He tried madly to get reception through the mould on the ceiling, but fungi are seldom receptive to horticultural black magic being as they are more intelligent than most other flora."

"The demon in the ivy, which had not seen the movie either, but had witnessed the worst excesses of Spanish Catholicism in the 14th century, decided to wing it and grew a thicker stem."

"The Geist found itself suddenly of a new opinion about the demonic procession of plant life. At least, in comparison to ecclesiastical clothing. He had realised, you see, that he would not simply have to make do with watching and make suggestions this time..."

"Indeed, perhaps one stem was not enough. There were options after all, and it had seen the internet, all those inventive Japanese cartoons with aliens in them..."

"There were a lot of screams, not oddly enough, though, all through horror. As noted earlier, Emmy Lou had once enjoyed a complex but very active social life. She was an imaginative and open minded girl herself in many ways."

"Afterwards, there followed a long chat about things, once she got used to the idea of talking to a plant that grew its own mouth to converse, and a deal was reached."

"You see, it turned out the ivy quite liked long

sunny days and frankly, it had also discovered it hated lawyers, which at least goes to show that even demons from the lower nether regions of Hell are not all bad."

"Emmy Lou never left the cottage on the hill, though not for the reasons you might first consider. The lawyer failed in his attempts to gain the cottage by trickery and black magic, and came to what for anyone else might be described as an unfortunate end."

"Indeed, it was a note in the small print of the demonic contract which caught him out. It turned out he did not read the small print either. And Hell has a special place for lawyers. They don't like them all that much."

"The ivy learned to control its growth."

"With its demonic host, it learned to control it quite well, in fact, much to Emmy Lou's delight and satisfaction."

"Quite a lot of satisfaction in the long run, as she had a leaning towards being tied up and was, it proved to be, surprisingly receptive to intrusions as she, too, had seen and enjoyed many Japanese cartoons."

"Though it has to be said, she did insist on using lubricant."

Richard was laughing. It felt good to laugh. The ridiculousness of the story had cut through his mood.

True it had been long winded, drawn out in Lyal's deadpan style for that one single payoff of the final piece of innuendo.

But it had been worth it all the same. He was not sure it would have been quite the tale had it not been told with Lyal's deadpan delivery.

Lyal laughed, too, as the final line was delivered. A strange laugh, the kind of laugh you got from someone who did not quite get the joke everyone else was laughing at, which was all the stranger as he had been the one to tell the joke.

Morn was laughing, too. She had come down to his end of the bar when Lyal started to tell his tale, her own laughter of a throatier, earthy kind.

Richard found himself smiling in her direction. She had a glint in her eye when Lyal delivered the last line, which added to Richard's smile.

"Good story Lyal, thank you," he said, feeling something was required of him, as well as feeling genuinely appreciative of the tale.

"You're welcome," Lyal said, picking up a glass to polish once more, still laughing at his own story. He wandered down the bar to serve a customer, leaving Richard with Morn.

"He doesn't know why it's funny…" Morn said, watching the barman go before turning back to Richard still smiling.

"I'm not so sure. I think he just wants us to think that," Richard replied. Slightly surprising himself with the insight.

"Possibly… you never can tell," Morn said with a shrug before picking up Richard's empty glass.

"You want another, or are you going to go earn your keep on the ivories?" she asked, with overtones to her question which suggested while either answer was fine the latter was preferable.

There was even a note of sanction to her voice, a suggestion of displeasure, which he tried to dismiss as his own paranoia.

He was tempted to have another anyway despite this, but he also knew he should not. Besides which, his dark mood had been broken for a while, at least, and he wanted to play once more. So instead he stood and returned her smile.

"I guess I should be playing," he said and started to turn, before realising he felt a little light headed from the bourbon.

"Any chance of a coffee?" he asked.

"Sure, all you need to do is go to the kitchen," she replied with a cheeky wink and turned to serve a customer.

Richard shook his head, half to clear it, half to hide his grin, then headed to the kitchen.

On his way his eyes were drawn to an odd patch on the ceiling, Darker than others--dark, with a red tinge. For a second, a flicker of a second at that, he thought he saw a face in the shadowy patch. A face with red eyes that seemed to leer out at him. He shook his head again in a vain attempt to clear it once more, then he made for the kitchen. Cursing his Pareidolia as he did so, he returned his gaze to his goal of the kitchen door and coffee.

Unaware that those red eyes followed him.

CHAPTER TWENTY

The Forest in the Cellar

"Richard, are you busy?" Morn's voice asked as he walked down the stairs, greeting him with a wide smile and a tilt of the head as he got to the doorway behind the bar.

His hair was still wet from the shower. He had stumbled into it half-asleep that morning after sleeping late and showered quickly. It had been another night staring at the ceiling in search of elusive sleep, though it had been easier to find than in the last few days. All the same, he had still woken feeling drained, tired to the bone.

"Not as such," he replied evasively, he wanted coffee. To be specific, he wanted black coffee loaded with sugar. He did not feel up to being dragged into anything until he had that coffee.

Possibly two coffees.

Expressos.

She came around the corner of the bar carrying two large old-fashioned watering cans. The large old tin things you never saw anyone use any more, except perhaps as decretive flower pots. From the sound of the sloshing as she carried them, these particular ones were intended to be used for their original purpose. They also looked rather heavy from the way Morn was struggling with them. On seeing he was still standing at the bottom of the steps, she put them down with a thud, causing some of the water splashed out onto the barroom floor.

"When you say '*not as such*,' what do you mean? Are you busy or aren't you? Because if you're busy, that's fine. I'll just have to manage on my own. But, to be honest, you don't look busy, and this would be so much easier with two of us," she rambled, tilting her head to one side once more in that strange way she did when she appeared mildly confused.

Quizzical was the word that sprung to mind.

"What would be easier?" he asked, suspecting that the coffee was now going to be much further in the future than he desired, his need to make Morn smile overruling his caffeine addiction.

He still felt a little guilty about the rift between them the argument in the garden had created several days ago. Though she seemed to have forgotten all about it, it still niggled him a little. The strange green haired girl's good graces were something he wanted to be back in.

"I need to go into the cellar to water the forest," she said, resting her hands on her hips, which made her seem a little frustrated with him. The way she often did when it seemed she was stating something she considered self-evident. Which was generally incomprehensible to him.

"Water the forest?"

"Yes."

"In the cellar?"

"Yes."

"You want me to come with you into the cellar to water a forest?"

"Yes, why are you repeating what I say?" There was more of a note of irritation in her tone now. It was clear she considered this a simple concept to grasp.

"With two rusty watering cans?"

"Well yes obviously, I mean, I know it seems like too much water, but it always spills on the way, so it's better just to take two instead. But they're really quite heavy, and so it's a lot easier with two people, rather than doing it on my own. Lyal normally helps, but he's having one of his… things… this morning."

"His…"

"Look never mind Lyal. Are you busy or not? Because if you are, then that's fine and I will just have to get on and do this myself."

Richard stared at her trying to make sense of what she was saying, resisting the urge to complicate things further by pressing her about whatever '*things*' Lyal was having one of. Morn already had a flustered look about her. She also had that odd glow about her eyes which always made him itch a little.

"Okay," he capitulated, with a sigh.

"Well fine, I'll do it myself..." she said in a voice that stamped its feet, and then bent down to pick up watering cans. There was a tiny note of anger in her voice as well as frustration. Her eyes flaring bright green in the odd way they did when her temper was getting the better of her.

"No, I meant okay I'll come with you," he said quickly, hoping to head off her anger.

"Oh... Good then that's settled," she replied brightly, tilting her head once more and adding a slight shake of her head, and no sense of irony. "I do wish you would try and speak more plainly sometimes, Richard. It would make life so much simpler if you tried to be clear with your words."

Morn picked up one of the watering cans and turned back towards the kitchen, sloshing water as she went.

Richard sighed to himself, biting back the urge to point out she had been less than clear herself. '*Water the forest in the cellar...*' he thought, shaking his head. '*This place will make sense one day,*' he added, with little real hope it was true.

Picking up the other watering can, he followed Morn across the barroom, wondering absently where the cellar door actually was.

It turned out to be a door next to the kitchen, which was one he had never seen before. This particular morsel failed to surprise him overly. You can get used to anything given time, and the doors in the Passing Place had a habit of only being there when you wanted to use them. Richard had reached a point where he ceased to be so easily surprised, mainly because it was that or spend his days in perpetual wonder.

Morn unlocked the door with a large brass key on a chain from her belt. There was a loud clanking sound as it turned as if the tumblers were huge mechanical things, hidden in the doors casing, which seemed somewhat ominous to Richard. As did the strange creaking sound that the door made as she turned the handle and pulled it open, like the opening of some dread portal or the entrance to some long undisturbed crypt in an old horror movie.

Needless to say, this did little to inspire Richard's confidence.

In the event it was a pleasant surprise to find the stairway, which the door revealed, was surprisingly light, airy and free of dust with, of all things, sunflower wallpaper lining the walls.

Morn flicked on a light switch, which refused to be in any way ominous, much to Richards's relief. There was, however, a heavy buzzing and loud 'thunking' sound as a contactor tripped into place and the basement lights came on one at a time. In the way much enamoured of movie directors when revealing secret warehouses under government buildings.

Richard found himself wondering what kind of cellar a passing place had. Just how deep it might go, given the size of the bar was somewhat indeterminable. *'It could be like the catacombs of Paris down there,'* he found himself thinking, then realised that thinking of it in term of the Parisian necropolis was a far from comforting thought. Morn, however, started down the steps, seemingly unperturbed by such possibilities.

Shaking his head at the foolishness of his own imagination Richard followed behind. While doing his best to mind his step and deciding quite firmly not to ponder how the stairwell--which obviously must be pushed through the kitchen--did not actually do so, because he was absolutely sure he had never noticed a stairwell wall running through the kitchen.

Their descent was lengthy, the cellar steps twisting back on themselves a couple of times at least. Eventually, they came out in a large cellar full of odd piping runs, create stacks and barrels.

The wine rack that lined one wall was impossibly long, disappearing off into the distant gloom beyond the light. Many of the bottles were thick with dust, as if they had been laid down many years before, an oenophile's dream collection. Richard was no great wine buff himself, but he suspected you could find vintages on that rack that were thought long lost to the world, *'or worlds…'* A stray thought at the back of Richards mind added. He had found himself thinking like that a lot of late. Making little mental additions to include it in his thoughts. Somehow among so many other strange ideas it seemed simpler than most to get his head around.

Crates of bottles were stacked against another wall, bottles of every size and shape, some with old labels that looked out of time. Others were the cheery, familiar ones Richard would have expected to find anywhere. Even so, it was an oddly mixed bunch from real ales and Belgium lagers, to American beers and spirits of every description.

He guessed, with a certain amount of resignation, it was what he should have expected in the bars cellar. If anything, apart from the strangely endless dimensions, he was a tad disappointed at the normality of it, though it was hard to accept the oddly wrong perspective of the endless wine rack.

What there was not, however, was definitely no forest. He said as much to his companion.

"Of course not silly, it's through here," Morn replied, putting her watering can down for a moment while she opened a hatchway in the floor that was half hidden behind a stack of beer barrels.

It turned out to be just the kind of hatch you would chain shut to keep the evil dead at bay. On seeing it, Richard had to suppress a slight shiver. A momentary flash of the name '*Ashley*' spoken in a broken woman's voice, hovering on the edge of his consciousness. He tried to put it down to the cold air in the cellar, and too many late night horror dvds on the sofa. Mostly he convinced himself, regardless of the hatchways ominous nature, and so he managed to ignore the gouges in the wooden floor that may have been made by heavy chains being rasped against them, but were surely just made by barrels been moved around…

Sighing once more, he shifted the heavy watering can from one hand to the other and followed Morn down the dusty wooden steps that led into the second cellar.

Where the first cellar was clean and well used, the second, deeper cellar, had a musty feel to it. The walls were dug into the dirt itself. Hard packed earth on which the bar must rest. At least it seemed like dirt--dark black earth. He could see old roots running through it like veins. Clumps of them hung down from the ceiling, dangling free like upside down bushes. Reminiscent of a tunnel cut into a hillside then left untended for years while nature slowly grew back down.

It felt warm down there, as well, while the first cellar had felt cold. He reasoned that there must have been coolers in the upper cellar he had not seen, It made sense after all, as it was used to store drinks for the bar. In comparison, the second deeper cellar felt close and dank.

Lighting had been jerry-rigged along its length, lines of yellow cable pinned to the ceiling, baton lights hung with bare bulbs every few meters along the string. They stretched down a corridor in little pools of illumination in the darkness that ran off away from the bottom of the stairs.

Richard followed Morn down the corridor, trying to avoid the urge to run his hand along the dirt wall. He had managed all of a few feet before he did so.

The earth felt warm, which he had expected, but not quite like it should all the same. Instead, it felt clammy and oily, not soil as much as a membrane, a living thing rather than earth. As he trailed his hand along it, he could feel the slightest of vibrations, a throbbing, like the echo of a pulse, with a slow, deliberate rhythm to it.

When he first felt it, he had an urge to pull his hand away. He fought the urge and kept his hand trailing the wall, fascinated and horrified at the same time, wondering if it was his imagination or if he really was, as he suspected, walking through a living thing.

But, no, that was a ridiculous idea, he knew that, and told himself so.

The walls were, more likely, just an odd kind of clay or something, and the vibrations… well, perhaps it was just some machinery of some kind sending vibrations through the earth.

He knew he was trying to rationalise, but was naggingly sure there was a more obvious answer, the one he was refusing to accept. The one that felt right, that he was in the belly of the beast, the inner heart of the Passing Place, he realised he should feel terrified by the idea. Walking inside a living thing, was that what he was doing? Then wasn't that the whole of Esqwith, the whole of the Passing Place. A living thing? His mind was repelled by the idea. Yet at the same time though it seemed right it was all the same; safe. He knew that somehow, he was safe here, though why he felt so he could not say.

"What is this place?" he asked quietly; more a question asked of the air, in truth, than directed at Morn, who was now some ways ahead of him.

If she heard him, she declined to comment.

He followed her down the strange corridor, occasionally running his hand along the wall once more. He was only half aware he was even doing so after a while. He felt an odd sense of calm descending over him each time his hand made contact with the surface, a feeling that left him as soon as he withdrew his hand, making him desire to do so again.

He tried to understand it.

The strange almost audible pulse, he felt more than heard--the warmth of the walls, their peculiar alive quality.

It reminded him of something he could not remember, no matter how hard he tried to grasp at it, a thing before memory, something at the core of his existence. A yearning for a forgotten place of safety that was once an absolute yet was now merely the memory of a memory forgotten. Something he knew he could never truly remember, yet had a longing for unknowingly all the same. An absence that he could not explain or express, only feel.

As they followed the winding corridor, it struck him again that this was perhaps the very centre of The Passing Place. The presence, the creature, whatever she was, that was Esqwith. This was close to the core of her.

It struck him also that there was something so familiar and yet so ungraspable about this place. To be inside another living thing perhaps, if that is what she was. To be within and yet not consumed.

To know that you're safe, secure, even loved maybe. To not know it or understand it. But to know where you were all the same. To know you were as safe and secure as you would ever be.

Then he realised what it reminded him of--the place he could not remember, could never remember, but had spent the first nine months of existence within.

He tried to shake the image, withdrawing his hand from the wall. To be within the womb, if that was truly what he was reminded of, seemed wrong in a new way, even if it was just a memory of a memory sparked by where he was.

He tucked his free hand into his pocket, to keep it from the wall. Trying to put the idea from his mind. But once he had come to this conclusion, it was hard to forget about it.

All the same, even with this realisation, it was hard to shake the feeling of safety. Where ever he was, he was safe, secure, wanted even?

He tried to shake the idea, focusing instead on following Morn who walked on ahead oblivious to the confusion that rolled through his mind. Also aware he had lost track of time, and how long they had been walking, the corridor seemed to just go on endlessly through the darkness. Following a trail of dim light bulbs hanging from their yellow cord.

After more twists and turns, which seemed to continue to descend deeper into The Passing Place, they rounded another corner and came to an opening in the wall.

Daylight, or at least the same kind of daylight he had found in Morn's garden, flooded in through the opening, blinding him slightly after the dimness of the corridor lighting.

Beyond the opening, there was a small terrace, and the void, that same deep engulfing black nothingness he had seen in the garden, which brought with it that self-same sense of vertigo he had felt there-- the swirling black run through with deep dark colours that were impossible to see. That familiar desperate sense of nothing.

There was another feeling too, something locked away that wanted him to remember it, adding to his vertigo. The vaguest of impressions of red, something red. For a fleeting second, the memory of it threatened to engulf him. Then he found himself shaking his head and the feeling past, leaving in its wake an odd feeling of relief...

The terrace that jutted out into the void some twenty meters was full of small trees. Bonsai's in small shallow earthenware in pots. Some truly tiny, others huge and ancient, in bonsai terms at least, rising to almost a meter tall, their canopies spreading out over the other trees.

Tiny pine cones clung to some, as small as the trees themselves. It was a forest in miniature, composed of pine, oak, ash, beech, yew and sycamore. Richard had never realised there was such variety in bonsai trees.

He found himself smiling suddenly. For all the strangeness of the place, at least he now understood how two watering cans could water a forest.

A small victory against the confusion of his daily life it may be, but a victory, nonetheless.

"Just put the watering can down over there Richard," Morn said, pointing to a small wooden trestle with tools and other assortments upon it.

He did as he was told, then found himself watching for a while as Morn started watering the trees, noting how she was carefully making sure not to pour too much in any one pot.

In part, he knew, he was keeping his eyes on the trees and the strange young green haired woman to avoid looking out into the void.

He knew why. He felt an aversion to looking into the blackness. Not just because it felt wrong, but it was more than that. It was not the absence of anything he feared, so much as something he expected to see within it.

He had the impression, once more, of red… something red… but for the life of him he could not remember what it was, or why he felt afraid of it.

He started to feel the silence hanging in the air-- a void like the one beyond the terrace--and felt the need to fill it.

"I like your forest," he said, grasping for a conversation starter, as Morn bent down to carefully add water to another pot. Consequently, he realised he was staring juts a little too much in her direction, pleasant though he found the view. So focused his attention instead on the miniature trees that made up the forest.

Not before Morn looked up from her watering, however, though if she noticed the lasciviousness of his gaze, she did not show it. Instead, she tilted her head to one side in that odd mannerism of hers, and looking slightly quizzical before she replied. It always slightly unnerved him when she did that, he had a feeling she was trying to look past the surface into his true self. As an idea it filled him with dread, ridiculous though he knew that was. He found it disconcerting.

"Oh, it's not mine. I just got asked to take care of

it by 'Bringer Of Things' the last time she went away." She chirped happily, smiling at him.

"Who's 'Bringer Of things?" he asked, knowing he was falling into obvious questions once more. He as unsurprised to see the puzzled expression cross the barmaid's face. He wondered why everyone just assumed he knew things, and almost sighed to himself.

"Bringer Of Things. She's the cat, didn't you know her name?" she asked, her surprise at least was quite genuine, he could tell. As was his own at the realisation that he did not.

"I...I never asked her, or anyone else..." he replied. The fact he had never done so surprised him even more than Morn, he suspected. Inquiring after the name of a person, or even a pet for that matter, was just something you did. And the cat was not just a pet, he was sure of that much, though, in truth, he never really thought of cats as pets anyway.

Dogs were pets. Cats, on the other hand, were more like lodgers you invite into your home rent free. Lodgers you supply with meals and clean up after. Until, before long you were putting the lodger's needs before your own, to be rewarded with the occasional unwanted present being dragged in through the cat flap.

But then who doesn't long to wake up to be greeted by an eviscerated mouse on the kitchen floor...

This cat, though-- Esqwith's cat-- she was as much of a person to him as anyone else in the bar. Yet despite this, it had never occurred to him to ask her name. Or even to call her anything but '*the cat.*' He felt a strange sense of shame wash over him for a moment, before something occurred to him.

"Sonny calls her 'Princess.' I thought perhaps that was her name." he said with all the sincerity of a drowning man grabbing for a life raft.

"No you didn't," Morn said, with a teasing smile. A tickle of laughter to her tone.

"No your right I didn't," he admitted, realising this was true even before she pointed it out. "It's just his pet name for her isn't it?"

"You have that right. Sonny likes to give everyone pet names. He liked to call me 'Green Girl' for a while till I asked him to stop."

"Green Girl?" Richard inquired fighting the urge to smile. It was an apt description after all.

"I know, it's terrible, isn't it? I mean, I am older than he is. 'Girl,' honestly it's ridiculous." There was a note of indignation in her voice, which was all but a verbal stamping of the feet.

Richard found himself looking hard at Morn once more, trying to figure out if she was pulling his leg. After all, she did not look like she was long out of her teenage years, if even that. Sonny was in his forties at least, possibly more. He found it hard to credit her words, but, as he looked hard at her, he saw little lines around her eyes that told a different story. Crow's feet on a teenager's face were odd, that was for sure. Perhaps she really was far older than she looked.

Not for the first time, he found himself wondering about Morn as he looked at her. She did not at times seem entirely human, which was, he found, too strange a concept to think about. People, at leats the none feline kind, were after all human, even the strangest of people in The Passing Place were still human. They had to be. Other possibilities were a touch beyond anything he wanted to consider. There was enough strangeness in his world already.

Instead of dwelling on the idea he tried to switch the subject elsewhere.

"So this... Forest... it belongs to the cat... Erm...To Bringer Of Things?" he reached. It seemed a safer subject than the one he was thinking of, for his own sanities sake if nothing else.

"Not really, she was just looking after it for a while after Li Lu left, before she asked me to keep an eye on it for her while she was away. I like doing it, so when she came back she just left me to it, I think. She's thoughtful like that."

"Li Lu?" he asked, the name vaguely familiar, though he could not place it.

"Yes, it was his forest of contemplation, before he left on his journey of enlightenment. We are looking after it in case he comes back," she said brightly.

"I know that name, just not sure from where," Richard said, thinking aloud rather than asking a question. He was still trying to get his head around other ideas: The heartbeat in the walls, the age of Morn, the cat who was not just a cat. There was always so much he struggled to get a grip on. He found himself swimming hard sometimes just to stay afloat in the oddity of his new home.

"Oh, that's probably from the story, you know.

It's one of those stories that people have always heard at some time," Morn said, and Ricard sighed noticeably. He felt on the verge of figuring something out. Or perhaps just figuring out all the things he did not understand, which was progress of a kind. The last thing he wanted right now was to listen to another story, though he was half sure he was about to.

"I'm not sure I know it," he said, before realising that was exactly the wrong thing to say, as Morn began telling a tale…

"Having searched for enlightenment in the darkest corners of the world. Talked at great length to the dragons of the four winds. Crossed the impenetrable mountains of the world pillar in broken sandals. Trekked through the forbidden forests of Lill. Dived to the ocean depths to talk to the sea serpents. Traversed all eight oceans on a raft made of driftwood. Spanned the grey dust deserts where all life flees in nothing but a loincloth, all the while carrying a thimble full of water but never drinking of it. Li Lu came at last to the erroneous conclusion enlightenment could not be found in the world and sat down on a solitary rock to die…" she began, and Richard felt the world begin to shimmer a little around the edges of his perceptions….

"Can you tell me this another time Morn…? I should probably be heading back upstairs," Richard interrupted, a little more sharply than he intended, in the hope of excusing himself.

"Oh, sure, if you like. Just follow the same route back. Leave the trap door open, if you will. It's a swine to open from this side," Morn replied brightly enough, though she looked slightly put out all the same.

Everyone in The Passing Place seemed to enjoy telling stories. Richard guessed Morn was no exception to the rule. He could see in her eyes that he had offended her ever so slightly. He ventured a narrow smile in an attempt to placate her feelings a little.

"I tell you what, you can tell me this evening after we close up," he said, mostly just to mollify her, though he was well aware he was setting himself up to hear the story.

"Okay, it's a date," she replied, answering his smile with a broad grin, and perking up instantly.

"Erm… that's not quite…" he started but realised that she probably meant no more than a date for a story, and felt foolish.

Not wanting to pour oil on troubled waters, he changed the track of the conversation once more, trying to extradite himself before he got himself further into trouble with the green haired girl. Besides which, a couple of questions had occurred to him that now niggled at him.

"You said the cat used to water this place before she left for a while. Where did she go?"

Morn shrugged. "Just away, I think she said she wanted to try something for a while. No idea what she meant by that. Bringer Of Things never really explains herself to me. No reason she should really. She was just gone for a while."

"How long was she gone?" he queried, not entirely sure why he asked, but it seemed important for some reason.

"Four, maybe five, years, I'm not sure. You know what time is like… It slips by," she replied, then smirked slightly. "Particularly here, as I am sure you've noticed."

He nodded. He knew that feeling of slipping time too well.

There was something else, though, something about five years. He was not sure what, however, but it rang a bell with him somehow. He felt on the edge of something again. It was frustrating, like glimpses of answers out of the corner of his minds eye that turned out be something else entirely when he looked at them full on.

It felt like he was trying to connect the dots on a blank piece of paper.

He turned to walk back upstairs, the desire for coffee suddenly all the stronger than it had been when he first woke that morning.

He was halfway down the corridor when the other question that had occurred to him came back to mind.

"How exactly did the cat water the trees?" he asked her, turning back towards the tiny forest.

The absurdity of a cat with a watering can struck him, though the weird mental image that accompanied it brought a smile to his face.

Morn shrugged once more, looking back at him over her shoulder.

"You'd have to ask her that," she said then smiling turned back to the trees. Singing something wordless but tuneful to them, as she got back to tending the forest in the cellar.

CHAPTER TWENTYONE

Power According to LaGuin

Richard made his way back through the cellar, feeling strangely bemused. He was not sure why this was the case. Something was bothering him, or rather, in all honesty, a collection of somethings.

Little things which added up in odd ways. None of which made much in the way of sense, if indeed any, come to that.

The cat was at the heart of it. The more he thought about it, the more he was sure that was the case. But he was certain at the same time that he was missing some of the pieces.

It was like grasping to remember something, some detail he had missed or forgotten.

That was the real problem, he was sure.

He had forgotten little things. Things he only knew he had forgotten because of the holes left behind. His memory was playing tricks with him, little grey spots, blank bits where there should be none. He was sure it was not just his paranoia playing tricks on his mind.

It was like being teased by someone, while at the same time, not quite being sure that was what was happening. Like an itch at the back of his mind that he needed to scratch, but could not reach.

There was something else as well, more a scar than an itch. Something he could not even begin to define. Something he had seen, or, perhaps, felt. Something menacing. Something hidden.

Something red.

When he thought about it, however, it slipped away from him. He would find his mind drifting off until he could not remember what it was that he had seen or felt, holding only the vaguest of memories.

There were things that were wrong in the Passing Place, of that much he was certain. Something a touch sinister that lay on the edge of everything. He felt his skin crawling as he tried to grasp at it. All he could put a firm finger on was the colour red.

Something red.

He was lost in these thoughts, or rather trying to grasp at them as he followed the organic walls of the corridor. They twisted and turned in odd ways, and he found himself paying little attention to the route he was following. He was sure he did not remember any side corridors on the way to the bonsai forest. So when he passed the first of them, he assumed he had just not seen it on the way to the trees. He was certain they had not turned off the main corridor at any point, so he just kept on walking.

By the time he passed the second turn off-- this one to the other side of the corridor that he was following,--he started to grow a little tense.

Lost in thought had it seemed, become just plain lost.

Richard passed a third turn off, then came to a halt when the corridor he had been following ended at a wall with a door in it.

He was certain they had not passed through any doors after the hatchway. All the abstract thoughts drained away, as he realised he must have taken a wrong turn.

His vague sense of paranoia was not helped by the fact that the door happened to be painted red.

He looked around the corridor with a certain desperation seeping into his mindset, trying to get a fresh sense of direction. The strangely organic walls offered no real clue. The odd root-like veins that seemed to run through it looked no different from how they had before. Too indistinct to pick out individual patterns that might help him recognise a patch of wall.

Except, that was, for the one nearest the door, which had a slight crimson hue in the darker parts. They, like the others, seemed to pulse slightly. But rather that it be benign the crimson ones pulsed in a more disturbing way, growing ever so slightly with each pulse. Slowly seeming to spread out from the doorway.

Richard tried to put that down to his imagination playing tricks. That same odd itch the colour red seemed to give him elsewhere in the passing place. Just his imagination putting things together. The red veins were not spreading like some infection in the roots...

Overactive imagination or not, however, he had no desire to turn the door handle and go through the red door. The thought of doing so alone felt wrong, bringing back that itch he could not scratch.

He turned back down the corridor and took the first turn he came to. Following a path that was much like the other, he passed more turn offs that led to doorways. Thankfully, though, none of them red.

Indeed, they all seemed to be universally dark brown in colour, much like the walls, which, if anything, made the red door all the more strange and disturbing.

All the same, he was still troubled that he had not seen all this before. The memory of that strange nightmare weeks ago, with the girl in the corridor, crossed his mind. But this did not have that same odd dream-like quality about it. It felt real, where the nightmare corridor never had. He knew he was awake, just lost. Whereas the girl in the corridor had just been a dream, after all, *'hadn't it?'* The questioning thought slipped itself into his consciousness.

'No, that was a dream, nothing more, this is real, strange yes but real,' he told himself.

Be that as it may. It was still frustrating to find himself lost in the cellar.

The next corridor he followed led to yet another door, so he backtracked once more and took another turn, stalking down the new corridor and feeling angry with himself for not paying more attention to the path when he came down with Morn in the first place.

He was also kicking himself for not making his way back to the bonsai forest when he first realised he had taken a wrong turn. Now he was not sure he could find his way back there either.

It was not as if he had been paying a great deal of attention when he set off back to the bar either, come to that. Now he was well and truly lost in the tunnels beneath the Passing Place. Lost in the engulfing gloom, lit only by strings of yellow cable and the bare light bulbs tapped into it.

Was it getting dimmer? Were those bare bulbs wider apart? Or we there just slowly going down, like the house lights in a theatre, but agonisingly slower?

He was not even sure how long he had been walking. It seemed like an hour or more, but it could not have been that long, could it? What was it Morn had said back at the forest?

'*You know what time is like… It slips by*'…

Was it slipping by now, were minutes passing like hours, or the other way around? He was sure it had not been that long. Though it was more than a few minutes, he was sure of that much, and he felt thirsty, more thirsty than he should. Perhaps it was the heat? It did seem hotter down here now.

He felt his temper was flaring--at himself, it was true, but no less angry for that. He stopped mid corridor and closed his eyes for a moment, trying to calm himself, to let himself think, if just for a moment. Then he could at least try and retrace his steps. *'Think damn it, did I go right first at the red door, or was it left? Calm, calm... Just think Richard, just think...'* he said to himself, or aloud, he was not quite sure... Any more than he was sure how long he stood there like that.

A moment, a few minutes, an hour...

His eyes were still closed when he heard a familiar voice. One which, in fairness, may have just been in his head.

'You really should have tied a piece of string at the entrance. That's the easy way, or so they say traditional as well come to that.' The cat sounded amused, and more than a little sarcastic. *'Or bread crumbs, they're supposed to be good, as long as the birdies don't eat them. Which they always do you know, you can't trust the birdies, nasty things they are...they do It just to fuck with people I am sure...'*

He opened his eyes, breathing out heavily, as much out of a sense of exasperation as anything else. He looked down to see the cat laying lazily on the floor of the corridor, its tail curled around its body. Eyes shining slightly in the dim light, she blinked at him before yawning loudly.

He found himself wondering, in an abstract way, which was stranger, a cat that talked, or a cat that swore. She seldom swore, which added impact to those rare times which she did. Yet somehow a cat swearing at you was oddly less surprising than one talking. Which did not make any sense at all, unless you knew cats, he supposed…

"Glad I am amusing you," he snapped, anything but glad to be the butt of her humour, but relieved to see her at the same time, which blunted his irritation a little.

'*No need to get all prissy on me, Richard, it's hardly my fault if you get yourself lost now is it.*' She seemed to yowl, though he suspected there was more amusement in her voice than anger. He took a breath and collected himself.

"Could you be so kind as to show me the way out?" he inquired in a more even tone, then as an afterthought he added, "Bringer."

As he now knew her name, he felt he should make an effort to use it.

She flicked her tail at him, rising onto her paws. Her tail flicked up to form a question mark of fur, and she began to prance down the corridor. There was an arrogance in the walk. Something that said, '*I know where I am going*,' which in fairness he had no doubt she did.

Sighing heavily, he followed as she made her way through the twisting half-lit corridors that wound through the cellar. Somehow they were a little less intimidating now because he had the cat for company.

Before long, little more than fifty yards or so, they came to the stairs up into the beer cellar. She pounded up them, in a series of leaps before coming to a halt at the top and looking down at him. If she had a readable expression, it was one of inquiry, though how he could tell, he was not sure.

As he put his foot on the first step she asked with an inquiring purr, '*You called me Bringer?*'

"Morn said it was your name, well part of it anyway, she said you were called 'Bringer Of Things'," he explained.

The cat tilted its head to one side, regarding him intensely. He paused in his ascent of the stairs, still with only one foot on the first step. He wondered for a moment if he had offended her in some way.

A moment passed until she flicked her tail once more and said plainly, '*Well that's a name she calls me, certainly. But it's not my name.*'

"It isn't?" he asked, finding himself wondering now what her name really was, if she was telling the truth, he was not entirely sure she would tell him the truth, he was not sure why that odd idea occurred to him though.

'*No, it's what happens when my name is translated into the language of her people and then back again. She's not half as good with human words as it appears at times,*' she replied, sounding slightly put out--irritated even-- he was not sure if it was with him or with Morn.

He was not sure why she was offended, though he knew people could be funny about names. It was something he understood well enough. He hated when people assumed it was alright to shorten his given name to 'Dick'. A name he found hateful for all the obvious reasons of a British childhood at a comprehensive school.

That the shortened version of his name was so easily used as an insult did not help, which may have been why it always felt rude to him to shorten someone's name unless they chose to use the shortened version themselves. After all, he always thought, your name was one thing that was certainly your own. He disliked nicknames for the same reason, at least unless people chose to be known by them. Even the pet names his wife used to call him rankled him a little at times. Irrational though he felt that was.

"I'm sorry, I just thought… What is your name then?" he stumbled, feeling now he had used an actual name for her, he should inquire as to the right one to use. He also hoped that in doing so he could undo any offence he had caused. He seemed to be finding little ways to offend everyone of late. It was starting to feed his paranoia a little.

He chose to ignore the odd reference to "human" as a language, letting it slip by him. It was probably just a cat thing after all. She probably just meant that Morn's first language was not English. He wondered absently where Morn was actually from. Her accent, now he thought of it, had a hint of Norwegian or Swedish perhaps. But only a hint at most.

'It's what I am called,' the cat replied cryptically, prowling back and forth at the top of the stairs. Then with a glint of amusement in her voice, she added, *'Have you ever read any Ursula LaGuin?'*

"Erm… Earthsea?" he dredged up the reference to the author. He had read some of her work as a teenager. He remembered enjoying the books but little else about them.

'Names have power, Richard. One must never just give away your true name. It gives someone power over you after all,' the cat said flicking its tail up into a question mark curl once more. He could have sworn that a grin crossed her face for a moment, in an almost human way.

She turned and stalked away from the top of the hatch, leaving him staring after her. He sighed heavily to himself, wondering if she was at times difficult just for the sake of being difficult.

He would not have put it past her. She had a temperamental streak to her that reminded him of Carrie. His wife would often be mysterious and obtuse for no other reason than she found it amusing.

At least that was always what he ascribed it to.

Thinking of Carrie, he was surprised how little such thoughts caused him to have a wave of grief. Perhaps it was simply because he was thinking of her in abstract, referencing the behaviour of someone else to her own. All the same, he found himself smiling at the memory, embracing it without the usual regret.

He was about to start up the stairs once more when the cat reappeared back in the hatchway and purred at him.

'I'll tell you when you're ready to hear it, Richard, if you choose to be told,' she said archly.

Then with a flick of her tail, she was gone.

CHAPTER TWENTYTWO

Striking the Wrong Cord

It was yellow, the sickly yellow of tobacco stains, and run through with tiny red veins. Yellow with age perhaps, but wrong even so, and all alone in a sea of white.

Just one key, alone among the others. Sitting there speaking without words of its wrongness.

Richard looked at it as he sat at the piano. It drew his eyes, as it had done the previous day when he first found it: a single key on his keyboard, one alone no longer pristine ivory like the rest.

It had just appeared among the others from nowhere, looking at first, like the key of some antique piano, merely yellowed with age, but wrong all the same. How does one key age faster than the others after all?

It had niggled at him throughout the previous day. That it was located at the furthest end of the keyboard was a saving grace. Something about it made his fingers feel itchy just looking at it.

He found himself avoiding the key, playing around it. If it had been a major key it would have been hard to play at all, but as a minor, it was at worst the cause of an occasional missed note, when he could not bring himself to strike it.

Which was a part of the problem. He had to force himself to play it. His fingers normally so quick to find notes would pull away, almost with a will of their own.

This morning the key was worse than it had been yesterday. The key was not only a little yellow with age but was now that sickly looking yellow that has started turning to orange. The tiny red veins that had yesterday been only the faintest of lines were more pronounced, thicker, raised lines which seemed to pulse slightly like arteries.

'A trick of the light,' he tried to assure himself, *'just a trick of the light.'* Though he was far from convinced by this explanation.

Those red pulsating lines reminded him of something as well. Something that seemed to itch at the back of his consciousness. That same something he saw everywhere, half hidden but leering out at him like a face in the darkness. That colour, that redness, that had come to suggest something threatening, dangerous.

That something he had seen somewhere else, felt somewhere else. In the garden, the cellar, at the edge of his vision, in the dark of the night and other places. Seen and then dismissed, or forgotten somehow, but seen all the same, of that, if nothing else, he was sure.

Seen, yet he could not bring fully to mind, which niggled at him each time he saw it, or felt it, come to that. That feeling of repulsion, of wrong, an odd anticipation about it that filled him with dread.

It was a wrong thing, something that should not be, could not be. Something from beyond everything, outside everything.

Something of a void.

And so, it seemed to him, was the key. Somehow it had become infected if that was the right word. Become a part of the void, a part of that something red which seemed to haunt the edges of his consciousness.

Sleeping the night before, he had dreamed of that single wrong key. Dreamt of it spreading like a bizarre sickness along the keyboard.

In the dream, it spread beyond the keys to the wooden casing, the sickening debasing the walnut panelling, blistering and warping the wood, the brass hinges turning green as it touched them, more disease than decay it devoured them. All the while in the dream he had played on, the sickness spreading through his fingers as they touched the keys, the piano screaming out twisted tortured notes of agony. The music as debased as the instrument. His own skin blistering and the red pulsing veins wrapping around his arms as they wound their way upwards. Yet all the while, he played on.

The tendrils of the sickness crawled out from the base of the piano, out on the barroom floor. As the sickness reached the bar and started to spread upwards, he could feel it wrapping around his throat, spreading around his face as it enveloped him, his vision swimming to that same red as it slipped into his eyes.

Yet, still, he played on--that sickening discordant music. All the while, in his dream, the red veins were pulsating and glowing as they spread.

The same red veins he saw now, on that single key.

It was unnerving.

He had woken in a cold, putrid sweat, his chest feeling tight and constricted as if the air had been sucked from his bedroom. Sitting bolt upright, his muscles felt clenched and rigid as he sat shivering in the darkness.

He had remained sat there while the last fading memory of the nightmare retreated remembering a pair of glowing red eyes he had seen before he woke. Glowing red like the veins in the key before him. Alien eyes that held an intrinsic wrongness in them. A stare that pierced through his soul.

Eyes, which even when he had awoken, he could see in the darkness of his room. For a long moment, he could not help but see them, for all he knew it was his Pareidolia playing tricks with his mind. He could not move, held within the grip of the nightmare still. Waking from one to another.

Finally, they seemed to fade into the darkness, as the dream finally slipped away, releasing him from its horrific grip. His heart which had bene pounding him his chest slowed at last and he felt himself gaining control once more of his limbs.

The cat had appeared not long after and leapt up beside him on the bed. Prowling and prancing, and demanding attention until he was distracted from the memory of the nightmare. He had dropped off to sleep once more while she curled up beside him purring and he scratched the back of her head.

He recalled wondering how she always seemed to know when he was restless in the night, a strange abstract that drew him further away from the nightmare, as he sank once more into the arms of the sandman's blessing.

He found himself remembering the nightmare now, however, while he looked at that one discoloured key before him. If not the details exactly, which were the whispers of the night, forgotten in the daylight. It came back to him all the same, at leats the memory of how it had felt. That strange terror which had gripped him so tight in the darkness.

"The imagination is a strange and wonderful thing," he muttered to himself, trying to brush off that feeling of being ill at ease, while he took a sip of his coffee. "It's just one key," he further advised, though, if truth be told, he was far from convinced. It was hard to shove it away to the back of his mind and just discount it. Dreams may normally be just dreams, but in the Passing Place, he was not entirely convinced that was true. Normal was not a description you could attach to anything within the bounds of Esqwiths mysterious embrace.

Regardless, he tried to put it to the back of his mind, letting the caffeine flood his system, and began to flex his fingers.

The bars main door opened, and he caught the scent of salt in the air. He heard the cry of a gull, and the gentle crashing of waves from beyond the portal.

Four men walked in, three of which wore like uniforms of canvas trousers and hooped blue and white shirts with white rags tied over their scalps.

'*Sailors,*' Richard hazard from the old-fashioned uniforms, '*jolly jack tars each of them*'.

In fact, he realised with only small surprise, they were almost parodies of sailors, dressed in uniforms you might see on the cover of a children's book. He gave a mental shrug, presuming that such caricatures had to be based on something.

The fourth member of the troop was dressed all in black, clothes that were also of a military cut but bare of all insignias. He sported a neatly trimmed black beard below a black peaked captain's hat, bearing a single insignia above the brim, a brass cap badge, which was repeated on the others uniforms. Shaped to resemble an elongated octopus or Richard thought, correcting himself, a nautilus squid.

He was unsure why description leapt to mind.

Sonny nodded to them as they passed him, in the traditional doorman's welcome. That noncommittal, '*welcome to the bar, have-a-good-*

time, but see you behave yourselves' kind of nod that is the hallmark of the doorman's invitation. Then he let the door swing shut behind them.

Richard watched them walking over to the bar. Overhearing the leader, who had a hard to place nowhere sort of accent, giving his men a lecture of sorts about the different fish of the Adriatic, and the freedom of the individual when not bound to state. All of this seemed odd and yet sparked memories that were ill-defined within the piano player.

Richard tried to shake his focus beyond the strange sense of dread that was still niggling at him and placed his fingers on the keys. He found himself playing some random melodies on the piano as was his practice this early in the day and was unsurprised when an old windlass shanty ended up in the mix, before being followed by an extravagant version of *'Drunken Sailor'*. He often found that the bar's patrons seemed to subtly, or indeed not so subtly, influence his playing. He would find himself playing tunes that just fit in with those around him. He was not quite sure why but he guessed it made sense all the same; A kind of subliminal empathy that directed his music.

For a while, at least, he was lost in the music. When he looked up next, he saw the sailors had been joined by a fifth seaman. One whom gaze was focused on the piano player. Looking straight back at Richard, meeting his stare with strange red eyes.

He found himself drawn to stare back, that itching in his mind starting again, the sense of wrongness he felt when he looked at the discoloured piano key with him once more. He found he could not break the stare of the fifth man. There was something menacing about the seaman. It made his spine shiver, that and the redness of the man's eyes. As he tried to ignore it and avert his gaze while playing on, he struck a discordant note that jarred him.

"Coffee?" Morns voice cut through his unease.

He snapped his gaze across to her in relief, in time to see her put the mug down on the piano lid with a delicate dip of her hips and a single extended arm. Then without breaking stride, she continued her mildly hypnotic walk to the bar, which grabbed his attention slightly, in ways he felt it should not.

"Cheers," he called after her retreating frame.

His eyes went, with some little resistance, back to the bar, where once again to his relief only the original four sailors stood.

He shook his head and cursed his over active imagination, and reached up for his fresh coffee, the hot dark brew had a solid reality to it. But as he reached for it something else struck him as wrong, though he could not place it at first.

It was still bugging him as he took his first sip, burning his lips slightly. He tried to ignore whatever it was. As he put the cup back down on the mat that always sat on the piano lid. Placing it carefully on the mat, he realised finally what struck a note of wrongness with him.

Morn had put the cup directly on the wooden lid of the piano. She never did anything that. She was always so careful with anything made of wood. The little ring of coffee marking the otherwise pristine lid of the piano was, however, evidence of her doing the opposite, something so completely of character for Morn.

A lecture she had given him a few days earlier when he had almost done the same thing still rang in his mind. The stern controlled anger in her eyes that blazed when he had been so careless as to risk scalding the wood leapt to his memory. For her now to go and do so herself struck him with that same note of discord as everything else seemed to have this morning.

Richard glanced up from his keyboard once more. His eyes seeking Morn out. He found her sitting behind the bar on a stool she had dragged through the hatch. He realised he had heard the scraping of the stool's legs on the barroom floor. He could see black marks on the floorboards where she had dragged it. More discord...

What was more, she was now absently playing with a corkscrew as she sat there. On her face a distracted, absent kind of look. She was tapping the point of the corkscrew against the wood of the bar top, to some odd rhythm of her own; A disjointed idle rhythm that gave Richard's inner musician the same kind of itch he felt when he looked at the discoloured piano key.

All of this was so out of character for Morn that Richards almost stopped playing, missing a note once more, for the second time in only a few minutes.

He felt the compulsion to go and ask her if she was okay. She was not entirely herself, of that he was sure. Normally she treated wooden things with a reverence other people might reserve for, well, other people.

He was about to stand and go over to her when she seemed to notice what she was doing and put the corkscrew down on the bar top gently. A pained look about her suggested she was shocked by her own behaviour. Her eyes met his for a moment, and he thought he caught the merest hint of red in her green irises. She looked troubled, almost on the edge of tears.

She was staring down at the marks she had made in the wood, something akin to grief on her face, and emotion he knew only too well.

She mouthed something, a word perhaps. Though too far away to hear her he was certain for a fleeting second it was *'Cutters.'* Why he thought that he had no idea, even when she did so a second time, a single tear tracing down her cheek. *'Cutters'*. He had no idea what it meant, or how he knew that was the word on her lips…

The corkscrew was now abandoned on the bar top. It too had a hint of red to it. Like the reflection of light from elsewhere in the barroom. A simple, normal thing to be sure, yet it gave him that same itchy feeling of wrongness when he caught sight of it. That same feeling of bile at the back of his throat, rising in his stomach.

Before he could stand to go over to her, a shout from the far end of the bar that caused her to stir from her malaise. Whatever had caused her in some strange distraction vanished, or was forgotten in the wake of this new diversion. That normal bright happiness returned to her eyes. She seemed to clear her head, whatever had happened in the last few moments forgotten and then she wondered off to serve a customer.

Behind her, the mark on the bar top still lay there Richard was sure. Just as he had a feeling Morn had forgotten about it completely. Why he knew this he did not know either, for a second or two, he almost convinced himself it had never happened.

As the tune he was playing ended, he rubbed his eyes and tried to banish the strangeness from his thoughts.

"It's all just my imagination," he muttered to himself, and he started playing some random tune he felt his fingers finding. For a fleeting second, he wondered what he was referring to. Was it the oddness about everything in the barroom on this particular morning. Or just everything…

He found himself allowing the melody to just drift along without playing anything in particular as the bar room began to fill. All the time trying to shake the feeling of discord, and trying not to be conscious of his desire to avoid touching that one yellow key.

A short time later he heard Jolene bustle through the kitchen door, a platter of hamburgers in her hand. The smile on her face was much broader than usual as she wondered through the barroom towards a pair of customers seated in an isolated booth.

He found his fingers slipping into '*Love me Tender*' without much thought, as he watched the southern belle lay out the burgers before the two half hidden patrons.

One was the epitome of an old southern gentleman. He had all the hallmarks of some long retired military man, a colonel perhaps. His companion, in contrast, was a large man, his hair oiled and coiffed, wearing a deep blue jumpsuit studded with rhinestones, his eyes hidden behind the type of round big seventies style shades that never quite came back into fashion. He was tucking into the hamburgers with a vengeance as Jolene took their order down.

Richard smiled to himself as he registered some confusion on the customers' faces. He realised what they did not, plainly, that been the quantum accountant- cum- chef's pre-emptive cooking had progressed all the way to table service.

The man in the Rhinestoned blue jumpsuit looked for all the world to be that once famous resident of Graceland. Richard, however, decided it was safe to assume it was just one of his many impersonators, mainly to be fair to him because the other option was a touch too surreal. If nothing else, though, Jolene seemed particularly pleased to be serving him.

She did not even mind when he reached over and pinched her backside as she leant in close to hear what the other man was saying, a cherry of a blush crossing her smiling face. Richard decided that if it made her happy, then he had no right to feel angry for her. Besides which, he knew Jolene could take care of herself should the booths residents stray further over the bounds of decent behaviour.

He slipped his gaze back towards the bar and saw a lone figure standing there a couple of stools down from the sailors. A figure with red eyes glowing and wearing an *'Elvis lives.'* t-shirt.

The strange sense of discord returned once more. His chest tightened, and he felt himself stiffen up. He felt a lump in his throat, shook himself, and dropped his gaze to the keyboard, still desperately trying to ignore the yellow key.

Another dropped note.

He started to play something which turned into a ragged version of '*Suspicious Minds'* while resisting the urge to sing along. He felt it would be wrong somehow, though he could not say why. But at the moment singing along to that song would have been a mistake.

Halfway through, when he looked up once more, the man in the t-shirt was gone.

He felt a strange kind of relief overrun him. His fingers loosened up once more, and his playing became freer.

Jolene finally returned to the kitchen after spending a suspicious amount of time taking the order for hamburgers, the smile on her face wider than he had ever seen before, bringing a grin to his own.

Only, as she passed closer to him the expression changed for a fleeting moment to one of discomfort, as if she had felt something pass over her grave. It threw him slightly, and as she passed he saw the two men in the booth looked different now; Colder perhaps, something dead about their eyes. There was a glow of red to the booth for a passing second.

Then Jolene smiled once more and the odd trick of the light, which was all it must have been, passed. The two men looked normal once more-- at least for a given quantity of normal, for an extremely convincing Elvis impersonator and his manager.

Richard tried to focus on playing once again, trying to ignore all the strangeness around him, for all the single discoloured key was still making him uneasy. He wondered if it was the source of the wrongness he could feel infecting the bar. Or if perhaps his perceptions were being shifted by it, causing him to see weirdness everywhere as a result of that single odd coloured key praying on his mind.

He was not sure which was the stranger notion.

He let the melodies take him further into his own company, trying his best to ignore his surroundings and just slip into the music, the desire to make it his only focus strong within him. All the same, after a few songs he found himself starting to look up once more, as much to keep that yellow key out of his peripheral vision as anything else.

His gaze found Sonny by the entrance, opening the door once more for some customer or other. As Richard watched the doorway, there was a sudden flare of intense red light. Shocked, Richard watched the doorman stare out into it for what seemed like an age, though he was sure he only played a few notes, hitting another duff one just before the door slammed shut once more.

Red, it was always red, that same dark red of

blood from the heart. Blood from the veins... the thought made him shudder, the mental image of Carrie in the bathtub on that fateful night washing over him. He tried to push the image away, not wanting to think of such things.

Shaken by these thoughts, he watched as the cat stalked over to Sonny and witnessed a strange kind of conversation of some kind between the two of them. Sonny looked flustered, lacking his normal aura of cool for a few moments. Whatever he had seen beyond the door had shaken him, Richard was sure of that, though the doorman regained his composure and that aura of self-assurance swiftly after he spoke with the cat.

Richard wondered at the exchange between them, but then his attention was dragged away by the shattering of glass near the bar.

Snapping his gaze around he saw Lyal had fumbled with a bottle of some kind. He was looking surprised at his clumsiness, staring at where the glass lay shattered on the barroom floor having left a red wine washing out across the floor boards from the pile of glass.

Grey Man came to the rescue from the kitchen with a dustpan and a mop and bucket. The monochrome man set about cleaning up the mess with his normal efficiency while Lyal watched on, his hands restless for want of his cloth and glass, the look on his face one of perplexed concern.

A ring on the barman's finger, Richard had never noticed before, flashed the red of a blood ruby. Then was gone, never there in the first place, he was certain. His mind still playing tricks with him.

Richard was glad the grey man had come to the rescue, if only because it restored a veneer of normality to the bar. Then he noticed there was something about the way the cleaner was acting that was just as disquieting. Richard struggled to understand what it was that seemed out of place about the grey man. His attention split as he changed into another song, he could not quite put his finger on what was wrong.

Morn was not helping the situation. Now back behind the bar, she was playing with the corkscrew once more. Tapping out a rhythm on the bar at odds to his own melody, She had that strange, detached look on her face once more.

Halfway through playing the next song, as Grey Man was sloshing around the mop, having finally finished brushing up the glass, Richard realised what it was that sat wrong with him.

Grey Man was not smiling.

For the first time that Richard could remember, Grey Man did not look happy in his work. Indeed, the monotone man looked simply miserable.

For a fleeting second, the liquid been mopped looked to Richard to be a deeper more viscous red than the wine it had been. The dark deep red of blood perhaps, he blinked hard, positive it was just a trick of the light. Still disquietened by the Grey Mans oddly sombre demeanour.

Determined to ignore the oddness once more, he played the opening chords of *'Norwegian Wood'*. But looked up to see Morn was now openly scratching at the bar top with the tip of the corkscrew. Mouthing the word *'Cutters'* under her breath.

He played on, watching with morbid fascination as she carved something into the wood, knowing in his gut he should try to stop her, but unable to tear himself away from the piano.

Then he saw her face change from one of dispassionate disinterest to horrified shock at her own actions. She all but screamed the word "Cutters." , a shocking anguish in her voice.

The corkscrew fell from her hand and she ran, distraught, across the bar room floor. She passed the piano and fled out through the kitchen door, her face a portrait of inner turmoil.

Richard watched her go, fighting the urge to follow her and ask her what was wrong, or try to offer her some comfort and solace. Aware he would probably fail, and somehow knowing he could not do so. He stayed rooted to the piano stool. Angry with himself for his inability to act. The anger he remembered from some other time, some other place, a bathroom awash with blood, a horror of his own. The vividness of the memory washed over him in torrid waves that felt like a sickness within him. He struggled to regain himself amidst it.

Why she would so unthinkingly damage the bar top was beyond him. He knew so well how much she respected the woodwork within the bar. She held it with a strange reverence, a kind of loving affection that went beyond that. What could lead her to do such an out of character thing? That was what he wanted to understand, not only because of Morn but because everyone in the bar was out of sorts. An ill feeling hung in the air, his own memories aside, something was wrong, something was very very wrong.

'*Norwegian Wood*' gave way to '*Hey Jude*' and he realised he was shuffling on his stool, finding it hard to get comfortable. With each glance at the keyboard, that oddly discoloured key stuck out all the more. What was worse, he found he was striking it more than made sense. It was too far down the keyboard to be a regular key, yet he seemed to be using it in every song he played.

A moment of hesitation crept into each melody whenever he needed to strike the key, a desire he could not explain, not touch the oddly discoloured ivory at its core. He found he would try to avoid it by playing the semitone instead. Striking the black keys, despite the sound being wrong. That note of discord with each strike. It all added to his sense of unease.

As he played '*Hey Jude*' he noticed the gunslinger had entered the barroom. The coincidence was not lost on him. It was at a second glance in his direction he realised it was not the same man, but someone older, craggier, even more, desert-worn than the original.

His mind went to the tale he had been told. A disquieting idea came to him, was the stranger from the story; The death incarnate of the old west. He found himself drawn to look closer and noticed the red glow to the man's eyes.

Unnerved, he pulled his gaze away, for a moment at least. When he glanced that way again, he saw the man was gone.

Questioning his own mind, more discordant

notes crept into the melody, the desire to not touch the yellow key becoming stronger. He felt himself getting dizzy, and the room began to swim, the strange dream-like quality of the day washing over him.

He wanted to wake up. To fall out of the odd nightmarish dream, he seemed to be living.

Only this was not a dream, he was sure of that, for all the strangely disjointed nature of the time.

He looked back down at his keyboard and saw a second key had started turning yellow, the same aged quality about it. The same little red veins running through it.

He stopped playing abruptly, mid melody, stood and closed the keyboard cover, experiencing a pressing need for fresh air, a need to centre himself, to take a step away from the oddity and find his feet once more.

His stomach churned and head throbbed with a headache that came from nowhere.

Slamming down the lid of the piano with such force that everyone in the bar turned to look at him, a wave of self-consciousness took hold. He found himself scanning the barroom as people turned back to their drinks and conversations. An odd sense of revulsion filled him. He sensed he was somehow being judged by these strangers, it was a thought that angered him.

What right did they have to judge him?

Who were they anyway?

These strange, odd people, out of time and place, gathered here as they passed through their lives, a moment's respite from the real worlds they came from?

Telling their stories, their damned stories, full of hints and mysteries, stories like the tellers too strange to be real.

How was any of this real?

Rage ran through him like fire in his blood, he was seeing red, everywhere, figuratively and in actuality.

Red, always red, something wrong, something red. That phrase echoed through his consciousness. Something red…

Then he saw her.

Just as he remembered her.

Just as he remembered seeing her that last time, before the mortuary, before the coffin.

Sitting there at the end of the bar, her skin pale as alabaster. Drained of life.

The red of her life draining from the cuts on her wrists.

'*Richard.*'

She looked at him, her eyes cold and dead. Empty of that spark, that vital essence, that was life itself, and staring right through him.

Her lips moved, but no words came from them. She had no breath for words to form but her lips formed the shape of words nevertheless.

The words were clear, '*Come to me.*'

An invitation.

A request.

'*Come to me.*'

An echo of the maiden of tears call.

'*Come to me.*'

And in that moment he wanted nothing more

than to go to her, wanted to join her in ending it all.

To take the final choice and be one with her.

One with her in oblivion.

In that absolute of ending.

There was something beautiful in it all, in her, always in her. The paleness of her skin, the dripping red of the blood from her veins as it spilt down on the barroom floor.

"Carrie…" he said, her name sounding strange on his lips, his voice arid and distant.

Richard climbed to his feet, the stool falling to the floor behind him. He could not tear his eyes away from her. She was here, he had found her once more. After all this time, he had finally found her.

'*Richard*'

Now, at last, he could join her. It seemed so obvious to him now, in this moment; the solution to everything, to all his grief, to all his loss, to that feeling of absence in his life, to that gaping hole within him.

He found his feet moving beneath him, taking steps towards her. His eyes fixated on the piece of shattered mirror she held in her hand. The glint of red upon it, her blood running over it.

Such a simple thing, a moment of pain, just a moment, followed by the ending of it all.

Just let all the red out of himself and join her…

Just let out the red …

The red…

Red…

There was something about red. It meant something, he was sure, but it was a distant thing now. He let it slip from his mind.

The urge to join her in oblivion was all that drove him.

As he walked towards her.

'*Richard,*'

The voice at his feet said with urgency.

He ignored it, like he had the first couple of times he had heard his name spoken since he saw her. His feet taking him forward, he stumbled into a table and spilt some drinks, but hardly noticed. Her name "Carrie…" a whisper on his lips.

'*Richard, stop!*' the voice said again, louder, more urgent. He tried to ignore it. It was only the cat, just the cat, it wasn't important now.

He moved closer. So close he could smell the perfume she always wore.

'*Richard. Stop. Stop Now… What's my name, Richard? What did Morning That Brings The Joy Of Delicate Sunlight Through The Leaves Of the Forrest In The Late Spring In The Ever Dale When The Gentle Wind Blows From The East And Unsettles The Blossoms Which Flutter In The Breeze, tell you was my name, Richard*?'.

He paused, turning his gaze to the floor where the cat stood beside him, her voice echoing in his mind. He was not sure why he stopped.

Perhaps it was the invoking of Morn's full name, more so than the urgency of her tone. The odd desperate note to her voice, an angry defensive note of urgency, he found hard to ignore.

He stared down at her, the little ball of fluffy life that was looking back at him in a fixed stare. But the urge to look back at Carrie drew at him all the same, more a need, than an urge. His head started to turn when the cat spoke again.

'*What's my name Richard*?" she hissed, that same angry undertone to her voice. But not anger directed at him. he knew that, but not how he knew.

"Bringer," he heard himself saying, distracted, his attention with the cat once more, confused that this tiny creature had gained his focus when Carrie awaited him at the bar.

"*My full name, my name like Morn's full name,*" the cat insisted. He could not understand what she was asking. He needed to get to Carrie; to join Carrie. Did she not understand that? Why was she asking him such questions? Now of all times?

"*My name, Richard,*' she insisted again.

"Bringer... Bringer of Things," he stuttered, feeling strange once more as he did so. He felt he needed to go somewhere, to someone, but for a moment he could not remember where or who.

'*Yes, think about that Richard. Think about Morn's name. Think about Morning That Brings The Joy Of Delicate Sunlight Through The Leaves Of the Forrest In The Late Spring In The Ever Dale When The Gentle Wind Blows From The East And Unsettles The Blossoms Which Flutter In The Breeze... What is it, Richard? What is Morn's name? Think Richard,*" she said, her tone softer now. His attention was with her, she was only trying to keep it now.

"Morning That Brings The Joy Of Delicate Sun..." he started to say slowly, each word a deliberate effort on his part.

'*No Richard what IS it?*' She asked.

He paused and thought about what it was he was being asked. What was this, some kind of riddle for him to solve? Why was she asking him a riddle? He thought some more, fighting all the time against the pull of something else, something less important now, but still out there, pulling at his consciousness.

This question, he realised, was important, he could tell somehow it was central to everything.

Important to the cat, to the bar, to it all.

He thought about Morn's name some more, and the name of the cat. They obviously had something in common. Something the cat wanted him to see. But what was it?

What as the cat getting at?

'*Think, Richard, think now…*' She purred softly now.

He did as she insisted.

Then it came to him in a rush.

"A description, her names a description," he said, a note of triumph entering his voice, like a child solving a puzzle for the first time.

'*Very good dear one, very good. So think now Richard, think on that, think about my name. Richard. What's my name?*' she inquired.

" It's Bringer of Things…" he repeated, trying to puzzle out what she was telling him.

'That is *what Morn calls me. Calls me in the way of her people, you see? A description, you understand? A description of something? Think now dear one, think*,' she said.

Whatever else had been on his mind, it was gone now. He found his gaze sweeping the bar and seeing nothing unusual.

He was buying time, seeking inspiration.

"Bringer of Things, a bringer of things someone who brings things, someone who carries stuff... Carries things. Carrie... your name is Carrie..."

As he said the name the enormity of it hit him, just as the last syllable past his lips.

The enormity and the horror of it.

Things clicked into place suddenly: the way she spoke to him, the words she chose, things she could not know but knew anyway.

What had Morn said? *"The cat had left the bar for four or five years..."*

The story of his band. She knew the lead singer's name. How could she?

There were other things, the little things that did not add up. That feeling of her been so familiar, that feeling of closeness in the night.

It was impossible, ridiculous, and insane. But it was, he knew with a certainty, absolutely true all the same.

A wash of vertigo swept over him.

"You're Carrie..."

Then there was a sudden desire to get away, to be outside this place. It overwhelmed him. He crashed through the barroom towards the exit, a desperate need within him to breathe in the open air. To feel the reality of the real ground under his feet.

He felt sick, his head whirling, nothing made sense. How could the cat be Carrie? How could any of this be real, was it all some insane dream?

He thrust his path through the crowd making his

way over to the main doors. Sonny looked up and smiled at him as he came alongside. Then after a glance at Richards' eyes, the doorman reached out and pulled open the door.

Richard did not pause to return the smile but stepped out into the doorway and saw the bright sunlight of the open street. The doorman followed on behind him a few moments later.

Richard gasped at the air. Hot and arid. The air of a desert.

"Oh," the doorman said behind him, genuine surprise in his voice as he looked around the street they had entered, "isn't this where you came in?"

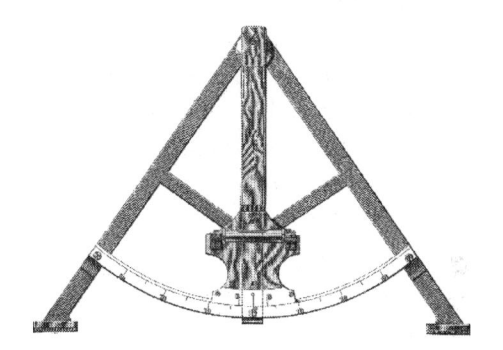

CHAPTER TWENTYTHREE

Back in the Middle Again

Richard looked out across a dusty desert town street, the mid-day heat making the air dry and arid. His mind still reeling from what the cat had told him.

'*What Carrie had told him,*' he corrected himself, trying to take in the enormity of it all.

'*No*' he told himself, '*it can't be true. It impossible, ridiculous.*'

Then he thought of that note. The note she had left behind before she took that final step. Before she went through with that final choice. Those words she had left him with. The words that had made no sense then or since.

I could not stay, it has grown harder each day.
Do not morn me. I am going home at last.
I will see you again in another life

'*Do not morn me. I am going home at last.*' Is that what she had actually meant?

Going home to The Passing Place?

Going back to being a cat?

It was an insanity too far, he could not comprehend it, make sense of it. Yet somehow…

She'd had no past. She had never spoken to him about her history; Not once throughout their entire relationship. It was just a black void she kept to herself, and he had learned not to ask.

Was that her secret?

The hidden thing she never shared?

That she was not even human?

He remembered how he had felt at times, those strange conversations in the night when her depression was at its worst. When she would accuse him of taking hold of her life, binding her to it, stopping her from moving on. That hateful accusation she would make about how loving him locked her into her life. Chaining her to living in the world when she should have returned.

Is that what it all meant, returned to Esqwith's, to her real life, to being a feline part of something so vast he still could only grasp at it?

What was Esqwith's, what was the Passing Place if not something from beyond the real world?

An intelligence, a creature, something magical, mystical, something beyond understanding?

Or was it his own personal insanity?

Was he in some padded cell somewhere, arms clutching at his folded legs, rocking and muttering to himself?

Wasn't, when all was said and done, reality just what you perceived it to be in the end?

'Carrie was the cat,

the cat was Carrie.'

What then was he, a figment of his own imagination? A face in his own darkness, a collection of shapes given form by some alien mind?

Everything about Esqwith's Passing Place was impossible. But, then, when everything around you is impossible, everything is possible. The rules of reality no longer matter, and you make your own.

'Carrie was the cat,

the cat was Carrie.'

All the stories, all the strangeness and the beguiling insanities of everything. All the fragments of other imaginings. All those familiar tales that twisted in on themselves. The redeemed man, the gunslinger, the grey world, the devil behind the bar, the dryad in the garden, the ageing waitress, the Eskimo's saga, the wolf that was winter, the girl in the corridor, Elvis, Nemo, Death, customers raked from the imaginings of humanity. All of it.

'Carrie was the cat,

the cat was Carrie.'

And what now? Accept it?

How could he accept it?

This madness he found himself at the heart of?

The world whirled around him in the dry desert

air. His mind span, that same feeling of vertigo hit him over and over again.

Till…

"Isn't this where you came in?" a voice he knew said behind him.

It took him a few moments to understand the meaning behind Sonny's words. His own thoughts still reeling, he tried to focus on his friends words if only to find some piece of reality to cling to. Something to grasp hold of. Something that might hold the insanity in check.

He looked out from the doorway trying to figure out what Sonny was referring to. Nothing seemed entirely familiar to him, and yet, then it hit him.

The last time he had been here it had been in darkness, After midnight in the middle of a thunderstorm. Rain lashing down as if it was the days of Noah once more. Which was why it took him a while to recognize the doorway of the Providence Farmers Union building across the street. The place he had used to shelter from that storm.

"Oh," Richard said, echoing Sonny's surprise, taking in the vista of the quiet noonday street.

It was little busier that it had been at 2 am in a thunderstorm. The odd badly parked car here and there along Main Street. A few of the townsfolk wondering about on various errands, looking either disgruntled or just uninterested in the world around them. No one seemed to be taking much notice of the bar. Which that had appeared in the vacant lot between 'Crazy Dave's' car lot and the Seven Eleven. If they saw it at all, and not a bare patch of scrub in a vacant lot.

"Well now. Guess it must be that time then my friend," Sonny said archly. Cryptic as ever, his face gave away little more than his words, though a frown creased his forehead and the big man looked concerned all the same.

Richard let the comment pass him by for a moment, breathing in the hot desert air while Sonny lit a cigarette and offered him one from the packet.

He took a cigarette, more out of an odd sense of politeness than desire. He had hardly smoked in the last few weeks. Once the white stick of tobacco was in his hand, however, he had the urge to smoke and took the proffered light, drawing deeply upon it, until he almost choked.

He felt a little calmer now. Still confused, but calmer with it. It all made some sense when he tried not to think too hard about it. Acceptance is its own reward, he guessed. If it was all true, then let it be true. He had found her after all

'Carrie was the cat,
the cat was Carrie.'

"Time?" he found himself asking after a few drags, not quite sure what it was he was asking, but not wishing to let the silence drag on between them. He did not want to ask all the other questions reeling around his mind. He did not want to ask Sonny to explain the inexplicable.

In response, Sonny drew on his own cigarette and gave him a quizzical look for a moment, obviously on the verge of saying something but gauging what response he would get while he chose his words with care.

"Time for you to make your choice my friend," he said finally, no less cryptic than before.

"And what choice would that be?" Richard replied, mildly irritated, for the day had been nothing if not odd and somewhat terrifying from the moment he sat at the keyboard. That strange sense of wrongness that seemed to be infecting everything in the bar continued to loom. That was before the cat, '*Carrie,*' told him who she was.

Now he felt lost, the last thing he felt he wanted was to negotiate being some cryptic conversation with Sonny right now on top of everything else

"It's like in a story. The good ones anyway, you know. It always comes down to the point where the protagonist needs to make a choice. Not just go along with things, but actually make a choice. Whether it's to go on, or turn back, I guess... Well, I think she, Esqwith, is giving you a choice now. Stay or go back to where you started. Least ways, I can't think of any other reason we would be back here right now. She's offering you a way out, and giving you the choice, you understand?."

'*I guess that makes sense,*' Richard thought. At least it made sense as much to him as anything made sense in his life right now.

Shake the fabric of your world then offer you a choice about it.

Had Sonny known? He wondered. Had he known what the cat would tell him, the truth about Carrie? Had he been in on it all along?

'*Carrie was the cat,*

        the cat was Carrie.'

Now he was telling him he had a choice and

somehow that made sense in the twisted strange logic of Esqwith's where stories were real, but at the same time, it answered nothing.

He said as much to Sonny.

"You expect answers? Don't you know life ain't about the answers, life is about the questions," Sonny replied, smiling that big, open, welcoming smile of his, the one that made it hard to so hard to think bad of him.

"That's very Zen of you, Sonny. But you know what I mean," Richard replied a little more sharply than he intended, unable to keep the bitterness from his voice.

"No my friend, can't say that I do," the doorman replied with a sincerity Richard could feel. It made him angry even so. Angry, frustrated and irritated all at once.

"Look, this place, it's impossible, right? I mean, it can't exist. You can't walk through a door and be in another world, another time. Buildings don't move about. Elvis doesn't pop in for a hamburger. Cowboys don't walk in from the desert and take a drink next to an Eskimo. Life ain't stories and cats ain't people," he raged, the last words with heartfelt anguish.

"What is life then, if it's not stories?" Sonny replied calmly, a smile in his words, despite Richard's anger. Calm in the face of the storm. That innate talent of a doorman to defuse a situation with soft words when a patron is being hot headed. Yet, without the proffered threat of the bouncer behind those soft words, just a case of genuine feeling between one friend and another.

"Oh come on, you know as well as I do all this is impossible," Richard said, still raging inside and looking around the dry desert town as he did so, trying to find some anchor in its reality.

'Carrie was the cat,
the cat was Carrie.'

"Yep, it sure is. Yet here we stand, in the doorway of impossible. Are you really so arrogant that you believe you know the limits of possibility? Hell, even when you have been living beyond them for weeks?" he said before dragging on his cigarette once more.

"Weeks? Has it been that long?"

"Hard to tell Piano Man, I gave up trying to keep track a long while back if I am honest, but you have been with us a while now. I know that much, gotten used to hearing you play. Seems like your just part of it all now, truth told. I am not sure I can remember a time when you weren't anymore. It's like that here; people come, and people go, but when they are here, they've always been here. Part of the fabric of the place, you know? Could hardly be a piano bar without our piano player now could we?" Sonny said, with that same sincerity he always seemed to have behind the smile in his voice.

Richard tried to dissect the words, the mild madness behind them. He knew it was all madness, but it made sense all the same. He found it hard to think of the time before, the life before. The endless bus rides, the grief of Carrie's death, their life together. It was all there, all part of him, and yet, at the same time, it was also another life, another time. A misty, greyed out, part of his life. He was the piano player in an impossible bar, and that's who he was. That other life had been someone else's.

Some other Richard, only half-remembered now.

"Doesn't it bother you Sonny?" Richard asked, calmer now that he'd had time to think, but frustrated all the same.

"Bother me? Shit no, man! Have you not worked that out yet Piano Player?" he said, the laughter behind his words barely disguised.

"Worked out what?" he asked with genuine interest. He knew it was because he was seeking a mystery to solve. Something that would distract him from the latest impossibility he faced.

'Carrie was the cat,
the cat was Carrie.'

"The thing we all have in common. All of us who live and work in the bar. In Esqwith?" Sonny explained.

"I don't know what you're talking about," Richard replied, though the germ of an idea was forming all the same. He tried to link up the things that the staff had told him over his time at the bar; Tried to find the common link between them. The thought struck him almost as soon as Sonny started to explain.

"Endings, you see, we had all reached them. The end of our stories I guess you could say. We had all at the end of our journeys, you see? One way or another. Hell, I was sitting in a cell, holding a piece of bronze in my hand and toying with the idea of beating the executioner to the punch by cutting into my wrists and letting it all flow out. Hell, for all I know, in reality, I am sitting there still grasping for that decision, and this is all a passing delusion. If reality is perception, then maybe we chose what to perceive. But given the choice... I'll stay with the delusion... Screw what's possible and what ain't. I'll take this over the alternative any day."

"Yer, but that's, well... That's your story," Richard said grasping, though it rang true all the same.

"Damn straight, and I know what you're thinking. You're thinking, that it's just that... a story I told you, no more true than any other. Hell, why should you believe it? Crazy as it sounds? But it's true all the same. True as I'm standing here, if I am... standing here that's is. But if I ain't then what's it matter, as long as I believe this is true?"

'Carrie was the cat,

the cat was Carrie.'

Richard thought, a dizzy logic to it all.

"And the others?" he asked, not really wishing to contradict his friend, or get into a metaphysical argument. Besides, he found it impossible to believe that everything he had told him was actually true. He knew at the same time it was a truth. Perhaps really was the truth. *'Perception of reality is reality,'* it made a strange kind of sense. Given Sonny's choice where would you be, in the death cell or in the impossible bar full of stories?

And besides that, it was where he was after all.

Impossible logic, but true.

"You've talked to them, what do you think? Grey Man thinks he is in heaven, and given the world he came from I can see why. He came to the end of his story, same as I did I guess. Never heard tell of how he ended up here, but I am damn sure the cat had something to do with it. Giving him a choice, a place to be, when he could not go on anymore."

"I guess," Richard said, deep in thought, though he felt a pang of pain when the cat was mentioned. It made sense, however, in its own way. If he had heard the tale the same way Sonny had, then Grey would have been faced with an end of some kind. It was hard not to see what that end may be.

He found himself thinking about that last bus ride through the desert. From the end of that long road from the yard sale to end them all, to a desperate little town in the middle of nowhere.

No money, no hope, no answers.

No choices left, the end of the road.

"Morn, now she's a strange one. But then she ain't entirely human I think. Her and her tree, well they are closer than lovers. Damn I tell you I think if the tree were felled then she would curl up and die with it. And as I heard it that was the other choice they had before they came here. As for Lyal, well, let's just say he doesn't so much wrestle with his personal demon's as he is his personal demon. But, from what I gather, he was at an ending too. Jolene, well, she has scars, though she hides them. Same goes for them all, I think. We're all here because if we weren't we would not be anywhere. Why we're here, well I don't let that bother me over much. I'm just damn thankful we are... I know I am."

Richard thought about this in silence as he drew on his cigarette, hardly inhaling any of the bitter tobacco smoke, as he was distracted by Sonny's words, trying to grasp their full meaning. All the while unsure the doorman himself really understood himself what it was he was trying to explain.

"You said choice?" Richard said after a while. Not a question really, just the nagging thought at the back of his mind.

"Yer, well, there is always a choice, I think. She gives it to us in different ways, I guess, but there is always a choice. She must feel it's time you made one," Sonny replied, a certain grim reality to his words.

"By she you mean the bar?"

"Esqwith's; yes, the bar, or whatever she is. Can't say I know the answer to that myself. Don't think any of us do… But then as you said, she's impossible. So how would we? She just is, some things you just need to accept," Sonny said, pulling out another cigarette and offering one to Richard, who waved the offer away with a smile.

"So what was yours then, your choice I mean?" he asked the doorman.

"You mean apart from staying in that cell?" Sonny asked, raising an eyebrow.

"You said she always gives you choices. I thought you meant afterwards. Like now, if I am supposed to make a choice, I guess it must be between staying and going."

"Oh I see, well, that's simple enough, I guess. You still got my medal? The one I gave you on the night you arrived?" the doorman asked.

Richard thought for a moment. He seemed to remember putting it down on the dressing table in his room at some point. But now that he was asked about it, he could not actually remember. He felt almost ashamed to admit it. The little piece of brass obviously meant a lot to the big man. He did not want to admit he had lost it. "Errrm."

Sonny smiled and fished in his pocket. "Don't worry, I know you don't," he said, pulling his hand free then opening his palm for Richard to see the sharpened brass cross in his hand.

"Don't matter what I do with it. It always comes back. Given it away must be a dozen times, threw it in a river once or twice. Hell, I threw it in the blackness beyond the garden once. You know, the void…? But when I think of it, it's always here in my pocket, always offering me my choice, I guess. She always offers me that choice. The choice to go, if that's what I want, and perhaps to remind me I have that choice. There's a kindness in there, I think."

It was yet another impossible thing, Richard knew, he could rationalise it easily enough. The big doorman must have taken it from his room a day or so after he had handed it to him. But at the same time, he found it hard not to believe him all the same. What was one more impossibility? After all, it made sense in its own way.

Perhaps there was a power in belief that worked here. That made its own kind of twisted sense too. If Sonny believed in anything, it was probably that sharpened piece of brass.

Richard looked out across Main Street. Thinking about all this as the world turned for a millisecond, Main Street, Providence, Nebraska became a small

North African township at the edge of a different kind of desert, then changed back again. A French legionary muttered "Pardon" as he walked between them into the bar room, his accent more Home Counties than Parisian French.

"What the hell?" Richard found himself saying.

"Just a customer, Piano Man. Happens if you're standing out here around the entrance. Occasionally, it needs to shift to let someone through," Sonny said, sounding unperturbed and taking in what view Main Street Providence afforded, which was, as ever, not much of a view.

Richard turned and watched through the open doorway as the foreign legionary walked up to the bar where he asked Lyal for water. The man looked like he had been marching through the desert for days, and drank the water in large gulps before asking for more.

"That happens a lot?" Richard asked, knowing the answer even as he did so.

"All the time, it's best not to hang in the doorway, to tell the truth. Took me some getting used to and I stand here half the time…"

"What happens if I step out?" Richard asked, concerned suddenly, as the thought struck him that once he stepped beyond the doorway, the bar would vanish behind him, as it probably did when most people left. He considered the legionary, desperate for water. When he left, he would probably think it had all been some form of mirage or other. Perhaps, if he were lucky, his thirst would not return, and he could finish his journey. He could hear him now behind them talking to Lyal, ever the listening barman; something about a cricket match and a debt of honour. A tale which would no doubt be told, or had been told before. Richard recognised some of the elements of it from somewhere in the recesses of his memory.

"Then you'll be back where you started, I guess. Or maybe not, maybe you'll know a little more. Maybe you have learned something, maybe you haven't. Maybe you'll forget all this, who knows?"

"And Esqwith's will be gone?" he asked, strangely pained by the thought. Another thought coming to him on its heels.

'Carrie was the cat,
the cat was Carrie.'

The wave of vertigo was less this time. The thought of leaving seemed worse somehow than grasping at that insanity.

"That, Richard, I cannot tell you. Truth being, I have no idea, though I doubt she would be that blunt. Tell you this much, though, if that out there were a Louisiana jail cell then I damn well wouldn't step through, just in case," Sonny said and started to laugh, clapping him on the back. "But no, I doubt she would do that to you. She likes you for a start, and I doubt she actually wants you gone."

"How can you tell?" Richard asked, though he was thinking of the cat: the Cat that was Carrie-- had been Carrie, perhaps. She wanted him here, he was sure of that. Or maybe he just hoped.

"You mean apart from you being here in the first place?" Sonny inquired, managing to sound genuinely surprised at the question.

"Well, yer, I guess there is that, but it still doesn't

explain why," he replied.

That same old question in a new form that he always seemed to be asking…Why?

"Why? Well, that's the thing, ain't it? Not sure any of us knows why. Chef has his theories, but I don't set much store by them. I think perhaps we are all here for a reason, but knowing that reason? Hell, I am not sure we're even supposed to know it. I don't think that's the point. Maybe we are here because stories need to be told and to tell them the Universe needs someone to listen. I mean, where do stories come from after all, when it comes down to it?"

"Books maybe, or writers I guess. People in general possibly," Richard hazard. All too aware he was grasping.

"You think?" the doorman said raising an eyebrow.

"No, I guess not… The imagination then I suppose," Richard replied, trying to think of an answer to what at first seemed such a simple question, yet knowing suddenly it was as complex as any that could be asked.

"Maybe, or maybe they come from out there. Everywhere. Since the first caveman wanted to talk about what happened on the hunt, or explain why the sun came up every morning. Or maybe they come from other places, and maybe the imaginations just a way of filtering them through. Maybe everything happens somewhere, and we all just tap into it somehow," the doorman philosopher said.

"That's a little deep for me Sonny," Richard

replied, not wishing to admit he was confused at the turn of the conversation.

"Well okay, think of Esqwith as a filter then, the place stories pass through between worlds. And I think she likes stories, likes people to listen to them, and that's why we're here. You and I at any rate, not the Universe as a whole. Rescued from the ends of our stories so we can share them and listen to others. Can't claim that's the truth of it but it's a truth, I guess. And one that I feel has a grain of real truth behind it, if only because I like it as a truth, something I can cling to. There are worse truths out there," the doorman said with all the sincerity of his heart.

"Okay, say I go along with that, then why the choice? Why am I looking out on Main Street Hicksville Nowhere?" Richard asked, still trying to wrap his mind around the whole concept.

"Because she wants you to want to be here, maybe. Or doesn't want you to be here if you don't want to be here... I don't know... I just know she's giving you a choice."

"Let me guess, the cat told you?" Richard asked a note of bitterness in his voice that caused Sonny to raise an eyebrow.

Sonny smiled anyway. "Perhaps she did, but if she did, can't say I remember."

Richard thought about this for a while, taking the earlier offered smoke from Sonny's packet. He knew what he was going to do. He'd known from the moment the choice was offered. He would turn around and go back to the piano in a few moments, play some melody and listen to the people in the bar talking.

Why did not matter.

Why never mattered when you came down to it. The choice of going back was no choice at all.

'*Besides which*.' he thought to himself. '*I made a date with Morn to hear a story.*' It seemed a thin reason to stay, but there were other reasons.

"Did you know her name?" he asked Sonny after a few moments silent contemplation.

"Whose?" Sonny asked, sounding confused.

"The cats," Richard replied, then added, "Carrie's…"

Sonny looked at him, his deep brown eyes looking shrewd for a moment. He seemed to be considering his answer, as if picking his words was going to be important. Richard found it hard to gauge if he had or not.

"Princess? Only name I know her by, but I guess that makes sense, be about right, time-wise, I suppose… Well, now ain't that a thing…" the big man said.

Richard looked for the glimpse of a lie to the doorman's words and could not see one. Or perhaps he wanted to believe his friend had not known. He was not sure he wanted to know anyway.

It did not matter.

Why did not matter.

He finished his cigarette and tossed it out into the street. Turning back towards the bar he saw a woman seated at the far end, a woman he knew. Or perhaps not a woman. But he knew her all the same.

Perhaps she would be who she was now for only a few moments, or a few days.

Perhaps she would change back to being the cat as soon as he crossed the threshold.

It did not matter.

He had found her, and perhaps found his why.

It did not matter if all the stories were just stories. Or if they had some deeper meaning he was supposed to find.

The Passing Place was a place to hear stories and perhaps to tell them.

It was also home now; home in a way nowhere else had been for so long. He was not sure he could leave even if he wanted to. Not really. He was not sure the place would let him go, though he could no more explain why he felt that than why he felt at home there.

She was here. In a way, she had always been here. And if all this was only real because he perceived it as such, well, that was as real as anything needed to be. He made to enter, then stopped once more and looked back at Sonny.

There was one other thing that was bugging him…The thing that had been bugging him all day, worrying at him like a dog with a chew toy.

It occurred to him now.

"Sonny?"

"Yer?"

"I've been seeing red all day." He said, it seemed as easy a way to explain it as any other.

"I know… There is something in the air," the doorman replied. For the first time, he sounded worried, a frown creasing his brow, a note of genuine concern in his voice.

"What is it?" Richard asked, disturbed more by Sonny's reaction than anything else.

"Something's ending, or something's changing. I'm not sure which."

"Something bad?"

"I wish I knew, Piano Man. I wish I knew," The doorman replied enigmatically, stubbing out his own cigarette and heading back inside.

After a few moments, Richard joined him, crossed the barroom and sat down at the piano to play '*Forever Autumn*' for the woman at the bar.

THE END

Coming 2017

The second Passing Place novel

Something Red

The scar in the wood was in the shape of the sign of the Cutters.

It stared up at her, accusingly...

Morn looked up from behind the bar, to see the woman before her waiting to be served. Then looked again, more carefully, tilting her head to one side, trying to see past the obvious...

"Why are you in that shape? She asked Bringer Of Things.

She did not ask how, how did not matter, how never mattered, why was always the important question.

The woman in front of her smiled..........

Also By Mark Hayes

Cider Lane: Of Silences and stars
Publisher's book club
Book of the month November 2015

A young girl is isolated by a hostile world. She watches a car burning, consuming all she knows. Grief-stricken she wanders, lost, and alone, her mind withdrawn into darkness. Fleeing from the world which has made her an outcast. Seeking only a refuge from other people.

Meanwhile a traveller, homeless, damaged by his past and living on the fringes. Seeks solace in solitude. Carrying the regrets of his yesterdays with him. Walking the roads to the lost places, as abandoned by the world as he.

Fate draws them together in Cider Lane, a place long forgotten by the world. Amid ruins of the past they must learn to trust in each other. If only they can. While the world is ever waiting to crash in on them once more.

Because the world never forgets anyone for long.

A novel of the lost and the broken. Of sharing the silences, talking to the stars, and the importance of tin openers.

ABOUT THE AUTHOR

Mark Hayes was born in Yorkshire on the day Julius Caesar was murdered. Though these two events are unrelated and separated by 1926 years, he has occasionally been known to mention the assassination in relation to his birthday all the same.
He now lives in Teesside next to a bird sanctuary he has never visited with a black cat called Boomer who likes to stop him typing by sitting on his lap and demanding his attention.
He has been known to occasionally update his blog, and even more occasionally manage to be insightful on Twitter, gets constantly distracted by Facebook, Netflix, and the internet in general. While studying for a degree with the Open University because he doesn't trust politicians and wants to know why. When he finds the time he works on the next novel, He would procrastinate more if only he could find the time to do so.
This is his second novel.
The first Cider Lane won the publisher's book club book of the month award for November 2015
He hopes to finish one of the other dozen or so he has started, which sitting on his hard drive leering at him.

Email: darrack@hotmail.com

Twitter: https://twitter.com/DarrackMark

Blog: http://writesrightsrites.blogspot.co.uk

Printed in Great Britain
by Amazon